Ride

To

Destiny

Scott Roker

This book is a work of fiction. Names, characters, places, and incidents either are the product of the author's imagination or are used fictitiously and any resemblance to actual organizations or persons, living or dead is entirely coincidental.

ISBN 978-0-9822092-6-4

Four Star Publishing
P.O. Box 2871,
Anderson, IN 46018
Tel. 765-635-9906
www.bookstore.fourstarpublishing.com

Acknowledgments

Cover photo taken by Tresha Moorberg

I would like to dedicate this book to my father who introduced me to the wonderful world of westerns. He showed me the path to follow and has always guided me down it. He will never know how much that has meant to me.

Thank you Scott

Visit Scott on the web at - **www.myspace.com/scott_roker**

You can also e-mail Scott at - **scott.roker@yahoo.com**

Scott Smathers

Regional Representative

Pheasants Forever, Inc. & Quail Forever

6140 S Richland Cr

Lincoln Ne 68516

Work: 402-261-4923

Cell: 402-314-3308

ssmathers@pheasantsforever.org

A VOLUNTEER IS A PERSON WHOSE ACTIONS ARE NOT FOUNDED ON ANY OBLIGATION OTHER THEN A PASSION TO ACT

Pheasants Forever & Quail Forever are the only national conservation organizations that empower local chapters with 100% control of their fundraising dollars.

Join our wildlife habitat conservation efforts today at:
www.NebraskaPF.com, www.PheasantsForever.org or
www.QuailForever.org

1

Doug is sitting on his couch watching a baseball game when the telephone rings. Without hesitation, he answers in his typical, “Hello.”

“Hey Doug, it’s Allen. I will be there in a few minutes; are you ready?”

“Yeah, I have the pistols and rifles by the back door; all we have to do is load them in my truck, and we are off to the range,” Doug answers.

“I was thinking,” Allen begins, “why don’t we go out to the farm instead. We always have a lot of fun out there, shooting pop cans.”

“That sounds good to me,” Doug agrees. “Hey, I need to let you go. I have to go downstairs and get the ammo we’re going to need. Just come on in when you get here.”

“Okay, I’ll see you in a minute.”

Doug climbs off the couch and goes downstairs to get the ammo they will need for an afternoon of target practice. Not long afterwards, he hears the back door open.

"Hey Doug, are you ready?" Allen shouts.

"How many boxes of shells do you think we will need?" Doug shouts back.

Allen thinks for a moment, and answers, "Four or five boxes each should do."

Doug grabs six boxes of shells for each of them, just in case they decide to shoot a little longer, walks back upstairs, and leaves the house.

"I have all the guns in the truck," Allen says, noticing Doug coming from the house and walking toward him.

"I have the ammo right here; let's get on the road," Doug says as he walks toward the truck where Allen is standing.

"Is Linda coming along with us?" Allen asks.

"No, she's at the lake for the weekend taking care of some tribal affairs," Doug replies.

"Is she still dealing with that?" Allen asks, surprised. "It has been almost a year since that week of our fishing vacation."

"I think this trip will take care of the remaining issues for the tribe," Doug replies with confidence. "She'll soon have her weekends free."

"Where is Linda going to work since she quit the ranger service?"

"She was hired by Game and Parks to head up their lake program."

"That sounds good; at least she'll be working in her field," Allen notes.

"Are we ready to hit the road?" Doug asks, changing the subject.

"Everything is packed and ready," Allen points out as he opens the passenger side door. "I am glad we started our Saturday target practice tradition. You know, I am getting a lot better with the rifle."

"It's a lot of fun and a good stress reliever after a long week of working in the E R," Doug agrees as he opens the driver side door." I appreciate the pistol shooting lessons you're giving me. I have to admit I'm a lot better than I used to be." Without saying another word, Doug and Allen climb into the truck. Doug fires it up and they begin heading out to the farm.

"I am glad we're heading to the farm, instead of the shooting club," Allen comments. "I kinda miss going out there and killing pop cans."

"It's funny you should mention that," Doug points out. "I have been planning to stop by the recycling center to drop off these pop cans. So it's a good thing I still have them. We will just have to turn them in with a few holes."

"Like I said, I thought it might be a nice change from the range."

"Sounds good to me," Doug acknowledges. "I need to check on a few things out there anyway. I packed some lunch for us," Doug continues as they pull off the highway and onto the gravel road. "I planned to come out here after we left the range, so this works out even better."

"What do you need me to do?" Allen asks, thinking ahead.

"What do you mean?" Doug shoots back, with a bit of sarcasm in his voice.

"Well, it seems everytime I go with you somewhere, there is a project you need my help with," Allen points out.

"Well, um, ah, now that you mention it," Doug replies, not sure he should continue. "I want to fix a hole in the roof of the chicken coop. When we get the house finished, Linda wants to raise a few chickens for eggs."

"I knew it! I just knew it!" Allen shouts back, and then looks at Doug, realizing what he had heard and asks. "Chicken coop? What chicken coop? What are you talking about? Where are we going?"

"Did I forget to mention that Linda and I bought the adjacent farm?"

"I don't think you mentioned that; I just assumed when we talked farm, we were going out to the spot where the hunting camp is on your place where we usually go."

"We'll always have that place where we can shoot and hunt."

"Where is this place you're talking about?"

"Just up the road a bit," Doug answers.

Doug pulls off the gravel road on to a long lane leading up to where the homestead's main farmhouse would be, among the various buildings that are already standing.

"How long is your lane?" Allen asks.

"It's about a quarter of a mile," Doug replies.

"Wow, won't that be fun in the winter?" Allen comments.

"When we bought the place, we bought the whole shooting match. The land, all of the out buildings, and the equipment," Doug explains. "I have a nice big tractor with a blade to move the snow in the winter."

"I didn't know you were even looking for a farmstead," Allen says in amazement. "I know you were always talking about it, but I didn't know you were serious."

"When Linda and I got married, we both thought it would be nice to have a house in the country," Doug continues to explain. "So, we started looking, and when this place came up, there was no question if we wanted it. We were able to finalize everything yesterday, and we signed the papers just before Linda left."

"We were never going to the range, were we?" Allen asks.

"Nope," Doug replies. "Well, here we are; what do you think of the place?"

"That is the biggest barn I think I have ever seen," Allen replies. "You can park a whole fleet of combines in that machine shed. But where is the house?"

"The couple we bought the farm from wanted to keep it," Doug goes on to say, "so they moved the house to town, and we're having one built. The crews start work next week."

"How many acres does this place have?" Allen asks excitedly

"This place has about five thousand acres; two thousand of it is in crops. A neighbor has been crop sharing those acres for a number of years. I met with him regarding it a few weeks ago. I told him I will keep the same deal he had with the last owner if he wants to continue farming the fields. He agreed. I may even talk to him about the other eighteen hundred acres I keep in crops on the place we use for deer hunting and the Pheasants Forever Youth Mentor Programs, but that's a thought for the next planting season. I do kind of like doing my own farming even if it doesn't make money. It's the joy of it. The wildlife needs it, so I am leaving it in until spring rather than harvesting it, to assure extra winter feed for the wildlife. The best thing about this place is that the rest of the acres are in timber. A creek runs through the timber. The property has two ponds, one small pond that will be good for horses or cattle. The other is about three surface acres. I think that the larger pond may make for some fun fishing. I would like to see Linda take that on, and see if it is doable for decent fish, not to mention, adding a small dock and maybe a spot where you can camp out on the bank. I am confident Linda can work that out. She would do well at this. It's her area of expertise."

As they walk across the yard, Doug continues his tour-guide role. "Allen, let's go over to the machine shed and I will show you the machinery that came with the farm."

"This building is so cool," Allen is quick to point out. "It looks like something out of a painting,"

Doug unlocks the shed and opens the two large doors.

"Holy, Doug! You have four tractors, two combines, and all the attachments that go along with them!"

Doug wants to laugh at Allen's amazement. "Yep, and we also have four ATVs. We no longer have to walk everywhere. Hop on that red one over there; the keys are in it."

Doug mounts a green ATV. They start them up, and out of the shed, they go.

Pausing for a moment just outside the shed, Doug asks Allen, "Would you help me with the doors? I want to lock the shed up while we are out shooting."

Allen and Doug close the doors. Doug puts the lock back on the door and latches it. They climb aboard their ATVs, and off they go, heading toward the timber.

Doug leads the way. They follow trails through the dense timber which the previous owner had cut out so you can get back to the big pond, surrounded by timber.

Doug pulls his ATV over and Allen is right behind him. They park in the shade of an enormous cottonwood tree that looks like it has been there since the dawn of time.

Standing there surveying the beauty, Allen says to Doug, "This is the neatest place. You can easily get lost out here and never go back to civilization."

"I know. The first time I was out here, I felt the same way," Doug agrees. "Let's go over there and set the targets up. There's a good back drop and we won't have to worry about stray shots going anywhere."

Allen and Doug set out cans for their afternoon of target practice. They walk back to the ATVs and grab the guns.

"What are you doing, Doug?" Allen asks.

Allen watches as Doug puts on a two gun holster for his two 44-40 pistols.

"I have been practicing my quick draw," Doug says as he loads his pistols. He readies himself, and then looks over his shoulder to Allen. "Say when." Doug waits for his cue.

"DRAW!" Allen commands.

Doug draws both guns and before Allen can say another word twelve cans are knocked off the log.

"Wow," Allen says in amazement, "that was fast. You must have been doing a lot of practice on your own."

"Every day for the past six months," Doug says with pride.

"Okay, let me take a turn." Allen loads the 30-30-caliber rifle, and then proceeds to take care of the rest of the cans which are left hanging on branches and on the log.

"So what do you think of that?" Allen asks.

"You have improved!" Doug replies.

"I snuck in some extra sessions at the range myself," Allen admits, and then continues with his confession. "Since LeeAnne and I separated, and while the divorce was being finalized, I really needed something to get my mind off of things. I just miss being around my boys everyday. However, they are old enough to understand the whole deal. LeeAnne is agreeable to a very liberal visitation schedule, which is helpful when it comes to heading out on rescue calls and when we go on our hunting trips."

They both go back to taking pot shots at the cans. For the next couple of hours they set up and knock down can after can.

"Hey Doug, what do you say we take a break and have some lunch?" Allen suggests.

"I hope roast beef is okay with you?" Doug asks as he goes over to the cooler and grabs the sandwiches and food he packed for the trip.

"That will do just fine," Allen answers.

Just at that very moment, a strong cold wind comes up out of nowhere. Then it starts to rain just as suddenly. Doug and Allen dive into some bushes and hide under an old fallen tree.

The rain begins pouring down. It is raining so hard there is no visibility, followed by lightning flashing and hitting all around them. The lightning crashes again, and again.

"Where did this come from?" Allen asks, confused by the sudden change in weather. "There was not a cloud in the sky when we got here."

Doug nods and shrugs. "Well, you know Nebraska; if you don't like the weather wait ten minutes and it'll change."

The storm rolls out as fast as it rolled in. Within minutes, there is a bright blue sky again. The wind dies down, leaving a nice spring breeze. Doug and Allen climb out from under the log. They look around, surveying for damage.

Then, they see one another.

"Doug, what are you wearing?" Allen asks.

"What do you mean? What do you call that 'outfit' you have on?" Doug asks.

They look at each other and themselves only to see that they are wearing what appears to be mid to late 1800's rugged-old-west attire.

Doug raises an eyebrow and slowly looks over to where the ATVs are parked, only to see two horses.

"NOT AGAIN!" Allen exclaims, seeing the same sight.

"I wonder who we have to help this time," Doug asks with a wry smile.

2

As the two walk over to the horses, they notice that they are saddled and ready to go.

"Where do you think we are supposed to go?" Allen asks.

"Maybe they know," Doug replies, pointing at the horses.

Doug and Allen climb on the horses and begin their journey, not knowing where they are going or why they are there in the first place.

"The horses seem to want to head northeast," Doug comments after riding for a bit.

"Well, I hope they know where they're going," Allen says. "I sure don't."

They did not ride for long, when they see what looks like a town.

"Maybe these two do know where they are going after all," Allen comments with relief.

"The surroundings seem kind of familiar to me," Doug points out, as they get closer to the town. "Maybe we've been here before."

"You have been here before; this is Avoca," Allen says, pointing to a sign on the side of the road.

Doug is surprised at the sight of the familiar town. "Wow, you know, this was a quite busy and well known town in its heyday."

The town looks just like one from a spaghetti western movie. There is a church and school at the top of the long easy slope that forms Main Street. At the bottom of the hill are the livery and a brothel. In between them are several blocks of businesses. There is the Post & Telegraph office, a mercantile, a barber & bath house, the Nebraska Territory Savings & Loan, The Avoca Hotel & Fine Dining, a Doctor's office, the Sheriff's office, and of course the saloon & dance hall.

There are people walking up and down the boardwalk; with horses, carriages, and wagons moving about town. It is a busy little town.

Doug is drawn to what he sees. He is half-pleased, half-disappointed. "I really can't believe the size of this town; it's bustling." He pauses. "And then to see what it will become." He shakes his head thinking, '*PROGRESS... Right.*'

Allen mumbles to himself and then aloud says, "I wonder what year this is?"

Doug shrugs. "I don't know. We will have to ask someone."

Allen rolls his eyes at Doug. "Right; they will think we are crazy, if we ask what year this is. What fool would not know what year this is?"

Doug thinks to himself a moment, and then says aloud, "Maybe we can find a newspaper and see the date on it."

"Good idea. But, where shall we look for a paper?" asks Allen.

As they ride into town a man who is walking down the street nods and tips the brim of his hat to them and says, "Good-day, Marshal."

Allen, although not sure of the comment, replies, "Afternoon, how are you?"

"Are you here to take Billy, the cattle rustler, back to Lincoln?" The man asks.

Allen just goes with it. "Yep, I reckon so."

They ride past the man; Doug leans over and asks quietly, "What the heck is going on?"

Allen is just as baffled. "I don't know, but we better find out."

Doug points ahead. "There is the Sheriff's office; why don't we go in and see if we can get some answers in there."

"We will just have to be careful how we ask certain questions," Allen warns Doug. "It seems like people know us and that kind of puts us at a disadvantage, if you know what I mean?"

Doug and Allen ride over to the Sheriff's office, dismount, and tie their horses to the hitching rail. Allen and Doug walk in to the office, and find a man sitting behind a big desk, with several wanted posters on the wall behind him.

The Sheriff looks up and says, "Afternoon Marshal. Are you here to pick up Billy?"

Allen, now assuming the Marshall role, replies, "Yes, we will be taking him to Lincoln in the morning. Is there room at the hotel for us or is there a boarding house where we can stay for the night?"

"Has it been a long ride?" The Sheriff asks.

"It seems like we have been riding a lifetime," Doug adds.

"Well hello, Doc," surprised by Doug's voice, the Sheriff shoots back. "Your usual rooms are ready at the hotel. I was told you would be here sometime today. So, I went over and made sure they have your rooms ready." The Sheriff rises from his chair, walking toward the door. "Well, I look forward to seeing you gentlemen in the morning. Have a good day."

Allen steps into the open doorway, tips his hat to the Sheriff, and replies, "You too, Sheriff. We'll see you in the morning."

Allen and Doug make their way out of the Sheriff's office and take their horses over to the livery where the blacksmith meets them at the door.

The blacksmith questions Allen, "How long will you be with us this time, Marshal?"

"Just for the night," Allen replies. "We'll be leaving first thing in the morning."

"You gonna take Billy to Lincoln?" the blacksmith asks.

"Yep," Allen barks back.

"You be careful," the blacksmith remarks as he moves the horses into stalls. "He has a lot of kin around here, and they're not happy that he's being sent to Lincoln to go in front of the judge and likely be hanged." He closes the stall and turns back to face Allen. "I am sure they'll try and stop you."

"I thank you for the warning. We will keep our eyes open for trouble, on our way to Lincoln." With that, Allen and Doug leave the stable and start walking back to Main Street.

"Well, Doug, how about we go and see if we can find the hotel?"

"How about we go to the building with the sign that says Hotel?" Doug says, pointing up the hill.

Allen, noting the sarcastic tone in Doug's voice, shoots back, "Funny; let's go up there and get our rooms and see if we can figure out who we are and where we're from."

Doug and Allen are making their way up the street toward the hotel, when a man flies out of the saloon. The man rolls onto the street, jumps up, and draws his gun.

Allen draws his gun and yells, "Hold it right there!"

"I was just funnin', Marshal," the man says. "I'm sorry; I'll go over to the Sheriff's office and turn myself in."

Allen looks over at Doug. "Why don't you go with him and make sure he gets there. I will go and check into the hotel. I'll see you when you get there."

"Okay," Doug says with a nod. "I'll see you in a few minutes, unless this young man gives me trouble."

The man turns and looks at Doug. Doug returns the man's gaze. The young man only says one word, "Doc?" as he turns pale and falls to the ground, unconscious.

"He's out cold," Doug notes. "I think he must have passed out."

"That makes your job even easier," Allen points out as he wonders if it was coincidence, or fright, that after exchanging glances with Doug, the man passes out. "Just throw him over your shoulder and carry him to jail."

Doug throws the young man over his shoulder and starts toward the Sheriff's office, while Allen keeps walking to the hotel.

Doug enters the Sheriff's office with the man over his shoulder. "Sheriff, where do you want him?"

Surprised at the delivery, the Sheriff says, "I'll open the cell. You can put him in there. Where did you find him?"

Doug tells the facts. "We were walking by the saloon and he flew out the door. He landed right there on the street in front of us. The Marshal and he had a few words. Then, before he could do anything else, the kid just passed out, and here we are."

The Sheriff grins. "I will keep him over night and let him out in the morning, as long as that's all right with you, Doc?"

"Yes, that's fine with me," Doug answers slowly. "I think he just needs to sleep it off. Thanks Sheriff; I will see you later."

****

Allen enters the front room of the hotel to see a young fair-haired lady behind the hotel's desk.

"Well, ain't you a welcome sight! Dan, I was wondering when you would be back in town," she says excitedly.

Allen looks behind him to see who she is talking to but no one else is in the room, except the two of them.

"You looking for someone, Dan?" Ellie, the hotel manager asks.

Allen, still confused by the 'change' of names, answers, "No ma'am; I just thought I heard something behind me."

Ellie comes running from behind the desk, jumps into Allen's arms, and plants a big kiss on him. She smiles and says, "It has been too long. Let me show you to your room."

At that moment, Doug walks through the hotel's front door and says, "Excuse me. I'm sorry, I didn't mean to interrupt."

Happily, Ellie greets him. "Doc, I didn't know you were going to be here too."

Doug shrugs, throws his hands in the air. "I could leave."

"Don't you dare!" Ellie shouts back, and then continues in her normal tone of voice "I was just going to show Dan up to his room; let me get the keys for your room too, and we'll all go up together."

She goes behind the desk to get the keys. Doug looks at Allen and asks, "So, 'Dan?' I assume you know her?"

"Right! We have been 'here' how long? I couldn't have seen her before in my life," Allen admits.

"Well, it seems like she knows you," Doug points out.

"Yeah, and that's what scares me," Allen agrees.

They quietly follow Ellie upstairs, both wondering *'What's next?'*

When they reach the rooms, Ellie says, "Here we are, gentlemen. Let's get you boys settled in. I bet you two are hungry. Why don't you get your things put away and come on down to the kitchen and I'll whip up something for you two to eat."

Doug is putting his things away when Allen comes into his room and says, "What am I to do with this Ellie woman? The way she acts, she wants to come into to my room and, well, you know what I mean."

Doug looks at Allen, not expecting such a statement. "No Allen, I am afraid I don't know what you mean."

"I think she wants me to take her to my bed."

"And that's a problem for you?" Doug asks.

Allen is a bit embarrassed. "Well no, but I don't know her."

"Once again, is that a problem for you?"

"You know what I mean," Allen shoots back.

Doug shrugs his shoulders and says, "I suppose. However, it's one way to get some information."

"I guess you're right, but I am doing it under protest," Allen strongly points out.

"Oh yeah right, now let's go downstairs and see what she has for us to eat."

Doug and Allen proceed downstairs to the kitchen where they find Ellie in her apron, frying steaks on the stove.

"How do you like your steaks?" Ellie asks.

"I like mine smothered in gravy," Allen pipes up.

"How about you, Doc?" Ellie asks.

"Without gravy and toward the bloody side," Doug answers.

"Coming right up, gentlemen." Ellie brings the steaks to the table and says, "Dig in, guys."

Allen and Doug start to devour the steaks when Ellie asks Allen, "So Dan, how long are you going to be in town?"

Allen almost chokes on his steak. "Um, just tonight, we have to escort a prisoner to Lincoln, so we'll be leaving early in the morning."

Ellie, with the sound of a woman with a mission in mind says, "Then we'll just have to make the most of tonight."

"Does the saloon still have the card table open tonight?" Doug quickly asks.

"You know it, Doc," Ellie remarks. "I guess I don't have to ask where you'll be tonight."

"Well I figured the two of you will want your privacy," Doug comments. "Besides I don't want to be number three in a twosome."

Ellie agrees with a nod. "Alright, see you in the morning, Doc," she says as she points and shakes her finger at Doug. "But, I'm telling ya, the town still hasn't forgotten the last time. So, try to keep your guns holstered this time."

Wondering what 'the last time' reference was about, he decides to worry about it later. "I will do my best," Doug acknowledges as he pushes away from the table. "Ellie, thank you for the meal; I think that was one of the finest steaks I have had in a long time. Now if you will excuse me, I have a card game to get to." Doug walks out of the kitchen into the hotel lobby and out the door to the saloon down the street.

"I will put these dishes away and meet you up in your room," Ellie says with anticipation and excitement. "I won't be long."

Allen hesitates for a brief moment, than says, "Okay, I am looking forward to catching up on all the latest news and gossip around town." Allen heads up to his room, trying to figure out just what the relationship is between them and what he is going to do about Ellie. Before he knows it, there is a knock on his door.

"Come on in," Allen reluctantly says. "It's open."

Ellie turns the knob and swings the door open. There stands Ellie, dressed in nothing but a corset and lace, holding a bottle of wine.

Allen is taken aback by the sight; he finds himself in the midst of a decision he needs to act on and quickly, by the looks of it. Allen stammers a second, and finally manages to say, "Ah, uh, uh, you sure look, ah, um, you look, um, nice."

"Dan, I do believe you are turning six shades of red," Ellie giggles. "You look like you have never seen me like this before."

"The way you look tonight it's like seeing you for the first time," Allen says, trying to regain his composure.

"Flattery will get you everywhere tonight, Marshall Dan," Ellie says as she runs over and jumps on the bed, placing herself cozily next to Allen.

She hands Allen the wine to open. While he is opening the bottle of wine, she reaches for the glasses on the table. Allen fills both glasses.

Ellie is the first to break the silence. "This is some of the best wine you can get around here." She takes a sip, giving him a smile. "And I was saving it for a special occasion, one like tonight."

Allen takes a sip and says, "This is very nice wine. Where did you find it?"

"I ordered it from a catalog. It comes from New York City. I thought I would save it for when you came back through town."

They finish the bottle. Allen tries to abstain for the night, but with the wine and Ellie's assertiveness, Allen gives in.

****

Doug pushes open the swinging doors of the saloon, and steps inside. As he stands there surveying the room, everything in the saloon comes to a halt. The piano player stops, and all conversation ceases. Even the card players take pause to see the man standing in the doorway. Doug walks over to a table where four men are playing cards. "Do you mind if I sit in?" He asks.

"Nice to see you again, Doc," a man dressed all in black sitting at the table replies. "Pull up a chair."

Doug grabs a chair and sits down at the table. "What are we playing tonight, gents?"

"Five card draw," Cisco, the man in black, replies.

"Sounds good; deal me in," Doug acknowledges.

As the card game gets into full swing, so does the music and lively conversation. The room returns to the liveliness it had maintained, prior to Doug's entrance.

"I was sure sorry to hear about your loss, Doc; my condolences," Cisco, the man seated across from Doug, says as he looks at him.

"Thanks, I appreciate it," Doug says, not having a clue as to what Cisco is referring to. "Now deal out those cards and let's get this hand going."

The game lasts into the wee hours of the morning, when through the doors of the saloon walks Allen. He looks over the dwindling crowd and spots the table where Doug is playing cards. He makes his way over to the table, placing his hand on Doug's shoulder, and asks, "Don't you think it's time to call it a night? We have to leave in just a few hours and I need you fresh for the ride."

Doug, although reluctant, looks up at Allen and says, "Let me finish this hand and I will be right with you." Doug lays down four aces to take the hand. He stands up, raking the pot into his hands, and says, "Well, fellas, it's time for me to turn in. Thanks for the game. I'll see you the next time I'm in town."

A man at the table stands up and looks straight into Doug's eyes and yells, "You aren't going anywhere until I win my money back!"

"Why don't you just sit back down and lick your wounds," Doug calmly says. The man again demands a chance to get his money back and Doug responds, "I could sit here all night; and the way you play, you would still go home broke." The man reaches to draw his gun. Before it clears leather, he lies dead on the ground. Doc stands over him, shaking his head. "Some people will never learn."

"I didn't even see you draw," Allen says, unsure if he saw what just happened.

"You need to pay closer attention next time," Doug points out.

"We are never going to have a quiet game with you around, Doc," Cisco comments, not surprised by what has just happened.

"I'm sorry, but I did give him a chance to walk away," Doug points out. "Besides he did draw first."

"Like that matters," Cisco comments. "As fast as you are, you could give a person a five-count head start, and they would still lose. Nonetheless, it was good seeing you again, Doc."

At that moment, the Sheriff bursts through the door with his gun drawn and shouts, "No one move!" He looks about the room. "What happened here?"

"This man drew on Doc and lost," Allen informs the Sheriff as he points to the dead man on the floor. "It was a fair fight. He drew first."

"They always seem to draw first," the Sheriff says as he is walking over to the group. "They always end up dead." He returns his pistol to its resting place and looks at Doug. "If you were not a U.S. Deputy Marshal, Doc, I would run you in."

"Sheriff, I did everything in my power to talk him out of it."

"I am sure you did, Doc," the Sheriff responds.

"Sheriff, that man was my brother," another man at the table says as he stands up and looks at the Sheriff. "As much as I hate to say it, Doc did give him a chance. My brother just wasn't smart enough to take the chance Doc was givin' him."

The Sheriff nods at the man, and then says, "Well, this man says there was a fair chance for him to leave it be. This man is the dead man's brother, and he says it was fair. I will have to say that's good enough for me." The Sheriff steps away from the group, looks at the patrons in the saloon, and announces, "Now, everyone clear out. The saloon is closed for the night."

Everyone has started to clear out of the saloon when the Sheriff stops Doug and Allen. "Not so fast. You two help me with this body; then get your things, your prisoner, and get out of town!"

Allen is shocked by the Sheriff's change of heart. "Sheriff, Doc has not had any sleep. And I need him sharp and awake for this trip."

"You should have thought about that earlier," the Sheriff comments.

Allen and Doug help the Sheriff move the body to the undertakers, and then head back to the hotel. Doug is in his room packing his things into his saddlebags, when Allen walks in.

"Doug, what are you doing?"

"Getting ready to leave."

"No. You just stop. You get some sleep. You're going to need it."

"What about what the Sheriff said?" Doug asks.

"You just let me worry about the Sheriff," Allen replies.

****

The sun is just peeking over the horizon, when Allen walks into Doug's room. He finds Doug up and ready for their trip. Doug smiles at Allen and says, "Good morning, are you ready to hit the road?"

"All packed and ready," Allen shoots back. "Let's get to the livery and get the horses, pick up our prisoner, and get out of here."

"Aren't you going to go and give Miss Ellie a kiss goodbye?"

Allen rolls his eyes at Doug, and then says, "I was kind of hoping to avoid that."

Doug and Allen quietly leave the hotel and head over to the stables to get their horses. The blacksmith has them already saddled, ready and waiting for them.

"Mornin," the blacksmith says when they enter. "I thought I would have seen you a few hours ago." He hands them their reins, then continues, "The Sheriff came down and told me you would be leaving earlier than planned and he did not look happy."

They paid the blacksmith without elaborating on the story then walk their horses down to the jail. They enter the Sheriff's office and find the Sheriff sitting behind his desk. His expression is that of a man, hotter than a fryin' pan full of chicken. "Did I not tell you to get out of town immediately?" The Sheriff snaps at them.

"Now Sheriff, you don't want to start your day like this, do you?" Allen asks, using a calm, cool tone, "Besides you don't want to get Doc angry this early in the morning, do you?"

The Sheriff tosses the cell keys to Allen and points toward Doc. "Just take Billy and get the hell out of here!"

"Sheriff, that's no way to talk to a U.S. Marshal," Doug points out. "You may need us down the road. Don't you think it would be better if we're on good terms with each other?"

Allen grabs Billy from his cell and escorts him to a horse the Sheriff has waiting out front. As Allen helps wrist bound Billy onto his horse, he points out, "Billy, if you try anything, I mean anything, my friend Doc there, will not hesitate to shoot you dead." Doc smiles and winks at Billy.

"I don't want any trouble," Billy acknowledges. "I tell ya Marshal, I did not do what they say I did."

Allen mounts his own horse, reaches over and takes the reins to Billy's horse. "It's not my job to judge. My job is only to deliver you to Lincoln."

Doug mounts his horse and the three of them head their horses west toward Lincoln. Doug begins figuring the distance and time for their ride and asks, "How far do you think we'll get before dark?"

Allen gives Doug's question some thought, then replies, "I hope we can make it in to Eagle before dark. We can drop Billy off at the Sheriff's office and get a room for the night."

"Don't you mean maybe another girl for the night?" Doug asks.

Allen furrows his brow at Doug. "Ha; very funny. No, I don't mean that."

Doug throws his head back and laughs. "Oh right, sure you don't."

"I can see this is going to be a long ride," Allen comments.

"These ropes are a little tight," Billy complains. "Is there any way you can loosen them?"

"I'll loosen them a little," Allen says, reaching over and releasing some of the tension on the ropes. "Remember what I said; if you try to escape, Doc will gun you down."

Doc is spinning his pistol around in his hand, and confirms Allen's warning. "Look Billy, I don't want to shoot you; and I am sure you don't want to be dead. So just behave yourself."

"Like I said, I don't want any trouble," Billy assures Doug and Allen.

They continue down the trail heading toward Lincoln. Doug is trying to figure out why people keep commenting they are sorry for his loss. He finds himself daydreaming, when a picture of two boys and a very attractive lady hanging from a tree flashes in his head. Doug halts his horse and gives out a loud, "WHOA!" He takes his hat off, runs his hand through his hair and says, "What the heck was that about?"

"What do you mean, Doug? No one said anything."

"I don't know. I just had a flash of a memory of something that I don't remember actually happening."

"Well, don't hold out on me now; what did you see?" Allen asks.

Doug places his hat back on his head and answers, "Just never mind. It's probably lack of sleep and the heat."

They have traveled about ten miles when Allen stops his horse and dismounts. He looks at Doc and Billy and says, "Let's take a rest for a little while; there is a creek here to water our horses and I know I can use the rest."

Billy and Doc climb off their horses and walk them down to the creek for a drink.

"How much further is it to Eagle, you think?" Doc asks.

"We should be there in three, four hours," Allen replies.

"We're burning daylight," Doc comments. "What are we waiting for? Let's get moving."

With the horses rested, the three of them mount up and continue on their way to Eagle.

"You know, Marshal; I really did not do what they said I did," Billy says, making his claim to innocence again.

"So, you tell us you're not to blame?" Allen asks. "Just what is it they're accusing you of?"

"They put me in jail for rustling cattle," Billy replies. "I didn't rustle them. I bought them from a rancher in Kansas, and brought them home."

"Alright, if you bought them, how did it turn into charging you, and convicting you, of cattle rustlin?" asks Allen.

"The man I bought the cattle from ended up dead the next day," Billy replies. "The law just figured, since I happen to have some new head of cattle that came from the guy, I killed him and stole his cattle. But, I swear Marshal, I did not kill him, or steal the cattle; I had a bill-of-sale."

"If you had a bill-of-sale, then how did it turn into this?" Doug asks. "Why didn't you just show the Sheriff your papers?"

"I couldn't. I don't know what happened to my papers," Billy quickly answers. "I had them in my saddlebags when I paid for the herd; and when the Deputy Sheriff looked for them in my bags, they were not there, so they tell me."

"That sounds like a sad story," Allen remarks. "But, as I said, I am not the judge; I'm just the man responsible for delivering you to the Sheriff in Lincoln."

“Marshal, maybe that is our mission,” comments Doug.

The three men ride in silence. There is no more discussion of Billy’s innocence, or the hows and whys that brought them to this day and time.

As they top a hill and look toward a densely tree covered creek, Allen informs the other two, “The way I figure it, after we cross that creek there, we will be about an hour’s ride from Eagle.”

Taking note of the thick wooded creek, Doc notes. “I think those have got to be the first trees I have seen in hours. It looks like they follow the creek.”

Allen gives directions. “We will go into that opening in the trees, and cross the creek there.”

Doc studies the tree line. “The trees are really thick here; looks like it would be some very good hunting.”

“My uncle owns this property and I have hunted this tree line a few times,” Billy points out. “There are a lot of deer in there.”

“Let’s get across the creek and get into Eagle,” Allen insists. “I’m getting hungry.”

They begin crossing the creek, and as they near the middle, riders appear on the other side, wearing masks.

“Hands up boys, or the next sound you will hear is harps playing!” the leader of the masked men yells out.

Doc, as always, not so diplomatic, asks, “What do you want?”

“We want your prisoner,” the man replies. “So keep your hands away from those guns and you will live to fight another day.”

Doc looks around at the men, smiles and says, “Do you really think you are going to get your man and get away with this?”

“Doc, let them have Billy,” Allen interrupts. “At this point we’re in no position to argue.”

“You are making a very wise decision there, my friend,” the man assures Allen. “Now, be still, and keep your hands in the air. My partner here will relieve you of your guns.”

As the second masked man removes their weapons, the leader says, “You will find your guns down the trail a bit. Once you have retrieved your guns, don’t try to follow us. We have many friends across these hills watching you.”

“Just take him and go about your business,” Allen shoots back.

The masked men leave with Billy and the lawmen’s guns, leaving Allen and Doc on their horses in the middle of the creek without their weapons and without their prisoner.

“Allen, what were you thinking?” Doc proclaims. “We could have taken them.”

Allen moves his horse up to the creek bank, and looks back over his shoulder at Doc. “Right, all of them, all fifteen of them.”

Doc follows him, still annoyed at the loss of his pistols. “I would have left one or two for you.”

“Let’s go and get our guns and get our hides to Eagle, and quick. I want to go straight to the Sheriff’s office so we can get a report filed with him immediately.”

Allen and Doc ride down the trail for a short time, and find where the masked band of men left their guns.

Doc being very annoyed, says, “If they put a single scratch on my guns I will kill them all.”

“Just relax, Doc, we’re still alive to tell the story.”

“Right,” Doc says in a condescending tone, “yeah, ah-huh. Well, it’s our first job since we returned to the Nebraska territory, and we can’t even complete it. We’ve gone and screwed it up.”

“Just shut up and ride,” Allen shoots back.” I can see Eagle up ahead. We can explain it to the Sheriff. I’ll have him wire the office in Lincoln, telling of our current situation. Then we’ll wait in Eagle for our instructions from Lincoln before we do anything else with this.”

As Allen and Doc ride into town, they see the Sheriff standing out in front of his office leaning up against the outside wall shaking his head. The Sheriff says, “I have been expecting you, but was under the impression that there was to be three of you.”

“Yes, that was the plan. We ran into a little trouble crossing that creek about five miles back,” Doc acknowledges.

Allen, quick to give the Sheriff the whole story continues, “As we crossed the creek, about fifteen men wearing masks jumped us, took our guns and then took our prisoner and rode off. They left our guns on the trail. After finding those, we continued to head straight here to your office. I thought it best to wire Lincoln, and inform them of the escape.”

Allen and the Sheriff walk down to the telegraph office and wire Lincoln the news.

The man at the Telegraph looks up at Allen and says, “I’ll get their response to you as soon as they send it.”

Allen nods and replies, “I’ll be at the hotel waiting.”

The Sheriff leads Allen out to the street and then begins walking toward the hotel. In a concerned tone, the Sheriff remarks, “Marshal, I heard about the trouble in the saloon over in Avoca last night. Can you tell Doc to take it easy tonight?”

"Why don't you tell him?" Allen says, pointing in Doug's direction, "He's right there in front of the livery."

The Sheriff shakes his head. "No, that's all right. I'll let you handle that. Let me know if you need any help with recovering your prisoner."

Allen turns back toward the Sheriff to shake his hand. "As soon as I hear back from Lincoln, I will let you know what the plan is." With that, he turns back, and begins to head toward the livery to reunite with Doug.

"I took care of the horses," Doug says, noticing Allen approach. "Now let's go to the Hotel, get a room, and find something to eat."

Doug and Allen walk down the hill to the hotel. When they enter, an older gentleman, standing behind the desk greets them. "Good-evening, gentlemen. Welcome, my name is Arlan. How can I be of help to you?"

Allen tips his hat brim at the man and replies, "We will need a couple of rooms for the night."

Arlan reaches for the register book for the men to sign. "All right, gentlemen, sign here. I think I have a couple of rooms available on the second floor. Let me get you your keys, and I will have Sherry show you up."

Arlan turns toward the office doorway and speaks loudly, "Sherry, can you come out here? We have guests."

A lovely young woman appears from the back and recognizes Allen instantly. "Dan! It's been a long time. I am so happy to see you again! Now you two follow me and I will get you settled in."

"Another town, another girl," Doug whispers to Allen.

Allen looks over at Doug with a scowl and shushes him, and then grins and whispers back, "When you've got it, you've got it."

When they reach the top of the stairs, Sherry turns, tosses Doug his key and says, "You're in this room, number eight. She then turns back toward Allen, smiles at him and says, "Dan, let me show you to your room. You will be in room six." Sherry walks to the room door, and reaches to open it. "Here, let me unlock it for you and help you get settled in."

Allen decides this time, *'why fight it'*. Once they enter the room Allen says, "That would be mighty kind of you, Miss Sherry. How can I thank you?" Then he slams the door shut.

Doug looks at the closed door, shakes his head and says out loud to himself, "Well 'Doc', looks like it's going to be supper for one."

Doug puts his things on the bed, walks back down to the front desk and asks Arlan, "Is there somewhere in town to get a hot meal?"

"You bet! The Flying Eagle Saloon across the street has a mean steak."

Doug tips his brim. "Thanks. Tell the Marshal, if he comes down, that's where I will be."

Arlan nods. "I'll be sure to let him know."

Doc walks out of the hotel and sees the Flying Eagle across the street, so he proceeds across the street and enters. Doug notices that once again, as soon as he enters through the doors, all activity comes to a halt. Doug reaches for his gun and everyone hits the floor. "Just kidding, folks," Doug explains. "Wanted to see if you were alive or not."

Sally, a lovely, sweet dance hall girl speaks up, "Doc, you shouldn't do that. You just about sent me to see the angels."

"Sorry, I was just funning; it was so quiet, I had to break the silence somehow," Doug explains. "Anyway, I came by because I heard that you serve up a mean streak here."

"That's the rumor," says Sally as she directs him to a table. "Doc, you just have a seat here, and I'll bring one out. Do you want the full spread with it?"

Doug smiles. "Sounds good. I think I'd like that."

After a few minutes, Sally returns with Doc's meal. She sets the food down on the table for him and pulls out a chair for herself. "Mind if I join you? I thought you could use some company. Besides that, I hate to see you have to eat alone."

"That's fine with me," Doug comments, motioning to the chair. "I appreciate the company." After a few moments of quiet between them, Doug asks, "Can you tell me if there's a card game tonight?"

"There's a card game every night," Sally replies with a grim. "When you're finished with your supper, I'll take you up to the game."

Doug looks about the saloon at the others. "You don't have a card game going down here in the saloon?"

"Yes, but the high stakes game is upstairs," Sally informs him, exchanging smiles with Doug, knowing he preferred a better choice of game.

Doug pushes away from the table. "That was sure good." He reaches for the back of Sally's chair. "Why don't you show me to that game?"

Sally leads the way upstairs to a room down the hall. She knocks on the door while opening it, and announces, "It's just me, fellas, and I have brought you another player."

As Doug enters the room, a very large man stands up, "Well, Doc, always a pleasure." After shaking Doug's hand, he returns to his seat. "What brings you to our little town?"

Doug is glad to know that someone else is pleased to see him. "Well, I have a few hours to kill, so I thought I would relieve some of you gentlemen of your money."

A man sitting at the table glances in Doug's direction, and mutters, "Fat chance."

Caught off guard by the tone and response, Doug questions the man, "Pardon me?"

"Never mind, Doc; he didn't say anything," the large man insists. "Come on over and have a seat, Doc, and we'll deal you in."

Fortunately, the man did listen to the large man. The man who appears to object to Doc's place in the game is 'One-Eyed' Jack Dollar, a man who doesn't listen to anyone. Doc reaches for a chair and prepares for a little relaxation.

"Good luck, Doc. Have a good time. You be sure to find me when you're done playing."

"You bet. Thanks again, Miss Sally." Feeling ready for a friendly game of cards, Doug looks back at the table and prepares for his first ante of the night while Sally closes the door.

Don deals out the first hand and as usual, Doc wins. As each hand starts and ends, Jack Dollar, who is seated to Doc's left, grows more and more frustrated at the outcome of each subsequent hand.

After three hours of losing, hand after hand, an angry 'One-Eyed' Jack stands up and says, "I am tired of yer cheating, Doc!"

Doc calmly looks up from the table and stares the man squarely in the eye. "Boy, you need to sit down, before you say something that's going to get you hurt."

Jack stares right back into Doc's eyes. "Why don't you stand up and we can settle this?"

Don, the gentleman, speaks out, "Jack, you need to sit and calm down, or Doc'll kill you."

Jack, unwavering from his challenge, states, "I am not afraid of this man." He stands rooted in place, continuing his protest. "He's just a man with a reputation. He probably has never even been in a real true gunfight."

Doc, now fully aware that this perfectly relaxing game of cards is relaxing no longer, takes a moment to allow the man one more opportunity to comply. "I am not going to tell you again. Sit down, Shut up, and let's play cards."

"If you don't stand up Doc, I will shoot you right there where you sit," 'One-Eyed' Jack Dollar states angrily.

Doc slowly rises from his chair, looks him straight in the eyes, and declares, "Alright boy, you want to settle this. We can settle this. You call the shots here. Say 'when'!"

Jack reaches for his pistol, but before he can even grab the grip, he finds the barrel of Doc's pistol between his eyes.

"Are you sure you want to do this?" Doc asks. "Now, why don't you back out of here and go home before you make me mad. I want to see you get those hands up, and keep them up until the door closes behind you."

Jack, with his hands above his head and the gun still between his eyes, starts backing out the room. "Now, go home, and sleep it off!"

As Jack backs out the door, he turns and starts to run down the hall. When he reaches the end of the hall, he stops and yells, "This is not over, Doc! This is far from over!"

"You better hope it is," Doc says as he closes the door, and then turns back toward the remaining men at the table. "I think I had better call it a night. I have a feeling it's going to be a long day tomorrow." He collects his winnings from the table, tips his hat and says, "Gentlemen."

Don nods to Doc. "Doc, you watch your back. 'One-Eyed' Jack Dollar is not a man to let things go."

"Thanks, I will keep that in mind."

Doc cautiously makes his way down the stairs, figuring one ambush today was enough. Sally sees him coming down, and walks over to visit with him. "Doc, where are you going to be staying tonight?"

"Across the street, at the hotel." He scans and rescans the room for Jack Dollar. "Tell me, Miss Sally, did you see the man who was playing cards with us come down here?"

Sally nods. "Yes, he left a couple of minutes ago."

"I think I am going to go back over to the hotel and try to get some sleep. I'll see you later."

Sally smiles, and touches him on the arm. "Good night, Doc."

Doug pats her hand while saying, "Good night to you, Miss Sally."

Doug turns and starts walking toward the saloon doors. When he reaches the swinging doors, he stops and looks out cautiously for his former card partner. He sees no sign of 'One-Eyed' Jack or anyone else so he steps out the saloon doors onto the boardwalk, glances up and down the street once more to make sure, and then proceeds across the street to the hotel.

He enters the hotel and approaches Arlan at the desk. "Has a wire come through for the Marshal or me?"

Arlan shakes his head. "No, I'm sorry. Nothin' yet."

Doug tips his head down. "Okay, thanks. See you in the morning. Have a good night."

Doug walks up to his room. He considers stopping at Allen's room; as he approaches, he can hear Sherry giggling and Allen laughing. He grins, shakes his head, and goes into his room for some much-needed sleep.

Doug has just lain down when there is a knock at the door. He instantly grabs his pistol, holding it ready below the sheet. "Who is it?"

"Doc, it's me, Sally; may I come in?"

"Yes, just a minute." Doug puts his shirt back on, turns up the flame on the lamp, and opens the door.

Sally steps in and looks at Doug, worried, "I just wanted to stop by and see how you are doing?"

Doug is not sure of her statement; he's learned in the last couple of days… 'Go With It'. "I am fine, Miss Sally. Why do you ask?"

Sally looks directly into Doc's cold eyes, looking for the other side. "I know it has almost been a year, and I know it still hurts but . . . . "

Doc cuts her off. "Well, sometimes you just have to pull up your boots and keep on walking."

Sally lowers her gaze, looks back into his eyes. "While that may be true, sometimes one still needs a shoulder to lean and grieve upon." They share a knowing smile.

"I thank you for the sentiments, Miss Sally; but really I think what I need is a good night's sleep." Doc gets up and reaches for the door.

Sally waits a moment, then gets up from the chair, following Doc's cue. "Okay Doc, I will leave you so you can get some rest, but if there is ever anything that I can do just let me know."

"Thanks, I do appreciate it, and the next time I'm in town I'll stop by and visit."

Doug opens the door. Sally steps out into the hallway, reaches for Doug's arm, and gives it a squeeze. "Good night then."

****

Doug is sleeping when the peacefulness of his sound sleep is interrupted by the dream of the tree with the lady and two boys hanging from it. It starts as flashes of scenes. Then he watches as if he is in a movie theatre.

He sees a group of masked men raiding and ransacking the house and buildings on the homestead. They drag the two boys bound and gagged from the house. They beat both the boys until they are no longer conscious.

The lady is being restrained by other members of the renegades and is forced to watch these beatings. The beauty fades from the woman's face, as she watches the violence.

When the men finish with the young boys, the tables turn. The once strong, now broken woman becomes the next victim. The men beat her into submission. Then a few of the men have their way with her. Once they feel satisfied with the havoc they have created, they hang the woman between both boys in the large oak in front of her home. The three men remount their horses and start riding down the lane. As they pass the tree, one man turns back and yells, "Maybe this time the message is loud and clear, Doc. And this time, don't forget it!"

Doug is suddenly awakened when the door to his room opens. Like a shot Doc sits up, pistol in his hand as he pulls the hammer back, pointing it in the direction of the door.

"Doug, it's Allen; don't shoot!" Doc's eyes are intent on the door. It is as if he doesn't see Allen there at all. Allen again shouts, "Doug don't shoot; it's Allen!"

Doc blinks, and things come into focus, finally seeing it is truly Allen in the doorway. Allen stands there, staring at the six-gun in Doug's hand. "Morning Allen, how are ya? Did you sleep well?"

"I slept fine," Allen replies, still staring at the business end of Doug's pistol. "I would feel a whole lot better if you would put the hog leg down."

Doug puts the hammer back into place and places the pistol back on the table. "Sorry, whew, I had ah, well; I guess you could say an interesting night."

"I heard you didn't shoot anybody," Allen remarks, leaning against the doorframe. "That's a surprise; I wouldn't necessarily call it interesting."

"Have we heard from Lincoln yet?" Doug asks as he starts dressing.

"Yes, actually the wire came in first thing this morning. Sherry brought it up a few minutes ago. It said they want us in Lincoln as soon as possible. Apparently, Billy was sighted northwest of Lincoln. It seems he has relatives out by Chimney Rock. They believe that he's headed out there."

“Let me finish getting dressed and I will be ready to go. I’ll meet ya downstairs at the front desk.”

Doug gets his things together and walks down to the front desk where Allen is saying his good-byes to Sherry.

Not wanting to listen to the salutations, Doug says, “I will go to the livery and get the horses ready. I’ll wait for you there.”

Allen looks at him and nods. “Alright, I’ll see you there in a minute.”

Doug walks out of the hotel and has started toward the livery when he hears a familiar voice calling out. It is ‘One-Eyed’ Jack Dollar, the angry man he encountered at last night’s poker game.

“Doc! Doc!” he shouts.

Doc stops in the street as he approaches the corner of the hotel on his way to the livery barn.

“You yella-bellied S.O.B.! I should have killed you last night.” Jack steps out into the open, standing on the edge of the boardwalk, then continues, “I am not going to let the opportunity pass me up today. Turn around so you can see the man who’s gonna kill you.”

Doc turns around slowly to face his adversary. An evil smile comes across ‘One-Eyed’ Jack’s face.

“That is much more to my liking. I want you to see the man who is responsible for killing the legendary Doc Gray.”

Doug decides to give the man one last chance. “Like I did last night, I am going to give you a chance to leave. So, now is your chance. Just turn around and go home.”

Jack steps off the boardwalk onto the street. “No chance of that, Coward. I am gonna kill you and leave your dead body for the coyotes, just like we did your wife!”

At that moment, Allen comes running out into the street from the hotel boardwalk, yelling, “Stop! Don’t shoot!” It is too late. In the time it takes the Marshal to say the words, Doc drops ‘One-Eyed’ Jack with a single shot between the eyes.

Doc looks in Allen’s direction and says, “I gave him every opportunity to walk away; he just wasn’t smart enough to listen.”

“What did he mean by ‘just like when we killed your wife?” Allen asks as he walks over to Doug. “Is there something you aren’t telling me?”

Doug shrugs. “I am not sure. I had a dream about a woman, two boys and a huge white house. I think it may have been Doc’s family. I am thinking they were murdered while the marshal and Doc were out tending to law business.”

Allen removes his hat and runs his hand over his head. “Well, I was watching and paying attention this time. I saw the gunfight. He plain did not have a chance. You, my friend, I have to say, are scary fast with a gun. I saw him go for his gun, his hand had barely touched the pearl handle, and then he was dead. His hand was on the handle of the still holstered pistol. I looked over at you and your gun was holstered. You were putting your coat back over your guns. I didn’t even see your hand reach for the gun.”

“I am kind of impressive as a gunfighter, huh?” Doug points out, with a ‘Cheshire cat’ grin on his face.

"Don't get cocky," Allen shoots back as he replaces his hat. "Let's get this guy to the Sheriff's office and get on our way to Lincoln."

Doug and Allen pick up Jack and carry him to the Sheriff's office. As they get closer, they notice the Sheriff running out the door and heading toward the sound of the gunfire.

Surprised by the dead man and his escorts the sheriff says to them, "I should have known it was you, Doc. Can't you go just one day without killing someone?"

"Sheriff, I'm telling ya, he came after me," Doug explains. "I tried warning him to give it up and go home but he reached and drew first! Honest Sheriff I tried to talk myself out of this gunfight."

"I saw the whole thing, Sheriff," Allen shoots back. "Doc was indeed trying to get out of the fight. But, our man, 'One-Eyed' Jack here, wouldn't let things go and reached for his gun first."

"Like it matters if he drew first or not; I have never seen anyone even get their gun out of the holster when they go up against Doc. Bring Jack in and set him in a cell. I'll have a couple of my deputies take him to the undertaker."

The two men haul the lifeless body into a cell. They turn to leave and the Sheriff stops them.

"Doc, I have five-hundred dollars for you."

Doug frowns at the Sheriff. "Five-hundred dollars for what?"

"Our friend, Jack Dollar here, had a five hundred dollar reward on him, dead or alive."

Doug smiles, and straightens his coat in confidence. He says to the Sheriff, "Well, I think that could have been the easiest five hundred I have ever made. Thank-you Sheriff."

“Sheriff, we’re heading out,” Allen interrupts. “I got the wire from Lincoln this morning. We need to get there as soon as we can. Is there anything else you need before we go?”

The Sheriff shakes his head. “No, I think we’re fine here. I would recommend that you keep your eyes peeled for the Dollar Boys. Jack’s band of men will not be happy when they hear of you killing their leader.”

“I hope they do try and come after us. I could always use some extra poker money,” Doug says with confidence.

Doug and Allen leave the office, and head to the livery. They retrieve their horses and head out toward Lincoln.

3

When Allen and Doug get to the edge of Lincoln, Doug chuckles. “Boy, Lincoln sure has changed since we left on Saturday.”

Allen nods and smiles, “The real question is, where do we live?”

Doug frowns. “It should be interesting to find out the answer to that question without raising too much suspicion.”

Allen smiles and points upward, having a bright idea. “Let’s go over to the Marshal’s office to see if we can find any answers there; after all I am a Marshall . . . .”

“That sounds like an excellent idea,” Doug interrupts. “Where exactly is the Marshal’s office?”

Allen looks over at Doug in a state of disbelief. Doug should know the answer to his own question. “It’s on the square where it has always been.”

"Just how do you know this for sure?" Doug asks, still confused by Allen's confidence.

"You know Doug, I really can't tell you. I don't know how I know it. It just came to me."

Doug scratches his chin and grins at Allen *'The Marshal'*. "You might be good for something after all; did the directions to where we live happen to pop into your head as well?"

"Not yet," Allen replies, shaking his head. "However, you never know when the right thing here in town will trigger something in my memory, and then we'll gain more answers."

"Okay, we're here," comments Doug, pointing to the front of the Marshal's office. "Let's go in and see if we can figure out a little more about these guys we're supposed to be."

Allen looks very seriously at Doug. "All right. But you just let me do the talking."

"Okay, you're in charge," Doug acknowledges. "I will leave it in your hands to find out who we really are, where we live, and hopefully, why we are here."

Allen and Doug get off their horses and walk into the Marshal's office where another man wearing a Marshal badge is pouring himself a cup of steaming hot coffee. The man looks over his shoulder. "Dan! I was wondering when you and Doc were going to show up in town!"

Allen tips his brim and greets his colleague. "Well, Bob! It's good to see you as well." Allen crosses the room and reaches for an empty coffee cup. "It has been an interesting couple of days. What information do you have for us regarding our escapee?"

Doug looks over at Allen with a curious look, wondering again how Allen knows the man.

Bob smiles, takes a sip from his cup. "As a matter of fact there has been word." Bob crosses the room to his desk and picks up a telegram giving the latest report of the whereabouts of Billy. "Well, according to this wire, Billy was spotted close to a small settlement northwest of town, riding with two other men." Bob pauses, sipping some more coffee. "We think these are a couple of his cousins, and they are heading to his uncle's, who has a place out by Chimney Rock."

Allen sets his empty cup down. "Okay, so what's the plan?"

Bob frowns and shrugs, looking at Allen. "I don't know. You're the boss on this one. We figured we would leave that up to you."

Allen, with his hands on his hips, paces the room for a moment. "Okay, well, Doc and I can use a good night's rest. So, why don't you get a few of the boys and have them ready to leave with us first thing in the morning."

"How many do you want me to get for the trip?" Bob asks.

"I think four should do; with Doc and me, that will make six and that should be plenty."

Bob nods, and reaches for a list in the top desk drawer. "All right then, I'll get the men ready for tomorrow; what time do you want to leave?"

"At first light," Allen replies.

Allen and Doug walk out of the Marshal's office, and Doug asks, "So Allen, how did you know Bob?"

"I really don't know," Allen replies, shaking his head. "Like before, it just came to me."

"That might just come in handy down the road," Doug remarks as he slaps Allen on the shoulder.

Allen knocks Doc's arm back, smiles and says, "I hope so, but I still don't have a clue where we live. That would be a good thing to come to me."

Doug grins, and taps a finger to his temple. "While you were talking to Bob I was snooping around the office and found a map of the area in and around Lincoln. This map on the wall shows all the ranches and homesteads. Our ranches are on this map too. If I am figuring my directions and distance correct, we only need to ride just a bit east and three or four miles south of town and we should be at the places we call 'home."

"Did you say ranches?" Allen asks with excitement.

"Yes, I said ranches. The map shows two big ranches, one with each of our names; and they're right across from each other."

"How many acres are they?"

Doug shakes his head. "I really don't know but they look pretty big to me."

Allen slaps his leg. "Hot Damn! That beats another night in a hotel!"

Doug starts laughing loudly. "Okay. We'll head there soon, but before we head out to the ranches, let's go to the saloon and see what they have to eat; I am getting hungry."

"I could eat also," Allen says as he steps off the boardwalk and stands in the street. I know where we can eat." Allen looks up and down the street to orientate himself about the town. They have walked a couple of blocks south of the square, when Allen speaks up. "I am puttin a foot down here; no gun-play, Doug."

"Why Allen, I am offended that you would think that all I want to do is look for a gunfight."

"Right, I know you don't have to look; they just seem to find you," says Allen, throwing a hand in the air.

"All right Marshal, Sir, I promise to be a good boy," replies Doug sarcastically

Allen reaches over and shoves Doug's shoulder. "Funny, real funny, just leave the pistols in the holsters. Remember we live here."

Allen and Doug are just about to walk into the Ninth Street Diner and Saloon when Doug stops a couple steps short of the doorway. He grabs Allen by the shoulder. "Hey Allen, watch this."

Doug pushes the doors open; as he steps through the doors all of the activity goes silent. No conversation, no piano, not even a coin or poker chip is tossed onto the game's pot. Everyone looks in the direction of the door, the patrons of the bar looking nervous.

Allen quietly leans toward Doug and whispers into his ear, "Does this happen every time you enter a saloon?"

Doug leans back and replies, "Yup. Every time."

"What's up with that?" Allen asks in amazement.

Doug starts walking through the room and continues, "I really don't know why I get that response, other than Doc must really be some kind of bad boy."

"Let's just find a table, and get something to eat," Allen comments.

They find a table in the corner and sit down, and the room resumes its flurry of activity.

A woman, with hair the color of fire-red walks up to the table. "Hello Dan, it's been a long time. What can I get you two?"

Allen smiles at the young woman. "What do you have on the menu today?"

"We have pot roast with mashed potatoes and gravy, fresh green beans, and fresh baked apple pie for dessert," the red haired waitress, Lisa, informs them.

Allen rubs his stomach. "Mmmm that sounds real good. You're right; we are in for a treat. Yep, we'll both have that."

Lisa smiles, pats them both on the shoulder. "Comin' right up, fellas. I'll bring you a couple of beers to wash it all down." Shortly afterwards she returns with the beers and two plates heaped full of food. "Here you go gentlemen, enjoy."

Doug reaches for a fork. "This looks good. Thank you, Lisa."

Lisa smiles. "You're welcome. If you need anything just holler."

Allen smiles at her. "I think we are good for now." They dig in to their meal and when they are finished with their pie, Allen rubs his stomach again for the second time since sitting down. "That really hit the spot. Now, what do you say we head out to the ranches and see where we live?"

Doug stands up, throws some money on the table for the eats. "Miss Lisa, thanks for the fine meal. Give my compliments to the cook." He heads out the door to catch up with Allen.

When they reach the street, Allen looks over his shoulder at Doug. "Bob said he'd take our horses to the livery and switch the saddles to a couple of fresh horses, and they should be waiting out front of his office.

We can get ours back when we come back in the morning and take these two we're picking up with us when we head out."

"Well then, let's ride," Doug says as he gets on his horse.

Without saying another word Allen and Doug, not sure what is going to come next, start out to their ranches.

"You know, that little red head was sure pretty," Allen remarks to break the silence.

Doug starts shaking his finger at Allen. "If I can't shoot anybody, you certainly can't go chasing after Miss Lisa."

Allen looks seriously at Doug. "How do you know her name?"

"I just know things," Doug replies.

"Yeah right," Allen snaps back.

"Actually I heard the bartender call her Lisa," Doug confesses.

"Oh," Allen says. "I thought you might be getting the same flashes of memory that I'm getting."

Doug shakes his head. "I wish I was getting those kinds of flashes. The only thing I am getting is dreams, the same dream every night."

Allen bows his head, and then looks back up at Doug. "Is that the dream about the lady and the boys?"

Doug gets a sorrowful expression, and his eyes take on a hollow stare. "The dead lady and the dead boys."

Allen, unsure how to respond says, "I think I will stay with my flashes. You can keep your dream."

As they are riding down the trail, Allen points to two signs hanging from posts. The one on the left side reads: the S-BAR-S Ranch; the one on the right side reads: Triple-J Ranch.

"I wonder which one is yours." Allen asks.

“The Triple-J is mine,” replies Doc, pointing to the sign.

Allen looks at the ground. “Are you sure?”

“Yep, absolutely,” Doug says, and then turns into the lane leading toward the ranch. “I am going there and see what I can find out about Doc’s past. Why don’t you stop by in the morning when you’re ready to leave and we'll head out from Doc’s, or should I say, my place?”

“Sounds good to me. I will see you in the morning.”

The two of them each go their separate ways, to their ranches, to their homes.

4

Doug rides down the long, long lane to his ranch. When he gets to the top of a rise in the road, he pauses and looks down. He sees a beautiful white plantation style mansion. The front entrance is grand. It has double front doors painted in a deep, deep blue which matches the shutters that flank the numerous windows of the manor. The front steps are set between four white pillars as tall as the house itself, with a balcony nestled in between the pillars on the second floor looking out to the front gardens. The gardens are magnificent. There are flowers, roses, flowering bushes, and fruit trees. The grass is lush, a beautiful green, and as soft to the touch as an Angel's wings.

He can see beyond the main house, a small one-story house, the caretaker's home. There are two barns and six other buildings, consisting of a bunkhouse, a blacksmith shop, and one building for storing equipment and supplies. However, he is not sure what the others are used for. He sees a large pasture with a corral containing about fifty or more horses. There are more pastures surrounding the farmstead with what appears to be hundreds, maybe thousands of cattle. Beyond the caretaker's home are beautiful green pastures which seem to drop off the map at the horizon. He cannot help but wonder how a U.S. Marshal's Deputy could afford such a place as this.

As he gets closer, a man steps out onto the porch of the caretaker's home; the man smiles big as can be and waves like wheat in the summer wind.

"John! Welcome home! I heard you might be coming back through Lincoln. I hoped you had time to come home for awhile." Doug rides up to the man who is now standing in the manor's side yard, next to the hitching rail. "John, you look like you can use a stiff drink."

"I just want to get off this horse and go inside and rest for a minute; it has been a long couple of days," remarks Doug.

Doug dismounts, and turns back toward the grand home. Just as he finds the beauty of what he sees as a wonderful peaceful place, he catches sight of the small burial plots. There are three headstones beneath a great big old oak tree, surrounded by a small iron fence.

Sam, the one-man welcoming committee, reaches for the reins. "I will have one of the men take care of your horse so you can come in and take a load off."

"That sounds good," Doug acknowledges, then holds up a finger, indicating that Sam hold off on the thought. Doug returns his gaze to the burial spots, and starts to walk toward it.

Sam reaches over and puts his hand on Doug's shoulder. "John, why don't you just come on inside; you know it's not good to dwell so much on the past."

Doug nods but can't take his eyes from the graves. "I will be there in a few minutes; I just need to… Well, um, you know."

Sam pats Doc's shoulder, trying to help with the overhanging gloom that is surrounding him. "Yes, I would, better than most."

Doug walks to the old oak tree where he finds three headstones. One is a bit larger than the other two. He stands outside the gate, removes his hat, and wipes the back of his hand across his forehead.

He reaches for the gate latch, and pauses as he starts to open it. He feels pain and grief that fills his chest. He gets his feet to move from their spot where they seem frozen to the ground. Doug steps through the gate and around the headstones, where he can read the inscriptions. He starts to read; the rush of what seems to be a lifetime of pain fills his entire body. He reads the largest stone first.

The stone reads:

Mrs. Julie Gray
Loving Wife to John
Caring Mother to Jacob and John Jr.

The first one on the right reads:

Jacob Gray
A Good Boy

The third, furthest to the right reads:

John 'Johnny' Gray Jr.
Taken Before His Time

John 'Doc' Gray is fully aware of the anger inside him, and what put it there. He stands there and bows his head, his hat in hand, grieving, grieving the loss of his family, grieving for the loss of his loved ones.

After a few moments alone with his family, John turns and leaves but not without taking one last look back as he closes the gate. He latches the gate and smiles; the unknown is becoming clearer, and he gives thanks to the loves of his life, his wife Julie and their two young sons. "Thank you, Julie; thank you, my sons."

Doc turns and walks toward the front door of his home. He now fully understands who the woman and young boys are in his recurring dream that is becoming a nightmare.

The poor souls who are left to die in this nightmare are not strangers as he hoped in the beginning, and has hoped in the days since he started having it. They are his wife and children. The next thing he needs to learn is why they died.

Although he encountered 'One Eyed' Jack Dollar and a couple of men who are part of his gang, now that he has put together the part of 'WHO', he has to figure out the 'WHY', why they were killed, why it was HIS family who became victims of the Dollar Gang's evilness. He can only hope when he talks with his property caretaker, he can fill in some of the blanks, without letting the caretaker realize that he doesn't know much, if any, of the details.

Doug turns the knob on the front door and steps into the front hall entry. He is taken in by the sight of the home's interior and wonders how 'Doc' Gray was able to build something this amazing, being a Deputy U.S. Marshal.

As he looks over the inside of the house, he notices a spiral staircase made of the most beautiful white oak he has ever seen; it leads to a balcony on the second floor.

"John," Sam says as he appears in a doorway on Doug's left. "Come on into your study and sit. Give yourself a break. Put your boots up and relax a little."

"Right behind you, Sam," Doug acknowledges. "You can fill me in on what has been going on while I've been away."

Doug and Sam make their way down a hallway, which is trimmed in oak, with crystal oil lamps on the walls to light the way, and step into the study. Along one wall, there is a roll top desk with a fancy leather chair sitting in front. On each side of the desk are built in bookshelves filled with books, papers, and manuscripts.

Sam crosses the room and sits in a chair. "Sit down John, and I'll get you up to speed on the ranch and of course the local gossip."

Doug walks over to the window and surveys the sights through its panes. He can see a pasture with a few cows with their calves. There are a couple of ranch hands moving more mother-calf pairs through a gate at the top of the hill. He begins to feel some excitement at this sight. He is starting to believe it; this is his ranch. This man Sam and those men out there work for him.

"It sure is nice to have you home, John," Sam says, interrupting his thoughts. "It's been so long since you have been home for a visit. I am sure you miss home, and the ranch. I have to ask, do you miss it?"

"Miss what?" Doug asks.

Sam points to a wall that is covered with framed diplomas, certificates, and awards that he, DR. JOHN GRAY, has earned and achieved. Doug walks over and glances at them a moment and then looks back at Sam.

"You know, your medical practice," Sam continues.

Doc looks at his friend, and tries to smile. "Yes, I guess sometimes I miss practicing medicine," and then thinks to himself, *'This is making more sense where and why I have the money for such a home and ranch.'*

"It seemed like when Julie and the boys were killed you gave up a whole lot of things," Sam points out.

Doc looks back at the window a moment. "Yes, this is true. Things have changed and things were taken from me. However, it would be nice to help someone rather than just putting them in the ground."

"Well, you know your office is still the way you left it in town."

He looks back at the wall, and then shakes his head. "I have other business that I must tend to for now."

Sam nods in understanding then says, "I hear you got one of the men who did this to your family."

Doc's eyes go dim, and the coldness returns to his face. "Yes, it was 'One-Eyed' Jack Dollar. I shot him over in Eagle. I didn't know at the time he was one of the men."

"Don't you think it's time you stay around here?" Sam asks as he stands up. "Maybe re-open your practice, and settle down."

"Not until the very last one of them is in the ground," Doc shoots back as his face turns from pale to amber with the thought of letting those men go on living, while his family is buried under the old oak tree.

"Hey, are you rested up enough to take a walk around the place?" Sam asks as he walks over to the window where Doc is standing.

“Ya know, I think I can muster up the strength to take a walk ‘bout the place,” Doc replies.

Sam and Doc exit the study, and cross the hall to the kitchen. Doug thinks to himself, *‘There has been a lot of cooking done here.’* Through the back door, they step onto a very large porch. The porch is covered with wooden boxes, and potted flowers. There are several benches for sitting, surrounded by a pair of well-worn rocking chairs.

They step off the porch and Sam takes the lead. Doc starts to follow. “John, I thought first we’d go over to the horse corral, and I’d show you the new colts. We have had four new colts since you left, all black. I think one of them is going to be a real good one.”

Doc smiles as he sees the mare and colts. “Oh yeah? Why do you say that?”

“Well, she started walking almost immediately and she was even trotting a little the next day.”

Doc gives an honest broad grin. “You don’t say? Well, looks like we will have to keep our eyes on that one. Did you name her yet?”

Sam shakes his head, then replies, “Naw, that one, I left it up to you. I had one of the men saddle up a couple of horses so I could show you all the new calves we have now.”

Sam and Doc get on their horses and ride out into the pasture. Sam begins pointing out all the new calves out in the pasture.

“So how many new calves do we have so far?” Doc asks.

Sam thinks for a moment, then replies, “Thirty three so far. We are expecting about another twenty to drop any day; that would bring the herd to just over eight-hundred and fifty head.”

Doc smiles, feeling proud of his cattle, and knowing his ranch is taken care of by a capable foreman. “Sam, it’s nice to know you and the hands are taking good care of things while I’m away. I probably don’t tell you enough how well you do and how much I appreciate it.” Doc reaches out and the men shake hands.

Sam, realizing what time it is getting to be, looks at Doc and says, “We better get back to the house and get cleaned up for supper. It is getting late, and you know Mary gets upset when we are late. Besides, she has something special planned for your homecoming.”

“All right, let’s get going. I want to stay in her good graces on my first night back home.”

The two men ride back to the barn where they put the horses away, and then head into the house to get cleaned up for supper.

Afterwards Doc walks into the dining room and finds Sam and Mary sitting at the table. Across from his seat is an attractive young lady. Unprepared for the newcomer, John feels a bit embarrassed and glad that he had taken a bath and shaved. Lord knows those are not daily luxuries when away from home.

Sam stands up. “Dr. John Gray, I would like you to meet Miss Audra Lee Randolph. She and her sister Amy recently moved here from Cedars Grove, Virginia. She and Amy are renovating the old hotel, the Exchange, I believe.”

Doc smiles and takes her by the hand. “Very nice to meet you, Miss Randolph. So you’re going to make that old hotel livable again?” He continues as he takes his seat across from his new dinner companion.

Audra smiles. “Yes, that’s right, Dr. Gray. We hope we can bring it up to New York style.”

"That's quite a challenge," Doc says to her. "I'm sure when you get it done it'll be the talk of the town."

"Thank you for the vote of confidence. We're trying to make it into a hotel and dinner theater. They are very popular back east. My brother runs one for my father in Chicago, which is very successful I might add. We hope it will be a place where people will come from miles around just to say they have stayed there."

"I wish you ladies well on your endeavor, Miss Randolph. If there is any way I can be of service to you, please do not hesitate to ask."

"Mary tells me you came here from Boston?" Audra asks. "And that you understand the tastes and preferences of those from the East, so I just may hold you to that offer."

Doc, Sam and Mary laugh at Audra's teasing. Doc cannot help but think that it may be the first in a long while since he had pleasantries at the dinner table.

Audra, unafraid to dive into heavy conversation, continues, "Sam and Mary tell me you are after cattle rustlers."

Doc reaches for the biscuits and passes them around after taking one for himself. "Yes that's true, but truth be known I am not sold on the story. From the story he tells, and a gut feeling, I think we might be after the wrong man."

"What makes you say that, Doc?" Sam asks, surprised.

Doc takes the bowl of sweet peas from Mary and hands it to Sam. "The story sounds fishy to me. Part of the story the kid tells sounds right, but I think there is something more to it. He either doesn't know, or is hiding the rest." Doc offers wine to Audra and his other dinner companions before continuing, "Sam, I will need the necessary supplies, and my horse ready, first thing in the morning. We have put a posse together, and we are heading out toward Chimney Rock"

Sam nods and says, "I will have your horse and supplies ready."

"I have to say, Dr. Gray, you have a most beautiful home. Mary gave me a tour earlier," Audra remarks as she sets her wine glass down. "Why so large? I mean, ten bedrooms? I have to ask, why ten. That seems like so many for one man."

"Please call me John, or Doc. At home, I am not much for the formalities. Before my wife, Julie died, she liked to entertain, and we would have dinner parties out here. She invited the people from the town board, and even the Governor came out once. She loved to entertain. The house was always full of some kind of activity on one day or another. Saturday was most often a day of something happening here. On many occasions some of the guests would stay the night. She wanted plenty of room for anyone needing a place to put their head down."

"John, I would love it if you would allow me to use some of your rooms for ideas to create some of the rooms in our hotel."

John smiles at the prospect that this lovely young lady would visit again. "Miss Randolph, I would feel honored if you would use some ideas from my home. So please, anytime you want to stop by feel free to do so; no invitation is needed."

Audra takes her napkin from her lap and places it on the table, then looks at Mary. "I must say Mary, that was such a nice meal. I want to thank you for inviting me."

"You're welcome, Audra. I always welcome having another female out here for company. It was so nice to have you come out and visit."

"John, Mary and Sam didn't show me around the grounds before dinner. I would be grateful if you would be kind enough to take me on a tour of your beautiful ranch."

"Miss Randolph, it would be my humble pleasure. Please excuse me a moment." Doc steps out of the room and returns with a torch lamp and her wrap. He walks over to her and pulls out her chair. "Please, follow me, Miss Randolph."

"John, I would be happy to. But, only if you are willing to call me Audra." She stands up and he places her wrap on her shoulders. At that very moment, she feels a tingle, a surge that goes through her whole body. Why did this man's touch reach into her soul? After all, he is virtually a stranger. She smiles and looks into his dark eyes. It is as though she has looked into them for a lifetime.

Doc looks at this lady's sweet smile. Looking into her face and her eyes gives him an almost peaceful feeling, a feeling he has not felt since that horrible day. She is a stranger but he welcomes this feeling. It has been so long since he felt so at ease.

"Audra," Doc says as he takes her by the arm and escorts her out to the back porch.

Sam stands and walks across the room to join his wife; they watch John leave the room with Audra on his arm. Sam hugs the love of his life, Mary, as she sheds a tear of joy at the sight of John, who has a smile and Miss Audra Lee Randolph on his arm.

"So, Audra, where would you like to start your personal tour?" Doc asks.

Audra points across the expanse of grassy yard. "Can we go look at the horses?"

"Horses it is." Doc holds out his hand to allow her to go first off the porch. When they reach the corral, they see the mares with their new colts.

"Oh, these are just marvelous, John. I have never been this close to a colt. I especially like that black one. How shiny it is."

"Yes, that black one looks to be an exceptional young girl. She pretty much came out of the womb walking and jumping. She's going to be something special."

"Does she have a name?" Audra reaches through the rails of the corral and strokes the neck of the colt.

"No, we haven't named her yet."

"She should have a name. Everyone needs a name," she says, then starts to rub the mother's neck with the other hand.

"Yes, I suppose she needs a name," he comments as he reaches through the rail, patting the colt and rubbing her head. "Name her," he tells Audra, surprising her and himself at the suddenness of his response.

"Really? I can name her?" She is thrilled at the idea of it. Names start flying through her head.

"Yes, Audra. Please, you name her," Doc goes on, happy to see her excited at the idea of the simple task of naming the colt. However, he can see she isn't taking it lightly.

"Oh, John, I can't think of a good name. I've never named a horse before."

"I tell ya what Audra, just take your time. I'll tell Sam that it is your decision to name her. And you can just let him or Mary know what the name will be when you decide." John feels a small amount of pride at the idea.

"John, you can be sure I will give her the utmost worthy name. Thank you for giving me the opportunity." She steps back from the rail and looks him in the eye. "I have never had the opportunity to ride a horse. I have always wanted to. My sister takes riding lessons, so she rides often."

Doc takes her by the arm, and leads her toward the pond. "Come; let me show you the pond." They walk between the huge barns and around another building to approach the pond. Doc directs her to the bench nestled under the cottonwood tree.

"This bench is one of the places I enjoy often on the ranch."

Audra can see why. It is a large several-acre pond, with lots of trees and bushes around it. The sound of the breeze through the cottonwood sounds like rain in the spring. As she is listening to the sound, Doc breaks her train of thought

"How about I give you riding lessons? I realize I am not a professional instructor, but I have spent many a day in the saddle myself. Besides it will be a privilege to teach you to ride."

"Oh John, that would be just wonderful!" she replies excitedly. "I'll be a dedicated student. Can we start the lessons just as soon as you complete your assignment?"

Audra feels as if she has jumped up and touched the moon itself. She cannot wait until he returns to start their sessions so they can ride together. They sit there in silence listening to the breeze and watching the last ray of twilight slip just below the horizon.

Afterwards, by the glow of the torch light, Doc escorts Audra back to the house, and when she sees the horses again she comments, "You have some beautiful horses."

Doc looks over at the corral and says, "Thank you. Yes, they are nice stock. However, more of the credit should go to Sam. He has more to do with the day-to-day operations than I do. I am afraid I'm not around much these days."

Audra stops and looks him squarely in the face. "Well John, maybe I can give you reason to stay a little closer to home." She turns and starts walking again. "I can't learn to ride without an instructor, now can I?"

He loves hearing the sarcastic tones in her voice. She knows how to have a fun conversation.

Doc smiles and says, "I'd say yep, that sounds like I will have to be close to home more often."

When they reach the rear yard, he motions toward the porch. "Well Audra, we probably should go back inside and see what Sam and Mary are doing."

"I really like Mary; she's nice," Audra says as they step onto the porch.

"Yes. Mary is a special woman," Doc acknowledges as he reaches for the doorknob, "She keeps Sam on his toes. They make a good couple; they've been married for twenty years now."

Audra removes her wrap and hands it to Doc. "They really do seem like they are a good match."

Doc opens a hallway door. "Okay, go to the rear parlor. Sam has a fire going."

With Doc close behind, Audra enters the parlor and begins looking around with huge eyes. "WOW! This is the most incredible room. Did you shoot all these animals yourself?"

Sam and Marry are sitting on a sofa in front of the fireplace. Sam can see that Audra looks amazed. "He sure did," Sam replies. "Why that buffalo over there was on the run at close to three quarters of a mile away and Doc dropped him like a stone."

Doc gives Sam the dismissive furrowing brow expression and says, "Sam, I'm sure Miss Audra here doesn't want to hear all the details of each hunt."

Audra looks at all of the trophies mounted on the walls and the animal skin rugs on the floor. "Actually, John, I would love nothing more. I have always found hunting intriguing. My father hunted some deer and bear when my sister and I were young. I always thought it would be fun to go out on a hunt. Maybe you can teach me after the riding lessons; take me on a hunt."

He looks at her, thinking, '*She isn't this refined eastern lady I thought she was. She has pioneering woman inside there somewhere.*' "We will have to see about that. I don't know."

Audra starts to get excited at the thought of the adventures she can encounter with John as her guide. "When you get back, we can start on the lessons, riding and shooting right away. Please don't make me beg you, John."

Doc looks at Mary and Sam. He can see what they were up to when they invited her here. He thinks *'A good tongue thrashing for both of them may be in order. However, they are right. She may be the right lady to enjoy some of my life's pleasures with.'*

"Alright, when I get back I will first teach you to ride, then how to handle and shoot a gun, and then how to hunt."

Sam looks at Audra and adds, "You're in for a treat, Miss Audra. Doc here is probably the best shot in the country. You put that Sharps rifle in his hands and he doesn't miss."

Mary looks at her husband with a smile, then at their guest. "Sam is right. If I mention that the cellar needs something, before you know it here comes Doc back from a hunt, with some sort of game."

The foursome talk and laugh for some time until Audra gets up from her seat and starts to go across the room. She stops suddenly. She notices the rug she is stepping on; she looks down and sees it's not a woven one. "Tell me about this bear skin rug."

"Dan and I went on a hunting trip a few years back," Doc begins. "We were hunting in the mountains north of Denver for elk. When this big ol' bear walks into camp, he stands up with teeth showing, men start running for cover, and there I was. I pulled my six shooters and let him have it with both barrels. The bear looked at me and dropped where he stood."

"Weren't you scared?" She asks in a concerned way.

"Yes, I was," Doc quickly replies. "I thought I was going to be his dinner, and that's when I thought it would be good idea to learn to shoot pistols a sight better." Everyone laughs at his musing. "Well, I best be heading to bed. We are riding out at first light, Sam. You will have my horse and things ready?"

Sam doesn't mutter a word. He just nods his head in acknowledgement of Doc's orders.

"I would love to hear more of your stories," Audra says to get back to the subject at hand. "Can't you tell just one more before you go to bed?"

"Sam will tell you about any one of those critters on the wall," Doc explains as he waves a hand toward the wall. "He is much better at telling them anyway."

"I am quite certain that he is a very good storyteller. But, I still would like to hear them from you," Audra points out, desiring to listen to John tell his stories.

"No offense, Sam"

Sam smiles and says, "None taken. John, tell her about the elk in the canyons southwest of Spirit Lake."

Doc inhales deeply, exhales loudly and starts to talk to his audience, as if he is telling a story to a group of children in Sunday school. "Alright, but this is the last one. Like I said, I have an early start in the morning."

"Thank you, John," Audra says as she sits down in a chair close to her host.

Doc thinks for a moment, and then begins. "Okay, well you see, Dan, Sam and I was overlooking a canyon in the mountains when we saw a bull elk. We spotted him on a little ledge across the creek and I took my Sharps out and took aim, pulled the trigger and we had elk for supper."

"Hey, you left out the best part," Sam points out. "We were going down the mountain to get to the elk when we see a young brave with an arrow sticking out of his side. He had been left for dead and by the looks of him he had been there for awhile. John patches him up and takes him to the nearest town where he takes the arrow out and makes sure the Doctor in town keeps him there until he is ready to travel. A few days later we went back to the Doctor, John paid for the brave's care, took the brave with him, and made sure he got back to his tribe."

Audra held her hands up to her mouth, as if to silence a gasp. "Weren't you afraid he or his tribe might try and kill you?"

"No, on the contrary," replies Doc, shaking his head. "He was in no shape to do anything to us, not to mention it was the right thing to do. When we found his tribe, we found out he was a son of the chief. So, the chief was grateful to have his son returned healthy." Stepping away from the fireplace Doc walks to the center of the room before turning back. "Good night all. Miss Audra, it has been quite a pleasure to meet you. I look forward to those lessons."

Audra smiles at Doc and says, "I enjoyed this evening as well." She then looks back at Sam. "I really want to hear some more stories, Sam."

"It is getting late and I need to get some rest too," Sam says. "I have to be sure I get up in time to get John's things ready. When John gets back ask him to tell you; he's really a better storyteller."

Mary stands and reaches for a lamp. "Come Audra, I will show you to your room."

"Thanks for a lovely evening, Sam."

When the two ladies reach the top of the stairs Mary opens the bedroom door and goes to the table to light the lamp. "I will wake you up in time for breakfast; good night."

"Good night, Mary. I have had the most wonderful time. You are right." Audra hugs Mary. "I can't wait for him to return home."

Mary smiles proudly like a mother would at her daughter and closes the door. Another tear of joy slips down her face.

5

Allen rides down the path leading to his house and finds a two-story Victorian style house, painted in various tones of green and tan. It has a large wraparound porch. The property also boasts barns and a couple of other buildings, and a cabin type home. There is an older man wearing overalls, waving him over.

"Dan! Great to see you!" he yells out when he sees Allen approaching. "I heard you were coming this way so I stocked the cellar. You should have enough to last you a few days."

Allen dismounts his horse and shakes the man's hand. "Thanks, Joe. I appreciate it. So how are things around here?"

Joe reaches in his pocket for a handkerchief, removes his hat, and wipes his brow. "It seems that we're getting rain just when we need it. The crops are off to a good start and the cattle are getting fat and sassy."

Allen smiles proudly and looks about his place as though it is just another day. "Looks as if things around this place are doing just fine."

Joe replaces his hat, takes Allen's horse, and ties it to the post. "So tell me, is Doc coming by for some poker tonight?"

Allen shakes his head. "I don't think so. He has some things to take care of at his place."

"All right, I guess I won't be setting him a place." Joe unties the horse from the post and heads toward the barn.

****

As Allen catches up on the happenings around town, and his ranch, he tries poking around for information from Joe about his friend and partner, Doc. "Hey Joe, lately some things really seem to have Doc more on edge. Anytime I want to talk about it, he grumbles, and looks at me with those eyes to say 'are ya beatin' a dead horse or what?' Tell me, do you know what happened that Doc seems to be so angry about? I know his family has died. But, it has to be more than that."

Joe looks at Allen a bit confused, not sure what to say at first. "I thought you knew the whole story. Well, you remember when you went into the Minnesota Territory after that gang of cattle rustlers who came up from the Kansas Territory last year?"

"Do I remember them? Hell yeah, I remember them. We spent what seemed like forever chasing them from one end of the territory to the other until they finally holed up about twenty miles east of here. It turned into quite a big gunfight. I lost a couple of good Deputies in that exchange of lead."

Joe nods and points at Allen. "Right, that's the one. In that fight you shot their gang's leader. He was gut shot real bad. They rode into town and went to Doc Gray's office for help. People in town saw them ride up to Doc's. Townsfolk said the gang was the one led by the Dollar brothers, Amos and Jack. Amos had been shot. They held Doc at gunpoint and told him he had better fix him up right good. Now, you know, Doc is a good Doctor, and he did everything he could, but Amos was hurt too badly and he died. Because he died Jack got extremely angry; he blamed Doc for his brother's death. So, 'One-Eyed' Jack Dollar, and the rest of the men, tied Doc up. They threw him over the back of a horse and hauled him out to his place. The only people at the Triple-J were Doc's wife and boys. I was working for him then. Sam, the foreman, the hands and I were out on the Southwest pasture, branding. The foreman's wife, Mary, was in town doing the shopping for dry goods and things; so when they got there they tied Doc to one of those pillars out front. They grabbed his wife and both of his boys and dragged them outside. By the looks of them, they had put up a fight, but both the boys were beaten almost to death. Julie was beaten, and several of them took a turn with her right in front of the house. Doc, tied up, was forced to see this evilness thrust upon his family. Once done ransacking the home and when the violence was over, they hanged Julie, Johnny, and Jacob from the big oak tree in the yard; there Doc was, left to watch their bodies go lifeless. He was completely unable to save the ones he loved and cared for more than life itself."

Allen removes his hat, and runs his hand through his hair. He pauses and gazes for a few moments at their feet. "Yes. Yes, that explains Doc's darkness, and the anger that surrounds him. I wish I had been here during that time." Allen puts his hat back on, and then continues. "I shouldn't have been away when that happened."

Joe throws a hand up at the Marshal as if to say no worry. He reaches for the cabinet, and pulls out a bottle of bourbon and two glasses.

"Yes, you were, but everyone knows that you would have been here if you knew it was going to happen." Joe pours each of them a shot of bourbon, and they sit down at the kitchen table. "The whole thing changed Doc. I mean really changed him. Doc was a peaceful man, not to mention one hell of a good Doctor before the killings. After you brought him back home from White Horse, all he could think about was getting the men who killed his family. You could hear gunfire every day. He would be out practicing with his pistols from dawn until dusk. I remember you riding out from town to see what was going on over there, because of the continual shooting; and he wouldn't even talk to you about it. All he said to you was, *'Those men took my family. Justice needs to be done. I have a job to do and I must be prepared for it.'* You tried talking him out of it, telling him to leave it to you; but it wasn't enough for him. That's when you deputized him and told him that if he was determined to bring these men to justice at least it would be proper and legal this way. He has been your Deputy who goes everywhere with you ever since, and now you know the whole story." Joe takes a drink of his bourbon, stands up and walks over to look out at the North pasture.

Allen stands and joins Joe at the window and pats him on the shoulder. "I remember the day I found him in White Horse. He was drunk. It was not easy getting him out of that saloon. Yeah, I remember when I went to see why he was shooting. It all makes sense now; but I tell ya, Joe, Doc is getting darker by the day. I don't know if I can stop him. It's as if he's going crazy with hate."

"I think he has something deep down inside him that will keep him from losing it all," Joe points out.

Allen smiles and says, "I have a hunch you just may be right."

"I kind of feel sorry for Doc at times though," Joe comments. "All this happened less than a year after his mother's death. It seems like a lot to handle in such a short time. If a person's brain did overload, it would make sense if Doc's certainly did."

"In the time I've known Doc, there is so much I don't know about him," Allen points out. "Doc doesn't talk about his past much; is he from around here? Or did he come from somewhere else?"

"For best friends, and riding partners, y'all don't talk much do ya?" Joe replies with a chuckle. "He's from Boston. His father is a world renowned surgeon there. People from all over go to Boston to see him."

"So he followed in his Father's footsteps?" Allen asks.

"Actually from how I hear it, becoming a Doctor really wasn't a choice," Joe replies." It was what John was groomed to be. His whole life was directed for him to follow in his father's footsteps. After John finished schoolin' and his medical training, he worked with his father for ten years. He was becoming the man, or should I say, the Doctor, his Father wanted him to be; but one day he told his family he was going to move west where he could bring modern medicine to people who did not have access to it. He moved himself and Julie out to Lincoln where they set up shop, and he built a beautiful house for her. He said she meant the world to him so he was going to try to give her everything she could possibly ever want, keeping her in the luxury she had been accustomed to in Boston. For him Julie was to want for nothin."

'I wish I had known and been here for all this,' Allen thinks to himself and then says, "I can see why he is so determined to catch the men who did this to his family. It makes more sense to me now, the reaction he had in Eagle when 'One-Eyed Jack Dollar called him out. Right there in the street he said to Doc, *'I'm going to kill you, and leave you for the coyotes just like we did your family.'* The look on Doc's face was one I have never seen before."

Joe's face turns pale at the thought of that street scene. "Let's change the subject to something more pleasant, shall we?"

Allen nods. "Okay, so anything new going on in Lincoln these days?"

****

Allen just finished taking a bath and shaving, and as he was walking out of the bathroom he hears Joe, at the bottom of the steps, hollering out to him, "Dan, supper is being served in the dining room."

"I'll get dressed and be right down," Allen says.

Allen goes to his room, gets dressed, and hurries downstairs. He walks into the dining room only to find an attractive woman sitting at the table with two place settings. He smiles politely and says, "Pardon me, ma'am."

Before he can utter another word, Joe enters the room carrying two plates of food. "I am sorry. Oh, where are my manners? Marshal, this is Miss Amy Lynn Randolph. Amy is new in town. I invited her to the ranch for supper before I knew you were coming in. I am so sorry; filling you in on ranch business, it slipped my mind."

Allen removes his hat and addresses the woman sitting at the table. "It is a pleasure, Miss Randolph."

Amy smiles and replies, "I have heard so much about you, Marshal. It is so nice to meet you. Please call me Amy."

Allen looks at Joe with surprise and says, "Joe, there are only two place settings. Aren't you eatin' supper? I thought you and Ruth were eating here tonight."

Joe sets the two meals down, and pulls a chair out for Allen. "I forgot that I need to tend to something in town, and Ruth is at Mrs. Marten's, some ladies' quilting square thing. So it will just be you two." The fumbling older man turns to leave the room, and then turns back. "Ruth made a cherry cobbler; it's in the kitchen, and there is more coffee on the stove. I've also started a fire in the parlor so you and Miss Amy may sit in there when you're finished with supper. I'll see you when I get back."

Allen, still not sure what is going on, nods, "Thanks, Joe. Thank Ruth for me." Allen takes his hat off and sits down across from Miss Amy. After she says grace, he hands her some cornbread. "Joe's wife, Ruth, probably makes the best cornbread in a hundred miles. I am at a disadvantage here. Miss Amy, you know who I am. So please tell me about yourself, and what brought you to Lincoln."

"My father recently purchased the old Exchange Hotel and the vacant building behind that has stables for guests' horses. It's on the square, right across from the Post Office, so business should be prosperous because of the location in the center of town. We're overseeing its renovations and we will conduct the daily operations once we open. We're not renovating only the hotel. We will be renovating the vacant building as well. Together they will be a hotel and dinner theater. You see, in the larger cities in states like Massachusetts, Northern Virginia, and New York they are quite popular. My father sent my brother to Chicago to try his hand there. It went quite well. Father thought since Lincoln is the last city of size going west, until Denver, maybe it would do well here too. We are going to rename it the Pioneer Hotel and Dinner Theater."

Allen finds himself mesmerized by this auburn haired stranger. He had not realized how much he missed a good conversation with a woman over dinner. It had been too long. Suddenly he realizes she has stopped talking, "Well, that sounds like a whole lot of work to accomplish. I have a feeling you know just how to run things since your family is already in the business."

"Yes, we have been busy trying to hire men to do the work. I am very excited about the changes. But, there are so many different things one can make . . . ."

"What kind of changes did you have in mind?" Allen interrupts.

Amy thinks for a few moments, then replies, "Well first, it's getting it updated, and keeping with the trends of places like New York, or Chicago, making it appealing and economical so people, who live here, even though they may not be staying at the hotel, may come out for an evening dinner show."

Allen reaches over and pours her some coffee, and puts their empty dinner plates on the sideboard. "Miss Randolph . . . ."

"Marshal, it's Amy," she cuts him off.

Surprised by her insistence Allen continues, “Right, Amy. That sounds like a wonderful concept and it wouldn’t hurt to add more class to this town.”

When they finish their dessert, Allen takes the coffee tray from the sideboard, and she follows him into the sitting parlor. Joe did make a nice fire before he left so the room has a cozy glow and feel to it, perfect for an after dinner conversation. They sit and watch the fire together in silence.

****

Joe mounts his horse and rides out over the pasture. He’s glad that Ruth talked him into this. She is right; there needs to be a Mrs. Allen. Joe stops his horse, and gets off to sit under a tree. He pulls out a small silver flask, filled with sippin’ whiskey that Doc had given him. He takes a couple of sips, and the memories of what happened to Doc and his family start to fly through his head. Memories so real, it is as if it happened yesterday.

It was almost sundown that day when the crew returned from the southwest pasture. Sam, Joe and one of the hands came up to the back porch and went into the house to update Doc on the branding. That was when they saw the devastation. The house was torn apart, things broken, furniture overturned; but what they found inside the house would in no way prepare them for the scene they would become witnesses to in the front yard and gardens.

Joe did not see Doc right away. He was scouring the house looking for Doc, Julie and the boys; he couldn’t find any of them. At first, he thought they might not have been here when it happened. He prayed that to be the fact. That prayer would go unanswered. He was crossing from the music room to the parlor when he could see the oak tree through the big windows, and the figures suspended within its bow. Joe yells out for Sam. He and Sam storm the front entry. The sight they would see would haunt them both for what would likely be the rest of their days.

There were Julie and the boys hanging like criminals in the tree. Sam tries to scream out, but there is no sound; he can't move. There hangs Julie, the daughter he and Mary always wished they could have had, and the boys with her. Those boys were their grandchildren, for all intents and purposes.

Joe cries out, "JOHN! JOHN!" However, there is no reply from John. Then he thinks, *'Maybe John is still in town?'*. Joe steps only a few feet when he finds John tied to the pillar, bound and gagged.

John is pale, and has been beaten by the vigilantes. Both Joe and Sam run to John. Sam reaches John first, pulls a knife from his belt, cuts Doc loose, and removes his gag. As soon as Doc is freed, he starts to scramble to the tree to lower his family.

Joe goes back into the house and instructs a couple of the hands to take two of the fastest horses, and move it as fast as they can to the Sheriff's office and the Marshal's office and get them both here just as fast as humanly possible. He turns back toward the front door and goes out to help John.

John and Joe cut Julie and the boys down from the tree. Doc throws himself onto the ground. He grabs all three of them and holds them, holding on for dear life.

Sam tries to get Doc to go inside; Doc does not respond. He just sits there holding his family. It is getting dark, and a little cool so Sam covers them with a blanket.

After the lawmen came and conducted their business, the undertaker unsuccessfully tries to take the family. John refuses to let go, he is still sitting there holding them. John sits there through the night. He is still sitting there holding them when the sun comes up the next morning, still silent and unresponsive to anyone.

Later that morning, Mary finally puts her foot down and tells Sam 'come hell or high water' she was going to get that boy to eat something. She takes John a bowl of stew, and a mug of coffee. Joe and Sam can do nothing for John, but stand and look on.

Mary would do what she knew in her heart she had to do. "John, my heart can't bear to see you like this. You have to let them go. I will do this for you, John. I will see that the undertaker dresses Julie in that dark gray dress, the one with the lavender lace. It was her favorite. I will have both the boys dressed in their Sunday best." Mary reaches over and strokes John's hair. "John, I love you like you were my own son, Julie like my own daughter, and the boys as though they were my own grandsons. So trust and believe in me when I say that it is time to let go John. They are with Jesus. And we're here together." John looks at Mary. She can see the tear stains on his face. "I thought we could bury them under the oak tree, here in Julie's gardens. I think she would like to be close to her flowers, her home, and you." Mary reaches for John again.

John's hand reaches out for hers. She helps him gently lay the three lifeless bodies on the ground. Together they cover them with the blankets. John grabs Mary and squeezes her.

"John?" Mary says, still holding him; he nods but doesn't speak. "Is that the way you would like them buried too? " John squeezes harder, and nods his head yes.

For the next several days, John sits in his room, mute, looking out the window watching Joe work under the oak tree.

"Sam? Can you go upstairs and see that John is okay, and ready for the services?" Mary calls out from the kitchen.

"Yeah, no problem. I see the pastor coming down the lane. I'm sure everyone else will be right behind him shortly." Sam climbs the stairs and when he reaches the top, he knocks on John's door. "John, it's time."

John rises from the seat at the window, and follows Sam down to the parlor.

Sam greets the guests that are there to pay their respects. Mary comes in and sits next to John. Ever since they cut Julie and the boys from the tree, John has not said a word. Mary has to talk for him and Sam has to handle all business for the ranch without John's input.

That leaves Joe to do more of the actual hands-on alone, or with the couple of hands they have working for them. Overall, the ranch runs well.

When it is time for the service to begin, Joe had done a nice job getting the stone markers and iron fence in so quickly.

Afterwards, everyone gathers for coffee in the parlor. Mary wipes her tears with her lace handkerchief. "Those were some of the most beautiful and touching scriptures, pastor. Thank you for such a compassionate service. John is very thankful you were here to do it. And Julie would have loved it."

After the last of the guests leave, Mary takes a plate to John. He shakes his head. “John, you have to eat. You can’t just starve yourself.”

John stands up, kisses Mary on the cheek, and heads upstairs. John remains there for the rest of the day.

The next morning Mary has a breakfast tray for John. She knocks on his door and goes in; his room is empty, and his bed had not been slept in. His carpetbag is gone and there is a note on the bed.

> Mary,
>
> I love you and Sam. I will be back soon.
>
> Thank you for the lovely service.
>
> You were right; Julie would have loved the scriptures.
>
> Please see that some yellow roses are planted there with her and the boys, will you?
>
> You know how she liked yellow ones.
>
> Respectfully, John

John had left under cover of darkness. Nobody knows his whereabouts. Joe goes to town, searching all over Lincoln, but he is nowhere. Nobody had seen him in any of the hotels, diners, or saloons. Joe gets a couple of ol’ boys from town to ride with him. They ride to each town within a day’s ride and to each camp in every direction. Doc is gone.

When Marshal Allen returns from the Minnesota Territory east of Omaha, Joe tells him the news of the horrible event, and Doc’s disappearance. Allen tells Joe not to worry. He will find Doc. Joe knows that he can. After all, the Marshal and John are close friends. The two hunt and travel together. He knows Dan would know how to find him and find him he does. Dan doesn't bring home John Gray who owned the Triple-J.

Oh, yeah, he brings home Dr. John Gray, but he is not the John Gray who left. The man who returned is not the same boss; he now mumbles orders. When you ask what he said he'll bite your head off. He won't go out into the pastures anymore. He stays up by the pond, sitting on that bench with his bottle of whiskey. He never goes back into his office in town again. Joe goes with Mary and they close it up tight. They arrange for another Doctor to take patients who come to Doc's office. Those needing medical attention find a note in the window which says they should go see Dr. Brendl because Dr. Gray had 'retired.'

Then one day, the gunfire starts. Sam and Joe are out in the calving pens when it starts. The sound creates panic for everyone on the ranch. They find themselves thinking that the devil has come back to strike again. They scramble towards the noise.

When they reach the pond they find Doc standing there sporting two shiny silver pistols with pearl handles. He focuses on the glass bottles set up on the fence rail, shooting the bottles off the rail one by one. The men stand there and marvel at the speed and accuracy that increases with each subsequent shot.

Joe asks him, "Why are you doing this?"

He simply says, "I have to."

From that day forth, Doc refuses to speak any further on the subject of Julie and the boys or anything connected to that day again.

****

Amy breaks the silence between her and Allen when she asks, "Marshal, I understand you ride with Doc Gray? Pardon my boldness, but how can a decent man like yourself ride with a cold-blooded killer like him?"

Allen sips his coffee, and then answers, "Amy, Doc wasn't always like that. He was a good, decent man when his family was murdered; it changed him."

"I didn't hear that part of the story," Amy remarks. "Please, tell me what happened."

"I'll just say this, his family was murdered, and Doc was forced to watch it happen." Allen pauses for a moment then continues, "That kind of a thing can change any man."

"Oh my God; that's terrible," is all that Amy can think to say.

"So tell me, Amy, what other changes are you making to your buildings?" Allen asks, feeling the need to change the subject.

"Well, a coat of fresh paint will do wonders, of course, and we need to do some remodeling on the inside to make it a little brighter. I have ordered some wallpaper books and some fabric books; and a furnishing company is sending their catalogs. I want it to be a place where people want to stay when they come through again, and tell all their friends or others they meet when traveling that we have the nicest place in town to stay. You know they could say, 'It's the nicest place between Chicago and Denver!' That would be the thing we need people to feel."

Allen smiles, noticing the twinkle she gets in her eye when she starts talking of something that makes her happy. "I expect that your plan will work. If you need any help when I'm in town, don't hesitate to ask. I've been known to swing a hammer on occasion."

"I might just have to take you up on that offer," Amy points out, then pauses for a brief moment and continues, "I would love to see the rest of your home."

Allen smiles, and then replies, "Where are my manners? Of course, please, I would be glad to show you the house." Allen takes Amy by the arm and shows her his office, the room with the piano and family things he has saved or had passed down to him over the years. Then they head up the stairs to the second floor. When they reach the top of the stairs Allen continues, "Ok, well, Amy I have four bedrooms and a bathing room up here. This room is my room," he concludes as he opens the door.

"Oh, my, my!" Amy exclaims, surprised at what she is seeing. "This must be the largest bedroom I have ever seen. This room must be larger than some people's homes in town."

"Yeah, possibly," Allen agrees." You see, this house was a gift. Doc had it built for me as a gift for my helping him out and such." Allen pauses for a brief moment then continues, "You see, Doc actually has a heart the size of Texas. I was living in a room in the boarding house across from the Marshal's office. Then one day he rides into town and asks me to go for a ride with him. He tells me he has something on his mind. Well, we ride out here. We were sitting out in front of the house when he asked, *'How do you like it?'* I said that's the biggest house I have ever seen. Doc smiled and said, *'I hope you like it, because it's yours.'* I did not know what to say, he smiled and said *'You're welcome. I hope you enjoy it.'* Then he said, *'Oh yeah, it comes with a thousand acres and a hundred head of cattle; thank you for what you've done for me. But thank you mostly for being my friend.'"*

"What did you do for him that he wanted to pay you this way?" Amy asks, surprised to hear of Doc's generosity.

"Honestly, I really don't know. Each time I bring it up, or when I ask him about it, all he will say is you were there when I needed a friend." Telling a lie always makes Allen feel terrible but he could not tell her the truth about Doc. She did not need to know about the man he found in that saloon in White Horse.

Amy looks out the window and notices lights in the distance. "Where are those lights coming from?"

"The Gray mansion," Allen replies, "as in Dr. John 'Doc' Gray."

She looks away from the window and says, "This night has really changed my mind about Doc Gray."

"He's a good man," Allen remarks. He's just misunderstood." Allen pulls the watch from his pocket and realizes that it is getting late. "Amy, it is quite late and much too dark for you to be riding back to town alone. Let me show you to the guestroom. You can ride back into town with Doc and me in the morning."

"Thank you, no. I should really get back to the hotel," she insists.

"It is quite all right," Allen shoots back. "I have plenty of room, not to mention you can ride over to Doc's with me. You'll get a chance to meet Doc. His foreman's wife, Mary, is a heck of a cook. She makes some of the best flapjacks!"

Amy thinks for a moment, and then says. "Alright Marshal, I must say you can be persuasive."

Allen shows Amy to the guestroom then returns to his room to prepare for bed. As he is getting ready for bed there is a knock at the door.

"May I come in?" asks Amy in a sweet voice through the door.

"Yes, come on in," Allen replies with a smile on his face.

Amy opens the door and enters. Being both bold and modest she says, "I know you have to get up early, but I need to talk to you about something." She steps closer to him. "I am afraid that when you leave tomorrow, I might not see you again."

"What do you mean?" Allen asks, looking at her confused. "Of course you will. This is my home. I have to come back."

Amy looks down, then back into his eyes. "Tomorrow you are going after that escaped prisoner; what if something goes wrong? What if you get or if you were to . . . ." She trails off not able to say shot or killed.

Allen reaches for her arm and squeezes it to give her comfort. "I am going to be fine. This is not my first time going after a prisoner."

Amy looks away and as soon as he releases her arm, she turns and walks over to the bed, takes her robe off, and slips into his bed, saying to Allen, "I don't know if this is proper. I have never done this before but I care for you so much already. I do not want to regret not having known the touch of your hand on my skin, not knowing how it would feel to wake up in the arms of the man who lives so deeply within my soul."

Allen walks to the bed, picks up the robe, and hands it to her. "Amy, while I would like nothing more than to do these things, I care very much for you. I think it would not be respectful to do such things to a lovely woman such as you. You are not a saloon girl who does these types of things. My God, Amy, you are probably the most intelligent, most beautiful woman I have ever had the privilege to meet. That's why I have to insist you get dressed and go back to your room. We will talk about this at greater length when I return home."

Amy reluctantly slips back into the robe. "But, what if you don't, and we nev . . . ."

He cut her off, putting a finger to her lips. "Shhh, don't worry I'll have Doc with me and he'll make sure I get back to you."

Allen walks Amy back to her room. He opens the door, and then says, "Now you go to sleep and stop worrying. I will be back in no time and then we will talk about this." Allen gives Amy a peck on the cheek then closes the door, walks back to his room, and jumps into bed.

6

The next morning John wakes up to the smell of freshly brewed coffee and the smell of cooking bacon. John smiles at the thought, *'Mary's up and cooking breakfast; bless her heart.'* He notices it is still dark outside so he looks at his watch to see that it is only five-thirty. He gets up and dresses to face the new day. As he walks out the door, he meets Audra in the hallway.

"Good Morning, John. I was just on my way to wake you."

John smiles. "Thanks. That's very kind of you but as luck would have it, I am already up."

Audra tugs a little at the lapel of his vest and in a teasing tone she says to him, "It may have been more enjoyable to let me wake you."

John runs a thumb across her cheek. “When I get back, that is a topic we will venture into.”

“I will hold you to that, John,” Audra says, looking into his deep dark, dark eyes.

“Let’s go down and see what Mary has for us to eat,” is all John can say.

They start down the stairs and Audra takes John’s hand and smiles. “You better be careful on this trip, John. You see, I have come to feel very deeply for you. I know it has only been a day but there is something about you that fills my heart. So, please be careful. I want you to come home to me.”

“I am always careful,” Doc comments as he helps her down the last step. “There’s no need for you to worry. I will be back; I promised you riding lessons and a ride in the country on horseback, and I never forget a promise.”

When they enter the dining room, John helps Audra to the seat closest to his and pulls her chair out. “Good Morning, Mary!” Doc calls out to the kitchen. “Everything smells terrific.”

“Thank you, John,” Mary calls out.

When Mary enters the room, Doc asks, “Why have you set out places for five?”

Mary laughs. “I figured Dan would be by soon. Since when have you known that man to ever miss a free meal?”

John laughs. “Mary, you are oh so correct. I am sure as soon as he smelled the bacon he was saddling his horse.”

“Is there something I should know?” Audra asks, not knowing what they are talking about.

Mary smiles at her and replies, “No, not really. I will introduce you to the Marshal when he gets here.”

****

Allen walks down the servants’ stairs and into the kitchen where he finds Joe talking with Amy. “What are you two talking about?” Allen asks as he reaches for the coffeepot.

Joe grins and winks at Amy. “Whether or not we were going to have to go up there and wake you up.”

“Very funny,” Allen shoots back. “Are the horses ready to go?”

“They’ve been saddled for almost a half hour,” Joe points out. “We’ve been waiting for you to wake from your beauty sleep.”

“Are you ready, Amy?” Allen asks as he sets his empty cup down.

“Yes, I am ready when you are,” she replies.

Allen reaches for her chair and pulls it out for her. “We better get over to Doc’s and get him up.”

Joe opens the door for Amy, and looks back at Allen. “You know as well as I that Doc has already been up for an hour, waiting on you.”

Allen pats Joe on the back and steps outside with Joe right behind him. “See you in a week or so,” Allen says as he mounts his horse.

“I’ll have the coffee waiting,” Joe says as he tips his hat brim and watches Allen and Amy ride away.

Fifteen minutes or so later, Allen and Amy reach the front gate to the Triple J. Amy looks at Allen and asks, “You will be careful, won’t you?”

Allen looks up at the full moon, then back at Amy. "I told you I will be back. As I said, I'll have Doc around to watch my back."

Because of the moon, when they reach the top of the small rise in the road, Amy can clearly see how large and beautiful Doc's house is. She is about to remark on it when she notices the horse and carriage tied to the rail on the side of the yard, next to another horse.

"That's my carriage!" she shouts. Realizing just how loud she was, a bit quieter she says, "That carriage is the one belonging to me and my sister!"

Allen thinks to himself about the possibility that Doc actually has a lady's company, and then dismisses it. No, there has to be a logical explanation. "I am sure there is a logical explanation for it being here." However, as they get a little closer, the only logical explanation is that her sister is there. "Maybe your sister is a house guest, visiting Doc."

"She better not be here to see that gunfighter!" Amy says in an angry tone.

"I thought you came to see the story behind Doc," says Allen, looking at Amy confused. "I thought you were all right with my friend, Doc?"

Picking up the pace a bit, Amy looks over at Allen. "Oh, yes Dan. I am fine about the man who is your friend. However, I am not fine with him putting his pistol spinning hands on my little sister, Audra!"

Surprised at her over protectiveness, he finds this sibling attachment touching. "Amy, I don't think you told me you have a sister, much less mentioning she is here with you."

"Well, I thought I mentioned her when I said that we had lots of plans for the hotel," she shoots back, defending herself.

When they reach the large manicured yard, Allen directs Amy toward the post where the carriage is tied. Allen dismounts first, and reaches to help Amy off her horse. For a moment, he lingers with her in his arms until he notices Sam coming out on the porch.

"There's Sam. He's Doc's foreman," Allen is quick to say. "Come, let me introduce you."

Allen sticks out his hand to greet Sam and says, "Good morning, Sam! How are you?"

Sam puts his hand in Allen's, almost shaking his arm off while saying, "Marshal Daniel Allen! Good Morning! If it don't beat all! Mary was right when she said as soon as you smelled the bacon you would show up!"

"Yes sir. Your wife, Mary, knows me all too well!" Allen replies. "Is there room for another lovely lady at the table?"

Sam tips his hat to Amy and answers, "Of course, Marshal. You know that any friend of yours is always welcome here."

Allen smiles. "Sam, allow me to introduce my lady friend. This is Miss Amy Randolph."

"Randolph, you say?" Sam asks, raising his eyebrows.

"Yes sir, please call me Amy," she replies, then smiles at Sam.

"Well, if that don't beat all," Sam remarks. "Please, the two of you, come on in. I'll let Mary know we need another place at the table." Sam steps over and opens the door, then looks back at the pair. "Tie up your horses and come join us for breakfast in the dining room."

''Is this really Doc's house?" Amy asks as they stand on the back porch. "This home is so large and beautiful. I have never seen a place like this. It reminds me of the ones in the Deep South, the old Southern plantation manors. You know, the ones that have all of the slaves harvesting and filling the tobacco barns and the cotton sheds."

Allen looks about the pastures; even though the sun has hardly begun its daily ascent he can see some of the cattle milling around the closer fields. "Yep, this is Doc's place. You see, he had it built for his wife. He wanted her to have all the comforts she had when they lived in Boston." Allen leads her into the house and as they walk to the dining room entry, he continues to explain. "You see, Julie loved beautiful things and when they lived in Boston she had the best of everything. So, when they moved out here Doc assured her that she would continue to have those very same things."

Amy is truly in awe as she looks about the room to see the exquisite décor and furnishings. "Maybe I could be wrong," she confesses. "Doc may not be as terrible a man as his reputation indicates."

When they enter the dining room, Audra is surprised to see her sister, Amy. "Amy Lynn, what are you doing here?"

"Audra Lee, I could ask the same question of you," Amy fires back.

"Yes, you could," the younger Randolph girl snaps. "But, I believe I asked you first."

Allen pulls out a chair for Amy and pours her a cup of coffee. "Well, if you must know, Miss Ruth from my bible group invited me out for dinner with the Marshal." She pauses as she sips from the steaming cup. "The Marshal and I were so caught up in conversation, time got away from us; so he had a room made up for me. He thought it would be best if I ride with him into town this morning. He thought it was inappropriate for me to ride alone so late into the night." Amy shoots a look at her sister. "So tell me, little sister, why do I find you so far from home in the wee hours of the morning, and in a stranger's home?"

Audra, offended by her sister's tone replies, "I came to visit Mary. When John returned home, she thought I should stay for supper and meet him. They insisted I stay over until morning. After all, there are ten bedrooms in this house. Mary said it has been a long time since they had guests. She was looking forward to something being a bit more normal around here. And how could I offend them and say no?"

Before either of them could continue their inquiries, Mary enters with two enormous platters of food. "Okay, will everyone please sit down?" Mary sets the platters down, and sits at the table next to her husband. "Sam, will you say grace before this meal gets cold?"

After they finish breakfast, John helps Audra and Amy into the carriage while Allen gets the horses. He ties Amy's horse to the rear of the carriage. Doc and Allen mount up, with Sam and Mary standing on the porch. The sun is just coming up over the horizon, the sunrise making the sky turn many colors, perfect for such a ride back into Lincoln.

Sam raises a hand to wave good-bye. "You boys, be careful; we look for you to be coming home right quick. And ladies, when they do, please come out and we'll celebrate their homecoming"

Both of the Randolph sisters wave goodbye, and off the four go, leaving only the slightest cloud of dust on the trail.

When they get to town they pull up to the stable at the rear of the hotel. Allen dismounts and ties the horse and carriage to the hitching post. "Ladies, this is where we must part company. It has been a pleasure. It was fine meeting you this morning, Miss Audra. Amy, I will see you when I return."

Allen has turned to remount his horse when Amy leaps down from the carriage, runs to Allen, and gives him a big kiss. With a tear in her eye, she looks at Doc and says, "You bring him back safe or you'll have me to answer to. You understand, John Gray?"

Doc looks down from his horse, and tips his hat at Amy. "Yes, Ma'am."

Audra looks up at Doc and says, "You know, there is some unfinished conversation between us?" Doc smiles and winks at her. "We will talk about those things when you return, okay, John?"

Doc smiles at Audra, tips his brim, turns his horse and starts toward the Marshal's office with Allen following.

As the two men ride, Doc looks over at Allen, "So tell me, what did the two of you do last night?"

"You would not believe me even if I swore on a bible," Allen replies, disregarding the insinuations and the tone of Doc's voice.

"Try me," Doc shoots back.

"I was a gentleman in every single sense of the word," Allen confesses, holding his head up with pride.

"Mm-hhm. Right, go on."

"I was in my room getting ready to lie down, when she came to my door," Allen begins. "She came in wearing only her undergarments beneath a robe. She crawls into my bed and wants me to take her, right then and there."

"So far, I believe you," remarks Doc.

"Well, I tell her as much as I would love to oblige her, I want to get to know her better. I hand her the robe, ask her to get dressed and walk her back to her room."

"You're right; I don't believe you."

"Really, that's what happened," Allen shoots back.

"Sure, well, I believe you might have actually walked her to her room when you were done, because you wanted the bed all to yourself."

"Believe it or not, I was a complete gentleman; I did not do a thing."

7

When they get to the Marshal's office, they see that the reinforcements have arrived. Doc greets the others. "Mornin' boys. We're here. Who do you have for us there, Bob?"

"Good morning to you too, fellas. I have recruited four of my best deputies to go along and round up Billy; and gentlemen, try to bring them back in one piece."

Allen looks over this group of young riders, then back at Bob. "We will do our best. Now let's ride, boys."

The six of them ride out of town, heading west. They ride hard all day; and just as it is starting to get late in the day, they see a town in the distance. Allen thinks it might be a good spot to stop for the evening, to rest the men and the horses.

"It's starting to get dark so let's ride into that town up ahead and call it a day," Allen instructs. "Doc and I will go over to the Sheriff's office and see if there is any news about Billy, while the rest of you go on over to the hotel and get some rooms for all of us."

When they enter the town, the four men go over to the hotel while Doc and Allen ride up to the Sheriff's office. When they enter, they see a man pacing back and forth across the room. Allen and Doc exchange glances, curious as to what has the man all riled up.

"Excuse me, are you the Sheriff here?" Allen asks. "We're U.S. Marshals in pursuit of an escaped prisoner."

The Sheriff looks at Allen for a quick moment and says, "Yep. I'm Tom. Thank God, you're here. I could use some help. I have a group of men runnin' amuck and terrorizing the town. I'd be much obliged if you can help me. They've shot three of my deputies already and told me if I step one foot out of the door again they will kill me too. I have been in here for several days. I tried to go out the door about four days ago but I got a hole in my hat for my attempt." The Sheriff takes off his hat and shows them the hole. "I'm sorry but I don't know anything about Marshals looking for an escapee."

Doc peers out the window to see if anyone is on the rooftops across the street. "Where are these guys hanging out?"

"Mostly at the saloon down the street," Tom answers.

"Tell ya what Sheriff, the Marshal and I will go down there and take care of the problem for you."

"It would be great if you can do that for me," the Sheriff says as he starts to relax a bit. "I know I cannot fight them alone. I will be in your debt if you rid my town of these fellers."

Doc, thinking about earning extra card money, asks, "There any rewards on any of these fellas?"

The Sheriff thinks for a moment, then replies, "Yes, I believe there is." The Sheriff begins rummaging through his desk. "Ah, here we go; well, I only have a couple of notices here. These are the ones I believe the men to be. On Carl Dyer, the reward is eight-hundred dollars; on Dux Godfrey it may be a thousand dollars or better. Drey James is a thousand dollars, and I can't be sure of the others. I can dig those up, if they have rewards on them, once I am sure who they are. These wanted notices state dead or alive; and at this rate I'd pay on them either way, just to get order restored to this town."

"Okay Allen, let's go and collect our money," Doc says with an evil smirk. "I need stakes for the poker game tonight."

Allen holds his hand out to stop Doc. "Hold your horses Doc; we need to figure out a plan first."

Doc winks at Allen and says, "I have a plan. We will go down there and stand in the street in front of the saloon. Then we will call them out. When they come out, we shoot them. After we shoot them all, we'll put them on horseback and bring them back here. After the Sheriff kindly verifies the men, and that they are indeed the outlaws who are on his wanted notices, we will collect our reward money from the Sheriff. Then we will go back to the saloon, have a bite of supper and a whiskey, and then sit down and play some poker with the reward money the Sheriff gave us. Is that planning enough for you?"

Doc does not wait for Allen to reply. He walks out the door and in the direction of the saloon.

"Doc, wait a minute," Allen says as he runs out the door after him. "We need to think about this."

Doc looks over his shoulder. "You just stay back; I'll handle this."

"If you are that determined to go after them, then I am going with you," Allen points out to Doc as they walk toward the saloon together.

Doc stands in the middle of the street, directly in front of the saloon and begins yelling to the saloon patrons. "You, in the saloon!" The sounds from inside begin to dissipate. "I repeat, you in the saloon, get your good-for-nothing tails out here!" There is complete silence in the saloon now. "Look, I know you men are in there, if I dare call you men. This is your last chance. Get your asses out here, and I mean NOW!"

There isn't a soul moving on the street. The town is so quiet, you can hear one lone pair of spurs jingle, as the first of the band of men moves toward the swinging doors in the front of the saloon, and then out the saloon doors.

The first man, a burly sort, walks out the doors. He stops just a couple of steps outside the doors. "Who the hell do you think you are? Talking to us like that? I don't particularly like that tone of voice yer usin' neither. So I 'spect that you take back them words, and get on out o' here, or I will see to it that you be meetin' yer maker soon."

Doc raises an eyebrow, as he looks this man square in the eye, then says, "I was assuming you'd be feelin' that way. Here's the deal, pardner; I will give you two options. Number one: you and all of your buddies, get on your horses and ride out of town, peaceful like, and not return here. Of course, if you don't like option one, I can give you option two." Doc pauses a second, waiting to see if this man will pop off before hearing the second option. "Now option two is simple; stand there, keep mouthing off, and you die right there. On the spot you're standing, you will be shot dead."

The burly leader steps closer to the rail at the boardwalk's edge and shouts back, "I don't think you are in any place to be giving us options. I stand here, lookin' out there, and I only see two of you. In no way can two of you out-gun five of us."

The remaining men begin filtering out the saloon door, standing side by side, facing the Marshal and Doc.

Doc looks over his shoulder at the Marshal and comments, "Well, it looks like they'll be choosing option two. Allen, you take the one on the left, shoot the next to the right if you can. I will start on the right, shooting to the left and take care of the rest."

The Marshal tilts his head in Doc's direction without taking his eyes off their opponents. "Sure, no problem."

The four men stand with the burly one on the boardwalk. The burly leader speaks up again, "Get this, boys; I think we'll add two Marshals to our list of lawmen killed." They all chuckle and laugh at the idea of five against two.

Doc reaches, and slowly moves his riding coat back to uncover the pearl handles in his belt. "So, is that it? You've made your decision? To me it sounds like you boys are choos'n option two." Doc glances in Allen's direction. Allen appears to be jumping in, both feet first, ready for this fight. Doc turns his glance back to the burly speaker. "All right, option two it is." Doc's hands ready themselves. "Just say when."

As the man reaches for his gun, Doc draws his pistols and begins firing. A few seconds' later, four men lie dead, all except the man on the far-left, who is still standing.

"Allen, are you not going to take care of your man?" Doc asks; and then, in less than a breath Doc fires again and the man falls back dead on the ground. "I guess not. Oh well, another job well done. Let's get these men loaded and delivered to the Sheriff and collect our rewards."

Allen and Doc load the men onto their horses and walk back to the Sheriff's office for delivery. As they approach the Sheriff's office a shot rings out and dirt flies up between Allen's feet. Doc quickly spins around and fires. A loud scream is heard as a gunman falls from the roof across the street. Doc puts his pistol back in its holster and comments, "That makes six today. This day just keeps getting better."

They continue walking and stop just outside the Sheriff's office, where the Sheriff is waiting for them. "Wow, that was close," the Sheriff says, looking at the Marshal. "An inch higher and you might have been singing soprannah."

Allen shakes his head and replies, "Why are they always shooting at me and not the Deputy?"

Doc shrugs his shoulders and answers, "Don't know, Marshal. Must be the badge; it makes a darn fine target."

"Very funny," Allen snaps back, then looks over his shoulder at the Sheriff as he starts to reach across one of the bodies on the horse. "We're going to need some help with the bodies."

The Sheriff nods and says, "I'll get some of the townsfolk and we'll get them to the undertaker. Just leave them. I'll see to it that your horses get to the livery barn. You boys have done this town a great service. You go down to the saloon and have supper on me. Just tell Sarah I sent you down and to charge me for your meals and drinks."

"There is a matter of the reward money on those fellas," Doc points out, referring to his poker money.

The Sheriff nods and tips his hat up a bit off his forehead. "After I get the bodies to the undertaker, I will double check the ones that I don't know against the notices. When I know who all of them are, and how much needs to be paid, I'll wake up the banker, and get the whole sum. I'll bring it to you at the saloon."

"Thanks, I appreciate it." Doc grins then continues, "I can always use more poker stakes and cattle buyin' money."

Allen shakes his head in disbelief, then says, "C'mon Doc. Let's just go and get some supper."

When Doc and Allen walk into the saloon, a huge cry of rejoicing comes from the saloon patrons. Allen leans over close to Doc and whispers, "This is not the welcome you usually get when you walk into a saloon."

"Nope, but, I have to say I kind of like this better," Doc comments as he follows Allen to a table and sits down.

The Sheriff walks into the saloon and over to the table where Allen and Doc are sitting. He lays ten-thousand dollars down on the table and says, "Here you go, Marshal; it seems they were worth a little more than I told you."

"Sheriff, we don't do this for the money," Allen points out as he puts his hand on the stack of cash. "After all, it is our job."

The Sheriff nods, puts his hand on top of the Marshal's, and pushes the stack closer to Allen. "I know but it does help. After all, you boys have expenses that the job doesn't always provide for."

Doc reaches over and takes the stack from Allen. "That's true, Sheriff. There are always things that one needs extra money for, like money to buy a few more cattle, feed for the winter, and maybe some horses as well."

"Don't you have enough livestock already?" Allen shoots back.

"Nope, a good rancher can never have enough livestock," Doc points out. "If you'll excuse me gentlemen, I have a card game to find." Doc picks up the entire stack of bills and puts them in the interior pocket of his vest.

"Enjoy your game," Allen tells Doc. "We leave first thing in the morning. See you then."

Doc gets up from the table and walks through a curtain-trimmed doorway at the rear of the saloon.

Allen looks back at the Sheriff. The Sheriff pours both of them a whiskey. "How long have those boys been here terrorizing your town?" Allen asks.

The Sheriff thinks for a moment, then replies, "Oh goin' on close to two weeks now. They have had their way with just about everything by putting terror into everyone." He gulps down his shot, then continues, "For the most part these men ate and drank anything they wanted, and didn't expect to pay. One bartender came to me and told me that another bartender told them that they owed him ten dollars for the bill for the first night's meals and drinks. Instead of paying the bartender, the bartender paid with his life. They shot him right here in the saloon. Two of my deputies were in the saloon at the time. They drew their guns, tried to arrest them, and were killed for their trouble. My best deputy went in when he heard the commotion and was shot; then they came down to my office, dropped all three of my deputies on the floor and said if I interfered I was next." The Sheriff pours himself another shot before continuing, "And let's face it, Marshal, I was defenseless. There was no way I was going to get anyone to deputy with me at that rate, and I couldn't get down the street to the telegraph to wire for help. When you two showed up, it was a big relief to have some lawmen who could take on these men."

Allen swallows his whiskey before answering, "You don't have to worry about them anymore. They're at the undertaker's now."

The Sheriff looks around slowly, moving only his eyes. "On the contrary, you didn't get them all. You only got six of them."

Allen starts scanning the room the same way. "What do you mean; we only got six of them?"

The Sheriff leans closer to Allen and whispers, "There were ten."

"Ten? You didn't say that to begin with. This complicates things greatly." Allen drinks one last shot of whiskey, knowing that this night was far from over. "If there are four more, where are they? Obviously, they know where we are, and who we are. I know Doc, he'll shoot first, ask questions later. So tell me where these men are.

"Right now, they're playing poker with your deputy, Doc."

Meanwhile Doc's luck is holding out as he wins another hand. "It looks like it is just not your night, fellows," Doc comments as he rakes in the money from the table.

The dark skinned man sitting across from Doc puts his hand on top of Doc's to stop him from moving the winnings. "I beg your pardon, but I don't think it's your night." The next sound Doc hears is a hammer on someone's pistol being pulled back. "After killing our friends do you really think you, the Marshal, and the Sheriff are going to make it out of here alive?"

Doc smiles and takes a loud animated sniff. "Hhmm, I thought I smelled the scent of another four thousand." The men start to stand, but the sound of Doc's guns ringing out sets them back down dead where they had been sitting. Doc rakes in the rest of the pot, stands up and says; "You boys need to learn that a Colt beats four of a kind every time."

The Sheriff and Allen are on their way to the room to warn Doc of the remaining four gunmen when the shots tell them Doc shot first, and asked last. Allen steps through the doorway. "Well, once again, I see you did not require my assistance."

Doc looks at the men at the table, then at Allen and the Sheriff. "Thanks for offering but I have everything under control. You know, Sheriff; you might have mentioned that there were four more before we came in the saloon."

The Sheriff pats Doc on the shoulder and says, "I was tellin' Allen here; I didn't realize it at first. You'd already left my office when I realized you only brought six of them to the jail.

"I see how that could have happened," Doc points out. "But, alls well that ends well. However, I think you had better go over and wake the banker again." Doc gives the Sheriff a wink.

The Sheriff laughs. "Yeah Doc, I'm on my way. I'll set it straight with you in the morning before you head out."

The Sheriff thanks Allen and Doc again. The three of them share one last shot of whiskey, and the Sheriff leaves the saloon. Doc and Allen decide to call it a night themselves and walk over to the hotel.

"So, Allen, what are you going to do with your half of the reward?" Doc asks as he hands Allen some cash.

Allen looks at the money in his hands. "Doc, what half? I did not do anything. You shot every last one of them."

"You've kept me company," Doc points out. "That in itself is worth half to me."

Allen shakes his head. "That is not the way it works. You did all the work; you take all the reward."

Doc takes the cash back. He can't fight with a friend. "Allen, I will make this right somehow, you know that."

Allen smiles. "Look John, you gave me my house and all the land that goes with it. I've got all that livestock to get my herd started. You, my friend, you do not owe me a thing."

"Look, this is how I see things," Doc begins. "You're my friend. When I need someone, you are there. When I need to talk, you listen. When I don't want to speak, you are silent. This is worth more than all the money in the world. Sharing this money is one of the ways I can show my appreciation. So, thank you," he concludes as he puts the cash back into Allen's hand.

Allen squeezes his hand around the cash, looking at his newfound wealth, and then back at Doc and smiles. "What are friends for?"

When they reach the hotel Doc looks at his buddy and says, "Well, I don't know about you, but I am ready for some shut eye. What do you say? Let's go on in and see if you have a wife for the night?"

Allen shakes his head and pats his friend on the back. "Nope, I am done with that. I have Miss Amy at home waiting for me."

Doc looks at Allen and chuckles. "I'll believe that when I see it."

Allen and Doc enter the hotel only to see a beautiful red haired girl. Her eyes light up. "Marshal Allen! It has been too long! I heard you were in town. I have a room ready for each of you. Here's your key for room four. You go on up and get all comfortable and I'll be right up." Next she hands Doc a key and says, "Doc it's always nice to see you. Here's your key for room six. It's in the back, so it should be nice and quiet for you. Sleep well, Doc."

Allen and Doc go up the stairs. When they reach the top of the stairs, Allen looks back down, thinking of the lovely girl who can share his bed. He smiles at Doc and says, "Maybe I will start tomorrow."

"Yeah that's pretty much what I expected you'd say," Doc says as he puts the key into his door. "Good night, Marshal Dan Allen."

Allen put his hands up in the air and shrugs, "Hey, if I turn two girls down in one day it might give you reason to fall over dead. You're my friend, and I am only looking out for your best interests, Doc."

"Thanks, but you don't have to do me any favors; anyway, good night and have fun."

"Yep. See you in the morning."

The next morning as the sun starts to peek over the horizon, Doc gets up early and goes over to the livery to get the horses. He returns to the hotel and ties the horses outside. Doc walks into the hotel, goes up the stairs, and without knocking, opens the door to Allen's room and shouts, "YO! Allen, it's time to get up." To Doc's surprise, he sees the covers pull up over two heads.

"Don't you knock? Allen snaps, defending himself and his guest.

"We gotta full day of riding ahead of us. We need to be hitting the trail soon if you want to make any distance today."

“Give me half an hour and I will be down.”

“Alright, I’ll take the boys over to the diner and get a hot breakfast. See you in a little while.” Doc starts to close the door but decides it is a good time to tease Allen a bit. “By the way, it was nice to see you again, Christy.”

Not surprised, Doc hears the sweet girl’s voice reply from under the covers on the bed. “Yes, it was nice to see you again, Doc.” Doc closes the door and laughs all the way down the hall, at his friend’s antics.

A few minutes later, Allen walks into the diner to find it empty, with only a man standing there nursing a cup of coffee. “Pardon me, but have you seen five guys anywhere around here?”

“They left a little bit ago,” replies the man. “They said you’d probably be lookin’ for ‘em. Said they’d be at the Sheriff’s office and that you’d find them there.”

Allen throws a two-bit piece on the table in front of the man. “Thank you. Let me buy your breakfast.” Allen turns and walks down to the office to join his deputies.

“Well, that was fast; we thought it would be awhile,” Doc says.

“Yeah, yeah, let’s get going; we’re burning daylight,” Allen shoots back as he mounts his horse. “We need to make up some time.”

“I wonder whose fault that would be?” Doc asks.

“Sorry boys,” Allen replies, trying to be sincere. “I, well, uh, never mind. Why don’t we just ride?”

As they ride out of town, Doc fills Allen in on the morning’s information. “The Sheriff gave me another twenty-five hundred for the four from the poker table. He did get a response from Lincoln regarding Billy.”

“Well, don’t hold out; what did he say?” Allen asks.

“Oh, you want to know?”

“Yes. I believe I would like to know if we have an update,” Allen snaps back at Doc.

“Oh, well, the Sheriff said the wire said there was no new information and to continue as planned.”

“Well, aren’t you a wealth of information? Thank-you.”

The other men in the posse start laughing at the Marshal’s slow uptake on Doc’s teasing. Allen gives them all a look of ‘enough of that.’

“Let’s ride hard,” Allen commands. “If we keep a good pace without pushing the horses too hard, we just likely will make it to Arrow Bluff by dark.” Allen uses his reins and gives his horse a slap and the horse picks up speed.

After Allen gets a short distance ahead, Doc looks at the other four. “Well, he wants to get to Arrow Bluff. Maybe we need to pick up speed.”

Doc and the four men laugh. They simultaneously pick up the pace to catch up with the Marshal.

8

As the sun starts to fade into the west, the lights of Arrow Bluff are still well off in the distance. Allen is showing signs of saddle fatigue.

"It sure is going to be good to get off this horse and not have to be sitting in this saddle for a few hours," Allen confesses. "I really can use a stretch."

"Yeah, not only that, but a good meal wouldn't be bad either," Doc points out. "I have to admit I'm feeling pretty hungry."

As they enter the town, they talk about what to do while in town. Then Allen interrupts, "Why don't the four of you go ahead and put your horses up. Get your sleeping arrangements at the boarding house taken care of. Doc and I will meet you at the saloon when we're done at the Sheriff's office. Then we can all have supper together."

Allen looks over at Doc who looks a bit more tired than usual. He wonders if Doc is sleeping much these days, but he knows that Doc won't tell him the truth even if he dares to ask.

"Doc, you and I'll head over to the Sheriff's office first and talk to him about Billy. We'll find out if he has any word. Then we'll stop by the hotel before going over to the saloon. What do you think?"

"Sure. That sounds fine. If I remember right, the hotel here in Arrow Bluff has comfortable rooms. Might be a good place to stretch out after this long ride, ya know?"

"That's what I was saying. I need to get the bend out of my legs. Hey, there's the Sheriff's office." Allen dismounts and heads inside, with Doc a couple of steps behind.

Inside the Sheriff's office, they find a slender man sitting behind his desk. The man looks up from his paperwork. "Evenin', gentlemen. What can I do for you fellas?"

"Evenin,' Sheriff, I'm Deputy Gray; this is Marshall Allen. We are searching for an escaped prisoner who goes by the name of Billy. He is likely with two other men. We think he is heading to the Chimney Rock area. We want to check and see if you have any word?"

"As a matter of fact I do have this," the Sheriff replies as he hands Allen a telegram. "I received this wire from an office out west this afternoon. They said there have been some men seen there who may be the men you're looking for, out by Spirit Lake."

Doc and Allen exchange looks. Doc thinks to himself; *"Spirit Lake? I remember that lake. I went fishing there. Didn't I take my dog with me? I remember Allen going too. What happened to that dog? What was his name?*

Allen reads the telegram and looks at the Sheriff. "We know where that is; we'll rest here for the night and be moving on in the morning. Thanks, Sheriff."

"I heard what you did last night," the Sheriff comments. "The two of you are making quite a name for yourselves these days."

"It seems like trouble is waiting for us wherever we go," Allen points out to the Sheriff. "We don't have to look for it. If trouble's around, it will find us."

The Sheriff nods in agreement, and then says, "I know how that goes. We have a few rough characters runnin' about in town today. They aren't hardened men, but you guys watch your backs nevertheless."

"Thanks for the warning," Allen replies. "We'll make sure and keep our backs to the wall."

"Are any of them wanted?" Doc asks. "Are there any rewards on these men?"

The Sheriff laughs. "I hear you like the rewards. Yes, the two of them are wanted for drunk and disorderly conduct. The men are nothing serious. The reward is only ten dollars for each of them when returned to the jail."

Doc puts a hand on his hip in jest. "Well it's their lucky day. Ten dollars wouldn't even pay for the lead if I have to use it."

"Well, you have a good evening, Sheriff," Allen concludes." We're off to get some supper."

If you want a good meal, go over to the hotel's restaurant for something to eat," the Sheriff points out. "They have a much better meal than the saloon; just don't tell anyone I said that."

"Thanks. Don't worry; your secret is safe with us." Doc pats the Sheriff on the shoulder as he walks by.

Allen and Doc make their way over to the hotel. The posse is standing in the street in front of the saloon, waiting to join them to have supper. Allen and Doc motion them over to the hotel, and then the group of six steps into the hotel's restaurant to have their first meal since they left the last town.

Doc reaches across the table to grab another piece of bread, and then asks, "You don't think the Sheriff sent us to the hotel so I would not go into the saloon?"

Allen, without looking up from his plate, replies, "Now Doc, why would the Sheriff do that?"

Doc looks at Allen as if he is having a lapse of memory. "No matter his intent. After supper I'm going over to the saloon to see if there is a good card game going on."

Allen looks up and points a finger at Doc. "I am going with you this time, to make sure you stay out of trouble."

After they finish eating, Doc, Allen, and the rest of the men head out to patronize the saloon, each of them looking forward to a quiet evening of relaxation.

As they are crossing the road over to the saloon, the Sheriff stops them. "Marshal, you guys are in for a treat tonight. We have a dance and music troop in town, performing in the other tavern. They're supposed to be very good."

Allen looks at Doc, then at the Sheriff. "Well it's a good thing you caught us. "We'll follow you there. I think musical entertainment just may be what 'the doctor ordered' for this evening."

The Sheriff smiles, and then says, "Great. You should enjoy them. I'm told they're quite good. They are from back East; I think someone said from Boston."

Allen throws a thumb up, pointing it at Doc. "Doc here, is from Boston." Allen looks at Doc. "Well, what do you know, Doc? They're from Boston. Maybe you will know some of them."

"Boston is a big city," Doc shoots back." I didn't know everyone there. And I haven't lived there for years."

They follow the Sheriff, and when they enter they walk into the sound of singing. As they look at the stage, they see a group of actors performing a musical.

They stand just inside the door until there is a break between numbers. The Sheriff sees an empty table close to the stage so they walk over and sit down to watch the show.

While the actors are getting ready for the next number a woman on the stage looks out among the crowd. As she brings her gaze to the table at the front, her eyes lock with Doc's. "Well, well. As I live and breathe, if it isn't John Gray." She steps over to the front of the stage and kneels down to get a better look at the familiar face. "John, I have not seen you in years; I just can't believe it!" She turns her head, and calls out to the rest of the group, "Look everyone, its Johnny!" Several of the members lean down and reach out to shake their old friend's hand.

One of the men in the music troop speaks up, "John, get up here and help us out. We're going to do your favorite song. It would be an honor for you to do the duet with Bonny, not to mention all of us sharing the stage with you again."

Doc sinks down in his chair. He pulls his hat down and looks directly into his lap after the man's invitation. Bonny, the woman on stage, yells out to the crowd, "Help us get John up here." People start applauding and cheering for him to join the group. Allen and the Sheriff grab Doc by the arm and take him to the stage.

Allen looks at Doc, and then at the Sheriff. "This should be very amusing."

With Doc on stage, the piano, fiddle, and banjo players begin to play. The first part of the song is a female part. Bonny begins singing. Her voice is that of an angel. Then it is Doc's turn to sing. John begins his solo part with a voice so deep and polished the whole room goes so silent that you could hear a pin drop. When the song is over, the crowd gives the duo a standing ovation. John shakes hands and hugs the group members before returning to his seat.

As Doc walks off the stage to take his seat at the table, Allen pats him on the back. "I have never heard a voice like that; where did you learn to sing like that?"

"When I was in college I took a music class. During the class, I had to sing. That's when I was asked to join the music club. We did performances throughout Boston and the region." Doc gestures toward the stage, and then continues, "These people were part of that same group. We performed for many events and for many prestigious people. One year at Christmas, we even went to perform for the President of the United States."

Allen shakes his head very slowly in disbelief. "Doc, I have known you for some time; and you amaze me every day."

The performers take an intermission break, and Bonny comes down to sit and catch up with Doc. Bonny sits down in an empty chair next to Doc. “Well John, what have you been up to?”

Doc grins at her and replies, “You know, a little of this, and a little of that.”

“Come on, I haven’t seen you in seven years and that’s all you have to say?”

Allen looks at this stranger, who knows Doc from his younger days. “You know, Doc here, ma’am; he is a man of few words.”

Bonny looks at John, and then at Allen, then back at John. “Then he has changed a lot in the last seven years. He used to be the life of the party; he was larger than life when he took the stage. I remember when this pretty little girl came to watch one of our shows. It was a holiday show for the Massachusetts Governor. Anyway, this little gal was seated in just the right place so you could see her well from the wings of the stage. During one of the intermissions, John sees her. He grabs me by the arm, and points her out to me. With that first look, he said to me, *‘See her? I am going to marry that girl one-day.’* I was crushed, because I had a crush on him myself. When I saw the look in John’s eyes when he was looking at her, I knew they would spend eternity together. I have never seen two people more in love than John and Julie.” Allen looks at John. He gives him a little shoulder shove. Doc looks a bit embarrassed, for this story told to the men at the table was his true history.

Bonny grabs John’s arm and squeezes it. “So John, how is Julie doing? I am sorry she isn’t here with you. When you get back home you tell her I send hellos and my best.”

Doc glances at Allen, and then looks back at Bonny with a smile. "I will do that. Tell me where are you going from here?"

"Well, this is one of the stops in between our trip from Chicago to Denver," she replies. "We'll be in Denver for several shows, and then we are going to San Francisco. After several shows there, we'll head back east to Kansas City, for only a couple of shows, then back home to Boston. The plan is to be home before winter."

"Sounds like you are going to see the country," Doc comments.

"We have seen so many nice and beautiful places since we started this trip," she goes on. "Some of the wide open landscapes are more beautiful than an artist's painting."

"You will have to stop in Lincoln after you leave Kansas City on your trip back," Doc points out. "I have a friend who just bought the hotel and opera house and that would be a perfect place to do your show. I have plenty of room at my house where you can stay. I would love to catch up while you're there for those few days."

Bonny thinks a moment before answering. "I think that can be done. That settles it. Yes, we'll stop in Lincoln on the way home. That sounds like fun; and I can catch up with Julie and see the boys and how big they're getting."

Doc reaches and squeezes her shoulder. "After the show we can sit down and work out some details. Then just send me a wire when you'll be coming through. I will handle the arrangements in Lincoln."

Bonny stands up and waves her hand in the direction of the stage. "Alright then, that sounds like a plan. I will inform the gang and we'll come to Lincoln. But, there is a catch."

Doc looks at her puzzled. "What's the catch?"

"You have to be in the show with us. It will stay a secret. When you bring Julie, she will get a thrill seeing you sing with us in the show again. We can make it our little surprise for her."

Doc stands up to hug his friend. "Sounds like fun; I will practice up for it."

Bonny looks directly into John's eyes. "Well we're starting up again so I have to go. It was real nice to see you again. How long are you going to be in town?"

"We pull out at first light, so I will see you when you get to Lincoln."

After Bonny returns to the stage, the show resumes. Allen leans over to talk to Doc. "Why didn't you tell her about Julie?"

"I thought it would be best to wait until they came through Lincoln. After Julie and I started courting, Bonny and Julie became like sisters. They were as close as could be. They did everything sisters do together. I thought it would be better to let her finish their schedule and not have to think about her dead friend. I know this will just kill her, and honestly, I thought she would have known about their deaths by now."

Allen reaches for his beer mug and swallows the last swallow. "Yeah, it is probably for the best that she concentrates on the show and not be grieving about Julie."

Doc looks down at the table. The melancholy is working its way through him again. "I will tell her when she comes to visit. Then she'll have me there for someone to talk to her about it."

The Sheriff brings a round of drinks to the table. "These are on me, gentlemen, in honor of the great song Doc just preformed for us. I have never heard something so moving in my life; you sure have some voice, Doc."

"Well thanks, Sheriff; but if it's all right, let's just keep this amongst ourselves."

The Sheriff slides the shots around the table. "If I had a voice like that, I would be singing loud for the whole world."

"I would just as soon the world did not know," Doc says, rubbing his temple.

Allen holds up his shot glass, and in almost a whisper he makes a toast, "To Doc."

The rest of the table follows his lead; in a whisper, "To Doc."

Two men walk by the table, staggering, and notice Doc at the table "Well, looky here Ronnie, if it isn't the songbird. I'm surprised he ain't wearing a dress."

Allen tips the front of his hat up to see the drunks better "Why don't you two just go and sleep it off?"

The man turns back and looks at Allen. "Do you think you are man enough to make us leave?"

Before anyone else at the table can move, Doc is on his feet with a barrel of his gun centered in each of the men's foreheads. "He may not be, but I am. I have twelve really good reasons why you should leave while you still can."

The two men slowly back out the door, muttering, "This is not over songbird; you will pay for this."

"I believe it is," Doc states as he spins his revolvers back into their holsters. "If it's not, twenty bucks is twenty bucks."

Allen stands up and announces to the table, "It is time to go." He then looks at Doc, who has lost the sadness from a few moments ago. How quickly he turns into the dark person he generally sees. "Let's go over to the hotel and let you cool off for a little while."

Doc turns and nods at Allen. "Yeah, I am getting a little tired and we do need to get an early start."

As Allen walks out the door, a shot comes from the street. Allen jumps behind the horse trough. Doc, with guns drawn, is standing in the doorway looking at the two drunks. "Now look, boys, you have had your fun; now go home and sleep it off. I'm only warning you one time."

"Let's make this a fair fight," one of the men yells out. "You against us, right here in the street, right now."

Doc takes a couple of slow steps closer to the street, allowing the Sheriff and the posse out the doors. Doc looks at the men, knowing they both are too drunk for a fight. "I have to warn you, fellas, I shoot a whole lot better than I sing."

"Yeah? Hear that, Ronnie? He says he shoots better than he sings." The two drunks start laughing. "Well, I guess we'll have to see about that. I thought your singing sounded like a dying coyote."

Bonny comes out of the saloon to see about the commotion. Allen sees her, grabs her, and pulls her down behind the trough with him. He instructs her "SSHHH! You just keep your head down and let Doc take care of this."

"Marshal, that's your job," Bonny pleads with Allen. "You need to go out there and help him. He is going to be killed."

"He'll be fine. Besides, it's only two of them." Allen reaches to keep her head down.

"He is a Doctor! Not a gunfighter!" Bonny says with tears in her eyes.

"It has been a long time since you have seen him," Allen says, still holding her down. "Just do as I say. Trust me." As Allen holds Bonny behind the trough protecting her, the conflict continues in the street.

The one man shouts out, "Hey Ronnie, I think we're going to have fried songbird for supper."

"Last chance here boys," Doc shouts. "Which is it? Walk away or am I twenty dollars richer?"

Without hesitation, a man answers, "You're going to die, Songbird!" Doc pulls the hammers back on his pearl handled peacemakers. "Just say when, boys. Just say when." One of the men goes for his rifle; the other reaches to draw his pistol. Doc fires his colts. Both men fall back and lie dead on the ground.

Bonny breaks free from Allen and runs to Doc. She grabs him and hugs him. "I thought you would be the one dead. You could have been the one killed, John. What just happened? The Marshal said you'd be okay; 'there is only two of them,' what does that mean, John?"

Doc grabs hold of Bonny by both arms and pushes her back to see her eyes. "Bonny, how about you finish your tour and I will explain everything when you get to Lincoln. For now, let's just say I had a career change." He pulls back the breast of his riding coat to reveal his U.S. Deputy Marshal badge pinned to his vest.

Bonny looks at Doc, confused. "Career change?"

Doc nods. "Yes, a career change."

“All right. John. I will be expecting the discussion in Lincoln to explain absolutely everything I’ve just seen here.” She turns and goes back in to finish the show.

The Sheriff walks over to look at the two drunks, dead in the street. “Well, I know they just died five minutes ago, but they have been dead for a long time; they just did not know it. I guess the stories about you Doc, are true; you have to be the fastest I have ever seen. I guess I owe you twenty dollars.”

“Naw. You give it to Bonny; it will help cover some of their traveling expenses.”

“We need to get to the hotel before you shoot someone else,” Allen says as he reaches over and pushes Doc toward the hotel.

“Evenin,’ Sheriff. Thanks for the drink,” Doc says, then looks at Allen. “Before I shoot someone else? Don’t you mean so you can find your wife for the evening?”

“Very funny, Doc, very funny; besides this hotel is run by an elderly gentleman.”

As they enter the hotel, a lovely blonde gal is standing behind the desk. Doc looks at her and then back at Allen. “That is the prettiest old man I have ever seen.”

Allen looks at her, then back at Doc. “When I was here earlier there was an old man here.” He looks back at her. “There was an old man running the desk earlier. Where would he be?”

The young blonde desk clerk says, “My uncle? He has gone home for the evening. But, I can take care of whatever it is you need, Marshal.”

“Excuse me, miss,” Doc says.

“Yes Doc, what can I do for you?” Ellen asks.

"Well, I just was wondering, how well you know my friend, Allen over here?" Doc asks as if he has no clue.

Ellen smiles as she hands Doc the key to his room. "I know him well enough to know he likes his eggs over easy, just like his women."

Doc lets out a deep belly laugh. "Yeah, that's pretty much what I thought; I'll see you two in the morning." He tips his hat, and starts up the stairs.

9

As the sun begins to rise over the bluff, Allen, Doc, and the rest of the posse leave town. The men are on their way to Spirit Lake, to see if they can find any clues as to where Billy might be.

"It is about half a day's ride to Spirit Lake; we can stop there," Allen points out. "We can water the horses and take a break. We can also search the area some to see if there is any sign of Billy and his partners, before heading to Westhaven, where we'll stop for the night."

Doc, still trying to remember the last time he was at Spirit Lake, asks, "How far is it to Westhaven from the lake?"

"It's about the same as it is from here to the lake," Allen replies.

"In other words, another half day's ride," Doc says.

"Exactly," Allen answers.

****

The sun is reaching close to mid-day. Riding along, around and on the stone bluffs, you can feel the heat reflecting off them. The temperature is different in the shade of the bluffs. It is cooler, and the men are thankful for the times they are in the shade. As they approach the lake, they are on the top of one of the bluffs looking down at the lake, when one of the men shouts out, "Hey Marshal, there's an Indian village down there. It's best we start keeping an eye out."

Allen quickly corrects the man's assumptions of the local tribes. "The tribes in this territory and on the lake front are those of a peaceful people. They will not create war with anyone not harming or troubling their people." The group stops to look down below. "Also I have had dealings with this tribe before; they will not be alarmed by us, and the people will be friendly and hospitable. We will not be concerned by their movements throughout the territory here."

Doc points over to an Indian on a horse. "Hey, that's Howling Coyote up there on that trail; I'm going to ride ahead and see if he has seen any white folks around here."

Doc rides up to meet with Howling Coyote, to see if he has any information for them. After a few minutes, Doc rides back. "Howling Coyote said he saw fifteen to twenty white men ride through here yesterday and they were all well armed."

One of the posse boys speaks out; "That will probably be Billy's kin. We had better watch out for them."

Doc shakes his head. "No, I don't think so. We already know that's not like them. They are more the 'let's sit down and talk type,' not the ambush type."

"Well, you could be right," remarks the posse rider. "However, I think we have to be prepared just in case it is them, and they are waiting to jump us somewhere along the trail."

"I agree with Doc," Allen pipes in. "But, with them being heavily armed, we should be cautious since we really don't know who these men are, and what their intentions are." Allen moves his horse toward the trail that leads down the bluff to the water's edge. "Now let's go down into that valley over there and let the horses rest and get a drink

They make their way down the trail into the valley below. When they are near the water's edge Doc speaks, feeling uncomfortable, "Not to tell you your business, Allen, but this would be a good place for an ambush."

Allen nods, as he scans the high bluffs that surround most of the lake. "I thought that too. I scanned the bluffs surrounding the valley before heading down, and I did not see anyone."

"That makes me feel so much better," Doc says sarcastically.

The men climb off their horses and the sky fills with the sound of gunfire. They all scatter to find cover behind boulders, trees and brush on the valley's floor.

"I say, Marshall; you might have missed those guys when you were doing your scanning," Doc says in an angry tone.

"That attitude is not helping," Allen shoots back.

Doc crouches behind a boulder, and lies down on his belly. He peers out a little, looking for his horse. Spotting his horse, which hasn't moved, he says to Allen and a couple of other men, “I need you to cover me so I can get the rifle off my horse.”

Allen and the other men start firing while Doc runs to his horse, grabs his Sharps, and dives behind a boulder next to Allen.”

“Now this should even things out,” Doc says, looking in his ammo satchel. “I have a hundred rounds. We should be able to hold them off for awhile.”

Bullets are flying all over; the sounds of them ricocheting off the rocks is deafening. Every time one of the men looks out, four or five shots ring out and bullets start flying around again. One of the men jumps out from behind the rock which is his cover and empties his revolver, only to take a bullet in the shoulder.

Doc yells out to the fallen deputy, “Take your bandana and put pressure on that wound; I will get there as soon as I can, to help fix you up.”

Doc finds a nice groove towards the top of the boulder, from which he can aim. He sets the long barrel in the groove to steady it, takes aim on one of the outlaws and fires. The bullet finds its target. The man grabs his chest and falls forward off the bluff.

Doc grins. “One down, nineteen to go. This could turn out to be a profitable day.”

Allen pops up, shoots and then pops right back down. “I’m glad someone is enjoying this.”

Doc sees the fire coming out of another gun on the ledge. Once again, he takes aim and fires; and another man finds his way to the bottom of the valley.

“This could take all day at this rate,” Allen points out.

"If you have a better idea, let me know. At the moment, I don't really have a better plan for this shootout," Doc says.

Allen pops up, empties his rifle at the men on the bluff, and slips back below the boulder's top. "Right now I am thinking the plan is: just keep shooting."

"I am hit in the leg, but I'll be fine," another one of the deputies yells out. "I can't stand up for awhile."

Doc reloads his Sharps and takes aim, with four bullets in between his fingers and one in the barrel. "Allen, cover me."

Allen opens fires with two pistols. Doc stands up and fires another bullet, which finds its target. He shoots again, then again. It sounds as if he is firing a pistol, by the speed at which the bullets are leaving the barrel. Doc runs out of bullets, so he ducks back behind the boulder, grabbing for some more shells.

Allen looks at this daring man. "Did you get anybody?"

Doc looks at him with an eyebrow raised. "Five rounds fired. Five outlaws dead. Give me a minute to get these bullets in between my fingers and I will be ready for round two." As Doc starts to stand, Allen begins the cover fire. Doc once again sends five more to the valley's floor.

"Are you ready to go again?" Allen asks, getting the hang of this little plan of Doc's.

Doc slides fresh shells between his fingers. "Give me a second and I will be ready; ok, go." Doc stands to shoot, hears the sound of war cries and sees his friends from the lake charging the rest of the outlaws. He continues with his rifle. Between his friends from the tribe and the shooting he is doing with Allen and the posse members, they are able to finish off the remaining outlaws in quick order.

Once the shooting is over, Doc climbs aboard his horse and rides out to greet one of the Indians, who is wearing a large headdress composed of many eagle feathers. It is Running Wolf, the tribe's chief. The two spend some time talking, while another member of the tribe tends to the two wounded deputies. Another rides in to greet Allen.

Allen greets the tribesman. "Flying Hawk, I really appreciate your man tending to my wounded."

Flying Hawk extends his hand to shake the Marshal's. "What are friends for? If my people were in similar trouble, you would do the same to save them."

Doc returns from visiting with Running Wolf. He gets off his horse and looks at his wounded posse men. He examines them closely. "Thank your man for me, Flying Hawk. I appreciate the medicine your man has given to our wounded. Allen, we need to get going. I have to get these men to the Doctor in Westhaven. The shoulder injury is very bad. I think it's best if we treat it in the doctor's office instead of here."

"You heard Doc," Allen says as he looks at the rest of the men. "We have to get to Westhaven."

They start to make their way around the valley's rim, heading toward Westhaven. Allen looks over at Doc. "What did you and Running Wolf have to talk about?"

"I will fill you in later," Doc replies.

Allen rides by one of the dead outlaws. He looks down at the dead man. He recognizes the man as one of the rustlers he was chasing a couple of years ago. They were the same rustlers who ran with Amos and

Jack Dollar, men from the same band who caused the terror and murder on the Triple-J. This man on the ground below his horse killed Doc's family. These men are not Billy's kin. They are hardened outlaws. They are women beaters, thieves, and cold-blooded murderers. He thinks about this and decides not to tell Doc that he is aware that these men are tied to those events. Allen gets a chill, causing his whole body to shudder. He gives his horse a kick and hurries to catch up with Doc.

Doc is going over the events of the shoot-out in his head. The actions of one of the men in the posse don't add up. Doc slips back to ride with him. He looks at the kid. "Why were you shooting into the walls of the bluffs, instead of at the men on top?"

"Doc, I was scared," the young rider admits. "I really wasn't looking; I was just pulling the trigger."

Allen thinks about the earlier conversations regarding the white men seen by the tribe. The kid Doc is questioning said it had to be Billy and his kin.

"These men are not Billy's kin!" Allen hollers out, pointing back at the dead man he recognizes. "This is one of the men who visited your family the final day of their lives. They are those unwelcome visitors, Doc!"

Doc draws his pistols and points them at the deputy. "What do you know about this?"

A scared deputy answers, "Nothing, I swear!"

Doc pulls the hammer back. "Wrong Answer! I'll ask again, only once more; what do you know about these men, these men who were shooting at us?"

"I swear, Doc. I don't really know anything. I was just supposed to get you here and blame the attack on Billy's family, and that's all I know."

Doc pulls the hammer back on his other pistol; now both pistols aim right at this man's forehead. "Are you sure that's all you know?"

"Yes, I swear that's all I know; I swear!"

"Wrong answer!" Both hammers fly forward on the guns. The man is blown off his horse and he is lying dead on the ground with the rest of the outlaws.

Allen takes his hat off and slaps his leg with it. "Aw-damn-it Doc; what are you doing?" Doc rides back toward the fallen outlaw Allen recognizes as being involved with his family's murder. He stops beside Allen.

Sitting on his horse over the man, Doc stares at him. He pulls out one of his pistols and shoots both of the man's eyes out, telling the dead man, "I hope you rot in hell!"

"Doc, get a grip!" Allen yells at Doc. "It doesn't matter now; they're dead. Let it go. Let's get going; we have a long way to go and we need to get these guys to the doctor in Westhaven."

Doc spits on the man with no eyes. "Yeah okay, I'm right behind you."

They all take off at a gallop to make up some time. As night begins to fall, Allen and his posse arrive in Westhaven. Allen looks at Doc. "Okay, here's the plan; Doc why don't you take these injured guys, and find the town's doctor. I will go to the Sheriff's office and report what happened at the lake. Then I'll see if this Sheriff has any information about Billy."

Doc nods. "All right; I will meet you in the saloon for supper."

As Allen walks into the Sheriff's office, the Sheriff has a surprised look on his face.

This brings concern to Allen. "Evenin,' Sheriff; is everything alright?"

The Sheriff gives Allen an odd look. "I'm just surprised to see you, um, just to see you here, so, ah, soon."

Allen looks about the office, without moving his head. "You were expecting us?"

"Well, um yes, well I just . . . ." The Sheriff goes for his gun; Allen sees him grab it, and draws his pistol. Two shots are heard coming from the Sheriff's office. When the smoke clears, only one man is standing.

Doc, hearing the shots, tells the town doctor, "I have to go. You look after these two, and I'll be back."

As Doc runs into the Sheriff's office, he sees Allen standing there, holding his upper arm with one hand, his pistol still pointing at the dead Sheriff in the other.

"Allen, what happened?" He asks.

Allen shakes his head. "I don't know. He pulled his gun and shot me so I shot him."

"I think we found the only man who is a worse shot than you, thank God," chuckles Doc.

"Hey, I am not that bad of a shot," Allen protests.

Doc grabs the hand Allen is holding over his arm. "Move your hand and let me take a look. It's nothing. I have had worse cuts shaving."

"Yeah, well it really hurts," Allen says as he looks at the blood on his hand.

"C'mon. I got to get back to the doc's.'

They walk into the doctor's office. Doc tells the doctor, in a teasing tone, "I have another patient for you, Doc."

"These are the most patients I have had to treat in weeks," the doctor replies.

"Kind of fun, isn't it? Let me introduce us. This is Marshal Dan Allen. I'm his deputy, John Gray."

"Yes, it's kinda fun," The doctor remarks. "This man with the shoulder is a tricky one; the bullet is buried in-between his nerves, almost in the joint and I am afraid I will do more damage if I go in after it." He wipes his hands as he reaches to shake Doc's hand. It's nice to meet you gentlemen. I'm Dr. Donald O'Leary, but, please just call me Don."

John walks over to the man with the shoulder injury and looks at the wound. "Give me a minute. Let me go out to my horse and grab my medical bag. I want to be able to look at this better." As he steps outside Don looks at Allen. "Is he really a Doctor?"

"Yes, he used to be one of the best doctors in Boston," Allen replies.

Don looks at Allen in disbelief. "From what I hear, he is one of the most feared men this side of the Missouri River."

"Well, I guess you can say that Doc here is, well, he's just multitalented," Allen points out.

Doc Gray walks back in with a large black bag, grabs some instruments out, and walks over to the man with the bullet in his shoulder. He lays the instruments on the table next to the man. He washes his hands and picks up a couple of other tools he may need from

Don's supply. He looks at the wound and then says to the injured man, "We have been riding together for a couple of days now; I don't think I got your name. I like to know the name of my patients. So who am I about to work on?"

"Yeah Doc, my name is Stan. You know, I don't want to die tonight."

Doc wipes the wound. "Relax; you're not going to die tonight. This is a simple procedure. It will only take a minute or two; now look over there out the window." Stan turns to look and Doc hits him on the head with the handle of his Colt; Stan is out cold.

"Um John, I have some ether you could have used."

Doc looks over his shoulder at Don. "Now you tell me."

Don walks over to watch Doc work. Doc skillfully removes the bullet and repairs the tissue. He does it with such ease, that Don is completely amazed.

"John, I think that is the best work that I have ever seen," Don comments. "Can you show me how to do that?"

"I just did." He looks around the room at the other men. "I don't think we are going to have any volunteers to take a bullet in the shoulder so I can teach you this technique."

"I suppose you may be right. Anyway, I don't think I could do as well, even if you show it to me a hundred times."

Doc wipes his instruments and wraps them in their coverings. "It just takes a little repetition and practice."

Allen looks across the room at Doc Gray, thinking how odd it seems watching him remove a bullet and fix the guy up. His disposition is different with those surgical tools in his hand. He seems so cool and relaxed, almost at ease. His use of the medical instruments is that of complete control, something so opposite of the 'Deputy Doc Gray.' It is almost as if a different person is inside his head, doing the doctoring.

Allen looks over at the country doc. "Don, I just had a run in with your Sheriff and had to shoot him; I was wondering if you could shed some light on what was going on with the man."

Don shrugs. "I really didn't know him. A group of men rode in a couple of weeks ago and shot our Sheriff. The Sheriff you met today was someone left behind from those men, to fill the spot. He kept to himself; he was kind of a nervous sort. We usually don't have any trouble here, so he didn't have anything to be nervous about." Don notices the fresh wound on Allen's arm and takes a look at it. "Is this from your run in with him?"

Allen nods. "What do you mean? He was nervous?"

Don finishes cleaning Allen's wound and wraps a cloth around his arm. "That will be fine, Marshal. It's superficial. You can take this off in a couple of days; after that just keep it clean. About the Sheriff, he did not talk to anyone, ate by himself, and spent most of his time in the office. He was always down at the telegraph office, checking for news about something. Then this morning, over at the diner, I overheard that he received word that a Marshal from Lincoln might be coming. He became more nervous. I didn't understand it at the time. I am sure you can fill me in on that now."

"Well, you see, we were ambushed at Spirit Lake by a group of outlaws," Allen explains. "It's likely that he was in with them."

Don takes a look at the other man's flesh wound to his thigh, and bandages it. He looks over at Allen. "That would make sense. I guess the town's going to have to wire for another Sheriff."

"I will leave one of our deputies behind until you get a replacement," Allen says as he looks at his posse.

"That would be great," Don says. "Like I said, we don't have a lot of trouble around here; but it would be nice to have someone here just in case."

"Thank you for fixin us all up, Don," Allen says. "Now is there a good place to get a meal around here?"

"At this hour? Hmmm well, the saloon is as good as any."

Doc, Allen, and the only able-bodied posse member leave and walk over to the saloon to grab some supper. As they enter the saloon, there are three men standing at the bar.

The man in the middle stares at Allen with a smile on his face and says, "I hear you shot our friend, the Sheriff?"

Allen looks at the short, hefty man. "He gave me no choice in the matter, and he drew first."

"Well, I really don't care what you have to say in the matter; you're going to pay with your life for what you did," the man replies.

Doc walks around Allen and looks at the man. "Well, are you going to talk about it or are you going to do something about it?"

The man next to him whispers into his ear, and the stocky man blurts out, "I don't care if you are the guy called Doc Gray. You will die too, if you stick your nose in where it doesn't belong."

Doc puts his hand against the pearl handle in his belt. "You know, buddy; usually I would give you the option of leaving peacefully, but I am not in the mood for negotiating today. So draw now or shut up. You're annoying me." All three men go for their guns; before any of the three clear leather and get off a shot, they all lie dead up against the bar.

Allen stands there looking at the three heaps against the bar. Then he glances toward Doc. "I could have handled this, you know."

"Yes, I know you could," Doc smirks." However, you have already had a lot of fun with the Sheriff and I felt the need to play a little myself. Now let's find a table and get something to eat."

Allen wrinkles his face at the thought of food. "How can you think about eating after this kind of thing?"

"Easy; put the food on your fork. Place the fork in your mouth. Chew, swallow, and repeat."

"That's not exactly what I meant."

Doc pulls out a chair at an empty table. "Look, if after every gun-fight or watching someone die, I did not eat, I would die of starvation."

Allen reaches for his chair and sits down. "Well, I suppose you got a good point, looking at it that way."

"Did the Sheriff give you a choice of whether or not to shoot him?" Doc asks.

Allen shakes his head as he slides back into the chair further. "No, I suppose he really didn't."

"All right, then. It was either you or him, and I think you made the right choice. Now, I'm hungry. Let's eat."

After they finish their meal, as usual they find a poker game to finish off their day.

Allen stands up from the table. "Well, you guys cleaned me out so I am going over to the hotel."

“I am right with you,” Doc agrees. “Well gentlemen, it has been a pleasure. We have to head out early, so I better get a bit of shut-eye. Have a good rest of the evening.”

When Doc and Allen enter the hotel, they find a lovely young woman there named Betty.

Doc tips his brim to her. “Evenin,’ Miss Betty. Could I trouble you for my room key?”

Betty smiles at Doc and hands him his key. “Yes Sir, Doc. It’s room two. You get a good night’s sleep now.” Betty smiles seductively at the Marshal and says, “You won’t be needin’ a key, Marshal. You’ll be staying with me.”

Doc waves at the two over his shoulder as he climbs the stairs. “How did I know that was going to happen? Okay, you two have a good night. Marshal, I’ll see you bright and early in the morning.”

Allen and Betty disappear into her room down the hall from the front desk. The two enter her room. She turns up the lamp, and sits down in a chair next to a small table in the corner. Allen sits down on the bed and takes his boots off, in preparation of the evening’s upcoming activities. Betty then says something that he is unprepared for. “Allen, I need to talk to you about your mission.”

He pops his head up and looks at her like she’s crazed. “What are you talking about, Betty? Talk to me about what mission?”

She holds a finger up to her lips to shh him, then gets up from the chair and sits next to him on the bed. She speaks quietly, almost in a whisper, “Well, I am originally from Avoca. I know Billy. I know his kin. I know that you are looking for him. I also know that Billy could not and would not do what they have accused him of doing.”

Allen scoots back on the bed to get a bit more comfortable. He then leans in to get a little closer to her. "Why don't you tell me a little about Billy and his family?"

Betty leans into Allen, and starts to tell the background of why she has come to be there in Westhaven. "Okay, you see, Billy's grandparents on his father's side, along with his grandfather's two brothers and their wives came from back east, West Virginia actually. They came to get a fresh start here in Nebraska. They came to stake their own claims and start some family farming and ranching. When they arrived in Avoca, they applied for and received their land deed. Almost immediately their trouble started. You see, the land that the three brothers bought had already been looked at, and was about to be purchased by the man who runs the bank in Avoca, Mr. Sutton. He had plans to buy the ground to expand and increase his cattle operation. Billy's relatives bought it, and received their deed before he could get the land for himself. This is why many of us who know the family believe Mr. Sutton is behind all of the trouble that Billy is being blamed for." Betty pauses, and then holds a finger up as if to prove her point. "Okay now, I think you have to ask yourself, could a sixteen-year-old be the mastermind behind a cattle-rustling operation?"

Allen scratches his chin, contemplating all the evidence he just heard. "Betty, you have given me a lot to think about. I will try to figure all this out before we bring him back to Lincoln. It sounds to me as if he has been set up. I am not the judge. I only make sure they get to have their day in front of the judge. I will see that we do what we can to get the wrongs turned right." Allen reaches for Betty's shoulders. He grasps them, and eases her onto her back on the bed. "Now what do you say; let's get down to some business of our own?"

Betty smiles, reaches out and pulls Allen closer to her, and says in a breathy tone, "That sounds good to me."

****

The sun is rising; its light could be seen coming over the horizon. Doc is up and dressed. He grabs his bag and heads down to the front door. When he opens the door, there in front of the hotel is Allen. He is on his horse, with Doc's horse in tow.

Allen hands Doc his reins, then says, "Good morning Doc, I thought you were going to sleep the day away."

Doc takes the reins from Allen and mounts his horse. "I am surprised to see you up so early, not to mention you sure are in a good mood. Allen, what happened to you to cause this?"

"Well, I guess you could say my eyes were opened last night."

"Oh, learn a little something exciting with the new wife, huh?" Doc asks, never missing a chance to get a dig in on Allen.

"No. It's about our business," Allen shoots back.

Doc straightens up in the saddle like he has just been scolded. "Well, are you going to let me in on your little secret?"

"Not right yet," Allen answers. "First of all, I don't know who can and can't be trusted in this town. I want to wait 'til we get out of earshot. Now let's get back over and meet up with our two deputies and get on the trail."

Allen rides over to the livery, and the two men ride out of the barn, ready to head out on the trail.

"Are you ready for another fun filled day?" he asks.

"I hope it is not as exciting as yesterday," one of the men answers. "I don't know if I can withstand another one of those days."

Allen looks at him in agreement. "I am right there with you; as I mentioned to Doc here a bit ago, I think the majority of our troubles are just beginning."

"What do you mean, Marshal?" the young rider asks.

"Let's get on the trail," Allen orders. "I'll tell you the story as we ride."

The four men start through town, passing by Doc O'Leary's place. Stan and the doc are on the front porch, waving good-bye. Doc looks over at Allen. "I hope things stay quiet for that young man. His shoulder is gonna be hurting for a while."

Allen waves to the wounded deputy. "Yes, he'll be fine. He's only got about four days or so, and the new Sheriff will be here from Omaha." Allen kicks his horse and takes off.

"Well, looks like he's leaving us in the dust again," Doc says as he and the two deputies pick up the pace to catch up with the Marshal. The four men ride in silence for most of the morning. They come to a nice shady stream about midday. Doc speaks up, "Hey Marshal, let's let the horses cool, and get a drink huh?"

"You're right, Doc. That's a good idea. I can use a stretch. The way I figure it, we have a little over half a day yet and we'll be in White Horse. If we keep up this pace we can maybe be there before sundown."

Doc walks over to the stream, kneels down, and begins splashing water onto his head and face. Afterwards he looks over his shoulder at Allen and says, "Hey, why don't you tell us about the things you learned that you couldn't tell us in town? I don't think anyone can hear you here."

Allen sits down in the shade before he replies. "Good idea, Doc. Alright. Now you have to realize that I still need to get more information than I have right now to completely authenticate this, but this is what I heard and have verified so far. Last night I talked with someone who says the person behind all the trouble in Avoca is a very powerful man, with many connections. She is sure that Billy did not rustle those cattle. This powerful well-connected man is the banker in Avoca, and he is the one responsible for it all."

"Why would the banker want to rustle cattle?" one of the deputies asks. "I am sure he can afford to buy them."

Allen reaches into the stream and gets some water to wet his face. "I thought the same thing at first. You see, it's not so much about the cattle as it is about the land which Billy's parents, grandparents, and uncles own."

"I am not sure I am following," says Doc, looking at Allen confused.

"It seems that the banker had plans for the land before Billy's family staked their claim and was given a clear deed to the property," Allen continues as he puts his hat back on. "Mr. Sutton wanted this property for himself, but Billy's family got it first. It seems Mr. Sutton finds that it would be easier to take it from them rather than to buy it out-right from them."

"Are you sure she wasn't trying to throw us in the wrong direction?" Doc asks as he stands up to stretch.

"I know what you're saying; I thought the same thing," Allen replies as he stands up next to Doc. "Last night I wired Lincoln to confirm the story. It checks out. It turns out their family's property dissects Sutton's, meaning Sutton owns the land on three sides of theirs."

Doc nods; he understands what Allen is saying. "You are thinking that if they convict Billy of cattle rustling, they can convict the rest of the family as accomplices. That leaves only the women left on the land, and he will drive them off that way?'

"I think that is probably the plan," Allen replies as he mounts his horse. "But, like I said, we need more evidence and information to prove this theory of mine."

"Then we need to find Billy before Sutton's people do," Doc points out as he too mounts his horse.

Allen grins; thinking for once Doc is a step behind. "That's the plan. So maybe we should pick up the pace a little, boys?" The deputies re-mount and they all start toward White Horse.

Doc looks back at the deputies and asks, "The man I shot yesterday, when did he start serving as a deputy with you guys?"

Steve, the tall lanky one of the two deputies, replies, "Well, Harvey was killed in a bank robbery attempt a couple of weeks ago. There was a shortage at that point. Because of something going on, they needed extra deputies in Omaha, and Mr. Sutton sent one of the men from his operation to fill the job. Nolan was only a deputy a couple of weeks."

Allen takes his hat off and slaps his leg with it. "Well, isn't this a fine mess we find ourselves in the middle of? Hey Doc, doesn't the east and south sides of your land butt up to Sutton's land?"

Doc's face was turning amber, thinking that Sutton's greed for land may force him to have to protect his property. "Yep, and if that arrogant S.O.B. thinks he can run me off, or rustle my cattle, he's going to have a rude awakening. It may be at the business end of my peacemaker."

"I guess we'll have to cross that bridge when we come to it," Allen comments, not sure what else to say.

"I have been with the Sheriff for about five years," Steve says defensively. "In all that time Mr. Sutton has always been a very generous man; he has helped with many community improvements and has always given loans to any who needed them. I find it hard to believe he has anything to do with this."

Doc is taken aback by the kid's thinking. "That may be so, but money and power do strange things to a man. I have seen many a good man go bad because he is always seeking more power and more riches."

Steve looks down at the ground and shakes his head before commenting, "You may be right, Doc. I just don't know."

Wes, the other deputy, picks up where Doc left off. "Steve, think about it a minute. Almost all the land Sutton owns, he got from foreclosures on the loans he gave to settlers."

"Yes, you're right," Steve says, realizing that Wes has a point. "I remember a story Nolan told me about things he did while he was working for Sutton. Nolan told me that one time Sutton sent him out to a section of land, to throw the settlers off because they were behind in their payments. He was there on the bank's behalf, foreclosing on the land. Nolan hated having to do it. He said it was the hardest thing he ever had to do."

"This story is making a lot more sense by the minute," Allen says as he looks sideways at Doc. "Boys, we better get a move on; let's pick up the pace, so we can get in to White Horse before night fall. I 'spect we may have someone waiting for us."

Doc looks at the two deputies, and then back at Allen, and says, "You think they are going to set up an ambush for us in White Horse?"

"I honestly don't know what to expect," Allen replies. "I think it is best to be prepared. If we need to fight, to do it during the daylight is best. Let's hit it!" Allen flicks his reins against his horse's flank, to get the horse to pick up speed. The others follow.

They leave a big cloud of yellow dust behind them, as the four men head for White Horse.

10

As they enter White Horse, the sun is beginning to set. Allen scans the rooflines and balconies of the buildings as they near the outskirts, in an effort to prepare for undesirables. “We made good time, boys. Why don’t the two of you take the horses into the livery, and Doc and I will go down to the Sheriff’s office to see if there is any news about Billy’s whereabouts.”

“Maybe we better make sure this is the real Sheriff and not one of Sutton’s people this time,” Doc points out.

Allen, still scanning the buildings as they stop by the hotel, answers, “Well, how do you suppose we find out that information without raising suspicion?”

“Allen, why don’t you go in to the hotel, and ask your girlfriend?” Doc is quick to answer.

"Funny Doc, very funny." Then it hits him; Doc is serious. "You know, that might be a good idea. I can use my 'way with the ladies' to our advantage."

Doc and Allen dismount their horses in front of the hotel while the two deputies head off to the livery.

"Okay, let's go in, and you can work your magical Marshal charm!"

They enter the hotel; there behind the desk is Nancy, a beautiful young brunette.

She is tall and very shapely. In a heavy southern accent, she greets them. "Why, hello boys; Are y'all here to stay for the night?"

Allen likes this girl already. What man doesn't have a weakness for a southern drawl? "Yes, ma'am, I reckon so. It's been quite a while since we been through; how have you been?"

"Oh, you have no idea," she replies as she turns and reaches for two room keys. "I have been so lonely. It has been far, far too long. I have been counting the days since you left."

Allen holds out his arms and says, "Well, I am back now. What do you say you get our room keys and we can catch up?"

Nancy runs out from behind the desk, runs past Allen's open arms, jumps up, and makes Doc catch her. She lands in his arms and then she plants a deep passionate kiss on Doc's lips. "Doc, I can't believe how long it has been since you left. I have missed you so much; where have you been?"

Totally at a loss by this turn of events, Doc has no idea how to react. "Well, you know being a deputy. I've been busy the last few weeks chasing down outlaws."

Nancy kisses him again. “Yes, I understand and that’s fine, just fine. Darling’, you’re here with me now. I have our room key right here. We have all night to make up for lost time.” She flings Allen’s key at him. “Here is your key, Marshal. It’s for room eight. You sleep well now. We’ll see you for breakfast in the morning, okay?”

Allen is standing there in complete shock. The expression on his face goes right along with it. “Ah, okay, um, uh, good-night then. I’ll see you in the morning, Doc.”

Allen walks over to the saloon to get a drink. He is hashing over what he has just seen in his head. He doesn’t remember her from the last time he and Doc traveled through White Horse. As he makes his way into the saloon, he spots Steve and Wes sitting with another fellow around a table, playing cards.

Allen walks up to them. “Do you mind if I join you?”

Steve looks up. “Not at all; pull up a chair. Marshal, this is Gabe; he’s a local. Surprised to see you here already; we figured you’d be at the hotel with your wife for the night.”

“I might take that from Doc, but you best leave me alone about the women in my life,” Allen shoots back.

Steve holds up his hand as if to stifle the mood. “Marshal, I was just kidding. Relax and play cards. I’m buying the next round.”

****

Nancy and Doc enter their room. Nancy pulls him close, and speaks to him in a hushed tone, “Doc, you better be careful tonight. Two suspicious looking characters rode in about two hours before you. They have been acting particularly odd. It looks as if they are waiting for someone. I suspect they are lookin' to stir up a bit o'trouble for someone."

"I am sorry, but I think I had better get over to the saloon and make sure the Marshal does not get into any trouble. I will be back later," Doc says as he strokes her beautiful chocolate hair.

"You will be coming back to me?"

"Yes, I will be back as soon as the Marshal and I make sure those two men are not here in White Horse looking for us."

"Of course, your safety is most important, Doc. I will be waiting here for you to return. Please wake me if I happen to fall asleep. We have far too much catching up to do." She kisses him again before he slips quietly out the door.

Soon afterwards Doc leaves the hotel. As he is walking across the street, he sees a man exit the saloon. The man quietly slinks back into the alley, and then Doc enters the bar.

"You better take that back, Steve, or I am going to give you another hole out of which to breathe," Allen yells at Steve as he stands up.

"Marshal, I was kidding. Really I didn't mean anything by it."

"Stand up, you no good cheat. We are going to end this right now," Allen insists.

Doc makes his way across the room. He stands directly behind Allen without Allen knowing it. "Marshal, maybe we had better get you back to the hotel so you can sleep this off."

Allen turns around and pokes Doc in the chest with his finger. "This does not concern you. Maybe you had better stay out of this before you get hurt, Doc."

"You need to come with me and cool off right now!" Doc reaches to grab Allen's arm and Allen jerks away.

"Do you think you are going to stop me?" Allen asks as he takes a step back from Doc.

"Marshal, don't start something that you can't win," Doc answers as he tries to reach for Allen's arm again.

"Oh yeah? Doc, just say when," he says to Doc as he prepares to grab his peacemaker.

"When." Allen goes for his gun, only to find it in Doc's hand and pointing directly at his chest.

"How did you do that?" Allen looks at his holster, then at Doc, and then his holster again.

"I am not drunk and I am a lot faster than you will ever live to be at this rate." Doc spins Allen's gun and put it into his own belt. "Now let's get you to the hotel. You, fellas, I will see in the morning."

"Thanks Doc, we appreciate it." Steve says, relieved.

Allen and Doc leave the saloon to make their way over to the hotel. Doc is holding Allen up as he helps him cross the street. A man is leaning against the post in front of the general store next to the Hotel. He rolls tobacco in a paper, looks over at the two crossing the street, lights his smoke and says, "It's comforting to know that the Marshal who is supposed to protect us is a drunk."

Allen reaches for his gun only to find an empty holster. The man sees Allen go for his gun and goes for his. Doc sees the man go for his gun and quickly reacts by saying, "It would be in your best interest to leave the hog leg holstered, if you would like to see the sunrise tomorrow." The man takes his hand off the grip of his pistol, turns, walks around the corner of the store, and disappears into the night.

Doc takes Allen into the hotel and up to his room and puts him to bed to sleep off all of the whiskey he drank. Allen is out for the duration of the night.

Suddenly Doc notices he can hear voices coming from his room next door. Doc pulls his pistol and slowly opens the door into the hall. He tiptoes to his room. He reaches for the door handle, and turns it very slowly.

"It's all right, Doc, darling," Nancy calls out to Doc when she hears the handle turn. "Please do come in."

Doc enters the room, closes the door, and locks it.

Nancy stands up and gives Doc a big hug. "Doc, please let me introduce you. This is Horace, and he is here to talk to you about Billy."

Doc reaches out and shakes Horace's hand. "It's a pleasure, sir. Nancy, how did you know that it was I?"

"Doc, darlin', I heard you in the Marshal's room next door. So I knew you would be here before long."

"You need to be careful who you trust, Nancy," Doc points out as he sits down in a chair at the small table. "There are some suspicious characters running around. Now why should I trust you, Horace?"

"Darlin,' give him a chance." Nancy says as she pats Doc on the shoulder.

"All right, Horace, what do you need to get off your chest?"

"Doc Gray, let me start at the beginning of what I do know. When that man, Mr. Sutton, came to Avoca, he promised he would put the town on the map, making it a big city like Chicago, or Kansas City. You've seen the town; you've been there Doc, and it is almost as big as Lincoln. Sutton started out with some good ideas. People were settling all around the area. Why, the people were flourishing for some time. Everyone had a few coins in their pocket and food on their table, while other families like mine even had money in the bank for surviving winters. However, as Mr. Sutton grew richer, he grew in power too. This wealth and power changed him."

'This man is telling the truth,' Doc thinks to himself. This he has already learned. "How do you mean, it changed him?" he asks.

"You see, Doc; Sutton started giving loans to people he knew could not pay them back. When the settlers couldn't pay, he would foreclose on the property, taking most of their personal possessions too, to pay off the back payments. He saw this as highly profitable, so he started to rely on more underhanded ways to acquire more and more land, livestock, and anything that has value."

"Okay, I see this, Horace. But, how is it that you and your family have been able to keep all of your land and livestock?"

"Our land was not mortgaged through the bank, so Sutton couldn't use his foreclosure methods. My family is large, so up to now Sutton has not wanted to tangle with us. Then he found what he thought was the perfect plan. He would make us out as cattle rustlers and thieves by arresting us fer that. One by one, he could run us off our land."

"I thought Billy had his day in court to prove his innocence?" Doc is quick to ask.

"He had his day alright; that judge, Greiser? Well, that yella' man in a lawman's boots is one of them that is on Sutton's payroll. And the jury? All of those men work for Sutton too."

Doc pushes up the brim of his hat and slides back in his chair to recline and stretch out his legs; he crosses them and folds his hands in his lap. "Well, isn't that convenient?" Doc says with a chuckle.

"I know that Mr. Sutton is the man behind the trouble that has plagued you as well," Horace points out.

Doc immediately sits up, tense, his hands clinched into fists. "What do you mean, behind the trouble plaguing me?"

"I hate to anger you, Doc. Please except my apologies. I happened to hear him while I was doing some banking. I was close to his office door. The door wasn't closed all the way, and I could hear the discussion between him and a couple of his 'hench' men. After I heard the beginning of it, I knew I had to listen. So I stood there awhile and listened. He was telling the men that he wanted your land. He knew there was no way you would sell to him; and even if you did, you wouldn't have sold it for a price he would pay. That's when he and his men came up with a plan that if your family was killed, you wouldn't want to stay here. You'd pack up, leave everything, and go back east where you came from. Mind you, this would be after your family was gone. He was sure that after you had taken off, no one would know where you had gone; they would think that you were gone for good. Then the Marshal found you, and brought you back. With you back, they needed to come up with a new plan. That was when they were trying to figure up a plan to rid you from the land and the house. He wants that house badly. He is jealous of that house. I could hear that in his voice."

Doc clinches his fists together tighter. His jaw is clamped so tightly it feels like it would never open. In an intense deep gruff voice, "Are you sure of what you heard? Horace, are you absolutely certain of these words?"

Horace holds his hand up as if to swear before God in church. "Dr. John Gray, as I sit here before you, breathing the same air you breathe, I am certain. If I lie about a bit of it, may the good Lord send me to the ground right here 'n now."

Doc sits forward in his chair, gripping the arms. "Why have you waited until now to tell me this?"

Horace looks at the floor in shame, afraid to look Doc in the eyes. Talking to the floor he answers, "Doc, You were in such a depression before the services; and with the rage that came back with you, I was afraid you might shoot the messenger."

Doc stands up and starts to pace the room. "I can't believe this. Sutton was at my house on many occasions. We had him, his wife, and children over often. His boys and mine played together all the time. He was over at the house after the killings to offer me his condolences; he came to the funeral services, and he was there anytime I needed a friend to talk to. I thought he was just trying to be a friend when he told me if I decided to go back east, he would give me a fair price for my ranch. I thought that offer was just one way of 'being nice' to a grieving man, not this. Never did I think of something like this." Doc looks out the window, and then holds his head down for a time; with one swift swivel he turns back to face the center of the room. "That man, Richard Sutton, is going to pay for his grave transgressions. He is going to pay and pay dearly."

Horace doesn't look Doc in the eye, feeling he has hurt and betrayed a good and decent man. "Doc, all I want, all my family wants is for my nephew Billy to have a fair trial. I can assure you that Billy will turn himself in, if you will promise me he will get a second chance, a second chance for a fair and honest trial."

Doc steps over to Horace and pats him on the shoulder. "Where can I find you later?"

"I guess here in the hotel, why?"

"Horace, you let Nancy know where to find you. I'll need to talk to the Marshal about all this. Just stay close, all right?"

Horace stands up and shakes Doc's hand. "Alright, I will be waiting in my room to hear back from you. Thank you for hearing me out, Doc."

"I am sure with this new information you have told me, the Marshal will help," Doc points out. "We can do something to help get this right. I'll see you in the morning."

Without saying another word, Horace leaves the room with Nancy.

Doc reaches into his bags and grabs a whiskey flask. He takes a good long pull from the silver plated bottle. He lays his guns on the floor and hangs his hat on the bedpost. He looks out the window again. He takes one more sip from the bottle, and then puts it back in its home. He runs his hand through his hair, shakes his head, lies back on the bed, and looks up at the dark ceiling. His eyes close almost immediately from sheer exhaustion.

Nancy returns to Doc's room only to find him asleep. She pulls the covers over him and gives him a kiss goodnight. In a sweet loving whisper she says, "You poor grieving soul. You sleep well. You need good sound sleep. I will see you in the morning, darlin'."

The next morning, as the sun is coming up, Doc enters Allen's room and begins shaking Allen's feet. "Hey, time to rise and shine!"

Allen stretches, and rolls out of bed, "What time is it?"

"It is six fifteen and you need to get up. We have a few things to discuss."

"Yeah, yeah, I know I owe the deputies a big apology for that outburst. I need to thank you for not shooting me last night; Lord knows I deserved it."

"Yeah, well, never mind about that; you were drunk. We all have been known to cut loose once in a while and last night was your turn."

Allen stands up to gather his things, and the hangover he is going to have for the day makes itself known. He sinks back down, groaning, holding his head in his hands.

Doc can't help but chuckle, knowing that look and how it feels. "Marshal, what we need to sit down and discuss is Billy, Mr. Sutton in Avoca, and so much more. You see, last night Billy's uncle, Horace, came to visit me in my room and he told me an interesting story."

As Doc fills in the details of the conversation he had with Horace, Allen gets dressed and ready to meet the day. When Doc is finished Allen shakes his head with both hands on his hips, and then looks up at Doc. "I am amazed by your restraint there, Doc. After hearing that last night, I'd have figured you would have headed right back to Avoca in short order, leaving me here to sleep off last night's whiskey."

"You know me well, Allen. You are right, I did think about it, and I decided that if Horace is telling the truth, justice needs to be served right. If what we have encountered already is anything like what we're likely to encounter on our way back to Lincoln, you are gonna need me, Allen. I think Sutton will stop at nothing to keep us from bringing Billy back alive."

“I appreciate you staying around; it sure keeps the odds in our favor. C’mon, let’s go meet with Horace and get on the road. We still have a long way to go.”

A few minutes later Doc and Allen go to Horace’s room and Doc knocks on the door.

“Come on in. I’ve been waiting for you.”

Allen walks into the room with Doc following. He shakes the man’s hand and says, “Horace, it’s nice to see you again, but unfortunately not under these circumstances. Doc filled me in and I believe your story. You have my word as a U.S. Marshal that we will take Billy back to Lincoln and see to it that he gets a fair trial this time. I ‘spect Doc and I will be paying a visit to Sutton as well.”

“Thank you, Doc. Thank you, Marshal. I will take you to Billy. We have him hidden out in the canyons outside Destiny.”

“I appreciate you wanting to come along and help but it’s going to be dangerous,” Allen says with concern for Horace’s safety.

“I understand, Marshal,” Horace says as he grabs his bags and belongings. “Billy is kin. You ain’t gonna get near him without my help, at least not without a fight. If you two are going to risk yer hides trying to get him back to Lincoln, to set things straight for him, then by God, I am going right in with you to help.”

Allen looks at Horace with doubt in his eyes, but sees the determination in his, “Alright then, Horace; let’s get going.”

The three men leave the room and head to the livery to meet up with the deputies. When they open the front door to exit the hotel, a shot rings out. Splinters fly from the doorframe right next to Doc’s shoulder. Doc ducks back around the door, Allen and Horace dive under the stairs. Doc reaches for both pistols and returns fire. Allen sneaks out from under the stairs and crawls under the window to get a better look at the street.

"Hell, I didn't think it would start so soon," Allen comments.

"You were too drunk last night for me to tell you. We had visitors expecting us when we arrived last night," Doc points out, "I figured those two were up to no good. It looks like they rounded up some other friends during the night, to come in and help me out."

"Help you out to do what?" Allen asks, as he looks at Doc, confused.

"Fill my pockets with gold, of course. Men like this are likely to have a bounty on their heads."

"Crying out loud, Doc, is that all you think about?"

"Actually, no, I have other things on my mind."

Windows are breaking from the bullets flying around the hotel; the two deputies are pinned down at the livery down the street. Doc knows that something has to be done and fast. "Allen, you two stay here, and keep them busy; I have a plan."

Allen looks over at Doc between his taking shots. "Are you going to let me in on it?"

"You just play your part," Doc instructs Allen, "Keep them thinking we are still all here; just keep returning some shots and, by all means, keep your heads down!"

Doc takes off up the stairs to the back of the hotel and looks out a window to see if it is clear, just in time to catch a man climbing up and over the balcony. Doc climbs out the window, sneaks up behind him, and introduces the outlaw's head to the butt end of his colt. The man drops to the floor; Doc drags him into a room and ties him up on the bed.

Nancy runs into the room in a panic. “Oh my God! Oh heavens, Doc! What is happening? What are we to do?”

Doc looks at her and speaks quietly, “Sshh, calm down.” He hands her the unconscious man’s pistol. “Take this pistol and if he moves shoot him. I’ll be right back.”

“Doc, where are you going?”

“To collect on an old debt,” Doc answers as he climbs back out on the balcony and carefully creeps around the side of the hotel where he sees two of the outlaws firing at the livery. Doc aims his rifle and fires twice; both outlaws drop to the ground. As he makes his way up the side of the building to the front, he spots three more across the street in front of the saloon, crouching behind the horse trough. Doc takes aim and patiently waits for his quarry to show itself. Finally, one of the men stands up and is dropped quickly. Another makes a break for the saloon; another round exits Doc’s barrel, sending him on his way to an undertaker’s box. The last man stands up to fire at Allen and Horace, only to find a round from Doc’s rifle in his chest. As Doc makes his way to the front of the hotel, he sees the two men from last night on their horses trying to escape. Two shots ring out from the 44-40 against Doc’s shoulder. The shots find their mark, knocking the men off their horses and to the ground. Doc continues scanning for movement, yelling to Allan and Horace, “I think it’s safe to come out now. I count seven down, and then there’s one tied up. Nancy has him at gunpoint upstairs.”

“You could have left one for me,” Allen says, feeling left out.

Doc holds his hand up and shrugs his shoulder. “Sorry Marshal, but I was just trying to clear the way.”

Suddenly a shot comes from inside the hotel.

"Nancy!" Doc yells.

He spins around to get to the room where he left her and her prisoner. Doc goes up the exterior stairs, taking them two at a time. He reaches the top and jumps through her window with guns drawn. He sees Nancy holding a smoking gun and the man in bed with blood on his ear.

"She's crazy! That dag-blame-woman almost shot my ear off!"

Doc starts laughing at the whole sight. "Yeah, well, if you keep talking like that in front of this fine lady, I might let her finish the job."

Allen and Horace come busting into the room from the main hallway. "Is everything alright?"

"Oh Marshal," Nancy says still a little shaken up. "Why, we are all fine. Well, maybe not this swarthy gentleman with the wound I put on his ear. But otherwise Doc here and I are no worse for wear."

"Okay, all is under control in here," Allen comments. "Well, let's go down and make sure the town's Sheriff can handle the clean up."

"Yeah, I need to see if there is money coming my way," Doc points out. "I discussed your run in with the last Sheriff. Miss Nancy here said last night that the Sheriff has been here for going on ten years and he is a good, honest lawman."

When the three exit the hotel, they find that the Sheriff and a few of his deputies are already moving the bodies to the undertaker's shop. Allen walks over to the Sheriff and tips his brim, "Morning, Sheriff. What a way to start your day, ain't it? Do you need any help?"

"Morning, Marshal. Naw, I reckon we have all the help we need. It looks like I owe someone about ten-thousand dollars for these men. Although we don't have that much in our bank here, I can have it sent by courier. Where do I send the money?"

Doc is quick to speak up. “That would be me. Just send the money to the Marshal’s office in Lincoln. They will take care of it, until I get there to get it. There is one more of this band tied up in room five. Miss Nancy is keeping an eye on him, but you might want to be sending someone up there. She seems to have an itchy trigger finger.”

The sheriff chuckles at the thought of that sight, a soft spoken, proper acting, southern lady, holding a prisoner at gunpoint. “Okay. I’ll get one of my men to take him off her hands.” He waves a hand to direct one of his men up to the room. “Well, thank-ya guys. Good luck catching up to your prisoner.”

The Marshal and his posse mount up and head out of town.

Doc looks over at Allen, and gives him a wink, “Where are we headed to?”

“White Cloud,” Allen answers.

“Do you think we’ll be there before nightfall?” Wes asks.

“I hope we can reach White Cloud before nightfall,” Allen replies. “White Cloud will put us just about a day’s ride from Destiny.”

“That sounds like a great plan, Marshal; but White Cloud isn’t quite a half day’s ride from here,” Steve points out, not sure if the Marshal is serious. “Don’t we want to get a little further than that today?”

“Naw, I was already figuring on stopping in White Cloud before this morning,” Allen answers. “Doc and I have discussed it. He thinks it sounds like a good idea to him. We have been on the trail almost a week now. Thanks to Horace, we will have Billy back in custody in a couple of days. We all could use a bath, a shave, and some good relaxation before getting to Destiny, and starting back toward Lincoln.”

“We still need to keep our eyes peeled for Sutton’s men,” Doc points out. “I’m sure we have not heard the last of them.”

Steve points off ahead in the distance and says, “Marshal, there is a pass about five miles ahead which would be a perfect ambush site. Would you like for me to ride ahead and check it out?”

Allen motions for Steve to ride up to the front, and starts pointing at the landmarks up ahead. “Why don’t you and Doc ride up and take a look. We will slow up and give you some time to check things out. We’ll swing out to that side a bit, and meet on the other side of that bluff over there. I figure we’ll be about twenty minutes behind you.”

Doc looks over at Steve. “Alright then, c’mon boy, let’s ride.” Doc and Steve ride off at a good gallop, to put some distance between them and Allen. Doc remembers the argument between Steve and Allen last night. “What was all the trouble between you and the Marshal last night?”

Steve shrugs his shoulders. “It was nothin’ really. I was giving him a hard time, you know just some jokin’ around; and he flew off the handle. It happened to be right about the time you walked in that it was really getting out of hand and you know the rest.”

Doc looks over at the young man. “I thought for sure he was gonna shoot you.”

“Yea, I kinda thought so too, Doc. Man, I sure was glad when you showed up. Hey, I have to know how you did that trick with the Marshal’s gun. I have never seen that done before.”

Doc shrugs his shoulder and answers, “I would love to tell ya kid, but truth be known, I don’t really know myself. When the Marshal went for his gun; I guess instinct kicked in, I got there first.”

Steve stops his horse and points toward the bluff ahead of them. "We are just about there; you see that big bluff over there? Well, we need to tie the horses up at the bottom and climb up there. When we get to the top we will be able to see if there are any surprises waiting for us on the other side of those trees." As they make their way up the bluff, Steve grabs Doc's shoulder, "Wait, stay here a second, let me take a look." Steve crawls the last few yards to get a look with his spyglass. Steve holds his spyglass up, looking through it, watching their awaiting foe. He looks back to Doc, holds a finger to his lips, indicating 'sshh' then motions for Doc to come closer. He whispers, "Doc, come over here and take a look. It is as I suspected; there are six men spread out over that bluff there."

Doc looks through the spyglass and sees the men ready to ambush them. "I see them. Steve, wait here; I need to go get my sharps off my horse and I will be right back." Doc slides quietly back down the backside of the bluff. In a matter of a few minutes, he returns with his sharps and looks at Steve. "Okay, see the one on the far right? I will start with him first. And I will work my way toward the one who is over by that hollow tree."

"Is that the smartest way to go?" Steve asks.

"The way I figure, you can reach the two closest to us. So why should I worry about them? And with any luck, we'll get them all before they high tail down the back of that bluff."

"Okay. That's a good idea. You just tell me when to start shooting."

Doc loads his cartridges between his fingers and loads one in the chamber. Doc steadies his Sharps in the direction of the first man. "When you hear my first round, start shooting."

Doc takes aim at the man farthest from them and fires; the man falls down to the valley below, Steve fires his dependable lever action and his target falls over backward.

"Nice shot, Steve; keep it up." They continue firing, hitting everything they aim at, and four men lie dead. Two of the men escape on their horses. Now they are riding right toward Allen. As Steve and Doc climb down, five shots can be heard in the distance. Steve and Doc jump on their horses to go and see what happened. Allen, Wes, and Horace ride out from around a small bluff.

Allen looks at the men and says, "That worked well, gentlemen. We got the remaining two outlaws. They came around from their hideout; they looked so surprised to see us, and even more surprised when we began shooting."

"They were right where Steve thought they might be," Doc adds. "We took them by surprise. He and I managed to get four of them ourselves. There were six total. You took care of the two who got away from us."

Allen looks at Steve and asks, "Do you know if there are any other ambush spots on the way?"

"No, I can't think of any," Steve replies. "I think we have a clear trail all the way to White Cloud."

"Well, then, let's make up some lost time," Allen says as he takes hold of his reins and slaps his horse.

****

As they enter White Cloud, Allen turns toward the men behind him and says, "Take the horses to the livery and meet us at the saloon.

Steve rides up beside the Marshal. "If it is alright with you, sir, I would like to go out and visit my aunt and uncle for a little while. It has been some time since we have seen one another. My mother will have a fit if she learns I was this close to her only sister and didn't stop in and see them, at the very least just to say hello. They have a ranch a mile west of town. I can be back by supper. Where should I meet you?"

"Steve, you go on. You give my best to your aunt. You show back up at the saloon for supper. We are having a special dinner. Doc here, if I can talk him into it, will do us up a beef brisket in a fire pit. It is something you can't miss," Allen concludes, rubbing his stomach.

Steve tips his hat to his superior. "Thank you, Marshal. I will be back for supper." Steve gives the horse a jab, and off he goes west, in double time speed.

"Brisket?" Doc asks, giving Allen the single raised eyebrow look.

Allen smiles. "Yeah, Doc, brisket. I knew we'd have time, so I wired an old friend, Bobby, who runs the saloon. I told him to round me up a brisket, and rub her down with seasonings. He should have it ready for you when we get there."

Allen and Doc make their way into the saloon to talk with the owner and find out about the brisket. "Hey, Bobby, how are you, old man? Did you round up the beef I wired you about?"

The man wipes his hand with a bar towel, and extends one to shake the Marshal's hand. "Yep, sure did. I got it from Hadley's farm over outside of Minitare. That man has some of the best beef in these parts. He says they butchered about ten days ago so this meat is good and aged. It should cook up great. I rubbed her down as you asked. I had a couple of kids dig a pit. Amazing what three cents for each of them got me." He motions for them to follow him, and he leads them to the back door. Outside behind the saloon is the pit. He points over at the pit and the pile of wood next to it. "This wood is some good hardwood. So it should work well. If the pit is big enough for you, we should be set."

"Bobby, this looks great! Show me to the brisket. Let's get it started," Doc says, after looking at the pit and firewood.

Allen and Bobby watch Doc do his 'pit beef' magic. Allen notices all of the activity going on. "Bobby, what is with all the activity and people in town today?"

"Today is our annual White Cloud founder's celebration. We have all kinds of fun things for adults and children. There is a huge picnic at the Church. All the ladies bring the most wonderful food. A couple of the ranchers donate a pig, some chickens, and some guys to roast them. For the kids there are games. They do a piglet catch. If you have never seen that, it is the funniest thing. They put about a dozen piglets in a pen. They make the pen real muddy, and then the kids go in and try to catch a pig. It's a lot like catching greased pigs, but funnier. The kid who gets a pig first wins a dollar. For the men, there is a horse race, a couple of different shooting competitions; and of course, there is the pie-eating contest. I won that last year. In fact, that's how I met my wife. She makes some of the best blueberry pie."

Doc finishes getting his wood fire going, puts the meat in, and covers it all up. "That sounds like just what the Doctor ordered, we need a day like this to rest up a little. We all need to recuperate from the last few days. When does all this get underway?"

Bobby pulls out his pocket watch, looks at it, and then replies, "Let's see, the kids have a foot race in about fifteen minutes, and then they'll do the piglet catch. The pistol competition will be after that, and then the horse race. After the picnic, there's the pie eating contest and a few more kid's games; and the town playhouse puts on a number. Looks like the 'big boys' games start in, oh, 'bout an hour."

"Well Doc, I don't know about you, but I think a hot bath and a shave is in order," Allen comments. "I think I'll sign up for the horse race."

"Have a good time today, Marshal; from what I have heard you guys could use a rest," Bobby concludes as he steps back in the doorway.

"Hey Doc, do you need any help with this?" Allen asks.

"No, I have it under control; all I have to do is cover it up and leave it alone. It should be perfect by six."

"Okay, I'm going to sign up for the horse race. Like I said, I think a bath and a shave would make the day perfect."

"I agree," Doc says. "That's where I am heading as soon as I sign up for the shooting competition."

"I am sure the other competitors will appreciate it," Allen chuckles.

After finishing with the brisket Doc goes over to the hotel, gets his things together and walks across the street to the barbershop & bathhouse. He sits down in the chair, and the man begins to give Doc the full treatment. After the man finishes giving Doc his shave, Doc goes into a room in the back.

A young Negro boy helps him off with his boots and fills the tub. "Sir, here are cloths to dry with and some soap. My name is Josiah, Sir, if'n you need anything."

"No, I believe things are fine, Josiah; thank you." Doc gives the boy a shiny nickel. The young man is beaming as he turns to leave.

Doc undresses and slides into the steaming tub of water. He soaks for a bit before reaching over to his bag to get the soap which Mary made for him. He likes it because it smells like the air after a spring rain.

When Doc unwraps the soap, a piece of paper and something frilly falls out. He looks down at it, and picks it up. It is a letter and a lace handkerchief. He smells the handkerchief. He knows right away, by the scent, that it is Audra's. It smells like lavender and vanilla, just like she did the night he held her. He knows he doesn't have time to read the letter, but, he has to; after all it is from Audra.

My Dear John,

I know we only met a few hours ago. But, it seems like I have known you forever. Please be careful on this trip.

I decided that you should name the colt Spirit, because she is beautiful, a wonder, and contains plenty of Spirit. I hope you find this name satisfactory.

I will be waiting for you, John. I will pray for you each night.

Keep this with you, and think of me, until you return home safe and sound.

Until I see you again,

With Love,

Audra

Doc pauses for a moment to remember that night by the pond. He remembers the color of her hair and her eyes. How she reminds him of the good times he had shared with Julie. She made an impact on his heart, one that he thought would never happen after losing his reason for living. He speaks while he inhales the aroma of her from the handkerchief, "Yes Audra, I will keep this with me, always."

Doc finishes his bath and carefully returns the handkerchief and note to his bag. He drops his bags off across the street at the hotel, and heads off for his afternoon of 'true' fun.

A man is standing on a wagon out behind the hotel and general store. He is shouting out the rules for the shooting contest. "A man will throw a bucket from the roof of the General Store. You will draw your pistol and see how many times you can hit the bucket, before it hits the ground. The man who can hit the bucket the most times, before it hits the ground, will be declared the winner!" Men begin lining up in preparation for the contest.

The first man steps up to the line and the bucket is tossed. The man draws and fires at the bucket, which reacts to each hit by altering its flight just a little, and then hits the ground.

The announcer yells out to a young boy, "Jeb, go out and get that bucket so we can count the holes."

Jeb returns with the bucket. The announcer and the other man on the wagon count the hits. The announcer gives the results, "The bucket has four holes in it!"

As the competition continues, men step up to the line and fire; the hits are then counted.

Then it was Paul's turn. He was the town's favorite, and an excellent marksman. The thrower on the roof waits for Paul's signal to throw. When the signal is given, the bucket goes up, the shots are heard, and the bucket hits the ground. Jeb fetches the bucket, and the announcer yells, "It's a perfect six shots!" The crowd of spectators yells and cheers for the hometown hero.

Doc steps up and the bucket is thrown. Doc pulls out both his guns and keeps the bucket in the air for all twelve shots. However, Doc's first turn was disqualified. He is only allowed to use one pistol. Doc steps up to the line again, with his reloaded pistol. He nods to the thrower; when the bucket hits the ground Jeb runs out and retrieves it.

The announcer gives the results, "We have a tie! Doc has a perfect six shots!"

The final three men shoot, although none of the remaining contestants are able to hit a perfect six shots to the bucket. "Okay folks, since we have a tie, we will have a shoot off between Paul and Doc."

The man on the wagon begins explaining the rules of the shoot off. "The target will now be smaller. We will shoot these glass balls." He holds up an amber colored hollow glass ball, the size of an apple. "This will be a best of three. Each man will get to shoot three globes. The one shooting the most wins; if the men continue to tie, the objects get smaller. Paul will be the first to shoot."

Paul steps to the line, nods his head and the first ball flies up. He shatters it. He signals for the second, and then the third. He shatters both of those balls too.

Doc steps up to take his turn. He nods, one up, two up, three up; they all come down shattered before reaching the dirt.

"We still have a tie! We will do another round!"

The men continue to shoot at the glass balls; neither misses.

After five rounds, the announcer says, "In this round," the announcer reaches to the bench behind him, picks up a silver dollar, and holds it up in the air, "each man will be given a silver dollar to shoot. They will have the opportunity to shoot five times."

Paul shoots first. He and Doc alternate turns. Ten silver dollars go up and then come back down, each containing a hole from a contestant's bullet.

"Okay folks, we now will make things a bit tougher." The announcer holds up a glass marble. "Each man will shoot until one misses. The one who does not miss the marble will be the winner!"

The crowd cheers. Paul is to shoot first. The crowd becomes silent. Paul nods and the thrower sends the marble up high. Paul starts to line up the marble with the tip of his pistol. The marble reaches the 'right' spot and Paul fires. The marble hits the ground.

Jeb picks it up and announces, "He missed, sir."

A big moan of disappointment comes from the crowd. Paul hangs his head in disappointment. Doc steps to the line, nods, and the marble is thrown. Doc aims, and just as the marble reaches its peak on its upward trek, Doc shoots. The marble shatters into dust high above the crowd.

The announcer hollers out, "Ladies and gentlemen, I think we have our winner!"

The man once again steps up onto the wagon. He presents Doc with a medal for the pistol competition and the ten silver dollars. "Congratulations, Doc."

The man then announces, "The horse race will be starting in ten minutes, in front of the saloon. The rifle shooting competition will follow."

Paul walks over to Doc and reaches out to shake Doc's hand, then says, "Congratulations. That was some damn fine shooting, Doc."

Doc smiles. "Me? That was fine shooting yourself; you got a good eye there."

"Thank-you, but you are the better man," Paul says, looking at the ground in disappointment.

"If you keep it a secret, I'll tell you something, Paul."

"Sure Doc, I can keep a gunfighter's secret"

Doc leans close to Paul and whispers in his ear, "I don't know how I hit that marble. I think it was luck."

"Aw, Doc, you're teasing me."

"Look Paul, when it comes down to it, you are a skilled shooter. This competition proved that. Practice, and next time you will hit that marble. Trust me."

Doc walks over to the saloon. He wants to see how the Marshal does in the horse race. Several of the young boys are coming over to him and saying how good he is, and they want to be like him. He reaches into his pocket and pulls out several of the silver dollars. He hands each boy one and says to him, "Okay, each of you has to make me a promise. You have to promise that you will listen to your mamas, do your chores, go to school, and say your prayers. If you promise to do these things until you are an adult, you can each keep yours."

They all say they promise and thank him, and the four boys go running down the boardwalk talking and laughing.

The contestants and those gathering to watch the horse race are at the starting line. The announcer is standing on the wagon in the street, at the intersection in front of the saloon. He starts to tell everyone the rules for the race. "The rules of this race are simple. The first one to finish is the winner. You will start here, and finish here. This course is going to be five miles out and back. The entire course is marked with red ribbons. You will find them tied to trees and bushes. If there is not a tree or bush to tie to, a post with a ribbon tied to it will be in that spot. Contestants, you will start when the pistol is fired."

He raises his pistol above his head and fires; the racers take off, all twenty-five of them, in a cloud of dust. Allen finds himself in the middle of the pack. As the riders make their way around the course, men are knocked off their horses and a few of the horses lose their footing and drop out of the race. When they reach the five-mile turn around, Allen is in fourth place. In the final half mile, Allen is running neck and neck with another rider. Just as he and the other rider reach the last one hundred yards, Allen inches out in front and maintains the lead to the finish line. The crowd erupts with cheers as Allen crosses the finish line first.

The announcer congratulates Allen on his fine horsemanship and fast horse. He then hands Allen the reins to a fine black stallion and says, "You have won the race and we have for your prize, this fine young horse!" Allen shakes hands with the announcer and waves to the crowd. The announcer then announces, "The rifle shooting competition will start in fifteen minutes down by the grain and feed market."

Allen, feeling pleased with the performance of his faithful gelding, gives his new horse a rub on the forehead, then takes the reins of his two horses and leads them to the livery.

The announcer's wagon moves to the north side of the grain house. Several tables are placed in a line to create shooting rests for the contestants' firing line. "May I have everyone's attention, please? Contestants, I need you over here for the rules reading."

The contestants gather at the tables to hear the announcer read the contest rules to them. "Gentlemen, here are your rules; a plate like this," he holds up a white plate, about seven inches in diameter, "will be your targets. The first plate will be set at a hundred yards. You have one shot to break the target; those who hit their targets will move to the next round. The second round will increase by fifty yards. The third round also will increase by fifty yards. Each round after that will increase by one hundred yards! The prize for this contest will be this two-year-old bull donated by Tom and Sissy Hadley from the Rocking–H Ranch! "Okay, can I have the first group of shooters on the line for round one, please?"

There are thirty men lined up to take their shot at the targets. The first ten shoot, then the second ten, and then the third and final group. At the completion of the first round, half of the competitors are eliminated.

"Alright, we are down to seventeen men. Everyone reload. Can I have the first ten to the line, please?"

The targets are moved out another fifty yards. The first ten men shoot, followed by the remaining seven. Out of the seventeen men, twelve move to round three. The targets are moved out fifty more yards. The contestants take aim and fire for their third round. Ten hit their targets. For the fourth round the targets are moved out another one hundred yards.

"Okay, men, you are now shooting from three hundred yards." The rounds continue, advancing one hundred yards each round. "Okay, folks, we are at round number eight here. We are down to three men!"

The crowd applauds and cheers. The targets are set at the seven hundred yard mark. The announcer gets the crowd excited. "Okay, we are at an incredible distance here. These men are the best of the best; they will be shooting at targets that I can't even make out at that distance. Are you ready for this round, folks?" People cheer. He speaks up again, "Fire when ready, Gentlemen."

Three shots ring out but only one finds its target. "Well, folks, it looks like there is only one flag waving at the other end! We have a winner!" The crowd erupts; hats go into the air. "Congratulations, Doc! It looks like you win again!" Doc thanks the announcer, and waves to the onlookers. "Would you like to have this bull sent to your ranch in Lincoln, sir?" Mr. Hadley asks.

Doc turns around and shakes Mr. Hadley's hand, "Yes, sir, that would be mighty kind of you. Could I trouble you to see that the black horse the Marshal won gets there too?" Doc reaches in his pocket and hands the man several bills to pay for the relocation. "I hope this will be enough to cover the expenses of getting them to Lincoln and the return of your men back home."

Mr. Hadley takes the cash from Doc and says, "That will be more than enough, thank you. I would like to talk to you about trading some cows in the future. I would like to get some of your cattle into my line."

"I tell you what, Mr. Hadley, I will wire my foreman and tell him you want some new cows; he will take care of this deal for me. Feel free to speak to him as you would me. He's my right hand, and he will accommodate."

"It'll be a pleasure doing business with the Triple-J," Mr. Hadley comments and the two men shake hands again.

Doc tips his hat, and says, "If you'll excuse me, I have some brisket to check."

Doc walks into the saloon and sees the group of riflemen; as he walks by them he says, "Good shooting, everyone; I had a great time."

As the kids are finishing their games, everyone is heading to the churchyard for the picnic. A makeshift stage has been set up for the community players. They will be putting on a play for the town's entertainment, following the pie-eating contest.

Doc, Allen, and their group are seated together, enjoying the fine meal which has been created by everyone in town, including Doc's brisket.

"Doc, I got to tell ya this is the best you've ever done," Allen says, licking his fingers. "You have out done yourself this time."

"I'm glad you are enjoying it; this turned out to be a great day, didn't it boys? This was something we all needed."

"Yeah, but I have a gut feeling we are going to pay for it tomorrow. I am sure Sutton has a surprise waiting for us in Destiny."

As the day breaks on White Cloud, Allen and his posse are riding out of town, heading for Destiny.

Allen turns, looking behind him at Steve, and asks, "How well do you know this territory?"

"Sorry, Marshal, but my expertise of the landscape ended at White Cloud."

Allen looks at Wes and points. He just shakes his head. "Sorry, Marshal. Until this run with you, I'd never been west of El Dorado."

"Doc, you've been this way on hunting trips, haven't you?"

"Yeah, I have. It has been awhile and I don't remember much about the landscape, not to mention, hunting and outlaws are two totally different subjects."

11

The ride to Destiny goes without a hitch, much to their surprise. Once in town, Destiny seems normal and peaceful. They ride up to the Sheriff's office. Allen looks at Horace. "Let's have you go in and see if this sheriff is legitimate or one of Sutton's men. You know the folks in these parts, so you may be our safest bet."

Horace gets off his horse, and looks back at the Marshal. "Unless something has changed Marshal, the Sheriff here is a good man. I'm sure he'll help us with Billy."

"In that case, I'll go in with you." Allen looks at the other three and continues, "Why don't you guys head down to the saloon and get something to eat and we'll be down there as soon as we finish our business here."

Allen dismounts, as does Horace, and they walk into the office.

A short time later, Allen and Horace walk into the saloon to see Doc, Steve, Wes and another man already involved in an intense card game. Allen walks over to the table. "Well, it did not take you guys long to get a game going; is there any room for us?"

"Not in this game, but there's one getting started over there," Doc replies without looking up from his hand.

Allen looks over at the other table and decides against it. "I think I'll just grab a plate of food, then head over to the hotel and get some sleep."

"All right Allen," Doc acknowledges, still not looking up from his hand. "I am going to play a few more hands and I'll be heading in that direction as well."

Doc finishes playing the hand and decides to call it a night. When he walks over to the hotel, he finds Allen at the front desk flirting with the girl there.

Doc clears his throat to get Allen's attention. "Allen, I thought you were coming over here to get a room and go to bed."

"I am working on it," he replies.

Doc walks up to the desk, glances at Allen and says, "Well, if you will excuse me." He looks at the girl and tips his brim before continuing. "I will need a room for the night, ma'am."

The little tiny dark haired girl smiles. "Coming right up, Doc. Say, that was some real fine shooting yesterday over in White Cloud. I enjoyed watching you. You're a fine marksman."

Doc smiles at the young ladies compliment. "Why thank you kindly, ma'am. I sure had a lot of fun doing it."

The girl reaches back and takes a key from its hook. She hands the key to Doc and looks right into his eyes. Her eyes are almost as dark as coal. "Here's your key. It's room three. Room three has a very large comfortable bed. My name is Cassie, so if you need anything just give me a holler." Doc takes the key and walks upstairs to his room.

"Well, Cassie, I am going to need a room too," Allen points out.

"Oh, of course; here you go. You are in room five. You be sure to get a good night's sleep, Marshal."

"Well, what if I need something? Do I just come back down to the desk?" Allen asks.

Cassie looks at the stairs, then back at Allen. "No, I will be in Doc's room; just knock on his door."

Allen takes his key from Cassie and says, "Thank you, Miss Cassie."

As Allen is walking up to his room, he wonders why his luck is changing for the worse. When he reaches the top of the stairs and takes a few steps, Cassie comes running by Allen, opens Doc's door, and runs inside.

Loudly and passionately she says, "Doc, it's been too long; I hope you're rested up, because this may take all night." She then jumps into his arms and buries her face in his neck. With her free hand she reaches for the door and closes it.

"Was that okay?" Cassie whispers into Doc's ear.

Doc whispers back, "That should work fine; I am sure we got him wondering now."

Doc sets her down on the bed. She straightens her dress before saying, "This is so mean, to tease him, but I like it."

"My partner deserves a little lesson in humility every now and again." Doc sits down in the chair and looks out the window overlooking Main Street. "I appreciate you're playing along on this little joke, Cassie."

The little trickster winks at Doc. "I was happy to play along. I will wait another half hour, then sneak back downstairs to my own room."

"No. Why don't you just actually stay with me tonight?"

Her eyes get bigger and appear darker when she opens them wide. "Well, Doc, is that an invitation?"

"Well, not exactly; you see, I was thinking that if Allen sees you walk out of here in the morning it will be more believable."

"Yes, I can see where you are going with this." She winks at Doc. "I will stay on my side if you stay on yours."

Doc stands up, removes his hat, and bows to her in the 'Old English' style, "Madam, you have a deal. Sleep well. I'll see you in the morning."

The next morning, the sun is already up in the morning sky when there is a knock on Doc's door. "It's Allen; are you awake in there?"

Cassie is sitting at the table with Doc, as they share morning coffee. "Yeah, what do you want?" she answers.

"I was just coming to get Doc up. We need to go to the Sheriff's office and talk to him."

"I will wake him up and send him over." She looks at Doc and winks."

"Thanks," Allen answers.

"Wake up, Doc. Allen needs you at the Sheriff's office," Cassie says, making her voice sound as though she is trying to wake Doc.

Doc sits there, shaking his head and smiling at how well his coffee companion can play the 'humility game.' He finally adds to the conversation. "I heard him; I am getting up. That man sure knows how to mess up a good thing."

Cassie once again winks. "Yeah, I know. Anyway you had better get going. I want to hear what he has to say about last night."

Doc stands up and reaches for his gear. "Thanks for this, Cassie. I'll stop by before we leave and fill you in on his 'attitude.'" He kisses Cassie on top of the head, as he would his sister.

Cassie looks up at him and points her finger. "You had better go. You may want to leave something here, so he believes your reasons for stopping back."

Doc hands her a bag, tips his brim, and leaves. He walks to the Sheriff's office. When he opens the door, he finds Allen, Horace, and the Sheriff waiting for him.

"Nice of you to join us," Allen is the first to say.

"Yeah, yeah, I am here; now, what's the plan?"

The Sheriff looks at the three men in bewilderment and then says, "Okay, here's what I think the three of you need to do. I think it will be in our best interest to ride out to the farm with all of your boys and my deputies and bring Billy back here. Once he's here in the jail, I can protect him here overnight. Then, you can get an early start tomorrow morning, before sunrise. That would be best, but that is not my call any longer. That would be yours, Marshal."

Allen thinks about the plan for a few minutes before answering, "That sounds like a good plan to me; what are we waiting for? Let's get moving."

When the men leave the Sheriff's office, the stage is pulling into town and the driver is yelling, "Sheriff! Help! Reb's been shot! The stage was robbed!"

The men run over to the stage to see the driver, Slim, with Reb, his lookout, slumped over at Slim's feet.

"Easy, Slim. Let us get Reb down. What was taken?" he asks as Horace and Allen help get Reb off the stage and Doc starts tending to his gunshot wounds.

"They got Miss Cora Bryan and the money that was being transferred to Cheyenne to the B&R railroad company."

The sheriff's face turns deep maroon. "What are they thinking, sending the territorial Governor's daughter along with railroad money on the same stage? You know very well we have been having trouble with stagecoach robberies lately. I would have expected you to know better than to let that happen."

Slim climbs off the stage and removes his hat. "Sheriff, I couldn't agree with you more, but it was Miss Cora. She would not listen to me; I tried to warn her that there has been a lot of danger, and she would be a lone passenger with that kind of money on board the stage. She just would not listen to me, Sheriff. She insisted she had to be in Denver right away, and the next stage to Denver was not due through for another four days. That was not acceptable to her."

"Why did she need to go to Denver in such a rush?" The Sheriff asks, hotter than a bull.

"Well, she said her father, the Governor, is in Denver on business. She was going out there to spend a few days with him. He was going to take her about town, shopping, or at least that's what she said."

The Sheriff looks at Horace and says, "Go to the telegraph office; wire Denver and let the Marshal's office know what has happened. Have him inform the Governor as well." He turns and faces Allen. "Marshal, I need you and Doc to help me get the Governor's daughter back, safe and sound."

Allen looks the fellow lawman in the eye and replies, "No problem. Getting Cora back is much more important than Billy, at this point. Besides, he is in hiding, and safe."

The Sheriff looks back at the stage driver. "Slim, can you take us to the place where you were robbed?"

Slim throws his hat back on his head and quickly replies, "Yes. Just let me run over to the stage office and grab a saddled horse, and I will ride out and show you. It's not that far, just a couple of miles from here."

Horace runs back from the telegraph office. Out of breath, he says to the Sheriff, "Sheriff, your wire was sent."

Allen looks at Horace and says, "Horace, you and the deputies go out and help your relatives keep Billy safe until we get back."

Horace nods and asks, "How long do you think you'll be?"

"It might take a couple of days, maybe more. When we get back, I will have the Sheriff bring us out to the farm to meet up with you for the return trip."

Slim returns on his horse and leads the Sheriff, Allen, Doc, Wes, and Steve to where the stage was robbed. "The crazy thing, Sheriff, was it seemed almost as if they just came out of nowhere. I didn't want to say anything in town, but they seemed more concerned about getting Miss Cora, than in the money and gold in the strong box."

"What do you mean?" Allen asks.

"It's like I said, Marshal; they seemed like they only wanted her," Slim replies. You see, they grabbed Miss Cora and started to ride off. That is when one of them said, 'We need to grab the strong box.' It looks to me that their main concern was Miss Cora."

"I tell ya, if they harm one hair on her head, I will kill them all," Allen says, angry at the thought of Cora's disappearance.

Doc leans over toward Allen and whispers, "Allen, tell me you did not take Cora to bed."

"Well Doc, she was at one of your parties, and you do have all of those rooms. We really hit it off that night."

Doc shakes his head at the thought of what kind of scandal it could have created. "I should have known this sort of thing could have happened. My friend, if you were a woman, you would be working for yourself in town or at the Saloon."

Allen grins and then shrugs. "It's a tough job but somebody has to do it and that somebody might as well be me."

Slim stops his horse and announces, "Here it is, this is where we were robbed."

Doc looks around at the dirt. "They didn't try to cover their tracks very well; it's almost as if they want to be followed."

Allen examines the tracks, looking in the direction the robbers went before commenting, "It would not surprise me if Sutton set this up as a diversion, knowing that Doc and I would have to go after Cora, knowing that would leave Billy out there for his men to reach while we are off after them."

The Sheriff pushes back his brim and says, "You could be right, Marshal. But Billy and Horace's family will not make it easy. Sutton's men will need an army to get past the lines." The sheriff pauses for a minute then continues, "Slim, you ride out to Billy's uncle's place and warn them that there may be trouble coming their way."

"You got it, Sheriff. I am on my way," Slim comments, then turns his horse around, and off he goes.

"Let's follow these tracks and see where they lead us," says Allen.

They follow the tracks through the valley, keeping a watchful eye on the bluffs in the distance for any possible sign of trouble.

Allen points off in one direction. "Steve, you go over to the bluffs to the east and I will ride to the ones on the west. We can cover the Sheriff and Wes better from up there."

"Okay, I will get there as fast as I can," Steve acknowledges. "Doc, you guys, be careful."

Doc nods at him in acknowledgment, then says, "If you see the outlaws who took Cora, don't miss."

"Yes sir. I may not be as good of a shot as you, Doc, but I can hold my own." Steve then gives his horse a kick, and off he goes toward the east bluffs.

They pass through the bluffs without incident. The Marshal and Steve rejoin the other three, and they continue. As the men ride, following the outlaw's tracks, it begins to get dark so they decide to make camp for the evening.

Doc sits up from the fire and announces, "I will take first watch. After three hours or so, I will come and get you, Steve, and then we will let Allen finish the last watch. For now, you fellas get some rest and I will come and wake you in a few hours."

"You watch your back, Doc," Steve says as he reaches for his blanket. "There's no telling where they could be holing up."

"Don't you worry about me; you just get some sleep."

Doc pours himself a cup of coffee and sits on a rock formation just out of the fire's light. Allen wakes to see that Doc is still on watch. He didn't wake Steve, so he put on some more coffee for himself and Doc. He pours Doc a fresh cup and takes it to him.

"See anything on your watch?" Allen asks.

Doc takes the steaming cup, and shakes his head. "Naw, it has been pretty quiet. I figured I would put some coffee on here soon, then get you boys up and get ready to pull out. Thanks for the cup."

"I will get everyone up while you finish your coffee."

As the Sheriff and Steve gather around the fire to fill up their cups, Doc climbs on to his horse. "I am going to ride ahead a little and see if I can spot them."

A few minutes later, the rest of them mount up. They proceed in the same direction they saw Doc head. Steve sees Doc's horse tied at the bottom of the bluff. They ride up to find Doc and as they dismount, they see Doc crawling down off the bluff.

Doc turns to Allen and says, "We have to move fast, or Cora is in far more grave trouble than we suspected."

Allen grabs Doc's upper coat sleeve. "What do you mean grave trouble?"

"We don't have time for questions," Doc shoots back. "Sheriff, you, and I will ride around the bluff and I want Steve, Wes, and the Marshal up on the bluff. Don't make a move until I tell you, got it?"

"Yep, we got it," Steve acknowledges as he dismounts his horse.

Allen, Steve, and Wes make their way up the bluff, while Doc and the Sheriff ride around it; when they arrive on the other side of the bluff they can see four men holding Cora down. A fifth man is attempting to pull down the front of his pants. She is gagged, so she can't cry out.

Just as the man is about to get on his knees, Doc pulls the hammers back on his colts and says, "Not a very wise idea, my friend." The men turn and see Doc and the Sheriff with their guns drawn. "Now, you stand up and pull your pants up, and you four let her go." Because of their positions, none of the men are able to draw a gun in defense. They have no option but to release her. "Cora, you come over here." Doc nods at her, then to the Sheriff. "Sheriff, if anyone goes for his guns, we open up on him. Got it?" The Sheriff grunts a response. Cora makes her way over to Doc's horse. He reaches down and pulls her up onto his horse. "Alright now, if anyone has any stupid ideas to try and shoot at this point, my friends on the bluff will cut you in half with their firepower." At that time, you can hear the Marshal and the other men cock the actions on their rifles. Doc starts pointing at the men with a pistol, while holding it steady on the man whose pants are still not fastened. "Now, all of you throw your guns into a pile in the middle over here. And you might live to see another day."

One of the men looks at Doc and scowls. "You are dead and the whore is too." He reaches for his gun. Doc, with gun in hand is much faster. Doc places a bullet between the man's eyes. This jump-starts a flurry of gunfire. Bullets are flying everywhere and outlaws drop like flies.

When the fifth and final one of them drops, the Marshal hollers out from his spot, "Is everyone alright?"

Steve is the first to reply, "I caught one in the shoulder; Doc needs to look at it. But I think I will survive."

Allen crawls out and over to Steve. "Yeah, you need to stay down and have Doc look at it." The three men crawl off the bluff and join Doc and the sheriff below. Allen reaches to help Cora down off Doc's horse.

"Cora, are you alright?" he asks.

Cora hugs Allen, and then brushes the dust from her fancy traveling clothes. "I'm just fine, Allen. Our friend, Doc here, took very good care of me."

"Marshal, what do you want to do with these men?" the Sheriff asks, referring to the dead bodies on the ground.

"Hell, I say let the buzzards take care of them," Doc suggests. "We need to get to Billy before the rest of Sutton's men do."

Allen agrees with Doc, so everyone saddles up and rides to the family ranch where Billy is hidden.

"We will need to go by Horace's place first," the Sheriff explains. "Billy is hiding close to his uncle's ranch. That's just a few miles north of town. If we cut straight across the valley, it will save us some time."

As they draw close to the ranch where Billy is hiding, they can hear gunfire.

"C'mon boys, let's pick up the pace!" Allen shouts as he kicks his horse. "We need to get over there in a hurry. Horace and the boys need our help!"

"There are twenty-five relatives out there, not including the deputies we sent out there. I think they have the situation well in hand," the Sheriff is quick to point out.

They slow down a bit to keep the horses off a dead run, but continue to make a quick pass across the valley's floor. As they arrive at the ranch, there are ten men lying dead and five tied to a tree.

Allen reaches over and pats the Sheriff on the back, "It looks like you were right, Sheriff." he laughs. "I figured they would be able to take care of themselves." The Marshal gets off his horse and walks up toward the house. "Now, where is Billy? We don't have much time, and Doc and I need to have a little talk with him as soon as possible."

From a shed across the yard a voice yells out, "I am over here." Billy steps out of the shadows. He crosses the yard to the Marshal. "We can go inside the house and talk, Marshal."

The three of them walk inside the house, close the door, and sit around the kitchen table. Billy looks directly into Allen's eyes. "What do you want to talk about, Marshal?"

Allen takes his hat off and runs his hand through his hair. "Alright Billy, we know that you say you bought the cattle. Then you were arrested; they couldn't find the papers or your bill-of-sale, so they arrested you for rustling. You say that you didn't rustle the cattle; fill us in on the whole story. We want to hear your side of the story."

Billy nods, and looks down at the floor for a minute to collect his thoughts. "My Pa sent me and two of his best men to go and purchase some cattle. Pa was in touch with a cattleman from Kansas. They had been exchanging letters to work out a fair price for the cattle and a new seed bull so we could start our own cattle breeding operation. When they reached a price, my Pa went to the bank and drew out some of his savings to pay the cattleman."

Doc realizes another coincidence, a visit to the bank before something bad occurs. "Did your Pa happen to speak with Mr. Sutton that day at the bank?"

Billy thinks for a moment, then answers, "Yes he did. Pa said that Mr. Sutton was very interested in where we were buying our cattle. He said if Pa was happy with the cattle, he might have to talk to the cattleman himself. Pa gave him the address so Mr. Sutton could get in touch with the cattleman."

Allen nods in agreement and then looks at Doc. "Things are starting to become a lot clearer now."

Billy continues, "The morning we were leaving for Kansas to go and pick up the cattle, my Pa gave me the money to pay for them. I put it in my shirt pocket for safekeeping and then the boys and I rode south. It was a four-day ride to get to the cattleman's ranch and when we finally arrived, he had the cattle in a holding pen for us. I thought it was funny that there were only three people at the ranch, but the owner said all the ranch hands were on their way to Kansas City to buy some more cattle. I saw about a thousand head around the property and asked, 'Don't you already have enough?' He said he had to replace the ones he was selling to us and a couple of other ranchers."

"So what did you do after you spoke with the cattleman?" Allen asks, anxious to hear the rest of the story.

"We went into his house where I gave him the money, and he wrote out a bill-of-sale that I put in my jacket pocket." Billy jumps up out of his chair. His excitement spills into his voice. "I know where the bill-of-sale is now! It isn't in my saddlebag like I thought. I had forgotten that I had put it in my coat. I didn't have my coat when they came after me for rustling, because, my cousin Tommy borrowed my jacket on the way back. When we got close to home, he split off to head toward home. And the rest of us headed to our place."

"Is Tommy here?" Allen asks.

"Yes, he is outside with the rest of my relatives, but don't you want to hear how we were attacked earlier?"

"Finish the story, then we will talk to Tommy," Allen replies.

Billy looks out the window to gather his thoughts, the terror of that night's events still raw in his memory. He clears his throat and begins, "We were about a couple of days ride from reaching home. We set up camp for the night in a little canyon. There was a storm coming in from the southwest, so the cattle were acting nervous. We doubled the nightriders, and kept rotating turns keeping watch, trying to keep the herd as calm as possible for the evening. When morning came, we were all exhausted from the long night. It was almost sun up when we broke camp. We had started out of the canyon, pushing the herd around toward the north face of it, when we saw a group of men in long riding coats appear over the hill in front of us. Pa's Ramrod and three others rode out to see what the men wanted. While they were talking, the men in the long coats shot all four of them, and then yelled at us to drop our guns. We all threw our guns down and put our hands in the air. They accused us of cattle rustling and said we were going to Avoca for trial. I told them that I had bought these cattle in Kansas and I had a bill-of-sale. When I went to get the papers for proof, I didn't have them. I searched everything, but I could not find the papers. The man doing all of the talking said he was a Sheriff, and a cattleman from around Abilene had wired him that a group of men had stolen some of his cattle and rode off to the north.

They found us with cattle wearing his brand and no proof that we bought them. That must mean that we stole them. I denied it, but they arrested me and hauled me in anyway."

"So Billy, what you're telling me is the man you bought the cattle from gave you a bill-of-sale. Then after selling you the cattle, he accuses you of stealing them?" Allen is quick to ask.

"Yes sir, Marshal, that's exactly how it happened."

Allen looks at one of the deputies at the door. "Go out with Billy and bring his cousin Tommy in and let's take a look at that bill-of-sale."

The deputy and Billy walk out of the house to find his cousin; meanwhile Doc and Allen sit at the table to discuss Billy's story.

"What do you think, Doc?" Allen asks. "Do you think the kid is telling the truth?"

"I know this cattleman he's talking about. He has done deals with Sutton before. I think they have some sort of friendship or business relationship. I went with Sutton once, down to this man's ranch, a couple of years ago. Sutton went to pick up two bulls because the man owed him some money on a loan. The cattleman gave him the two bulls for payment and Sutton said that will do for now but he was far from being paid in full."

"Doc, you don't suppose Sutton called in his loan and this is how the cattleman paid up on his remaining debt?"

"Maybe, but if Billy has the papers, how will they be able to explain the bill-of-sale versus the cattle being stolen?"

"That's a good question. I don't know; when we take a look at the paper maybe that will answer the question."

At that moment, Billy walks in with a tall, thin young man. Billy introduces the young man. "This is my cousin, Tommy; he has the bill-of-sale that was in my coat, which he has."

Tommy walks over to Allen and hands it over. "Here you go, Marshal. I am sorry that I got Billy into so much trouble. I didn't know it was in the pocket until just now when Billy told me."

"It's not your fault, son; thanks. We have it now and this will help prove your Cousin Billy's innocence."

Billy sits down across from the Marshal. "I hope so, 'cuz I did not do what they said I did; and now they have gone and killed every person who could tell the truth, 'cept Tommy and me."

Doc reaches over for the document in Allen's hand. "Let me take a look at that bill-of-sale, Marshal."

Allen hands over the bill-of-sale to Doc. "This is Hank's signature. I remember seeing it when he signed a contract with Sutton, when I went down there with him."

Allen looks at the document, and then back at Doc. "How can you be so sure, Doc?"

"It's the way he makes his H. It has a curly-que tail on the bottom. I remember thinking how strange it looked the first time I saw it. That it looked elaborate, uncommon for a man. And that seemed odd to me."

Allen shakes his head. "It will be hard to prove it's his signature in a court of law, even if it is his signature."

"Yeah, and it'll be very hard to prove that Billy stole those cattle, with this bill-of-sale," Doc points out to Allen,

"That's why Sutton is sending so many men after Billy," Allen says as he stands up. "He knows if we bring Billy back, with this document, his goose is cooked and the truth will come out!"

"I'll hold on to this for you, Billy," Doc says as he takes the bill-of-sale from Billy. "If I have it, I can make sure it makes it back to Lincoln in one piece."

Billy nods at Doc and hands him the bill-of-sale, all the while carrying some doubt of the man. After all, Doc is holding the piece of paper that means life and death for him. "Please don't lose it, Doc. I don't want to end up with a hemp necktie after I get to Lincoln."

"That will not happen as long as I am still alive," Doc assures Billy.

Allen steps toward the door and then looks back into the room. "Billy, get your things together. Be ready to leave at first light. Doc and I will come and get you in the morning."

"You don't want me to come to town with you?" Billy asks.

"I think you will be safer here, where all of your relatives are here to protect you," Allen says. "I'll leave my deputies here as well."

"Okay," Billy nods in agreement. "I'll see you first thing in the morning."

Doc, Allen, the Governor's daughter, Cora, and the Sheriff climb onto their horses to head back to Destiny. They leave the Deputies at the ranch to stand watch over Billy, Tommy, and the others until morning.

Doc looks over at the Marshal. "We need to be prepared for the possibility of another ambush when we get to town."

"If you see anything, or hear anything, we need to get Cora to safety." Allen then looks at the Sheriff. "Sheriff, if we encounter trouble, I want you to take Cora to the jail and wait for us there."

The Sheriff nods and replies, “Okay, Marshal; I will keep her out of harm’s way.”

“Sutton could use Miss Cora as a bargaining chip if he gets his hands on her,” Doc points out.

“Do you really think he would stoop so low as to kidnap the Governor’s daughter?” the Sheriff asks.

“Hey guys, I am right here,” Cora says. “I don’t mind sayin’ you’re kind’a scarin’ me.”

“Sorry Cora, we are just concerned for your safety and we don’t want anything to happen to you,” Allen points out.

“I have had dinner with Mr. Sutton and my father many times,” Cora goes on. “I even worked in his bank for a couple of years as a teller. I don’t think he would do anything to me. He has always been caring and generous to me.”

“That is what I used to think of the man,” Doc shoots back. “That was before I found out he was the one responsible for the torturing and killing of my family.”

Cora puts a hand to her mouth and gasps. “Oh my God, Doc. I am so sorry. I had no idea he was behind that. I can’t believe what I’m hearing. I know Mr. Sutton was a friend of yours as well.”

“The word ‘was’ is the right way to explain my relationship with Sutton,” Doc comments. “When we get back I plan to pay him a visit. Sutton and I have some unfinished business to discuss.”

“I don’t think he’s going to enjoy that visit,” the Sheriff says.

****

It is late morning when they ride into town. The streets are empty. There isn't a person anywhere. Allen looks over his shoulder at the Sheriff and then says, "I think you better get Cora to the jail and protect her there. We're going to see what Sutton has in store for us." Allen looks at Doc, Doc nods back; and off they go, into the heart of town, in search of their fate.

As Allen and Doc ride farther into the town, a voice from inside the saloon breaks the town's silence, "Marshal! Turn Billy over to us or we are going to kill you! Then we will burn down this town!"

"That's big talk from someone who is afraid to come out and face me," Doc yells back.

A man emerges from the saloon and says, "I am not afraid of you. I just wanted to get your attention before I came out."

"I know you; you're Sutton's Brother, Shawn. What are you doing here?" Doc asks.

"Well, it's a family thing. My brother is in trouble and I am here to get him out of it." The man steps out to the edge of the boardwalk as he speaks.

Doc glares into the man's eyes, determining what his next move might be. "You've come a long way to die, my friend."

Shawn throws his hands up in the air to direct Doc and the others to look about. "You, Doc, are in no position to threaten me. Just look around; I have men on the roofs of every building on Main Street. So, you better ride on out of here and bring me Billy; or the town is going to burn, and your friend, Cora, is going to be our party favor for the night."

At the opposite end of Main Street, two armed men are leading the Sheriff and Cora out of the jail. Shawn points behind them to show his threats are not without truth. "I told you; you are in no position to make threats."

Doc pushes back the brim of his dark wide brimmed hat and says, "You don't seem to understand; you only have twelve men here. I have just enough bullets to kill them all."

Shawn laughs. "Doc, I believe your count is off by one. You seem to have neglected to count me. That makes thirteen. So, I'd say you are a bullet short, sir."

Doc scoffs. "Well, you see, the Marshal is going to take care of you. I will take care of the rest. Now, why don't you and your boys let the Sheriff and Cora go? Give yourselves up, and I won't have to clean my guns tonight."

The man puts a hand on his belt close to his pistol. "You actually think you can kill us all before any of us kill you, the Marshal, the Sheriff, and the girl?"

Doc gives the man a look of confidence and nods a yes. "I know I will get all of you, before you ever clear your guns." Doc looks around to make sure of the positions of the men in support of Sutton's cause before continuing. "If you have a wish to die today, it's time to make your play."

The man reaches for his gun. Allen fires the rifle that he had across his lap and Doc pulls his pistols and begins to fire. He first hits the two holding the Sheriff and Cora, and then moves to the men on the rooftops. After eight of them go down, the rest of the outlaw-gang throw their guns down and surrender to the Marshal.

"Take these men to the jail and then meet us at the hotel for some supper," Allen says to the Sheriff. "We will need a new plan."

Shawn Sutton is lying on the boardwalk, right where he had been standing, outside the doorway of the saloon. His gun lay just out of his reach. Allen calls out to the man, "Sutton, don't you even think about going for that gun."

"No, do; go for it. I still have one bullet left," Doc points out.

"You shot me in the shoulder and I am going to bleed to death if you don't get me to a doctor," Shawn pleads.

"I think we will let ol' Doc Gray take a look at you," Allen shoots back. "Now get your ass up and move it into the saloon."

As the men walk up to the saloon doorway, Doc looks at the younger Sutton and says, "Shawn, would you like to walk in first?"

"No, not really," he replies, shaking his head.

Doc grabs Shawn by the shoulder and says, "I didn't think so. Why don't you make sure the men you have inside throw their guns on the floor or the first shot is going to be in the back of your head."

"In the saloon," Shawn shouts, "throw your guns on the floor, now!" They hear the sounds of metal guns hitting the wood floor.

"Now, Shawn, you first and if anyone gets stupid, you die first," Doc says as they make their way into the saloon.

Inside there are six men standing up against the bar with their guns still in their holsters and their knives at their feet.

Doc looks over at them and says, "You men don't listen very well, now do you?"

One of the men in the middle takes a step forward, looks Doc straight in the eye and says, "I don't know. There are six of us and only two of you."

"Allen, you take Shawn and go over there out of the way. I will handle this."

The men who are leaning against the bar, each take a step forward, brushing their coats out of the way, revealing the hardware in their holsters.

Gus, the leader of the gang looks at Doc and says, "You are going to die an ugly death, Mister."

Doc smirks at the surly man and replies, "We all have to die some day, but I don't think today is my day."

"There are six of us; how do you expect to win?" he answers back as he looks across the line of his associates.

Doc holds his hand up with the palm facing the ceiling. He then swipes the air in front of him, as if he's swatting away an insect. "You are really starting to bore me. If all you want to do is flap your gums, we can simply take a walk down to the jail and you can talk to me from your cell. At least you'll still be alive."

Gus lets out a laugh. "Alright, I am just going to have to kill you to shut your smart mouth up; but before I do, I need to know your name so I can engrave it on my gun."

"You're not going to win this little battle so my name is irrelevant. Just say when." Doc reaches down and wraps his fingers around the pearl handle of his pistols.

As the men go for their pistols, Doc has already cleared his holsters and fire is shooting out of both barrels and all six men are slumping down to the ground; all except Gus. Doc had shot the gun out of his hand.

"Who the hell are you?" Gus yells out.

With a wry grin, John Gray answers, "Most people call me Doc."

Gus looks at Doc with raised eyebrows, and surprise. "You are Doc Gray? Oh hell. If I had known that, we would have taken your first option of jail; but why did you spare me?"

Doc puts one of his pistols in the holster but keeps the other pointed at Gus. "I need you. I want you to ride into Lincoln and tell Mr. Sutton we have his brother, and that any other attempts to kill Billy will end in his brother Shawn buying a bullet in his head. You see, we're going to wire him the message, but I think if you ride hard and tell him in person it might save Shawn."

"You might as well shoot me now!" Shawn shouts. "My brother Richard is in too deep and he will stop at nothing to silence Billy. Richard has already thrown Billy's family off their farm and put them in the Avoca jail. He's just waiting for the judge now."

Doc walks Gus out the door while Allen interrogates Shawn. "So Shawn, what does your brother have planned for us on our way back to Lincoln?" "All I know is that if Billy makes it back, Richard will be going to prison for a long time and he will do everything in his power to prevent that from happening."

"What happened to him; he used to be a good guy?" Allen asks.

Shawn shakes his head and looks down at the floor as he answers. "What happens to most men in his position? They get greedy and all he can think about is getting more money, more land, more, more, more!"

"That's too bad. He did help get the town of Avoca on the map when he first came to town," Allen comments.

"It has only been the last few years when he seemed to get worse, and it seems that this last year he has really gone over the edge." Shawn continues to hold his head down, looking at the floor as if he were ashamed.

"Why are you helping him?" Allen asks.

"One word; blackmail'. He's holding something over my head; if I don't do as he asks he will spill the beans, so to speak."

Allen looks about the room; he wants to be certain that this conversation is just between the two of them. Then, with every ounce of his will, he asks the question that has haunted not only him, but his best friend. "I have to ask, did you have anything to do with the killings out at Doc's house?"

"How did you hear about that? What would make you think I could have had anything to do with that?" Shawn's face goes pale.

"Someone overheard a conversation between your brother and one of the men he had go out and murder Doc's family." Allen removes his hat and starts rolling the brim in his hands.

"No, I had nothing to do with that. I was in Kansas City running an errand for Richard, thank God." Again, Shawn hangs his head in shame.

"That might just keep you alive. However, I said might. Remember that."

****

Doc and Gus enter the telegraph office and send a message to Richard Sutton to back off and leave them alone or he would be attending his brother's funeral. He is also to be waiting, as Gus would be delivering a message in person.

"Now Gus, I suggest you ride like the wind because if we get attacked again you'd be better off to find a new residence in Mexico."

"I will ride as fast as I can." Gus steps out of the office, and mounts his horse. Without looking back, he heads in the direction of Avoca, with the message that will not only save his life, but the message to save Shawn Sutton's life.

Doc walks back to the saloon and sees Allen and Shawn eating supper. "Allen, why is Shawn still here and not in jail?"

"Well, he has been giving me quite an ear full about his brother. It seems he does not really care for his brother anymore." Allen looks at Shawn with a convincing glare. "After Richard ordered the killing of your wife and kids, Shawn told him he was through, that he wasn't doing more. Richard has something he is holding over Shawn's head, forcing Shawn to help, or meet the consequences."

"It seems he was willing to help his brother when we entered town today," Doc points out, not buying this story.

Shawn raises his eyes to meet Doc's and pleads, "I had no choice; some of Richard's most trusted men were here with me. If I would have backed down they would have shot me."

"That may be true, yet if you make a wrong move I will put an end to your suffering," Doc points out. "Keep that in the front of your head.

Now, I am going to see if I can find a game of cards to get into." Doc turns and walks away.

Allen takes Shawn down to the jail and when he walks in, he sees the governor standing there holding his daughter.

"Marshal, I am glad to see you. Cora said it was because of you and Doc Gray that she is still alive." The Governor reaches out his hand to shake Allen's hand.

"I am just glad we could help," Allen says as he removes his hat and shakes the Governor's hand.

"I am shocked to hear that Richard Sutton is behind all of this," the Governor comments.

"Yes sir. It is quite the tale. I think he thought his plan would work and nobody would be the wiser. He didn't intend for Billy to live or the bill-of-sale to wind up in our hands."

With great interest, the man looks at the Marshal. "You have the bill- of-sale? May I see it?"

"No, I don't. Doc has it. He is unwinding with a game of cards. I have seen it and Doc says it is legitimate." Allen places his hat back on his head and smiles at Cora.

"I just can't believe that he was behind the kidnapping of my daughter."

Shawn, from his cell offers up, "Yes, it is the truth, Governor. I heard him give the order before I left to come out here. He said that the Marshal and Doc would hear of her kidnapping, and would have to go after your daughter. That would leave Billy without protection, and allow his men to kill him."

"He will pay dearly for this," the governor promises.

"With all due respect, sir, I think you are going to have to stand in line to get to Richard," Allen points out.

He looks at Allen confused. "I am not sure I am following you. What do you mean?"

Allen looks down for a moment, and then looks the man in the eye. A chill runs down the back of his neck. "Well sir, Doc just found out that Sutton was the true mastermind behind the massacre of his family."

The Governor is shocked. He looks down into the face of his daughter, telling her, "Darling, I think we'll take the train back to Denver and take you shopping and stay out of Doc's way. I think that will be the only place truly safe from the impending battle, and fallout."

"I was wondering how you got here so fast," Allen remarks.

"I took the train from Denver when I received the wire of what had happened to my daughter. The train passes just five miles north of here. I brought some horses with me and rode the rest of the way."

"Governor, are you really okay with Doc taking care of Richard in his own way?" Allen asks, wanting to make sure he understands the Governor correctly.

"The man is responsible for the killings of John's wife and young sons. Then he had my daughter kidnapped by men who almost raped her. I am thankful you men were able to save her, saving her virtue from such swarthy individuals. I would have to say, yes. I think it fitting that Doc would want to 'correct' things the way he deems appropriate." The Governor shakes Allen's and the Sheriff's hands, and escorts his daughter out the door.

Allen leaves the Sheriff's office and heads over to the saloon to make sure Doc is staying out of trouble. When he walks in the door, he sees Doc at a table, with three women, playing poker.

Allen walks over to the table and asks, "Hey Doc, got room for one more?"

Doc looks up from his hand and looks at the gals around the table. "I think we can make room, can't we, ladies?" The ladies look up at Allen and smile.

"What are we playing?" Allen asks as he pulls up a chair and sits down at the table.

"The ladies wanted to play five card stud," Doc answers.

"Sounds good to me," Allen says, and then smiles at the women.

After a few hands, Doc looks over his cards and says, "After this hand I think I am going to call it a night."

"What? You? Turning in before the sun comes up?" Allen asks, surprised at the comment made by his friend.

Doc looks over his cards before placing his final bid and says, "I'm a bit tired. I assume we're leaving bright and early."

Allen throws in a bid and nods. "Yes, I want to head out about five in the morning."

Doc calls the bid, and lays down a full house, aces over queens. He scoops up his winnings and smiles. "It has been a pleasure, ladies. I will look you up the next time I am in town."

Doc and Allen excuse themselves, and they head over to the hotel to get some rest.

When they enter the hotel, a young man is manning the desk. "Good evening, gentlemen. I have your rooms ready. Here are your keys; have a good night."

Doc takes the keys. "Thank you, have a good night."

As they make it up to their rooms Allen says, "Well, at least I will get a chance for a good night's sleep for a change."

Doc looks at him and grins. "Good night, Allen."

Allen opens his door, reaches for the lamp, and turns up the flame. He notices that someone is already in his bed. The young lady sits up and smiles. "Hello Marshal. I have been waiting quite a while. It's about time you got here."

12

Doc is up at five to prepare for the day ahead. He walks down the hall to wake Allen, when he notices a figure at the end of the hall.

"Doc Gray, is that you?"

Doc stops in his tracks and looks directly at the shadow. "Yes, it is. Long time no see. What brings you to Destiny?"

"I heard you might need a little help taking a prisoner back to Lincoln," says the shadowy figure.

Doc smiles, and then says, "There's no money in it."

"I don't care about the money. I was in Kansas. That business took me to Lincoln. That's when I heard about you and Allen trying to get this cattle rustler, Billy, back to Lincoln for trial."

Doc starts to walk toward the shadow. He is smaller than Doc, which makes Doc seem larger and more mysterious. He stands almost toe to toe with the man, looking down into his cold eyes.

"Yeah, he's a real hard case, this one. Did you hear who is really behind this?"

"Yeah, I did hear rumor that Sutton is behind it. I hear from the Sheriff down the street that he also was involved with the killings at your place. That was when I decided I had to help you get this kid back."

Doc reaches out, offering a handshake to the shadow. "Well, we sure can use an extra gun on the return trip, Levi; welcome aboard."

Allen enters the hallway, to see Doc talking with Levi. Surprised by the sight he asks, "What are you doing here, Levi?"

"Well, I was punching cattle down south around the Kansas Territory border, trying to catch the guys who have been changing brands on cattle so they can steal them, and like I was telling Doc, it took me to Lincoln. That's where I overheard a conversation about what the two of you have going. After hearing what was going on, I high-tailed it as fast as I could to get here to help."

"We do appreciate it. We'll need all the help we can find."

The three men make their way across the street to the livery where the Sheriff has their horses saddled and ready. Allen takes the reins of his horse from the Sheriff and says, "Thanks Sheriff, we appreciate all of your help in this matter."

The Sheriff tips the brim of his hat and says, "You gentlemen have always been good to come and help me when I need a hand. So, I figure I am just returning the favor."

Allen shakes the Sheriff's hand and mounts his horse. "We're gonna go out and pick up Billy and the rest of our men. Then be off toward Lincoln."

"Billy and your deputies are waiting for you at the jail," the sheriff informs Allen. "They arrived about twenty minutes ago. They thought if they hit the trail under darkness, they would be safer. They have been waiting for you in my office. I came down here to get your horses ready so you can get on your way before any of Sutton's men arrive."

Allen, Doc, and Levi ride to the jail. Steve, Billy and the rest of the deputies emerge from the jail when they arrive.

"Good morning, Steve. Are you guys ready to make some distance?" Allen asks.

Steve nods as he and the others mount up. "Yup. We're ready to get Billy to Lincoln and have a few days without gun play."

Doc nods and smiles. "This is the first trip in a long time that I have had this much fun!"

"Only you would consider this fun, Doc," Steve comments.

"You two have plenty of time for this debate," Allen points out." Gentlemen, let's get moving so we can make White Cloud by nightfall."

While they are riding out of town, Allen looks over at Doc and says, "I'll be glad to get back home and put all this behind me."

"Me, I am going to miss all the action," Doc comments and smiles. "But truthfully, how are you going to limit yourself to just one woman, Marshal?"

A little glance of resentment from the comment passes over Allen's face. "I think I will manage fine, Doc. How are you going to live without the constant gunfights?"

"There will always be outlaws to chase," Doc points out to Allen. "We're just finishing one job. I am sure there will be another one when we get back to Lincoln."

"That's wishful thinking on your part, Doc," Allen remarks.

Steve rides up beside them and points ahead. "Look on that bluff up ahead, Marshal. Do you see that little flash? That looks like a reflection off glass to me."

Allen looks and sees the flash Steve is referring to. "Doc, you and Levi circle around back and see if you can come from behind. We'll walk our horses for a little while to give you time to get around them."

"Okay, when the shooting starts you better come a running," Levi says to Allen.

"We'll be ready when we hear the first shot," Allen assures him.

Once Doc and Levi are behind cover, they make a break for it, riding around the bluff to get the men up on the bluff caught in a crossfire.

"So Doc, I hear you are making a name for yourself on this trip," Levi comments.

"I am just doing my job. But it has kept me busy on this trip," Doc answers.

"Who do you think is up there, Doc?" Levi asks as he studies the bluff which they are riding around.

Doc looks up at the tall rock. "I would guess it is more of Sutton's men. It could be someone hunting. I guess we'll find out when we get there."

The men find a spot where there is easy access to the top of the bluffs. Levi dismounts his horse and whispers, "Let's tie our horses to this bush and continue on foot."

Doc nods, and then whispers as he points to another spot further over. "Levi, you go over there to the right. I'll come up over here from the left and we will get them in between us."

"Okay Doc. Just keep your head down, and whatever you do, don't shoot me."

Doc smiles at his partner and says, "I'll try to keep you out of my sights; now let's go up, and see who's there."

As they make their way up onto the bluff, Levi finds the person responsible for the flash they saw from the prairie below. Levi sees a young boy lying on his stomach looking through a spyglass. He sneaks up on the boy and says to him in a hushed tone, "Hey there, young man, what are you doing up here?"

Without looking over his shoulder toward Levi, the boy answers, "Get down, Mister. And shhh. I am hunting elk. My family needs the food, and with the noise you're making you're gonna scare him off!"

Levi ducks down and lies beside the boy. He whispers so as not to disturb the potential harvest. "Sorry son, but I didn't see any elk when I came up here."

The boy slowly moves a hand to point in the direction of the elk. He hands Levi the spotting telescope. "It is bedded down under that pine tree down there." Levi and the boy are watching the bedded game, when Doc appears over the top of the bluff. Levi hears him and immediately signals him to remain quiet and motions him to get down.

Doc crawls over to where Levi and his new friend are sitting and asks, "What are we doing here, fellas?"

The young man looks at Doc and replies, "Like I told him, I'm hunting elk for my family."

"Aren't you a little young to be out here on your own?" Doc asks.

"I am fourteen! And I have been doing this on my own for the last three years," the boy snaps back.

"Where is your Pa, son?" Doc asks.

The boy doesn't take his eyes off his prey, but replies, "He was killed three years ago in a stampede. I had to take over for him and be the man of the family."

The bull elk hears the men talking and makes a break for it; the boy takes aim and fires, but misses. "See what you made me do? Now I will have nothing to take back to feed my Ma and my sisters." Doc stands up and aims down the barrel of his Sharps. "Mister, that elk is about six-hundred yards, if not further. You'll never hit it that far away."

Without looking down at the boy, Doc asks, "Do you want to eat or not?"

"Yes sir, but it is too far away now." Doc pulls the trigger and the elk drops to the ground. "Wow mister, you have to be the best shot in the world!"

Doc reaches down and pats the boy on the shoulder. He looks at the boy's smiling face. He can't help but feel the pang of loss at not being able to do this with his own sons. "You can make that same shot with a little practice, son."

The boy looks at Doc with admiration. "Do you think so?"

Doc looks into his young friend's eyes and says, "Yep, all it takes is practice and a little patience. Now what do ya say? Let's go and get that elk, and get it home to your family, okay?"

Allen and the rest of the men ride up the bluff from the other side with guns drawn. They see Doc, Levi and the young boy, Thomas, standing there talking about the shot.

"What do we have here?" Allen says, putting up his long-gun.

"We have a slight detour," Doc answers. "My young friend here needs a little help. We need to help this young man get his elk back to his family."

Looking at the faces of the Doc and the boy, Allen knows this is more important to Doc than any outlaw. "Okay, let's get it quartered, packed on the horses, and to his home so we can get back on the path to White Cloud."

They ride over to the elk and help Thomas prepare the elk for transport to his home. Doc reaches into one of his saddlebags and pulls out a small white cloth pouch. He lights a match and starts the pouch smoldering. He kneels down beside the elk. He recites a tribal prayer of thanks over the animal. When he finishes he looks up at Thomas, saying to him, "Remember Thomas, you always want to give thanks to the animal that gave his life to extend yours."

Levi looks at Allen, then at Doc and asks, "Where the heck did that come from?"

Doc stands up, looks at Levi, and replies, "I spent some time with a Sioux Tribe. I helped a tribe member who was hurt quite seriously. I lived with them for some time. During that time they taught me the ways of the tribe." He looks back at the boy and the fallen game. "I think we owe the game we hunt a little respect. You have a problem with that?"

"No, not at all," Levi replies. "You do what you have to."

"That's what I thought. Now, let's get this elk loaded on the horses and back to Thomas' house." Doc instructs.

"Where do you live, Thomas?" Allen asks.

"I live a mile or so north of here; it won't take long to get there," Thomas answers. "We can put the meat in the cellar. After that Ma and I can take care of it from there."

Everyone mounts up and follows Thomas as he leads them. A few minutes later, they approach the ranch and see a woman hanging clothes on the line. She stops and watches the men approach. When she sees Thomas, she comes running across the yard to meet him. "Thomas, I was so worried. You were gone for so long. Where have you been? What trouble have you gone and gotten yourself into this time?"

Allen removes his hat and smiles at the woman. Her face shows the days of work and worry that she has had to endure. He dismounts and offers a hand to shake. He notices her hands are callused, and she has grip strength like a man. He thinks, *'Poor woman. No woman should live here in this open prairie alone with her children.'*

"No trouble, ma'am," Allen says to the woman. "He was out hunting. We happened across him and stopped to help him get his harvest home."

She smiles at Allen, then at the others. "Well, I don't think I can thank you gentlemen enough. Can I offer you something to eat or drink?"

“No thank you, ma’am,” Doc replies. “We appreciate the offer, but we need to get this elk unloaded so we can get back on the road to White Cloud.”

Several of the men begin unloading the elk from their horses. They help carry the elk down into the cellar and then mount up to leave. They are about to turn around, when Thomas’ mother, Sally, comes out hurrying to stop them.

“Doc, please take this,” she says to Doc, displaying a jar of something she has put up.

He takes it and asks, “What is this for?”

“Thomas just told me the story about who shot the elk. We don’t have much to offer, but take this jam as a thank you, please.” Doc takes the jar. He rests his hand on hers as he takes it, in an effort to comfort the plainswoman. “Since my husband died many things have been hard on us. When the bank man came to call in the marker, we had to sell all of our cattle just to pay off the loan my husband took out on this place.”

Doc removes his hat, and then asks her, “The bank man himself came calling? Let me guess, the bank is run by Mr. Sutton, isn’t it?”

“Why yes, it is. How did you know?” she asks.

“Let’s just say it was a lucky guess on my part. Ma’am, don’t you worry too much more. I have a feeling your luck and troubles are about to change.”

Doc tips his hat, and waves to Thomas and his sisters watching from the porch of their log home. All of the men wave, and in a cloud of dust they are off.

Doc looks again over at Allen and says, "Allen, remind me when we get back to Lincoln to send a few head of cattle to Miss Sally to get her up and on her feet again."

Allen smiles at his usually dark companion. "That's awfully nice of you, Doc. Are you going soft on me?"

"Keep it up and you're going to find out the hard way why you shouldn't talk in such a way," Doc answers. "I thought it would be the right thing to do, sending her some cattle. I think there are going to be some cattle for sale soon, and cheap."

"Ahhh, you're talkin' 'bout Sutton's herd aren't-cha?" Allen asks.

"Yep, sure am," Doc replies. "The way I am seeing things, Sutton's luck is going bad, real bad, real soon."

The men are back on the trail to White Cloud, when Levi points to a man up ahead of them on horseback. "Do you want me to ride up there and see what he wants?"

"No. I know that man," Doc answers. "I'll see what he has to say." Doc rides up ahead of the rest of the men and greets his old friend. "Running Wolf, it is nice to see you. What brings you way out here?"

The man dressed in buckskins and wearing feathers in his hair, reaches out to shake hands with the white man he is proud to call friend. "I came to warn you. There are many white men with guns on your journey, who are going to try to harm you. The Spirit Warrior came to me in the sweat lodge. The spirit told me where to find you and that I must ride out and warn you."

Levi leans over toward Allen, "Who is that talking to Doc?"

Allen doesn't look at Levi as he replies. "That's Running Wolf. He is the Chief of the Sioux people. He is a very close friend of Doc's, and of mine."

Levi looks at the two men as they talk. "I suppose that is a story for another time."

Allen nods and smiles. "Exactly."

Doc looks about the land as he talks with the Chief. "Where are the men now?"

Running Wolf holds out a hand, and sweeps his hand across the skyline. "The Great Spirit Warrior tells me these vicious men are everywhere over the land between here and our village, and going east. I have brought six of my bravest warriors to help you with your journey."

Doc shakes his friend's hand and concludes, "Thank you, Running Wolf. As always, you are a trusted friend. My companions and I can use all the help we can get."

Running Wolf waves his hand about above his head, and twelve Sioux warriors appear from over the hill. "My friend, I am sending with you six of my most bold warriors. As you can see they are ready for battle." Doc looks at the twelve men on their painted ponies. Six of the warriors are dressed in battle clothes and painted in their war paint, prepared for battle. "You will take with you the six brave warriors in war-paint. The others will return to the village with me. John, I wish much success on your journey. I will pray to the Great Spirit to protect you."

"Thank you, Running Wolf. My friends and I are thankful for the help, and I hope to see you soon."

Doc returns to the others with the six braves. "These brave warriors were sent to go with us by my friend, Chief Running Wolf. These fine young braves will help us on our journey to Lincoln. The Spirit Warrior visited the Chief, and the Spirit told him of the dangers that lie ahead of us on our way to Lincoln. Running Wolf tells me there are many white men wandering around between here and their village. He wants to assure our safety."

Allen looks at the braves, then back at Doc. "Well, we can use the help, that's for sure. Let's ride, gentlemen. Let's make up some time."

The men begin to ride at a fair pace again in the direction of White Cloud. After some time, Allen puts his hand up to halt the men. "Doc, you, Levi and Steve ride ahead and make sure there are no surprises up there in those bluffs." He turns to the remaining members of the group. "You guys, dismount. We'll rest our horses for thirty minutes or so. This will give them time to scout ahead. Stay close, 'cause if we you hear shooting, we have to mount up and go!"

The three men ride ahead while Allen and the rest of the men get off their horses and walk them for a spell, allowing their horses to graze and water at a nearby creek. Allen keeps watching the three as they circle the bluffs. He looks back at one of the others at the creek. "Those bluffs just look like a good place for an ambush, and I don't want to take any chances."

As Doc, Levi and Steve approach the bluff a shot rings out from atop the bluff and a man yells down, "The next one will be right between your eyes. Hand over Billy and the bill-of-sale and we'll letch-ya live."

Doc looks over at Levi, and then yells up at the voice, "You're going to let us live if we do these things?"

The voice sounds out again. "That's what I said, ain't it? You can ride outta here in one piece if you hand him and that paper over!"

Doc looks back up the cliff. "Alright. What if I don't want to let you live?"

The man beyond the edge above answers, "Fella, I don't think you're in a bargaining situation."

Doc looks back where he, Levi, and Steve left the others, then up at the rocks above. "I do, so here's the deal; if you come down and head out peacefully, I will not kill you."

The voice yells down at him again, "Look, I told you and I am not kidding; if you do not give us what we want we'll start shooting!"

Doc looks at Levi and lets out a quite chuckle. "Levi, I am not sure, but I think the man just said 'when'."

Levi smiles and nods. "I do believe he did, Doc. I guess we're gonna have a bit o' fun!"

Doc and Levi pull their pistols and start to make their way up the rocks. Steve stays back to watch for someone coming up behind them. Just as they come around the first large rock, a bullet ricochets just above Doc's head. He and Levi take cover and make quick work of the outlaw band.

After the shooting is over, Doc asks, "Steve, why didn't you draw?"

"I was just about to, but by the time I reached for my gun the fight was over," Steve replies.

Levi laughs. "You have to react fast with Doc around or you won't get any fun for yourself; I learned that a long time ago."

The three start their way back down. Steve looks over at the other two and asks, "Where did you two meet, anyway?"

"We met a few years ago," Levi answers. "Truthfully, I don't remember Doc being the gunman he is now. He was this quiet little saw bones, practicing in this itty-bitty town not too far from Spirit Lake. He patched me up after I had a run in with some stagecoach robbers."

"So are you a lawman too?" Steve asks.

Levi opens his coat to show Steve his Marshal's badge.

Steve raises his eyebrows. "Let me get this straight; you met Doc before he was a Deputy Marshal?"

Levi nods. "Yep, before becoming a Deputy he was a surgeon with a good practice in Lincoln. He became a Deputy after that mess at his ranch. He became a changed man. To tell ya the truth, I can't say I blame him. I probably would have done the same thing. I just hope I will never have to find out."

Steve looks down at his feet, nods and quietly says, "Yea, me either."

When Allen and the rest of the posse catch up to Doc, Steve, and Levi, Doc says to the group, "Well it's about time you show up."

"We got here as fast as we could. What happened?" Allen, not sure how he should respond, asks.

"Well that gentleman down over there told us if we did not give him Billy and the bill-of-sale, they would kill us and take it," Steve replies. "However we had different plan."

Allen smiles and asks, "Where are the others?"

Levi throws a thumb up and over his shoulder and replies, "Trust me, they are up and over there. They probably are between the top and bottom in some rocks or on a ledge somewhere. A couple fell back when we shot at them."

"How many were there?" one of the men in the posse asks.

Doc and Levi ejected the empty rounds from their pistols. Doc looks up and replies, "I have five spent. How about you, Levi?"

Levi looks at his rounds. "I have four."

Doc shrugs. "Well, there must have been about eight up there."

Allen shakes his head and laughs a bit. "I'm beginning to wonder about you two." The Marshal looks at the men. "Steve, you and Levi go up there and make sure nobody is left up there to cause us trouble."

The two men ride up to the top of the bluff and come back a few minutes later. Levi reports to Allen, "All present and accounted for. We were able to pick up their horses. We can drop them off in White Cloud at the Sheriff's office, and claim them for official use."

Allen nods and answers, "Sounds like a plan. Now, let's get a move on so we can make White Cloud before dark."

****

As the men make their way into White Cloud, Allen looks over at Doc and says, "You and I will take Billy to the jail. We'll take turns guarding him for the night." Doc nods in response. "The rest of you go and get yourselves some rooms for the night. When Doc and I are done dropping off Billy at the jail, I'll meet you at the saloon for supper."

Doc shoots Allen a dirty look then says, "What do you mean, you'll meet them for supper?"

Allen looks wide-eyed in surprise at Doc and replies, "You have first watch." Allen then snaps his fingers, "Oh, I forgot to mention that, didn't I?"

“Um, yea, I think you did forget that little detail,” Doc shoots back.

“Sorry. Well, you have first watch,” Allen points out. “There you go, I told you.”

Doc rolls his eyes at Allen. “Thanks. Thanks a lot.”

Allen, Doc, and Billy enter the jail. Allen tips his hat at the man sitting behind the rail at a small desk. “Evening, I assume you’re the Sheriff?” The man nods. “I have a guest for the night. We won’t require any of your deputies though. We will be taking shifts ourselves to keep an eye on him tonight.”

The Sheriff stands up and reaches for the cell keys. “Are you expecting trouble?”

“Concerning this young man, you might say that there has been nothing but trouble since we left Lincoln,” Allen replies as the Sheriff puts Billy in a cell.

The Sheriff hands Allen the keys to the jail cell. “I’ll get a couple of my men to watch the outside as well; I’ll be right back.” The Sheriff walks to the door, opens it, and leaves with Allen hot on his heels.

Doc looks at the Sheriff just before he closes the door. “Sounds fine. I’ll be here keeping Billy company. Say, by the way, Sheriff, have there been any new faces in town recently?”

The Sheriff pauses for a moment, then answers, “I don’t recall seeing any strangers hanging around lately.” The Sheriff closes the door and goes to get the help he suggested for outside.

Billy stands inside the cell. He stands with his hands gripping the steel bars, looking helpless at his protector. “Doc, am I gonna see my family again?”

“Why would you ask that?”

Billy squeezes and twists his grip on the cold hardened steel. "Well, it seems like everyone is trying to kill me. I'm startin' to wonder if or when our luck is gonna run out."

Doc grins at the boy. "It has nothing to do with luck but a lot to do with skill. Levi, Allen, and I are skillful in what we do. So don't worry so much. Now, get some sleep."

Billy smiles with some reluctance. "Thanks. Ya know Doc, I really appreciate what you guys are doing for me."

Doc sits forward in his seat. "Don't mention it, kid. It looks like we all have a score to settle with Sutton. Go on now, and get some sleep."

A few minutes later the Sheriff walks back in with two men. "These are two of my best men. I also placed a third man in a second floor room, in the building across the street. That will give even better front coverage. I figure I can stay with you and cover the back."

"That should do. I must say you're helping out more than we expected," Doc comments. "We just need to keep a sharp eye on the street for Sutton's men."

The Sheriff turns to the two deputies and says, "Alright, you two, keep a lookout in front on the street; Doc and I will watch the back."

A few hours later, Allen and Steve enter the Sheriff's office to relieve Doc and the Sheriff. "Doc, why don't you and the Sheriff get some shut-eye. We'll cover the rest of the night. We can come and get you in the morning."

Doc looks over at the Sheriff and says, "Why don't we grab a cot here in the other cell? That way if there's trouble we'll already be here."

The Sheriff stands up and answers, "Good idea, Doc. I have a couple of bunks in the back room." He looks over at the Marshal. "Allen, wake us if there is trouble."

The next morning the sun is just starting to rise when Doc is awakened by the sound of Allen yelling at Steve. "What the hell do you think you are doing, falling asleep on your watch? If we all fall asleep, Sutton's men could come in here and kill us!"

Hanging his head in shame Steve answers, "I am sorry, Marshal. I was exhausted. You have been pushing all of us pretty hard."

Allen throws a finger into Steve's face. "You don't hear Doc complaining, do you?"

Doc walks out of the backroom, stepping in between the men. In a quiet tone he says, "Why don't you two announce to the whole world that we are in here. Now shut-up, both of you! Steve, you take a look down the street and see if it is clear."

Steve gets up and looks out the door only to find a pistol in his face. Steve freezes in his place.

The man holding the gun pushes the tip of the barrel into Steve's forehead. As the man starts to push his head back, he speaks to Steve, letting the hammer back into its non-firing position. The men all watch with hands ready for a shootout, when a familiar voice comes through the door's opening. The voice is Levi's, "Didn't Doc teach you anything? You never just stick your head out without first getting your gun out."

"Um, I guess he forgot to tell me about that," Steve answers.

Levi enters the room and holsters his pistol. "Doc, you need to teach these guys a little better. Well, anyway, I looked around town. There are some men hanging around the livery. I watched them for awhile and I'll tell ya, they look like trouble."

Doc walks across the room to the front door. "Well, what do ya say, Levi? How about you and I pay them a little visit? We can see what they're up to, and maybe defuse things."

Levi steps in line with Doc. "Alright Doc, let's go down there. I don't know about defusing. I'd rather see if they came to play."

As Levi and Doc walk down toward the livery, the men become aware of their approach. The men fan out on the street and start walking toward Doc and Levi.

As they get closer to the group of men, Levi recognizes one. "Bart, is that you?"

"Yea, who wants to know?"

"It's Levi and Doc Gray," Levi shouts back.

The tall willowy dark man answers back, "I didn't know you two were with the Marshal. We mean no harm. We were just going to the, uh well, um, we were . . . ." His voice trails off in a mumble.

Levi points a finger in the men's direction, then back to the livery. "You men were 'just' going to get on your horses and ride out of town."

The man looks at his companions, then at the two lawmen who continue walking toward them. "That's right. We were going to ride out of town, right now. You won't be seeing us again."

Levi puts a hand on the pearl handle of his trusty pistol. "If I see any of you anywhere between here and Lincoln, trust me, I will not be so nice. This is your only warning; now git!" The men turn tail and disappear without incident.

As Allen, Doc, Levi, and the other men gather at the livery to prepare for their ride to Whitehorse, Allen announces, "Okay men, we had better be ready for a fight on our way to Whitehorse."

Steve looks at Allen as he swings his leg over the saddle on his horse. "Marshall, it's only a half day's ride. You really think someone will be waiting for us somewhere between?"

Allen trots his horse into the street. "With all of the bluffs and hills around here, it is a perfect place to hide for an ambush. I am suggesting we had better keep our eyes open. Now, let's ride." He snaps his reins across his horse's rear quarter, and off he goes. The group of men follows, but each is on edge knowing he is not safe.

13

As they leave White Cloud, Levi looks over at the Marshal and speaks up. "Do you want Doc and me to ride ahead and scout the area for possible trouble?"

Allen surveys the landscape in front of them and replies, "That's a good idea, Levi. Why don't you take three of the braves with you in case you do happen to run into some trouble?"

Levi nods in agreement. "Good idea, Allen. We'll try to get about a mile or so ahead. If you hear shooting . . . ."

"Yes I know, I know," Allen interrupts, "If we hear shots, come a runnin'."

"You got it." Levi makes a gun with his finger and acts like he's shooting Allen as he gives him a wink. Then he turns and says, "Doc, let's go and find us some fun."

The five of them take off at a gallop to get up ahead of the rest of the posse. Levi turns and asks, "So Doc, I have to ask, do you miss being the good old country Doctor?"

Doc pauses in his thoughts before he answers. "At times I would like to go back to the good old days. But without my wife and kids, I don't think it would be quite the same."

Levi laughs as he says, "I can't believe how fast you have become with your pistols. The last time I saw you, you were still trying to hit that old barrel in your pasture."

Doc grins, knowing how it must have looked back then. "I have practiced some since then."

"I noticed that," Levi comments." You must have done nothing but practice since I saw you last."

That dark cold expression of Doc's angry side appears on his face. "I have had nothing better to do since the murder of my wife, Julie, and my sons."

"John, I sure was sorry to hear about all of that. Ya know, I really liked Julie. She was a very sweet and generous lady."

Doc holds his gaze toward the ground. After a few moments of silence, he looks up. His expression is blank. His eyes show the still present grief he carries for his family. "Thanks Levi. I really do miss her. She was a woman like no other. To tell you the truth, my friend, I thought all of this killing would somehow fill the void, the loss, and the pain of losing them; but it hasn't. Truth be known, it's only made it worse."

Levi looks back at Doc. "Yea, I know what you mean. After I lost my daughter, there has always been a hole in my heart."

"I forgot about that; how long has that been now?" Doc asks.

"It has been about five years now," Levi replies. "It seems like yesterday; I still expect her to come running out the door when I come home."

Doc nods, and raises his gaze to meet his partner's. "I know that feeling all too well."

They come upon a creek with trees all around it and tall bluffs just beyond the trees. When they get closer, one of the braves grabs Doc by the shoulder and points up toward the top of the bluff. "Look up there, Doc. Do you see that?"

Doc looks up and sees the sun reflecting off a rifle barrel. "Yes, I do." He stops his horse and looks among the men. "Why don't we split up?" He points to some of the men. "You three go around to the north; Levi and I will go south. That will get them in the crossfire."

As Levi and Doc make their way around to the backside of the bluff, the braves are making their way on foot up the northern face of the bluff. Doc and Levi climb off their horses and start to make their way up the south face of the rock. Just as they get to the top, there is just enough cover of bushes and trees to hide them.

While Doc is peering through the vegetation he whispers to Levi, "I see five of them. It's the same guys we chased out of White Cloud."

"I warned them, if I saw them again only bad things were going to happen," Levi whispers back.

Doc motions for the braves to take the three outlaws closest to them. Then he motions to them that he and Levi will take the two closest to them. As the rest of the posse rides closer to the bluff, the outlaws step out from behind their cover in an attempt to open fire on the men below.

To their surprise, they are recipients of the silent flying arrows from the braves in the bush beyond them. As the two remaining outlaws turn to see the fate of the other three, Doc and Levi begin firing upon the duo, laying them out next to the other three. Now, all five outlaws lie on their backs, motionless.

Levi bolts out and charges toward the slain men. He looks down into the face of the deceased leader, shoving the man's shoulder with his boot. "I told you if I saw you again you would regret it."

Doc is standing behind Levi, smirking and shaking his head. "Some people never listen."

The posse is directly below with Doc and Levi's horses. Allen shouts up to his friends, "Is everyone all right up there?"

Doc looks over the edge, back down at the Marshal. "There are five men up here you can cross off your 'to do' list."

Allen nods in acknowledgment, and then waves them down. "Why don't you-all come back down and we can get back under way."

Levi waves back, while shouting down to Allen, "On our way down. We just have to make sure none of these men will be returning to the trail; besides, Little Bear wants his arrows back."

Doc and the others climb down and join the posse. After a brief review of the events on the bluff, Doc suggests, "Why don't you guys rest awhile and water your horses?" He motions toward the river just a mile from their location. He then pats Levi on the back. "We'll ride ahead again. We'll see if anyone else is waiting for us between here and town."

Allen looks ahead in the direction of town, and looks toward the river, then back at Doc. "That's a good idea. I think we all could use a breather. How long do you want us to wait before we follow you?"

"Give us about twenty minutes or so," Doc answers.

"Alright. We'll see you in White Horse... if not sooner," Allen says.

Doc turns his horse in the direction of White Horse, looking back over his shoulder at Allen. "We will wait just outside White Horse for you. We want to go in as a group in case there are surprises waiting for us in town."

Doc, Levi and their war party go ahead to scout for possible trouble on the path leading to town.

Levi breaks the silence. "Well, I have to say, that skirmish was pretty uneventful. This is almost getting too easy."

Doc nods in agreement. "The more we practice, the easier it gets."

"Well Doc, the way you've been practicing, this should have been a breeze for you."

"That may be all well and good. Let's just hope the outlaws are not practicing."

Levi lets out a little laugh. "They never do. You know, they don't think they have to."

The group continues in silence for some time. Levi is the one who breaks the silence. "Well Doc, tell me, have you met anyone lately who could take your mind off your troubles?"

Docs face takes on an odd expression, one that is new to his friend. It isn't mournful like he has been accustomed to seeing on Doc's face. "You know Levi; there will never be one that will ever take the place of Julie. Julie was a woman who could never be duplicated. However, I did happen to meet a very nice gal in Lincoln recently. She is remarkably funny and sweet. She definitely has the right qualities, a gal that I can see myself maybe settling down with."

Levi smiles big and slaps his thigh in response to the news. "Well, I'll be. Doc does have a soft side. Seriously, that sounds good, Doc. Sounds as though it could be promising."

"Yea, it could be a promising thing," Doc admits. "But, it's a little too soon to tell if it has a chance of turning into something more. At least it will be time well spent. She may be the right lady for me at this time in my life."

Levi smiles at the thought of the possibility of Doc remarrying. "When we get to Lincoln you will have introduce me."

"I will make sure to do that," Doc replies.

Levi points over at an outcropping of rocks. "Doc, look up there on that bluff; see that big rock?"

Doc looks and replies, "Yes, what about it?"

They stop their horses. Levi takes out his spyglass, to take a closer look at the area. "Doc, there is someone up there. And that someone has a rifle."

Doc examines the landscape between them and the rock. "We must be popular today. Tell me, how do you want to approach this one?"

Levi studies the area, and then shares his plan. "Well, if we go around this hill over there and then stick to the creek, it will take us to the backside of the bluff."

Doc tightens up his reins, and readies for their approach. "Sounds like a plan to me; let's do it."

As they go down the creek, Little Bear makes a suggestion to Levi's plans. "Why don't you let us take this one? If we can do this with our arrows instead of bullets, no one will know we are here."

Levi strokes his chin, thinking of the idea and says, "That sounds like a good idea. Before you attack, be sure that you can overtake them. If you cannot handle them, come back and get us."

Little Bear nods. "Yes, we will be sure to do that, Levi."

As the little war party of three Sioux braves make their silent ascent up the bluff, the men hiding atop come into view. They spot only two men. Little Bear points to the farthest man behind a rock and tells one of his braves, "I want you to sneak over there quietly and do away with that white eye." He motions at the other outlaw. "I will see to this man over here, and you," he points to the third brave in his party, "stay here. There is a chance that there are others we cannot see. If that is the case, I want you here to protect us from them."

Little Bear clenches his hunting knife in his teeth and crawls behind a row of blackberry bushes to get close enough to the outlaw to take him out quietly. He looks over at the other outlaw. Behind the man, he can see the other brave in position to strike. Little Bear motions and they each grab a man. In unison they each place a hand on their adversary's forehead, and with the other hand, drag their knife blades across the men's throats. Now having successfully completed the task, they return to Doc and Levi, just as quietly as they departed.

Little Bear looks at Doc and says, "It is done. There were only two men, so it was easy and quick."

Levi pats Little Bear on the back, commending him. "Nicely done, men! We did not hear a thing down here, did we Doc?"

Doc shakes his head. “Well, let’s keep going. We can only hope that’s the last of them for awhile.”

The small group of men returns to the trail heading toward town. When they get near the outskirts of White Horse Doc suggests, “We are only half a mile from town; maybe we need to find the best way to sneak in. That will give us the ability to lurk a bit and see if there are any of those men hanging around.”

“Not a bad idea there, Doc,” Levi comments. “Who do we talk with to find out if there are any ‘non-townsfolk’ about in town?”

“I will sneak into the Hotel,” Doc answers. “I know a girl who works there named Nancy. I can ask her. She’ll know if there are any strangers in town.”

“Who is this Nancy?” Levi asks.

“Well, it’s kind of a long story. If we live long enough I’ll tell you.”

“Doc, I think you’re going to live forever,” Levi remarks.

The five men sneak out and around to the north side of town. As they approach the backside of the hotel, Doc dismounts his horse and hands the reins to Levi. Doc quietly sneaks in the rear door of the hotel. As he opens the door there are three men talking to Nancy. Doc ducks around the corner into the back hallway. He listens to the inquisition regarding if she has seen the Marshal or Doc and when she last saw them.

Nancy, knowing how to respond to them, answers, “They were here a few days ago, but I haven’t seen them since. To tell you the truth, I don’t think they’ll be coming back here anytime soon.”

“Why do you say that?” one of bandits asks.

"Well you see, they had quite the gun battle the last time through," Nancy replies. "It didn't go too well, and I think they said that they were going to take the southern route back, to avoid more trouble on the way home."

One man looks at the other. "She said ''think', didn't she?" The other man nods. "Even so, we are going to hang around town awhile. After all ten-thousand dollars is ten-thousand dollars." The three men turn and walk out the door. After they leave, Nancy hears a 'psst-psst' sound from behind her in the hall. She slowly peeks down the hall.

The shadow in the hall whispers, "Nancy, over here." She looks about the room, then proceeds to the nook in the rear hall.

"Doc, is that you?" she asks in a hushed tone.

"Yes," he replies as he reaches out for her as she closes in. "I heard the conversation between you and those three men. Nice job, by the way. How many of them are there in town?"

She leans into Doc, whispering, "Those three and I think about five more."

Doc squeezes her arm in thanks, smiling. "What was that talk about ten-thousand?"

"You don't know?" she asks, looking at Doc surprised. "Mr. Sutton told everyone that you and Allen are in with Billy on the rustling operation. He said that Billy did not escape, but was let go by you two. He has posted a bounty for the three of you. I'm surprised you didn't see the posters. They're all over town."

Rubbing his chin, thinking, he asks, "Where are these men staying?"

"They have been staying in the rooms over the saloon," she answers.

"Need I ask? What do they do at night?" Doc wants to know.

She smiles at the expression he gives her. "They all go to the saloon and drink until they can't walk. They also spend time going around town, boasting to anyone who can hear them how they are going to gun you down, and be rich because of it."

Doc comments, "Really, well, many have tried,"

Nancy snickers at his tone, nods in agreement, and says, "From what I have been hearing, many have died trying."

"When do these guys usually go down to the saloon?"

She thinks about Doc's question for a moment, then replies, "In about an hour or so they will be tired of waiting for you so they'll mosey on down to the saloon."

Doc grasps both her shoulders, holding her squarely in front of him. "Now listen, I am going to get back to Allen and the rest of the men. We will wait about an hour or so, and then return. I will need your help to know if it's safe for us."

"Okay. I will put a lit candle in the corner room window," she points toward the room she intends to use, "on the second floor. If it isn't safe, I will simply open the window to allow the curtains to blow in the wind."

Doc smiles at her as he turns, opens the door, and leaves. Doc is able to sneak quietly back out of town to where he left his horse with Levi. When he returns, he finds that Allen and the rest of the posse have caught up to them.

"What's the news, Doc?" Allen asks.

Doc takes a moment to answer. "Well, Nancy said that there are eight men in town who are looking for us." He pats his trusty gelding and mounts up. "She also says that they are spouting off around town how they plan to gun us down, and then they go to the saloon each night and get drunk as skunks. I think we should let them get good and drunk, and then we enter the saloon from the front and back and give them the choice to surrender or die."

"That sounds like a good plan, Doc," Allen agrees. "Give them option one or option two. I say let's make our way to the hotel, grab a bite of supper and wait for them to drink themselves into a stupor."

As they make their way into the hotel, Doc looks for a candle but sees none. The window is not open, either. Knowing this means that all is not well, he takes Little Bear with him and instructs the others to wait and stay out of sight.

Doc leaves Little Bear to cover the rear entry he used before and sneaks in the door of the hotel again. He ducks into the little nook that hid him from view earlier, and can see the front desk area.

He sees Nancy behind the desk and a man watching out the front door. Doc watches for a while before crawling behind the desk. Although surprised by his appearance, Nancy is careful not to let her captor know of Doc's arrival.

Doc tugs at Nancy's dress. She looks down, and whispers, "Shh, he's one of them."

Doc looks out around the desk and watches the man for a moment. Waiting for the right second, he leans around and looks down the hall. Little Bear is outside peeking through the glass in the door. He motions for Little Bear to come forward. Little Bear enters and readies his bow. On Doc's signal, he pulls back his bowstring and lets the arrow fly. The man drops to his knees and slumps over, without making a sound.

Little Bear steps forward from the hall and stands over the man and says, "That makes seven."

Doc returns to the door and motions to where the others are waiting, undercover. The others quietly enter.

Allen looks out the curtains of the hotel lobby toward the street. He turns back to Nancy and asks, "Where are the others? Are there any more in the hotel?"

Nancy held a finger up to her lips to indicate "Sshh". In a quiet tone she tells him, "Yes, there is one upstairs in the front room on the corner." She points to which corner they would find the man. "They came in unexpectedly and there wasn't time for me to get to the window and warn you."

Allen looks at Doc. "Doc, go up and take care of the problem, but do it quietly."

Doc nods and answers, "Not a problem."

Doc slowly makes his way upstairs and sees the man in the room, watching the street from the window. Doc slowly takes out his hunting knife and sends it flying thru the air. The knife lands deep within the man's shoulder blades, piercing his heart and killing him instantly.

Doc makes his way back downstairs. He looks at Allen and asks, "Was that quiet enough for you?"

"Perfect, thanks Doc," Allen replies. "Let's give the others another hour or so in the saloon. Then we'll take them by surprise."

The group sits down in the hotel kitchen for a much-needed hot meal as they wait for the outlaws to become intoxicated.

Doc looks at Levi and explains the situation. "Nancy says that Allen and I are on wanted posters all over town so we'll have to go in the back way, while you and Steve go in the front. Little Bear you and your braves, stay here with Billy and keep an eye on him. Give Allen and me a few minutes to get around back; we will sneak in and lie low until you make your move."

Allen and Doc slip out of the back of the hotel; they duck in and out of the shadows to make their way to the back of the saloon. They reach a corner just diagonal from the back door of the saloon. They can see the rear door. Guarding the door is an outlaw who is walking back and forth.

Doc whispers, "Think you can take him from here?"

"Why do you think I borrowed Little Bear's bow?" Allen answers.

"All that practicing you did a year ago should help us out now," Doc points out. "Just take your time, and aim for the throat."

Doc hands him the bow and arrows. Allen pulls back the bow and lets the arrow fly. It hits the man in his Adams-apple and sticks him to the door. Without a sound, another outlaw goes down.

The duo makes their way to the saloon door. After removing the man on the door, Allen quietly opens the door and looks in. They see that it leads to the storage room of the saloon. They creep through the room and around the shelves filled with dry goods. As they look around the bags of flour, they find a spot where they can see to the main floor of the saloon. From this spot, they see Steve and Levi talking with four men. They hear the threats being told to their associates. "If those guys come in here, I tell ya we're gonna skin 'em alive. An' when we're done, we'll drag 'em thru the streets for all to see."

As Doc and Allen lie in wait, two men come walking down the stairs and join the others at Levi's table.

Levi looks at one of the other men he has been talking to. "Who are these two simpletons?"

One of them looks at Levi. "We saw the wanted posters and wanted in on the action."

"Oh yeah? Who do you think you are? How do I know I can trust you?"

Levi notices the movement in the back and instinctively knows it is Allen and Doc; he plays off that. "I guess you don't know. I will tell you one thing. You have about a snowball's chance in hell of getting the drop on Doc."

The bearded man leans toward Levi as if he wants to intimidate him and says, "What makes you so sure?"

Doc stands up from behind the sacks of flour and says, "He knows me all too well." Doc has both of his pearl handled pistols pointed at the men around the table. "Now boys, as I see it, you have two options here. One is to slowly remove your guns and lay them there on the table in front of my friend, and then you can walk with us to jail and live to see the sunrise tomorrow. Your other option is to try your luck and wind up like your two friends in the hotel and the one out behind the saloon."

"What makes you think we can't outdraw you?" the bearded man asks. "There are four of us against you."

Doc steps a little closer. "If you want to die that badly, stand up and face me."

The man stands up and turns to face Doc. "I ain't afraid of you. I think all the stuff they say about you is all a myth."

Doc's eyes darken, as his pupils get larger; he looks the man directly in the eye. "Just say when." The man goes for his gun but Doc is faster.

Levi looks about the room at the remaining men. "Anyone else want to try their luck?" The remaining men unbuckle their gun belts, dropping them on the floor. "Very good choice, gentlemen. Steve, why don't you help the Marshal take these men to the jail?" Levi hands the gun belts to Allen, then looks over at Doc. "Now, how about you and I get in to a quiet game of cards, Doc?"

"That sounds good to me. I could use a drink too. I am kinda thirsty." Doc holsters his pistols and sits down across from Levi.

"Yea, I could use a shot of whiskey as well," Levi agrees.

After a couple of drinks and several hands of poker, Doc and Levi decide it is time to call it a night. They meet Allen as they cross the street and go into the hotel.

"Are you two really quitting before the sun comes up?" he asks.

"I think tomorrow is going to be a long day so we're heading to bed early," Doc replies.

Allen turns back toward the hotel and walks in step with them. "I think you're right."

They enter the hotel together and talk to Nancy about getting some rooms.

"The other fellas have already gone up to their rooms, but I saved two for you all." She holds out some keys and continues, "Allen, Levi here are your keys. Allen, you are in room five. Levi, your room is room six." Nancy then steps out from behind the desk, putting her arm into Doc's, telling him, "Doc, you will have to stay with me. There are no other rooms as they are all full. Oh, and Allen? There is something for you in your room."

"Umm Nancy, are you going to give me a hint?" Allen asks.

She grins. "Nope." She smiles at her escort. "Now, come on, Doc, we have some catching up to do."

Allen and Levi head to their rooms while Doc walks Nancy to her room.

As Allen walks into his room, he finds Nancy's sister, Cynthia, waiting for him. She smiles and greets him, "Evenin,' Marshal Dan Allen. My, it has been a long time since I have seen you!"

"Hello Cynthia! What a surprise to see you! When did you get into town?" Allen removes his hat, and gives her a hug. He motions toward the settee for her to have a seat with him.

"Yesterday," She replies. "I heard you may be coming back through on your way back to Lincoln. I had to come to town, because I needed to see you."

Allen's pulse quickens as she is sitting so close he can smell the sweetness of her perfume. He reaches over and takes her hand. "So you need to see me? Well, what did you want to talk about?"

Cynthia smiles and reaches for his hand with her other hand. She gives him a coy flirtatious smile. "Talk is so overrated, Allen; don't you think?"

****

Doc and Nancy enter her room. She leans up against the door as she closes it; looking at Doc, she winks at him and locks the door. "John, we were so rudely interrupted the last time you were here, you know. So, what do you say we do some catching up?"

Doc pauses a moment before answering. He sees the excitement in her deep gray-blue eyes. Still he answers, "Would it be all right if we do some of that catching up in the morning? The trail hasn't been easy and I am exhausted."

She crosses to him, removes his hat, and presses his head to her bosom. She just holds him and strokes his head for a while. Then she says, "Yes, John. You get some rest. You will need some quality rest for what I have planned for you."

The next morning the sun is starting to peek over the horizon when the sound of a bell is heard from the entry. Nancy sits up, expressing a few un-lady like vulgarities. "Oh my God, who can that be so early in the morning?"

Doc sits up and pats her shoulder. "Go back to sleep. I will go see who it is." Doc gets dressed, places a pistol in his belt in the small of his back, and proceeds out to the entry and front desk to answer the bell. Standing in the vestibule is a dark man wearing a long dark range coat. The man looks at Doc, spouting out, "Well, it sure took you long enough. I've ridden all night to get here. I need a room."

Doc looks into the dark hardened face. "I'm sorry mister, but we are full up until tomorrow. There are rooms available over above the saloon. They were just made vacant."

The man starts to become agitated. "What do you mean by 'they were just made vacant'? I know there are only four rooms over there, and I have friends taking up all the rooms."

The man turns back to the window and peers out. Doc takes the opportunity and grabs his pistol from his waistband. He places it under the desk, pointing at the stranger. "Sorry, Mister. That's just what I heard. The word out last night was that those men were taken to jail."

The man turns back and faces Doc, who is seated on a stool behind the registrar's desk. "Who took them to the jail?"

Doc shrugs. "I heard it was a Marshal and some guy who rides with him, one they call Doc."

The man raises an eyebrow, and gives Doc a wry half grin. "Really? Well, that's why I am in town. I was asked to meet up with my associates here in town. Then I was to put a bullet in Doc's and the Marshal's skulls."

"Well, I'd say your friends had a change of heart when they met up with Doc," Doc points out.

The dark coat man turns back to look through the drapes. "When I catch up with Doc, he will be sorry."

Doc tightens the hold he has on his pistol, which he has pointed at this angry dark stranger. "I overheard them talking about heading south to ride back to Lincoln thru Kansas Territory to avoid any more trouble."

The man turns back to Doc and says, "Thanks, stranger; I will just keep on going. I'll swing down thru Kansas Territory and just as easily collect on that reward there." He reaches over the desk to shake Doc's hand and asks, "By the way, what is your name, friend?"

Doc reaches up with his right hand to shake the man's hand, and in the same instance cocks his pistol in his left hand and says, "Everyone, especially my friends, call me Doc."

The man yanks back his hand and tries to go for his gun. Like many men before him, all he accomplishes is hearing Doc's pistol fire off a round, followed by a searing burning pain ripping thru his chest. He feels a severe burning in his chest. He grabs at the wound and falls to the ground. Doc stands up and looks over the desk at the man writhing on the floor. "Sorry about that reward money, fella; I think it's going to be hard to collect."

When Allen and the rest of the men hear the shot, they come running down the stairs to see what is going on.

"Doc, what was that all about?" Allen asks.

Doc steps out from behind the desk and looks down at his adversary on the floor. "He said he was with the men who were staying above the saloon, the same men you escorted to the Sheriff's special accommodations down the street. He told me he was here to carry out the deed to collect the reward on our heads. I just changed his mind, that's all."

Allen steps over and stands next to Doc, looking down at the stranger too. "I see that. But don't you think you could have done it a little quieter?"

Doc runs a hand thru his hair. "I don't know. I didn't have time for reason as he didn't give me much of a choice."

Allen turns and heads back toward the stairs. As he reaches the landing, he turns back and says, "Well, we better get our things together and get out of here lickity split. You know? while the getting is still good."

Doc nods and returns to Nancy's room down the hall. He knows Nancy will be hurt by the news he is about to break to the sweet woman. He knocks on the door out of common courtesy. "It's John," he announces.

"There's no reason to knock, John; come in," she answers.

He has to break the news to her quickly and without delay. He knows too well there is no time to waste. "Nancy, I have to tell you." He sits next to her on the bed. He can't help but look at her twinkling eyes, and know how hard she's going to take this. He takes in a deep breath, and then exhales loudly. "I, we, I mean the rest of the men and I have to leave. We need to leave quite expeditiously. The gentleman who rang the bell is a man wanting to collect on the reward on Allen and me, and my having shot him surely will alert others to our presence. We must be on our way while the trail is safe or at least get out of town safely. I'm sorry I have to leave so abruptly."

Nancy reaches up and runs a hand against Doc's several days old stubble, and she gives him a sad smile. "Well Doc, it hardly seems fair. We just seem to never get time alone together."

Doc leans forward and places a long sweet gentle kiss on her forehead. He strokes her upper arm and stands up. "I know. Well maybe next time when I'm in town we'll have to set aside some time for us to catch up."

A small teardrop slips out of her eye and runs down her cheek. "I am going to hold you to that. Goodbye John; be safe."

Without another word said, Doc packs his things and meets the rest of the men out in back of the hotel. They all mount up and head for the outskirts of town.

As they ride out of White Horse Allen looks at Doc and asks, “What is that between you and Nancy all about?”

Doc doesn’t look up. He simply replies, “Allen, I wish I knew. I really don’t know for the life of me what it’s about. I can’t remember her, and I am afraid of hurting her feelings. Last time we saw her and last night I just kind of put her off.”

Allen, the man with an endless line of female companions, tells his friend, “Smooth, real smooth Doc.”

Doc looks Allen in the face. “I really can’t tell her that I don’t remember her when she thinks we have or had something special. Maybe after awhile I will come to remember her and the time we shared. Right now I can’t recall her.”

“Well, how much trouble do you think is waiting for us today?” Allen asks.

Doc shrugs. “To tell ya the truth, I hope we can have a quiet ride for a change. How about having Levi, the three scouts and me riding ahead to smooth the way for you?”

With a nod from the Marshall, the five ride off toward the horizon, in search of something lurking just out of sight.

14

As the five men ride out ahead, Levi looks over at Doc. "You said you were going to tell me about Nancy if we survived our visit to White Horse. Well, it appears that we're alive and well. I 'spect it's time to tell your story."

"Levi, I wish there was something more to tell. But it's like I told Allen earlier; I don't remember her."

"You might be able to get away with that story with Allen, but I am not buying it," Levi shoots back.

Doc scans the horizon in an effort to avoid eye contact with Levi. After a few moments, he confesses. "All right, I'll tell you but this is between me and you and no-one else. I mean absolutely no-one."

"You have my word. Whatever you tell me about this will be buried with me," Levi assures Doc.

Doc takes a couple of deep breaths, scans the horizon a bit more, takes another deep breath, and starts his narrative. "Okay then. I trust you with this. You see, it was shortly after my family was murdered. I just lost it. You know, my mind and life were forever changed. I broke down at the funeral. In my head, I needed to be anywhere but where I was so that night I packed a bag, got on my favorite horse, and headed west. I rode that horse for days before stopping in a town. The first town I stopped in was White Horse. When I got there, I was exhausted and starving. I made my way to the hotel. I was in search of a hot bath, a meal, and a drink. That's when Nancy and I actually first became acquainted. That sweet girl took me in. She saw that I got cleaned up, she fed me; but most of all, she comforted me. She held me and let me be close to her. Then in a moment of weakness, and after having drunk probably a few too many shots, we found ourselves in her room. As nature presided over us, I found myself taken in by her beauty. This resulted in my taking liberties with her, if you know what I mean." Doc looks straight down over his horse's shoulder to disguise his humiliation. He is hoping that by avoiding Levi's eyes he won't see for himself his remorse over his behavior and the moments he shared with the woman named Nancy.

Levi can feel the anguish Doc has been harboring about his days spent in White Horse. "Look Doc, there is nothing wrong with what you did. It was a troubling time for you. You were grieving and needed someone to comfort you, and you found that sweet gal to help you heal."

Doc still doesn't look up to meet Levi's look. "I needed comfort yes, but sex with a woman I hardly knew, no. I mean, it was just weeks after I lost Julie and the boys. I had just buried them. The ground wasn't even settled over their graves yet. What kind of man would carry on like that?"

Levi directs his horse over closer to Doc and pats him on the shoulder. "Look Doc, my friend. It is done and over with; there is nothing you can do about it now. I suggest you get over it and concentrate on the job at hand. We have quite a distance yet between here and Lincoln."

Doc looks at Levi, consoled by the words of his friend. He is glad his friend is willing to let the subject fade away quickly. "I guess you can say 'I am over it.' However, I do feel a little bad for Nancy and the way I have treated her and dodged her. She's a kind and caring woman."

"Oh, somehow I think things will work out for her and she'll be able to go on without you."

"Yeah, you're probably right," Doc agrees. "Let's let this lie from here on?"

Levi nods, acknowledging that he understands.

Doc points up the trail. "Now, let's take a closer look at that valley up ahead."

As they approach the valley, Levi spots a rifle barrel sticking out from behind an old tree stump. He starts to scan the immediate area and announces, "We need to find some cover, boys, and I mean like when a husband comes home to you and his wife. I can see that there is someone in those trees trying to get the jump on us. His barrel is sticking out from that rotted stump." Levi redirects his horse toward safe cover. "Alright guys, let's get behind those rocks over there. We'll see if we can draw them out, then take them out."

They ride toward the rocks. Just as they are dismounting their horses, the men hiding in the tree line open fire on the posse. Bullets keep bouncing off the rocks each time Levi tries to look around the rock to get a shot off. Doc wheels around the rock he is standing behind and is successful at firing two rounds. Then he returns to the cover of the rock.

"Did you hit anything, Doc?" Levi asks.

"I think I got one of them, but I am not sure," Doc replies.

The three braves are making their way on their bellies toward the trees, keeping behind the cover of the rocks and in the vegetation of the valley floor.

Levi looks out from behind his rock to take a couple of shots. "I got one. He's not going to bother us anymore." All at once, the shooting stops and Doc peers around the rock to see the three braves out in the open, walking back to them.

Little Bear smiles "We took care of them. They won't be causing harm now. We should be clear all the way to Westhaven."

They mount up and wait for Allen and company to catch up with them so they can enter Westhaven in full force. As Allen is riding up, he asks, "Why are you guys not scouting up ahead?"

"There are only small hills ahead, and really there is nothing like rocks or trees to hide behind," Little Bear answers. "We decided it would be better to be at full strength going into Westhaven. If we meet up with more of them on the edge of the town, there is strength in numbers."

Allen smiles. "Sounds like a good plan. We probably should wait until dark to enter town anyway. I will slip into the hotel from the back and talk to Betty and see if we have a welcoming party waiting for us."

"The rest of us will wait at that pond on the south side where we have the cover of the trees and bushes," Doc points out.

The men approach the southern outskirts of Westhaven. A few lamplights are visible in some of the windows, showing there is still activity in town. The men escape the open by ducking into the tree line around the pond. After dismounting their horses, Little Bear and the other braves take the horses to the pond's edge for water. Allen waves a silent salutation and rides ahead into Westhaven.

When he arrives at the back of the hotel, he is just in time to catch Betty in back, dumping out a pail of water. "Pssst, Pssst, Betty, it's Allen. I need to talk to you."

Betty quickly looks about the area, then grabs the reins of his horse. "Marshal, you get down off your horse. Hurry and get into the hotel. There are men all over looking for you, Doc and Billy."

Allen climbs off his horse. He pauses only long enough to ask, "Men all over? How many would you guess there are?"

Betty ties Allen's horse in the shed behind the building. Turning back around, she tells him as she walks to the back door, "I'd say fifteen at least, but there could be more. They started filing in about two days ago."

Opening the door for her he asks, "Where are they staying? Am I safe here in the hotel?"

As they enter the door, she puts a finger to her lips to 'shhh', and they go down the rear hall to the storeroom. Betty shuts the door behind them. “You may be safe, but some are staying here at the hotel. Others are staying at the old boarding house, and there are a few in those ‘private-special’ use rooms over the saloon.”

“Are any of them here now?” Allen asks.

“No, none are here in the hotel right now,” she replies. “The others are at the saloon. There is a new dancer in town tonight. Many of them went to see her. Her show won’t be done for a couple of hours, so I’d say you have time on your side, not to mention the alcohol will be another factor in your favor.”

Allen reaches for the doorknob. “Thank you for the information, Betty. I’m gonna get back to the rest of the men. We’ll sneak into town and after we stash our horses, I’ll be back to see you and verify where everyone is.”

Betty reaches for Allen’s arm and gives it a squeeze. “Okay. I will see you in just a while. Be careful, Marshal.”

Allen rides out of town, back to the pond to join the rest of the men. When he arrives, they all gather and listen as he explains the situation in town.

When they ride into town, they go to the rear of the livery. They plan to leave their horses there, but a man appears from the shadows.

The voice is deep and quiet. He looks at Allen. “Are you Dan Allen, the Marshal?”

Allen nods. Meanwhile both Doc and Levi are reaching for ivory grips. “Yes, I am. Who’s asking?”

The man points at a hill to their right. “Allen, you and your men take your horses to the barn at the top of the hill. Betty is waiting for you there. She thought you would be safer meeting her there.”

Allen glances at the others, then back at the shadowy man. "Okay. Thanks, mister." The man silently disappears around the corner.

The posse continues on their way. They reach the old red barn where Betty is standing in front of the doors. "Hurry, hurry, you guys. You gotta get in the barn. There is an intermission in the show. Many of the men are in the streets, stretching their legs." The men hurry inside and Betty quickly closes the doors behind them. "After you left, Allen, three more men came riding in. Now you are up against eighteen in all."

Doc lets out a deep from the belly, "HA!" and exclaims, "Finally a good challenge!"

Betty looks at him with extreme concern. "These men are hired killers and bounty hunters. They are not your usual bandits, crooks and outlaws. Gentlemen, these are professionals. They are here for two reasons and two reasons only. Reason number one to kill you; reason two is to collect the high dollar bounties on your heads; nothing more, nothing less."

"We will not let that happen," Doc assures her. "We just need a plan to get them separated."

"Are the deputies still in town that we left behind?" Allen asks.

"Yes," she replies. "They haven't left the jail since these men arrived."

"Steve, you go down there and bring them up here," Allen instructs. "Those men will not likely recognize you, but still, don't get caught."

"Yes sir, Marshal, I'll do my best."

Steve mounts his horse and works his way down to the jail to get the two men they left behind. He stops his horse a couple of buildings over from the jail, and walks the rest of the way on foot. As he sneaks from one building to the next, he carefully stays to the shadows until he arrives at the jail where he knocks on the back door.

"Yeah, who's there?" a voice from behind the door asks.

"Wes, it's Steve," Steve whispers loudly. "Allen sent me here to fetch you."

"I'll let you in but I want you to come in with your hands where we can see them." Steve walks in with his hands raised; as he enters the jail, the men both take a deep breath. Wes motions Steve to put his hands down. "Boy, sure is nice to see a familiar and friendly face around here. Where are the Marshal and Doc?"

"They're all up at the old red barn over on the hill with all of the others," Steve replies.

"Who's all up there?" Wes asks.

Surprised that Wes would ask, he simply answers, "The Marshal, Doc, and Levi, another deputy marshal they know. Of course, the kid they were after, Billy, and his cousin came too. Then we ran into an Indian Chief who knows Allen and Doc. Guess it goes way back. Anyway, he sent six of his best warrior braves to help us get back to Lincoln. We don't have a lot of time. We need to get back up to the barn and get a solid plan together. It sounds like things may get real ugly."

The three of them make their way back to the barn. As they enter the old barn, Allen is standing up on a hay bale speaking. "Well, this is how I see it. We need to hit them as they leave the saloon. They will be drunk and will not suspect a thing."

"That could be true, but there could be townsfolk there watching too," Levi points out. "We don't want innocent people getting caught in the middle of a gunfight."

"You may be right there, Levi," Allen agrees. "I didn't think about that. Okay, anyone got an idea about what you think we should do?"

"We know that some of them are staying in the hotel, right? With Betty's help, we know what rooms they're in. We can wait until they get back to their rooms and take them out quietly, while they're sleeping," Levi suggests.

"That's well and good, but what about the ones staying at the boarding house, and the saloon?" Allen asks.

"We can be inside the hotel and set up an ambush for them when they start to file in, pick 'em off one at a time," Levi shoots back.

The Marshal raises his eyebrow, strokes the beard stubble on his chin, while thinking Levi's plan over. "Well, I'd say that doesn't sound like too bad of a plan to me. It could work. How 'bout you, Doc? What do you got to say?"

"Ask me, I think it will work. Maybe a bit cold blooded, taking them out like that. They won't even know they're walking into a fight. Hardly sounds fair to me," Doc replies.

Allen looks at Betty and says, "Betty, you go on back to the hotel. When the men are all in their rooms tucked in nice and tight, light a lamp and set it on the sill of your room. After you do that, leave the building. I want no excuses either. I don't need you caught in the crossfire. You hightail it back up here where you'll be safe. Agreed?" With a nod and a hug for Allen, she leaves and returns to the hotel, to set in motion the next chain of events.

While Betty is on her way back to the hotel, Levi takes charge and starts to give the men their instructions. "Little Bear, I want you and the other braves to go into the hotel and silently take out each of the men in there. However, I need you to save us one. We need one left to call out to his friends in the boarding house to come and help him. Doc, I want you and Allen across the street from the hotel on top of the general store, or a point around there, whichever has better access and advantage. Steve and I will set up in the alleyway on each side of the hotel and pick off those you leave us to rid. Then we'll just have to wait for our signal." Levi points at the deputies who came out from town, and says, "I want you men here to watch after these kids, all right? Betty will be here, and I, in no uncertain terms, don't want her in the middle of any crossfire. When she comes up here, your job is to look out for her well-being. Got it, gentlemen?" The group of men all nod and a harmonious sound of 'yeahs' is heard. "Now, all we can do is wait for Betty's signal. Wes, I want you to go out and watch for it."

"Yes Deputy," Wes says as he stands up. Without delay, he slips out the side entrance of the barn to wait and watch for Betty's lamplight.

A few minutes later, the show in the saloon concludes. The drunken scoundrels, outlaws, and headhunters file out of the bar. They stagger about the street full of bourbon and beer consumed while watching the dancing girls in the saloon. As they return to their rooms, Betty waits patiently for the right time to signal the men in the barn. Once the last one has reached his room, she tiptoes thru the hall to listen. She can hear nothing. She concludes the time is now. Betty slips down the backstairs, lights her lamp, and sneaks silently out the back.

After seeing Betty's signal, Wes returns to the barn from his viewing spot. "Hey Allen, there is a lamp in the window. You guys best get going." Steve and Levi jump up and start for the side door of the barn.

"Hold your horses, Steve and Levi," Allen commands. "I think we'll wait until Betty is in sight. I'll feel a lot better if she is here safe and sound before we start to carry out the rest of the plan."

"Allen, I think you're right," Levi agrees. "That's probably a better idea. I didn't think of it that way."

Not long afterwards, Betty returns to the barn. She hands a piece of paper to Allen. He looks it over and begins to give last minute instructions. "Okay everyone, like we talked about; Doc and I will make our way to the building across the street," he points at Little Bear and company, "while you six make your way to the hotel to do your thing. Steve and Levi, be careful not to be seen; and you two stay with Betty, Billy, and Tommy to make sure they're safe in case anything goes wrong. Stay inside and out of sight. Someone will come for you when it's safe."

Everyone checks and double-checks their gear one last time. The men start filing out of the barn and making their way to their objectives. Allen discusses the room numbers that Betty wrote down for the braves. The six braves quietly sneak into the back of the hotel and up the stairs. At the same moment that they are about to enter the first rooms, Allen and Doc have made their way to a balcony across the street. This vantage spot gives them a perfect shot line to the front of the hotel, while still having a view of the saloon and boarding house. As planned, Steve and Levi are in the shadows in the alleys beside the hotel.

As the first two braves make it to the first door, one of them puts his ear to the door and hears loud snoring. He slowly opens the door to see two men asleep on the beds. They each sneak over toward an outlaw and put a hand over the outlaw's mouth to ensure complete silence. They each slit a man's throat with their hunting knives. Not a sound is heard, as each brave completes the 'silencing' of an outlaw. They return to the others in their party in the hallway without saying a word; they look at one another and nod. Little Bear points to the next room where two of the braves enter to finish off two more outlaws. Little Bear himself then enters the last room to retrieve the last man who will be used as bait. He comes out into the hall with his hostage in front of him, one hand over the man's mouth while the other hand holds a knife to the man's throat.

Little Bear speaks softly into the man's ear. "Now mister, listen closely, listen good; I have the power to let you live to see the sunrise here in Westhaven. I need you to yell at the top of your lungs to get the rest of your friends to come and save you from the savages. As loudly as you can, tell the town that a band of savages are attacking. Now start yelling or I'll cut your throat!"

Little Bear walks the man to the window overlooking Main-Street at the end of the hall. One of the other braves opens it. Little Bear sticks the man's head out, holding him by his hair, with the knife still at his throat. He starts yelling, "Help! Hey, someone, we need help over here at the hotel! The hotel is being raided; we are being attacked by Indians! The savages are trying to kill us all!" Little Bear pulls the man back in, and looking out the window himself, he sees no movement or lamplights. He pushes the man out again.

This time he walks the man to the window at the end of the hall and tells him, "Louder. Keep yelling; I don't think they heard you." The man continues to call out for help until the men from the boarding house start coming out into the street.

Once it appears that the majority of them seem to be in the street, scurrying toward the voice calling out through the window, Doc and Allen prepare to begin their assault. In the side alleys of the hotels Steve and Levi prepare to do the same.

When the first man reaches the steps of the hotel, Allen takes aim and releases his first shot. In short order, he and Doc drop several men. Allen pauses only to reload. While reloading he says to Doc, "Ain't it just like shooting fish in a barrel?"

Doc and Allen continue with their cover fire. Meanwhile Levi is out with Steve, firing his pistols as fast as he can. The outlaws caught in the crossfire don't have a chance and are falling dead in the street.

In the hallway the hostage says to Little Bear, "I did what you said, Injun. I got all the others into the street for you. Now can I go?"

Little Bear releases the man, giving him a shove down the hall. "Yes, you go on out of here. You may leave now." The man starts to run down the hall. In an instant, Little Bear quickly takes out his tomahawk and throws it down the hall, burying it squarely between the man's shoulder blades, dropping him in his stride. Little Bear shrugs as he is looking at the other Braves. "I never said I was going to let him live. I said I had the power to let him see the sunrise." He sets off down toward the fallen man on the floor and retrieves his tomahawk.

When it appears that there are no more outlaws, Allen and Doc come down off their balcony perch to meet up with Levi and Steve in front of the hotel. Little Bear and the other braves join them in the street. One brave heads off for the barn to tell the others to come, that it is safe.

When the deputies, Betty, Billy and the others join up, and everyone is together, they enter the hotel.

Now that everyone is safe, Allen announces what the next phase will be. "Well done, everybody. That went better than I anticipated. I think we'll need to take shifts standing guard. Remember, there could be a few that didn't come out once they heard the shots and they may surface later in a sneak attack. I want to post a pair of guards to watch both entrances. We'll do this in three-hour shifts. We need to also be prepared for any newcomers who will straggle in tonight in the hopes of collecting the reward on our heads."

Levi is standing against the banister, leaning on one shoulder acting casual, spinning the chamber on his pistol and says, "Doc and I will take first watch. I have a business opportunity I want to share with him anyway. When you deputies finish moving the bodies off the street, head up and get some sleep. So Allen, why don't you and Steve relieve us in about three hours, okay?"

Allen starts up the stairs and remarks, "Sounds like a good plan to me. I could use a nap. You boys get those bodies taken care of, and then get some sleep. I'll wake you after my shift; then you can take yours. Goodnight, Doc. We'll see ya in a few hours."

Everyone retires to their quarters, leaving Doc and Levi alone in the hotel lobby. The two grab a couple of chairs and position themselves where they can see both entrances. Once they are set, Doc asks, "Alright, spill it Levi, what is this business you need to talk to me about?"

Levi leans forward in his seat. "Well, it isn't truly a business deal. It's more like doing some work together. Do you remember when I was working in Texas a while back?"

"Yes, I wished you could have come up when that whole thing with losing Julie and the boys happened, but that isn't what we're here to talk about. What does you're being in Texas, and now, have anything to do with one another?"

Levi shakes his head and says, "Absolutely nothing, but what I was wanting to ask was if there would be any way you and Allen would be able or interested in coming back down there and helping me track down a group of rustlers who are stealing cattle and changing brands. Of course, we need to get Billy back to Lincoln, get his name cleared, and put those responsible for this extensive pursuit behind bars, and in prison."

"That could be a possibility," Doc admits, "why don't you ask me when this is all over if we're still alive. Allen and I can discuss it and give you an answer then. Alright?"

"Okay. That's a plan," Levi agrees.

The two of them spend the remainder of the time in idle chitchat, talking guns, horses, battles and so on. Time goes by quickly; before either one noticed, their shift is over. They can hear Allen upstairs, thumping his boots.

Doc shakes his head as he stares at the ceiling. "I know he knows better than to make so much racket with his feet. Hunting with him is more about luck rather than stalking silently. Nevertheless, he's a great friend. What do ya do; ya know?"

A few minutes later, Allen and Steve come down and exchange pleasantries, then announce, "Levi, why don't you guys go and get some shut-eye? Steve and I will take over."

The two get up from their seats, and then Levi suggests, "Hey Doc, let's take a walk around town and make sure it is safe."

"I'll be right with you. I have to grab my rifle," Doc points out.

"Okay, I'll meet you out front," Levi acknowledges as he opens the lobby door.

Allen looks over at Doc. "You two, be careful out there. Remember, we don't know if we got them all, or who has ridden in since"

"That's why we're taking a look," Doc points out. "Aside from that, I could use a little fresh air before turning in."

Doc steps out the front lobby door to meet up with Levi. "Where do you want to start, Levi?"

Levi points up toward the hill. "Well, I thought we could start out from here and walk up to the old barn and check on the horses. Then we can swing around the other end and make our way back here."

"Sounds good to me," Doc agrees. "However, we had better be ready for a few surprises. Allen thinks, as do I, we might have missed a few." Levi nods in agreement and off they go.

As they make their way down the street, there is a strange glow coming off the trees as the moon shines through them.

"It sure is bright out here, considering it's almost midnight," Doc comments.

"I was thinking the same thing, Doc," Levi agrees. "Think about it; it will make it a little easier to hunt."

"Yes, that's true. But it's easier to be hunted as well," Doc points out to Levi.

"Always with the negativity, Doc," Levi shoots back.

"Well, it's the truth now, isn't it? So shut up and keep your eyes peeled. If I remember correctly, that's how you got shot in Texas, by not paying attention."

They continue around a curve in the road in silence. Then Levi says, "Yeah, that may be true, but it was also a lesson to tell me not to be anywhere near Allen when he has a scatter gun. You know what Doc? The only time I was shot was by a friend."

"Yeah, I don't think he has ever really forgiven himself for that."

"Remind me to talk to him; it's been five years. I don't hold any grudge about it, or at least not anymore."

Doc shakes his head, and pats Levi on the shoulder. "I think that might help some."

The duo is passing a small stand of bushes when they see a shadow. They can see lamplight in the barn. They both stop cold and stare at the barn's glow from within, and then suddenly there is a shadow moving about in the barn. Doc grabs the arm of Levi's jacket and pulls him toward the bush.

Ducking behind the shrub, Levi asks, "Doc, you did see that too, didn't you?"

Doc holds a finger up to his puckered lips. He whispers back, "Yes, I did. Okay, here's the deal; I'll go in the back door, you go in the front, and we will take him by surprise. When you hear me whistle like a red bird, you go bursting in the door. Got it?"

Nodding, Levi replies, "You see, I told you this moonlight would help us tonight. With this light, we can make our way around easily and more quietly."

"Yeah, yeah, let's do this. Let's take care of this guy."

Doc gets into position at the back entry. He can see between the slats of the barn. He can see it is Betty in the barn. She is brushing out Allen's horse. Rather than signaling Levi, he simply slips in the barn without her noticing him. Before he can get her attention without startling her, Levi bursts in the front door with both guns drawn.

Levi shouts out, "Reach for the sky, you low life!" Then he has a moment to see the sight before him.

Doc almost laughs, but poor Betty is as white as a sheet, from the start Levi gave her. "I think we have this under control, Levi. I don't think Miss Betty means us any harm here."

Levi lets the hammers down on his pistols slowly, his face turning several shades of crimson. "Well, I uh, I well, I didn't know it was her. And we were going to . . . ." He trails off a second before changing the conversation. "And just what do you think you are doing out here, young lady? Do you have any idea the danger at this time of night?"

Betty's color begins to come back, and she catches her breath. "I couldn't sleep and I went for a walk and just ended up here." She reaches into her pocket and pulls out a piece of paper. She holds it out to Doc. "Doc, I forgot to give this to you earlier in all the excitement. It's a telegram. It is from some woman named Bonny."

Doc takes the telegram and smiles. "I was wondering when she was going to get back to me."

Levi looks at Doc puzzled. "Who's Bonny?"

Doc is reading the note and smiles from ear to ear. His demeanor changes right there in front of Levi. He finds this interesting, since he forgot there was a 'lighter side' of Doc.

"Bonny is someone I knew back in college," Doc finally answers. "She and Julie were best friends and she introduced me to Julie; the three of us… why we were inseparable in those days. I ran into her a while back. Her music troop is going to go to Kansas City after heading to points further west. She says here that she is going to be in Lincoln, and going by this date that makes it in about three or four days, according to her wire."

"Why is she going to be stopping in Lincoln?" Levi asks. "Neither you or Julie are there."

"Well, she is with a group of performers who travel around. I talked to her about stopping in Lincoln on their way east, and possibly spending a few days out at the ranch."

Levi smiles at the prospect of something joyful, especially the thought of seeing that side of Doc, something he hasn't seen in some time. "That sounds like fun; can I come along? I would really like to meet someone from your past and kind of fill in some blanks about the 'young' Doctor Gray."

A shy kind of smile comes across Doc's face. "Of course, you're invited. This would give us a fun little breather before we start out on the next job you and I discussed."

Levi looks at Betty and then says to Doc, "What do you say we get this young lady back to the hotel and get a little sleep?"

"Sounds good to me, Levi. Betty, let's get you back to your room."

While they are walking back to the hotel, Betty decides to ask some questions. "Doc, where does a doctor learn to shoot the way you do? I have never seen anyone shoot like that."

"I learned from Levi," Doc replies. "He taught me the basics and then I spent a lot of time practicing."

Levi puts an arm out across the other two, stopping all three at once. In a hushed voice he says, "Doc, look up there at the hotel; do you see those two snooping around, looking in the windows?"

Doc pulls Betty by the arm and they walk silently backward into the shadows. "Yep, I see them. Betty, you stay here. You keep your head down. I'll come get you when it is safe. Don't move from here 'til then. Levi, c'mon; let's go see what their story is." Doc looks at his pardner, "Levi, do you want to have a little fun with these boys?"

"Of course. What ya thinking?"

"Just follow my lead."

When they are close to the front of the hotel, Doc speaks in a low quiet voice, "Hey, you guys. What are you doing? Who are you looking for?"

One of the boys looks at Doc and replies, "We're looking for Billy, so we can collect the reward on him."

Doc can see that these two boys can't be much out of their late teens. He knows they aren't hardened gunmen so he asks them, "Why would you want to get into that ordeal? You could get yourselves shot, you know." The taller of the two answers, "Well you see, our family is about to lose our farm because of the man at the bank making our mortgage payments due all at once. Our crops aren't ready yet, and our cattle were stolen. So we thought that with the money we could get from the reward, we'd be able to pay off the bank mortgage."

Doc presses his lips together tightly. Then says, "I think I can help you with your problem, and without you likely getting yourselves killed.

Just follow me and my friend Levi to the hotel. We'll sit down inside and discuss this."

"But the Marshal is in there," the boy points out.

"Don't worry, he's a friend of mine, and I think he'll go along with me on this." Doc steps over to the alley across the street. He calls out to Betty. "Betty, come out; it's safe"

Doc, Levi, Betty, and the brothers walk into the hotel. Allen and Steve are surprised to see that Doc and Levi's 'duo' has increased to five members.

"I think I might have found us a couple more recruits," Doc points out to Allen. "It seems that these boys are here to try and collect the reward on Billy to help pay off the bank mortgage and save their farm."

Once everyone is sitting around a table in the hotel's dining room, Betty heads into the kitchen, thinking coffee is what this group needs.

Doc starts to inquire about their situation. "Now, you boys tell us what bank, or banker, holds the deed to your family's farm?"

Bud, the brother who has been doing the talking, answers, "It's at the bank in Avoca, with Mr. Sutton, why do you ask? Why would that matter?"

Doc looks the young man in the eye, giving him a well-earned look of trust. "If you put your trust in my friends and me, and if you agree to help us, your loan will be taken care of. I mean, you will not owe the bank anything from here on out."

"How is that going to work?" Bud asks.

"Well, it seems Mr. Sutton has been using loans to acquire farm ground by calling in full payment on the mortgage total amount," Doc begins to explain. “In short, we intend to stop him and make sure everyone he has swindled gets their property back.”

The two brothers look at each other. Just by their expression, they come to an agreement. “Okay, how can we help?”

“What I need you to do is ride ahead into Arrow Bluff and scout it out to see who is there, as far as gunmen and such,” Doc explains. “When you find out, ride back to Spirit Lake, and let us know how many men there are in town waiting for us.”

Bud looks at his brother, then back at Doc. “Okay, we’ll leave at sun up.”

15

At sun up, Bud and his brother, Fred, ride out of Westhaven on their way to Arrow Bluff. Allen is coming down the stairs and sees Little Bear with another brave keeping watch. He reaches for the coffee pot and pours himself a cup.

He walks over to Little Bear and says, "Good morning, men. Are you ready to go to Spirit Lake and see your families and fellow tribesmen again?"

Little Bear smiles; he is quiet for a moment as he reminisces about his tribe. "It will be good to get back home for a day or so before we leave for Arrow Bluff; I miss my family and my tribe a great deal."

Allen smiles at the idea of his friend having so much to go 'home' to. "I am looking forward to going to the Sioux village myself. I will be glad to have some buffalo for a change and from what I remember, it is very good."

"Yes, it is a wonderful meat. Many of the men, including myself, were preparing to go to the buffalo prairie when Chief Running Water sent us to be with you. So there will be much meat in our village when we return."

Doc, Levi and the rest of the posse come down the stairs all packed and ready to go. Doc looks over his shoulder at the others as he reaches the front door. "Levi and I will go up and get the horses ready."

"Sure thing, Doc; the rest of us will meet you there as soon as we finish up at the general store. We need to get a few supplies."

Levi, Doc, Billy, Tommy, and the braves head up to the barn while Allen, Steve, and the deputies head over to the general store to get the supplies they will need for the rest of their journey.

While Doc and Levi are saddling the horses, Doc makes a startling discovery. "Um, Levi? You are not going to believe what I found over here."

Levi, thinking it was going to be something like, 'Doc found a dead mouse in his satchel,' responds nonchalantly, "Well, what did'ja find there, Doc? Or are you going to keep me guessing?" Since they are a few stalls apart, Levi cannot see Doc's expression at first; but when he steps out of the stall, he can see the Cheshire cat grin all across Doc's face. "Well, spit it out, Doc. Are you going to tell me what it is you're grinning about or what?"

Doc motions for him to come closer. "Look! I found a case of dynamite over here buried under some blankets."

Levi claps his hands and massages his palms together. "Hot damn, Doc; let's load that in the saddle bags. You know, I think that just might help give us the edge we have been looking for."

They finish preparing the horses and carefully packing the dynamite before the others arrive with the food supplies and bullets from the general store. They load the supplies on a spare horse, and they are set to head out to Spirit Lake and the Sioux tribal village.

Allen looks at everyone after climbing up on his horse. Once seeing everyone is mounted and ready, he gives the command. "Alright, let's move out; I want to be at the lake by mid-day." He stays back a moment and thanks Betty for her help and hospitality. She, of course, tells him to be safe and return soon. He promises that he will; and with a crack of his reins against his chestnut gelding, he is off. He only looks back for a moment to wave good-bye.

Not far down the trail, Allen notices the mood between Doc and Levi. He can't quite make it out. It reminds him of two schoolboys who put a frog in the teacher's desk. He can't take this childlike behavior anymore. So finally he demands an answer from them. "Alright, you two, what gives? Just what are you two so happy about?"

"Let's just say you will be very happy with what Doc and I found," Levi answers.

"Are you going to let the rest of us in on what you found?" Allen asks.

Levi points at one of the Marshal's saddlebags and replies, "Just reach into that saddlebag and you will know."

Allen looks at Levi, then his saddlebag, then at Levi again. "This isn't one of those 'there's a snake in my bag jokes', is it?"

Levi shakes his head while motioning at the saddlebag.

Allen reaches in the saddlebag and pulls out a stick of dynamite. His eyes almost pop out of his head. “Where in the… holy… just where did you get these?”

“Oh, I found them in the barn,” Doc replies. “We thought they might come in handy down the road.”

“Well, it could or should make our job a little easier anyway,” Allen comments as he places the stick of dynamite back into the saddlebag.

“Not to interrupt your conversation here, boys, but you see that pass in between those trees up there?” Levi points out.

“Yeah, what about it?” Allen asks.

Levi stops his horse and points before answering. “Look to the right of the big rock; do you see the reflection down there? If you watch over there, you won’t only see that reflection; you’ll also see a hat right above the reflection.”

Allen, having stopped his horse, takes a good look at the suspicious reflection. “Oh yeah, I see what you are talking about. So what’s your plan, Levi?”

“Well, I think we need to split up the posse as usual and slip down there under the cover of the hills, over there on the left. Then once we’re out of sight, one group will slip quietly into the trees and take care of the problem, then meet the others on the other side of the pass.”

Doc looks over at the braves. “I think it would be in our best interest to split up the braves too. Allen and I will take three; you and Steve take three; and we will leave the deputies with Billy up here. That will ensure his safety during crossfire.”

Levi looks at Doc and says, "You have a good idea; I think the braves will add some stealth to our attack."

Allen looks over the landscape and trees. "Well, enough chattin'; let's go and get this done."

The two groups break off from the third. Once they reach the hill, each goes their separate way. After riding a little bit, Allen looks over at Doc and asks, "Do you have a specific plan once we get in the timber?"

Doc nods. "We let Little Bear and his braves take the lead and we will keep them covered. If the braves can take them with arrows it will be silent, and we won't draw any attention to us."

Once they reach the right spot, Doc directs Little Bear and his braves to take the lead. They didn't go far into the edge of the tree line before dismounting, and then they crawl into the timber. Allen and Doc stalk silently behind them, preparing to cover them with gunfire. Going only a very short distance into the trees, Little Bear and the braves become virtually invisible. While waiting for them to return Doc finds a tree, in which he has ample cover, and can cover them from above. It is not long before Little Bear and one of the braves return. Doc climbs down from his spot and meets them outside the trees.

Little Bear speaks softly. "Doc, we must leave here very quietly. There is no danger here. It is a small hunting party from my tribe. This small group is hunting for deer for this night's feast. We must go quietly and quickly so as not to disturb the game."

Each man works his way silently back to the waiting horses and rejoins the others. Allen explains the situation. They decide to stay wide of the trees and passage. While riding around the area Allen leans over toward Levi, telling him, "I am glad it was just a hunting party from Little Bear's tribe. I didn't want another fight."

"Oh c'mon Allen, where is your sense of adventure?" Levi asks.

"I have had about as much adventure as I can stand for one trip," Allen replies.

"I've never been to the Sioux village. How far away are we from there?" Levi asks.

Allen looks around at the landscape. Determining their location before replying, he says "We're about an hour or so away from the village. When we get there we can rest and get a good night's sleep. While we're there, there will be no reason to worry about being bothered by bounty hunters or Sutton's men."

"How can you be so sure he won't send someone to invade the Sioux village?" Levi asks.

"Oh, about two hundred braves," Allen replies.

They continue in silence, with Little Bear and the five other braves in the lead of the group. Not long afterwards, they can see the village and the excitement among the members, as they get closer. They see the women busy preparing the food for the evening's festivities. The men from the hunting party brought in game from the hunt and the kids are playing games.

The group reaches the corral, dismount from their horses, and begin walking among the many tepees of the village. After walking silently and absorbing the serenity of the village, Allen looks at Doc and says "This brings back memories, doesn't it, John?"

"Yes it does, my friend. It seems like we just left."

Allen pats his comrade on the back and says, "What do you say? Let's go over and see if there is anything we can do to help out."

"I better get back to my mare. She needs a good brushing. I haven't done right by her the last few days. Just let me get the saddle off, comb her down good and then I'll be over."

Allen walks over to sit with Chief Running Wolf. After enjoying the feel of the village, he looks at the chief, smiles and says, "On behalf of those in my party, I want to thank you for letting us stay here for the night. After many nights of unrest with those who are looking to profit in our deaths, a peaceful night of rest will be refreshing for every one of us."

The wise leader smiles at the white man, who is his friend, and says, "You are welcome here anytime you wish. Our village will always welcome you."

Doc finishes with his horse, walks through the village, and finds Little Bear, the braves who traveled with them, and many others, discussing the adventure the six had just returned from.

Doc comes into the circle and sits with the men. Giving Little Bear a show of respect, he then says to him, "I want to thank you and your braves for helping to protect us and helping us get Billy back to Lincoln."

Little Bear gives the same show of respect to Doc. "Doctor John, we are proud to help you and Marshal Allen. This man, Billy, is accused wrongly. It is only the proper thing to help the man prove his innocence."

Doc smells the heavenly aromas lofting about the village. He asks, "Those smells; I can smell things like that everyday. Tell me what have the women prepared for this homecoming feast?"

Little Bear smiles, knowing the differences between them are part of what brought his people and Doctor Gray together to forge a long and prosperous alliance. "Well my friend, we have buffalo, elk, and deer for the meats of the feast."

Doc inhales as deeply as he can, taking in the aromas thru his nose then exhaling loudly out his lips. "MMMmmm. This morning Allen stopped off at the general store before we left Westhaven. I can bet he picked up something for tonight. I had better go over and talk to him about what he brought." He gets up from the group and goes to join Allen and the Chief at the fire in front of the chief's tepee. "Allen, I was just talking to Little Bear about tonight's feast. I know that you stopped at the general store; did you happen to pick up anything for us to prepare and share for the feast?"

Allen smiles and looks surprised that Doc assumes he'd picked up anything. "How did you know it was not just supplies for our trip?"

Laughing Doc replies, "My friend, we have been riding together for some time. Some may say maybe too long."

Allen gets up and motions Doc to come with him. He waves good-bye to the chief and the two go back to the packhorse to get the goods. "Well, I picked up some flour, sugar, and other dry goods. I thought if the women had fresh berries maybe they could make blueberry cobbler. The shop also had a large shipment of potatoes from a local farm. So there are a couple of large bags that can be baked in the pit."

Doc unties the packages and drops one, then reaches to untie another. "Well, we had better get started or they will not be done in time for the feast." While they lug the load over to the prep area, Doc asks, "So Allen, what were you discussing with the Chief?"

"I was asking him what, if anything, he or his men may have heard about many strangers in and around Arrow Bluff."

"So, what did he have to say?" Doc asks.

"He couldn't tell me very much. He said he heard there has been a lot of activity around the town lately. However, he was not certain as to what the activity was about or if there were any newcomers there."

"Well, we're covered there," Doc points out. "That's what Bud and Fred are supposed to find out."

"Let's just hope they don't get caught snooping around for us," Allen shoots back.

We'll know how things are if they show up safe and sound tomorrow afternoon," Doc is quick to point out.

The two men make an odd pair working among the women, preparing food. They both work quietly. Allen scrubs potatoes for baking. Doc assembles the dry goods for the cobbler, while one young girl is helping to clean berries.

With the supper projects underway, Levi feels the need to come over and visit with them. He walks up and asks, "Hey Doc, do you need an apron?"

Doc fires back a not so nice, "As a matter of fact, I don't. Do you need an ass whipping?"

Levi backs up in his tracks. "Whoa. No, I think I will pass on that. Wow Doc, you sure are touchy today."

Without looking up to meet Levi's gaze Doc says, "Look, I just have things to do here. I don't have time for lolly-gaggin'. Besides that, don't you have something you should be doing?"

"No, as a matter of fact, for a change I have the afternoon off," Levi replies, shaking his head.

"Then why don't you go down to the lake and catch us some fish for the feast?" Doc suggests.

Levi strokes his chin and nods about the idea. "You know Doc, that's an excellent idea. I haven't been fishing for quite some time now. Are there fishing poles and bait around here?"

"Go ask Little Bear," Allen informs him. "I'm sure there's something around here, as he too enjoys fishing."

Levi walks over to talk to Little Bear and then the two men walk off toward Little Bear's tepee and emerge with stick and string, and they make their way down to the lake.

"Well, at least he'll be out of our hair for awhile," Allen comments. "How're the cobblers coming along?"

Doc smiles at his assistant, Singing Yellow Bird; he then replies, "I think my helper here, and I, have it well under control. We should have warm blueberry cobbler just in time for supper."

"Fantastic," Allen says. "I think these potatoes are good to go. They'll be ready in plenty of time. Hey Doc, when we're done here, what do you say we go and have a talk with Running Water? I'd like to catch up on what he's been up to."

Doc and Singing Yellow Bird finish the last of the cobblers and place them in the hot stone shelter to cook. After thanking her in her language, he turns back to Allen, "Hey. That sounds like a good idea. I'm finished here; let's head on over to his tepee."

Allen and Doc walk over to where Running Water is seated in front of his tepee at the fire. He greets and welcomes his white-eye friends.

The three of them share stories of their escapades. They joke and laugh for hours. Before they realize it, the afternoon has grown to evening.

The Sioux tribe and Allen's posse gather together to share the fruits of the land; sharing gifts from mother earth to sustain their souls, while they enjoy the camaraderie and energy of the giving people of the Sandhills.

While Levi helps himself to a second dish of meat he remarks, "These people sure know how to throw a party."

Allen looks over at Levi and nods. "Yes, but this really isn't a party. It is a celebration of thanks. These people are very good hunters, not to mention the women folk are good cooks. I have learned much from them during the times I have come to stay with them."

Levi sits down next to Allen before saying, "You know Marshal, in the time I have known you I don't remember you talking about spending time with these people before."

Allen thinks about it, and then says, "Well, it all started when Doc and I were hunting along the shores of Spirit Lake. A winter storm came in. It was early for such a storm. We were trying to return to our camp, but you could not see through the blinding snow. In the storm, we got lost. While we looked to find a place where we could take shelter, we wandered into their village. The kind souls of the tribe took us in. They gave us food, clothing, and shelter. They kept us in the village until the weather broke and it was safe for us to return to our camp."

Levi looks around and sees why they are special people. "Well, that was quite neighborly of them."

"That's what we thought. For the first couple of days I was wondering when they were going to kill us. Doc was the opposite. He trusted somehow, as if he had the knowledge that these people were good people. From the first moment they helped us he knew they were people of the earth and sky, and peaceful loving people.

"Well, how was he so sure?" Levi asks.

Allen shrugs then answers, "Ya know. I really don't have a clue. I can tell you he wasted no time getting to know the tribe's medicine man. Those two became very close."

Levi looks over at Doc who is sitting with Flying Hawk, the medicine man. He can see that Doc is in deep conversation with the tribal medicine man. "Wow, that was some story. I will have to ask Doc about it sometime."

Upon the end of the meal, the dancing and singing commenced. The first ceremonial dance has all the men in the village singing. Allen takes the time to explain each dance and it's significances to Levi, Steve, Billy and the others from the group. "This is the dance to thank the spirits for a great hunt and the bounty for the year ahead."

"Do they have a dance for everything?" Steve asks.

"I am not completely sure. They do have one for those things that are most important to them," Allen answers.

****

Doc finishes his talk with Flying Hawk and walks over to speak with the Chief. "Running Wolf, our journey back to Lincoln is going to be hard. There are many evil and greedy white men out trying to send Allen and me to the Great Spirit. I would be grateful and honored if we could use some warriors of your tribe to help protect the man we need to return to Lincoln. Would you grant this request, my friend?"

"Doctor John, you are a respected friend. The answer to your request is yes. I give you my permission to take with you as many warrior braves as you feel you need."

"If it is all right with you I would like to take the same men who have been riding with us, if they are willing."

The tribal chief smiles at his treasured white-eyed friend. "That will be fine with me; do you expect more trouble along the way?"

With a half nod he tells the chief, "There could be. I will be able to confirm the answer to this question tomorrow." The two men laugh and share a good time, talking and watching the others singing and dancing. Feeling tired Doc decides to retire before the end of the celebration. He bids good night to Running Wolf and leaves his friend to retire to his tepee for a good night's sleep.

The next day Allen is up at sunrise, brewing a big pot of coffee. Levi is awakened by the smell of the fresh boiled coffee.

Levi steps out of the tepee, stretches, and takes in the view of the countryside. He walks up to Allen and asks, "Is the coffee ready?"

"Sure is," replies Allen. "I just poured myself a cup. It tastes pretty good if I have to say so myself."

Levi pours himself a cup and watches the steam rise from it. He takes a deep sniff from the cup. "Where's Doc? Still sleeping?"

"You know Doc; he has to be up with the chickens," Allen answers. "He left with Running Water a couple of hours ago to get in some fishing. It's something they enjoy doing together."

Allen and Levi enjoy their coffee in silence. Allen is mesmerized at the mist which rises from the lake each morning. It is always beautiful to watch. While he's stares in awe, he sees the two fishermen round the rocky outcrop. Pointing toward the rock he says, "Levi, look over there. There they are now and look at that mess of fish they have."

"Is there anything he doesn't do well?" Levi s asks.

"Not to my knowledge," Allen answers.

Doc joins the others around the fire while Running Water hands their fish to Little Bear.

Doc reaches for a cup and pours himself coffee. "Mornin' fellas. How are we feeling this morning?"

Levi responds first. "We're doing fine I'd say. After all, we all had a quiet night of sleep. I was just asking Allen where you were."

"Why, did you need something?" Doc asks.

"No, not really," Levi replies. "You weren't out here with the others, so I was just wondering."

Their morning chat is interrupted when the sound of thundering hooves can be heard getting closer to the village. Experience says it is the nighttime scouts coming in. The gathered men turn to see the scouts come over the rise behind them. They see it isn't just braves. The braves have two white men with them. As the braves ride up to the group, the gathered men notice the two white men are the two brothers that Doc and Allen sent ahead as scouts to Arrow Bluff.

Bud looks at Allen and pleads with him, "Marshal, will you please tell them that we're with you?"

Allen stands up to talk to the riders and motions for them that it is okay. "These boys were to meet us here. They are coming to give us information. Get off those horses and come tell us what you were able to learn in town."

The two men dismount their horses and walk over to the campfire. Fred reaches for a coffee cup while Bud starts telling of their trip to Arrow Bluff.

"First we just walked around town. When we walked past anyone, they just stared at us; so we went into the saloon. We figured we could just sit there and listen to everyone. That was the right idea. You guys were all them fellas could talk about. You were on everyone's lips. The guys were all bragging how they were gonna get the reward for you, and how they'd spend it. It seems that the reward has gone up on you guys."

Allen looks concerned, looking at Doc then back at the boys. "Really? Worth more? What're we worth now?"

Bud didn't say anything for a bit. Then with an expression of fear, he tells them, "Well, the rewards are now for dead or alive on all three of you."

"Three of us?" Levi interrupts. "You mean there's one on me too?"

"Nope," Bud replies. "Doc is worth twenty thousand dollars. The Marshal is worth ten thousand and Billy is now worth ten thousand as well."

Doc has an evil grin on his face. While he is listening, he pulls a pistol from his belt, spins the cylinder on his revolver, and then says, "Don't get any ideas of collecting them, Levi."

Levi is grinning as he looks at Doc. In a voice full of sarcasm he says to his buddy, "The thought never crossed my mind, friend."

Allen, still looking concerned about the news, asks for more information about what's in town. "How many gunmen are there waiting for us?"

Fred scratches his head while he calculates it. "Well, I can't be positive. We can only estimate it. But from what we could tell only about fifteen or twenty guys are out to collect."

Allen seems surprised by the young man's laid-back attitude about it all. "Only? That seems like enough to me; what do you mean by only fifteen or twenty?"

"From what we saw in Westhaven, we figured twenty would not be much of a challenge for you, Doc and Levi," Bud points out.

Levi starts laughing. "The kid's right, Allen. Twenty does not sound like too much trouble if we do it right."

"Just how do you plan to pull this one off?" Allen asks. "As I remember we got kind of luck the last time."

Levi gave Allen a playful swat on the arm and says, "Luck has very little to do with it. It was careful planning and execution that made the difference."

"If you say so," Allen comments. "I assume you have a plan for Arrow Bluff as well?"

"Not right now. But by the time we get there I will," Levi assures his worried associate.

By mid morning, the group decides it is time they break from the village and head to town. After exchanging farewells with Running Wolf, Running Water, and Flying Hawk, Doc saddles his mare and mounts for the ride. Since no one else has mounted, he shouts out to the guys, “Are you two ladies about done gabbing; or is the plan to stay here all day flapping your gums?”

“Now you listen here ,Doc, I was just trying . . . .”

Doc cut Levi off in mid sentence by saying, “I really don’t care. We need to get this show on the road. Now get saddled up and let’s get going.”

Everyone mounts up. They wave goodbye to the tribe and head in the direction of Arrow Bluff.

16

As they are leaving the Sioux village on Spirit Lake, Allen knows that they are in for one heck of a fight when they arrive in Arrows Bluff. He worries that 'the next gunfight' could possibly be the last one for one of them.

Doc rides up beside Allen and asks, "What has you all worked up?"

Allen shakes his head, takes a deep breath and replies, "John, it's just that we have been so mighty lucky up to this point. I'm concerned that our luck is going to run out."

"It won't run out," Doc assures Allen, trying to rebuild the man's confidence. "Not as long as I am around, it won't."

"What if something happens to you? What will we do then?" Doc reaches up and taps Allen's hat brim down in an effort to break his stress. "Allen, you worry too much. We need to face each conflict or trouble spot one at a time. Let's just deal with what comes our way when we cross paths with it."

"If you ask me, Levi seems a little over confident for my liking," Allen says, still not feeling better about their situation.

Doc sits up taller in his saddle and says, "When we get to town we'll assess the situation and deal with it then; for now just enjoy the ride."

For a while, Doc rides in silence next to Allen. Slowly and a little at a time he drops back to be able to talk with Levi and not bring more concern on to Allen. "I think Allen is worried about Arrow Bluff," Doc informs Levi. "He thinks that our luck is about to run out."

Levi nods, "I wondered what was up with him. He seemed a little off this morning when I joined him for coffee."

"I think I'll keep him close by when we get to town," Doc comments. "Hopefully it will help him feel more confident."

Stroking his horse's mane, Levi says, "That's a good idea, Doc. Just make sure he doesn't panic and get you killed."

"I think once we get there he'll be fine. I think the time to think of the 'what ifs' is working him up. But just in case, I will do my best to keep my head down."

The trail makes its way from atop the hills into a lush valley leading to a beautiful prairie. Descending, the Marshal and his posse are approaching the last of the bluffs. Levi is using his spyglass to see if there is danger in or around the bluff. While examining a group of thick trees, he sees something that doesn't seem right.

He jumps off his horse, grabbing his rifle on the way down. He yells out, "Doc, Allen, everyone; take cover!"

Everyone jumps off their horses and takes cover behind some rocks off the side of the trail. Little Bear takes the initiative to lead the horses back to the last hill for cover.

Before they have time to take a breath, bullets are flying through the air at an incredible pace. They are ricocheting off the rocks behind which they are trying to take cover.

Levi looks over his shoulder between shots and asks Allen, "Where did Doc go?"

Allen looks around and then replies, "I don't know; I thought he was right behind me."

A couple of shots later, Little Bear has crawled up to join them and is sharing in the return fire. Allen asks Little Bear, "Have you seen Doc?"

Between shots he answers, "Yes. He rode past me on his horse, heading around that hill."

Thinking to himself, he says out loud, "What exactly is he up to?"

With the clue Little Bear gave, Levi realizes where Doc went and what he is doing. Levi looks at Allen, gives him a sideways smile and a wink, and says, "Wait for it."

"Wait for what?" Allen asks. "What is he . . . ."

A large explosion interrupts Allen. It came from the backside of the bluff. They look at the face of the big rock to see rock, dust, vegetation, and men flying off over the front ledge of the bluff.

Levi stands up, swings his hat in the air, and yells, "Woo Hoo! For that!" Placing his hat back on his head he looks down at Allen. "I had a feeling that was what he was going to do. I knew he would have to try it out before too long."

While they are waiting for Doc to return, they hear gunfire coming from the area where Doc was heading for. Levi takes off running with Steve close behind. They make it to their horses as Doc and two of the braves are riding back to the posse.

Levi is grinning from ear to ear when he says to Doc, “I just knew you couldn’t wait to try out your new toy.”

Doc dismounts and replies, “Uh, well, I had to see if they were still good after sitting in that barn for who knows how long.”

Allen, still worried about their luck and timing asks, “I see that they still work fine. What was the gunfire all about?”

“Nothing really,” answers Doc. “There were a couple of guys left after the explosion. They just would not listen to reason. I gave them a couple of choices. But, it turns out they needed some convincing, so I had to help convince them.”

Levi laughs, then asks, “Are they convinced now?”

“Yep,” Doc answers.

Everyone mounts up and soon afterwards they are on their way to Arrow Bluff. They ride for about three hours after Doc’s discharge demonstration when they come upon a familiar farmstead. Before they reach the lane leading to the house and barn, the farmer runs out, waving to greet them.

“Hello Marshal, Hello Doc. I was hoping to see you pass by on your way. I need to warn you about the men waiting for you in Arrow Bluff.”

Allen smiles while looking down at the man from his horse. “We already know we have a few ‘new friends’ waiting to be our welcome wagon.”

"You fellas come in. I heard you were coming through. I thought it would be today. I'll have my wife get the rest of supper together and we'll feed you boys a good home cooked meal."

Allen dismounts and shakes the man's hand. "Well, that's awful nice of you, Robert. How did you know we would be coming by today?"

Walking with Allen, they lead his horse to the corral. "I was in town this morning and I overheard two men talking about having seen you two days ago in Westhaven and they were assuming you would be in Arrow Bluff yesterday. I knew that if you left when they said from Westhaven, you would stop at Spirit Lake for a visit. I just knew it would likely be today. Then I figured you might be coming by my place. Leona and I thought you might enjoy a home cooked meal. So we prepared one for you."

"Leona's cooking, now that sounds like a good idea," Doc comments. "We accept your invitation. It will be much better than trying to eat in town at the saloon, I'm sure."

Without saying another word, they climb off their horses and take them to the watering trough to let them drink. Then they leave the corral and head for Robert and Leona's kitchen.

Robert invites them to sit around the small table. Within no time, Leona has a huge platter of beef for the men. She turns around and sets an enormous bowl of fresh picked green beans on the table.

After Robert leads his guests in a prayer of thanks, Leona tells them, "Dig in boys, there's plenty more where that came from; we just butchered yesterday. I also have mashed potatoes and gravy. Just give me a moment and I'll have those on the table in a jiffy, along with some fresh baked biscuits."

“This sure smells good, ma’am,” Allen comments. “I haven’t smelled anything like this since we last ate Mary’s cooking before we left Lincoln.”

Doc was enjoying the meal. It reminded him of home. It was obvious that Leona and Mary both inherited the cooking gene from their Mother. “Leona, you have outdone yourself with this. I want to thank you. Really, thank you so much.”

Leona smiles at Doc, wipes her lips with her napkin, and says, “It was no trouble at all, John. After all of the times Robert and I came to visit my sister and you let us eat and sleep in your home, feeding you and these men is the least we can do.”

Doc smiles at her and says, “The next time you are in Lincoln visiting Mary and Sam, you know you’re welcome to sleep in the house just like always, even if I am gone.”

“Thank you, John. I will be sure to write Mary and tell her of your visit.”

The rest of the men are quiet. The only sounds are the knives and forks clicking against their plates. Leona stands up, surveying the food supply on the table. She tells the group of hungry men, just before she returns to the stove for more food, “There is plenty more if you want seconds. If you save room, I have fresh baked pie for desert. I had some cherries I put up last fall and I have been saving them for a special occasion like this”

“Thank you, Miss Leona,” Little Bear says. “I will make sure and leave some room for your pie, ma’am.”

Everyone finishes their meal and to Leona’s surprise they take their plates and cups to the pan of water in the kitchen. They even wash their own plates and cups for her. She smiles at Doc. She knows that these men are good men, and he is one of the best.

Allen is the last to finish. He gets up from the table and looks at both Robert and Leona in gratitude. "Thank you so much for the fine meal. Miss Leona, you never fail to put on a terrific spread. As much as we would like to stay and visit, we must be going. We have to get back on the trail if we want to make Arrow Bluff by nightfall."

"We really enjoyed the company, and I am glad everyone enjoyed the meal," Leona says as she walks to the door with Allen.

"Everything was just fine," Allen says, rubbing his belly. "You're a mighty good cook, Leona."

"We didn't finish our discussion about what I heard in town today. I need to tell you what I overheard at the Livery this morning," Robert says as he walks over to Allen, then continues, "Like I started to say, I needed to go see the blacksmith and there were two men in the Livery, talking. They were talking about how they were going to wipe you and Doc out. They also were discussing how there were many men all around town waiting for you."

Allen pats the elder man on the back and says, "Well, we will just have to be careful when we arrive."

"I know you boys are capable. However, I am worried about this one, Allen." Robert goes on, "These men could easily overpower your small group. If you want my opinion, it may be better for you to skirt out and around Arrow Bluff and camp out by the old fort. You know the one. It's deserted and it's up on a hill. It being where it is, you boys would be able to see anyone approaching for miles."

Doc and Allen exchange knowing glances. Allen pats the man's shoulder again. "You know, Robert? I have to say that's a great idea. I think we just might have to do that."

Leaving Robert to join his wife on the porch of their quaint and warm little Sandhills home, Allen and Doc join the others at the corral. Allen and Doc mount up and start off for the lane leading to the trail. Each man waves a big good-bye to Robert and Leona as they pass the porch. Doc rides up to the porch, shakes Robert's hand, and leans down to kiss Leona.

A little tear can be seen in the corner of her eye. "John, I am praying you and the others make it home safely. You watch out, okay?" Doc nods, turns his horse, and gallops off to catch up with the others. Doc looks back once more to wave goodbye from the end of the lane.

The band isn't far from the homestead when Allen suggests the change of direction. "Hey fellas, how about we head to the old fort and camp there for the night? We might just avoid some trouble."

"We are going to have to face the gunmen waiting for us sooner or later. So, why not tonight?" Levi asks.

"I just think it would be better to avoid as much confrontation as possible until we get Billy back to Lincoln," Allen shoots back.

"Allen, I am sure we're going to meet trouble no matter where we go," Doc says calmly. "Staying at the fort is a good idea and it's a reasonable plan. Why don't Levi, Little Bear, the braves, and I ride ahead and scout out what trouble lies ahead?"

Allen looks down at the ground to think a moment and then says, "Alright, but you guys be careful."

"Give us about thirty minutes' head start and we'll clear the way." Doc, Levi, Little Bear, and the braves head out to the abandoned fort, several miles to the Southeast of the main trail.

While they are riding around a large sand gully, Levi looks down into the wash out. He thinks to himself, *'How are there so many of these in the landscape.'* It amazes him how, when riding, they haven't been surprised by gunmen hiding out in one. He looks over the opposite way to Doc. "Do you have a plan to take the fort yet?"

"Yes I have, but the fort should be abandoned. I don't know if there will be trespassers inside. I think we need to wait until we can examine the situation. We may need to wait 'til dark for a sneak attack on the inhabitants."

"That sounds like it should work. We should be getting there around sundown," Levi concludes.

Doc waves Little Bear up. He speaks in native tongue to him. Little Bear nods and rides off with his braves.

"What did you just say to him?" Levi asks, surprised. "What the heck are you doing?"

Doc gives Levi a sideways grin. "Relax, relax. I have a plan. We need to attack the problem from all four sides. That's what I told Little Bear and the braves. They're going to split up and we are going to assault the fort from all sides."

Levi wipes his brow. "Oh all right; that sounds better. I thought maybe you were sending them back to Allen."

"It sounds like you are a little apprehensive about this one?"

Levi didn't raise his eyes to meet Doc's gaze. "Well, we are assaulting a fort here, Doc."

Doc throws his hand in the air and shrugs. "Not like it's the first time we have done this."

"Yes, that's true Doc, but that time we had a whole lot more people with us to do it," Levi points out.

"Don't worry, we'll be fine. Remember, we didn't have Little Bear and his braves with us that time either. Trust me when I say they are very good at what they do."

The sun has dropped behind the horizon, bringing on the welcomed cover of darkness. Doc and Levi are closing in on the fort. As they reach a small rise, they can see everything in and around the fort. They pause on the rise to survey the area.

"You see?" Doc asks as he points toward the fort. "We don't have to worry too much. At this point, all we have to do is make our way to the fires; the majority of the men will be around them. Now, let's get off these horses and make our way on foot to the fort." Tying their horses to a small tree, the two men make their way toward the fort.

The two were making their way closer to the fort when Levi puts his arm out to stop Doc and whispers, "Look over at that rock. When was the last time you saw smoke coming from a rock?"

Doc nods and replies, "I see it. I'll go right and you circle around to the left. Let's see if we can't take him without making any noise or shooting to let the rest of them know we are here."

Levi makes his way to the left side of the rock, while Doc moves toward the right side. The man behind the rock is asleep with a cigarette hanging out of his mouth. Levi knocks him over the head with the butt of his rifle to make sure he does not wake up. Doc comes around just in time to see the action.

"Nice shot there, Levi," Doc comments. "We need to make sure there are no more people out here on watch." They bind and gag the unconscious man.

Agreeing, Levi answers Doc. "Alright, I will go this way and you go that way," Levi instructs. We'll meet back here at this rock."

Doc and Levi soon meet back at the rock and Doc looks at Levi and asks, "Did you see anyone?"

"No, I didn't," answers Levi. "This must have been the only one."

Doc double checks the ties and gag on the man, and then says, "Now that this guy isn't going anywhere, Levi, let's go over the wall there." He points to a spot that looks like it should be easy to scale.

The two men are almost to the wall when Levi stops Doc with a "Psst." Doc stops to listen, "Just how are we supposed to get over that wall?"

Doc pats his rear hip and says, "I brought a rope. We'll lasso that pole there; then we can scale the wall and get over the top. When I get up, just follow me."

"Alright, get going; I'm right behind you," Levi says.

Doc throws the rope up, lassoing the pole on his first attempt. He gives it a pull to make sure it will hold and up he goes. When he reaches the top, he peers over and sees the gunmen have a sentry on the catwalk. Doc can see he is walking away from him. It allows Doc to carefully crawl over the top of the wall. He quietly creeps up behind the man, takes out his knife, and with one-hand covers the man's mouth while he slices his throat. Levi comes over the top and sees Doc slowly lowering the man onto the walkway. He looks over across the compound to witness that Little Bear and the braves have scaled the other three sides in unison. They too have overtaken their opponents. Doc begins giving hand signals to the braves. With everyone ready and in position, Levi is getting into position to make the assault on the men below in the fort courtyard. Doc lets his arm fall and arrows start to fly. Levi and Doc are picking outlaws off as fast as their repeating rifles will go. The outlaws, with nowhere to go for cover, drop in quick order. The surprise assault is over in just moments.

Little Bear and a brave climb down to seek out any outlaw left hiding. Doc, Levi and the other two braves stay on the upper walks to keep watch. After completing a room-to-room search, Little Bear gives the all clear signal. Doc and Levi climb down. The two braves remain above to watch for any undesirables approaching. One brave whistles, alerting the others he sees incoming riders. The men prepare for it to be more headhunters. Then the brave announces that it is the Marshal and the rest of the group. Little Bear and a brave open the doors to let them inside.

After exchanging welcomes, Allen looks down at Little Bear. "Any trouble taking the fort?"

Shaking his head no he tells the Marshal, "No, they moved things against the walls so when we came over the walls, they had nothing in the yard to hide behind."

"That was stupid," Allen says as he dismounts.

Little Bear nods. "Yes Marshal, we all thought the same."

Allen looks around for the others. "Where's Doc?"

Little Bear points up to the walkway. "He is up on the walk with Levi and two of my braves, keeping watch."

Allen climbs up the ladder to go visit with his pal. “Doc, do you think you made enough noise? We knew the fort indeed wasn’t abandoned, by the noise. We heard you three miles away.”

“Hey, partner. I’m sure you could hear it. After all we were out numbered about four to one. So our needing to shoot as many times as we did, went without saying.” Doc turns and looks back out across the dark landscape before continuing. “If you think you could do it better, then next time we’ll let you go in first.”

Allen holds up his hand to wave off the comment from his riding partner. “Doc, no, I ah… I did not mean that I could uh, well, you guys just frustrate me sometimes.”

“You have always been quick on the uptake, Marshal,” Doc shoots back.

Allen’s face turns amber in anger. He lets out a grunt saying, “One of these times Doc, you and I are . . . .”

Levi cuts the comment short by saying, “He’s going to slap you silly for getting him into all this, Doc.”

Doc climbs down the ladder, looking back up at the Marshal. “When we go into Arrow Bluff, you can go in first. Levi and I will back you up; how’s that sound?”

The braves are standing watch while the rest of the posse gets some sleep. As the sun is coming up, Levi climbs the ladder to relieve one of the braves.

When Levi sees several riders approaching, he yells down, “Doc, Allen, Steve! Hey everybody, we got company a’comin. I suggest you get a move on and get up here!” Everyone jumps up and in a hurry takes a place along the wall of the fort, on the walk, and on the ground below.

Doc runs up the ladder and asks, "What is it? What do we have comin'?"

Levi reaches into his rear waistband and pulls out his trusty spyglass. He points where he sees a cloud of sand dust on the horizon. "Look over there on top of the hill. I can't be positive, but it looks to be about fifteen to twenty riders."

Doc looks, only to see the dust cloud. He turns and looks back down at the Marshal, asking for his help, "Allen, will you go and get my saddle bags off my horse? Then carefully bring them up here?"

Levi smiles and looks over at Doc. "Are you thinking what I think you are thinking?"

"You throw, I'll shoot," Doc replies.

"That's what I thought you had in mind. I gotcha."

"What do you need these for?" Allen asks as he arrives with the saddlebags.

"Just watch and learn, Junior," Levi replies.

The men continue across the prairie, pistols and rifles drawn. Some of them yelling, others are shooting.

Doc sets his saddlebags down in front of Levi, and then gets himself into a good spot for aiming and shooting. He looks at Levi and asks, "Are you ready?"

Levi reaches into the pouch and replies, "I am ready if you are."

Doc points out to the prairie and says, "When they get to that bush, start throwing."

When the riders get to the appointed bush Levi starts throwing. He gives the first stick of dynamite a good heave. The stick lands almost exactly in front of the men. Doc shoots the stick just as it hits the ground.

That first stick goes off, completely surprising the group, throwing half the riders to the ground. Levi throws a second stick. Doc opts to shoot this one mid flight. The second explosion sends the remaining riders back from where they came, riding off like they had a tornado chasing them.

Levi screams as if they can actually hear him, "And don't you come back if you know what's good for you!"

Allen is laughing and doing a little jig. "I have never seen anyone ride that fast. That was the best plan you guys have come up with yet."

Levi smiles, and then says to Allen, "I suppose we need to head into Arrow Bluff. Those left in town will know we're here now. What do you think, Allen?"

"Well Levi, I think you have a point. Now we'll be too vulnerable on the trail with those guys headed back to town like a Kansas tornado. So I guess we're off to Arrow Bluff." After giving directions to all of the other men of the posse, the last to mount up is Doc.

Doc climbs on his horse and looks at Allen asking, "I suppose you want Levi and me to clear the way again?"

"If you don't mind," Allen replies. "We need to keep Billy safe."

Levi and his horse come to the front of the group. "It seems we discussed you scouting the trail ahead last night, Marshal."

Allen's face shows his shock from the comment that just crossed his ears. The color also drains from his face.

Before Allen has the chance to respond, Levi laughs and follows up with, "A scout's job is never done. Come on, Little Bear, we need to make sure Arrow Bluff is safe for Billy."

Levi and Doc take off to assure the safety of the others in their group. They follow the same route the men who tried their sunrise invasion used for the return trip to town. They agree that this trail would be the best, since they can take out any men left behind as they follow them.

While the ride remains uneventful, Levi asks, "Doc, I have to ask a kind of personal question of you."

"Oh, yeah? What do you want to know?" Doc takes a deep breath, preparing to hear the inquisition.

"Just who is this Audra person?"

Doc whips his head in Levi's direction and gives him a look of irritation. In a not so pleased tone, he says, "How did you find out about her? What did Allen tell you?"

"No, no, no. It was nothing like that." Levi answers. "I found the sweet smelling handkerchief and note in your saddle bag."

Doc leans over and reaches into his saddlebag, grabs the letter along with the handkerchief and puts them in the breast pocket of his vest. He looks over at Levi and says, "Did you read the whole thing?"

"No, I saw it when I was getting the dynamite out," Levi replies. "I shoved it in my pocket while we were throwing and shooting the dynamite. When we finished, I glanced at it as I was putting it back in the pouch. That was when I saw it was from someone named Audra."

"Well, it's kind of a long story," Doc shoots back.

Levi can tell by Doc's reaction that the note is important to Doc. "We have an hour or so before we get to Arrow Bluff, so let's hear it," Levi goes on.

Doc takes a deep breath, gazes off over the prairie, looking over the blowing grass that sparsely covers the sands of the territory.

He rides in silence for a few minutes before taking one more deep breath and starting the narration of his new beloved. "When Allen and I returned to Lincoln, we took care of our business in town and rode out to our ranches. When I came down after cleaning up for supper, stepping into the dining room, I find seated at the table a nice, lovely young lady named Audra. Mary invited her to supper. She and I talked well into the night. We discovered common interests in things like plays, books, and you know. In short we discovered each other and how much we have in common."

"That's it? You're kidding me, aren't you? Levi asks, wanting to hear more. "Come on Doc, there has to be more than that."

"We left it at that because I had to help Allen with this matter. When I get back we'll see where it goes."

"I still think you're holding back something, because no woman writes a note that touches a man like this did you when they just talk. So what haven't you told me, Doc?"

"Nothing," Doc replies. "I didn't have a lot of time to get to know her. When I get back, I hope to spend some more time with her, which I am looking forward to, I might add. After some time together, I'll let you know if there's anything between us that I need to tell you about."

They stop talking when Little Bear rides up and then reports, "I have seen some men up ahead; they don't look happy."

"Where are they?" Doc asks as he stops his horse.

"They're waiting at the bridge that crosses the Platte River, just outside of town," Little Bear replies.

“How many would you say there are?” Doc asks.

“I saw four men,” Little Bear replies. “Only two of them are on horseback.”

Doc nods and then points to two of the braves and says, “We need you two to go along the right fork of the river and cross back to the bridge.” He looks at Levi and Little Bear and continues, “Alright now, let’s send you and Levi in from the left side, but don’t cross the river before me if you can avoid it. As for me, I’m going to go straight in, go right through as though I’m going to cross the bridge completely unaware. I’ll be heading straight at them.”

“I see,” Levi comments. “Get them in a three-way crossfire and we should have the advantage; I like it.”

The men separate, and Doc heads for the bridge. Doc approaches the men on the bridge.

One of the men on the bridge speaks out, “Hold it right there, Doc. If you move a muscle my man over in the trees there,” he points to Doc’s left, the area Levi and Little Bear are sneaking through, “will put a hole in your head.”

Doc looks over at the trees where he points. At that moment, a man falls into the river, with his throat cut.

“Who, that man?” Doc asks, as Little Bear’s kill comes floating by.

The man looks at the floating body and sees Little Bear step out, pointing a rifle directly at his head. The man looks the other way toward the rocks and sees Levi holding a pistol to the head of one of his other men.

Doc chuckles. “Well, I see the roles have changed, so let me tell you of the options you have here. Option one: you go for your guns and we shoot you down and you get to float your way to the Missouri. Option two: you drop your gun belts and you two dismount your horses, and then all of you turn yourselves into the Sheriff."

The men unbuckle their belts, dismount, and walk over the bridge into town. Doc, Levi, and the braves escort the three men to the Sheriff's office where they quietly turn themselves in.

Doc, Little Bear, and Levi step out of the Sheriff's office. Levi looking toward Doc, says, "That was almost too easy."

Doc looks back through the Sheriff's window to see the three men locked up, and he smiles at their small triumph. "Yeah, I know what you mean. I can bet you this is not all we will see here in Arrow Bluff. I wonder where the Sheriff is though."

"What do you say? Let's go up to the saloon and wait for the others," Levi suggests as he starts walking up the boardwalk.

"Sounds good to me," Doc agrees. "We could use all the information we can get about the status in Eldorado."

When they step up onto the porch outside the saloon, a man confronts them. "Levi! I thought I told you if you ever came back here I would put a hole in your heart."

Levi smiles and says, "Well I am just passing through and I really didn't come looking for a fight."

"Too bad; you have found one!"The man shouts as he put his hand on his pistol.

Doc steps in front of Levi and announces, "Stranger, if I can quote a card player I once had the pleasure of playing with, 'I'll be your huckleberry.' You see, I did come looking for a fight."

"I have no quarrel with you, Gray; so step aside," the man shoots back.

"I beg to differ," Doc calmly says, trying to make his point. "You were with the gang who killed my wife and children."

The man looks at Doc like he is crazy. "That was a year ago. Besides all I did was hold her down."

Doc steps a step closer to the man and declares, "That's enough to get you dead. Now draw, you good for nothing S.O.B.!"

Levi tries to pull Doc back by grabbing his shoulder, before saying in a calm voice, "I realize you have your beef with him Doc, but he did call me out, so this is my fight. The thing is I shot his brother in a fight last fall."

Doc doesn't move an inch. He keeps his glare locked with the gunman. "Levi, I have thought of you as a mentor for some time now, but if you don't get the hell out of my way, you'll be waking up with a nasty headache."

Levi looks out of the corner of his eye at Doc. "What are you talking about, Doc?"

Doc draws his pistol and thumps Levi over the head. "Sorry Levi, but this man is all mine," Doc remarks as Levi falls to the ground.

Doc makes eye contact with the villain. "Draw, boy, or I will shoot you where you stand."

The man goes for his gun; he clears his holster as Doc draws and shoots the gun out of his hand, leaving a hole in the man's palm. Doc displays a dark evil grin. "You still have one gun left, and you better reach for it."

Again, the man goes for his gun and again Doc shoots it out of his hand with another hole in his other palm.

The stranger hits his knees; he looks at his pistols and contemplates picking one up again. He looks back at Doc's face. He reaches for one and Doc shoots the pistol and sends it skidding across the boardwalk. He looks back up at Doc. "Come on, Gray. Give me another chance. Have some mercy."

Doc walks toward the man and declares, "I'll show you the mercy you showed my wife." Doc stands directly above the man and uses his boots to push him up so he is kneeling on his knees. He makes the man look him in the face as he puts his pistol to the man's forehead. The man starts to shake. Doc pulls the hammer back, and the man starts to weep like a child.

Just as Doc is about to pull the trigger, Little Bear grabs him by the shoulder and whispers into Doc's ear. Doc stands there, not moving for a minute. Then he puts his gun away, turns, and says to Little Bear while poking him in the chest at the same time, "That's your one and only!"

Doc turns away and enters the saloon. Little Bear picks up Levi and carries him into the saloon. The stranger is still on his knees, weeping.

Little Bear puts Levi in a chair and throws water in his face, waking him up.

"What happened?" Levi asks.

Doc throws a shot of whiskey down, and then pours himself another. Holding up his shot glass, he says to Levi, "Your friend out there won't be holding anything for a while. I think his gun-fighting days are over."

"What did you do?" Levi asks.

Doc swallows his second drink. "I shot him in the hands, right after you passed out."

Levi rubs the back of his neck and says, "Passed out, my ass; just what did you think you were doing out there?"

"Collecting on an old debt," Doc replies.

Allen and Steve walk through the saloon doors. Allen asks, "Hey Doc, there is a guy out there with bloody hands, on his knees, sobbing; what gives?"

Doc looks toward Allen and gives him a grin, and replies, "He heard you were back in town and he is dating the girl at the hotel."

"Very funny Doc; what is really going on?" Allen asks, not amused by Doc's joke.

Doc slams his fist on the bar. "I shot him!" he shouts at Allen.

"Why do you feel the need to shoot someone in every town we come to?" Allen asks.

Doc steps over to Allen, grabs his coat lapels, and yells into his face, "He was one of the men who came to my ranch that day and killed my family!"

Doc releases Allen. Allen stands there for a second, absorbing the statement. "Do you want me to go out there and finish the job?" Allen asks.

Doc shakes his head. "No, his shooting days are over. He'll suffer for it now. I think we should just keep riding for Eldorado. That's a day's ride from here and it is still early."

Allen reaches and pats Doc on the back, trying to console his friend's frustration and grief. He tells his friend, "Sounds like a good idea to me. Let's hit the trail."

The men mount up and head out for Eldorado. Levi is still rubbing his head when he rides up to Doc. “I did not even see you draw; how did you get that fast?”

Doc smiles and replies, “I had a good teacher, and followed his instructions.”

Allen looks over at the two men and asks, “Are you going to tell me what happened to Levi?”

Doc simply replies, “We weren’t seeing things the same, so I solved our disagreement.”

“Just like you did with me in that saloon?” Allen asks.

Doc starts to laugh. “Yes, just like I solved our disagreement. Now, let’s get a move on so we can reach Eldorado today.”

17

The group of unlikely partners rides along an abandoned Oregon Trail route. Much to Allen's relief there is no trouble along this forgotten and little known trail. The trail crosses a small stream; it is at this junction Allen decides that the horses can use a break. He holds a hand up in the air saying, "Hold up; we need to rest the horses." The men get down off their horses and lead them to the stream.

Allen walks over to Doc and asks, "About how far is it to Eldorado?"

Doc points to a hill in the distance. "It is on the other side of that hill in the valley below. I sent Little Bear and the braves ahead to scout it out for us."

Allen squats down at the stream, cupping his hand to get a drink of water and wet down his head before saying, "Okay, that's good. We'll wait here until they get back, and then decide what to do with who or what is in the town of Eldorado waiting for us."

They wait for the scouts for a couple hours. Allen is beginning to worry about the amount of time that has passed. Allen is pacing the creek bank talking to himself, *'Experience says this ain't good. They're not gonna make it back in one piece; I just know it.'*

Bud and Fred notice dust coming from the hill that Doc pointed out earlier. They alert Allen and everyone stands ready because it may not be friendly riders. Allen and everyone are relieved to see Little Bear and his braves crest over the hill.

Little Bear rides up to Allen and Doc and reports, "I have seen many men in town. They are making the town look like they are preparing for a war."

Allen, looking concerned, asks, "What do you mean they look like they're preparing for war?"

Little Bear points to the hill and answers, "Buildings have windows boarded up. They have wagons turned on their sides in the street. They have placed tables on their sides in front of the stores. There are saloon tables on the roofs of two or three other buildings."

Doc smiles as he strokes his chin. "How many men would you say there are?"

Little Bear talks to the other braves in Sioux. After making their determinations he replies, "There are many men, Doc. It is like when we watched the Army Calvary pass through the bluffs by Spirit Lake. All of the gunmen seem to be working as a group. From what we could see, there can be as many as forty men."

"Did you say forty men?" Allen asks.

“Yes, but there can be more,” Little Bear answers. “There were men watching on all sides of the town’s borders. We could not get too close without being seen.”

Allen motions for the men to gather around, and then announces, “I think we’ll camp here tonight and move in on the town at first light.”

“If we wait until the sun comes up they’ll see us coming and pick us off as we enter town.” Little Bear points out.

“Leave that to me,” Doc replies. “I have a plan to make sure that does not happen.”

“Are you planning to let us in on this or are we just supposed to follow your lead?” Levi asks.

“I’ll tell you the details in a minute,” Doc replies. “Let’s wait to see what Allen has to say first.”

Allen looks over at Doc, shakes his head, and says, “No, actually why don’t you tell us what it is you have planned first. When we know what you are going to do, I’ll come up with a plan.”

“Okay,” Doc agrees, “I’ll need Levi, Little Bear and the braves. A couple of hours before sun up, we will sneak into town and take out the guards. This will allow us access to the areas like the roofs where the outlaws so graciously set up barricades for us. We should be able to provide cover fire for Allen and the rest of you from there.” Doc pauses for a moment, looks at Allen, and continues, “Well there, you go. In a nutshell, that’s my plan; now it’s time for yours.”

Allen breaks a piece of twig and starts scratching something in the dirt. “Here is a drawing of the town; what I think we should do is try to get to the jail first. There we will drop off Billy, Tommy, and Fred. I realize, boys, that you did nothing to be locked up; but this is not your battle. I feel the jail will be the safest place for you. We can hit each storefront one at a time. We can start with the store across the street from the jail. If we are slow and careful it should work for us, and then make our way up to the other end of town." Allen points to Doc and Levi, and then continues, "If you guys can keep them busy, we will be able to clear each store as we make our way up the street."

"We're going to be out in the open when we move from one store to the other," Steve is quick to point out. "Exactly how do you plan to do this without getting killed?"

Allen points at the various buildings to signify who is where, doing what, "Well, I thought if Doc and Levi with Little Bear and his braves can provide cover fire as we move ..."

"I understand that Doc and Levi are good shooters," Steve interrupts, cutting Allen off in mid-sentence. "But they can only keep a few of the outlaws busy at one time and that leaves a lot of them to shoot at us."

"If we did it as one group, maybe, but if we split into pairs, with one pair going in the front door and the back of each store simultaneously, we cut our chances of being shot considerably," Allen explains.

"Okay, that sounds great. Marshall you still have not answered my question," Steve points out.

"Any ideas how we can do this without getting everyone killed?" Allen asks Doc.

"Yep. It's not a problem, buddy," Doc assures Allen. "It's called dynamite and we have a lot of it. You guys get to the jail; get the boys locked up good and safe. Then I want you to head to the gunsmith across the street. You stay there and wait until we clear a few obstacles out of your way. Do you have anything to add, Levi?"

"Just be ready and wait for our signal," Levi adds. "When we signal, you move, because we're gonna raise some hell. They will have our racket to worry about, and they won't be concerned about you."

Allen takes his bedroll from his horse, unrolls his blanket, and then looks to all the men, "That sounds good to me. Now, let's be sure the horses are tied and secured for the night. I think everyone should turn in and get some rest. After all, we want as much done before daybreak as we possibly can." He throws his saddle down at the end of his blanket; he stands up pointing at a couple of deputies. "Steve, why don't you grab one of the deputies and take first watch? I'll have someone relieve you in a few hours." The rest of the men pick a spot of prairie and call it a night.

Doc wakes up about four hours before sun up. He walks over to warm himself by the fire. Wes, who is sitting guard, says to him, "I made the coffee about an hour ago. Want a cup?"

Doc sips on his coffee, then grabs his saddle and throws it on his horse. It isn't long and the others start to rise and pack up their gear.

Levi is cinching up his saddle when he says to Doc and Little Bear, "Are you guys ready to even the odds a little?"

Doc mounts his horse, then answers, "Yep. Okay boys, this is a big one for us. Let's slowly make our way around Eldorado so we can try to hit all the men guarding the town at once. It is important to be as quiet as a mouse in church. We just can't afford to wake anyone. When we get that done, we will have to get to the rooftops and take care of those men. Then, with Allen and the boys, we hit 'em like they've never been hit before."

"Well, It's been a pleasure working with you gentlemen," Levi says, tipping his hat to his partners

Doc gently puts his spurs into his horse. "Last one to the saloon buys."

Levi swats his horse's hindquarter to catch up. When he gets beside Doc, he looks at his friend and says, "I'll hold you to that, Doc."

They part company and ride off in opposite directions.

Doc approaches a grove of trees. He dismounts and ties his horse to one of the trees and creeps through them. As he thought, there is a man standing watch just on the other side. He watches and waits for the man to walk in front of him. When the man finally comes toward him, Doc steps out of the bush and, without a sound, grabs the man from behind. Placing one hand on his forehead and one on his chin, he twists the man's head around, snapping his neck and taking him to the ground. Doc then drags the man into the tree line.

As Doc emerges from the trees, he sees a man walking toward him. The man is carrying a rifle and Doc finds himself in an interesting position. Just then the man asks, "Joe, is that you?"

In a muffled voice Doc replies, "Yep"

"Have you seen anything?" the man asks, standing several yards away.

Doc answers, "Nope, not a thing."

The man starts to walk closer to Doc's position. Doc reaches into his boot and pulls out his hunting knife. As the man approaches, Doc hurls his knife into the man's neck and the man drops without a sound. Doc drags him into the trees and proceeds into town.

Levi is already off his horse and crawling up behind two of the guards who appear to be in the middle of an argument.

"If those idiots come into this town, I am going to gun them down no matter what I have to do."

The other man says, "Yeah? Well, I'm waiting for the Marshal. It is just a bonus for me that he has a bounty. That no a'count slept with my wife and he's going to pay by seein' my pistol in between his eyes!"

Levi quietly stands up from around the corner of the livery barn where they are patrolling. He reaches out and puts a hand on each of their shoulders, asking them, "Is everything all right here, fellas?"

Startled by Levi, the men jump. The angry husband says, "You almost scared me to death. Yes, so far everything is quiet. Are you here to relieve us?"

Levi still has his arms around the men and replies, "Something like that." He grabs each man by the hair and smashes their heads together, knocking them out cold. "Consider yourselves relieved," he says to them as he drags the two men in to the livery, gags them, and ties them to a post in a stall.

Little Bear and his braves have succeeded clearing out the men posted in the other areas. With all their tasks completed, it is time to go vertical. Levi quietly goes up the stairs and finds two outlaws on the roof, asleep. He makes his way to the first one and quietly puts him to sleep for good. Levi then makes his way over to the second and gives him a real close shave. He then takes his place on the roof where he can provide cover fire.

Doc slips onto the roof of the gunsmith's building where he finds two men, one asleep and one at the far end overlooking the town. He climbs on to the roof, grabs the man by the neck, and with a snap he breaks the man's neck. Doc turns to the sleeping thug and pulls out his knife, using it to cut the man's throat.

Little Bear takes his place with one of the braves on a roof. The other two braves find themselves a cozy overlook. All they can do now is to wait for sunrise. The small band sits and watches from their perches, anticipating the coming morn.

It isn't long after the sun starts to peek over the vast sandhills that Doc sees movement in the street below. Now that there is enough light, he can scan the rooftops. He can see that his associates are the only ones on the rooftops. He smiles, knowing this first phase is a complete success.

Little Bear is on top of the hotel with one of his braves. As soon as they are finished checking the views from the rooftop, they start tying dynamite to some of their arrows.

Levi takes advantage of the additional ammo and firepower. He places the pistols and rifles of the men he's eliminated around the rooftop in strategic positions. He then checks them and insures they are fully loaded and ready for the upcoming battle.

Doc can see Levi's activities. He likes the idea, so he decides to follow suit. Now they are ready. The only thing to do is to wait.

The sun is coming up over the horizon and there is more movement on the boardwalk below. Little Bear, the braves and Levi look over to Doc, waiting for the signal to begin the sunrise assault. Doc holds his hand up to say, 'wait.'

Doc is evaluating the goings on below. He happens to look up the street to see a couple of outlaws come out of the church. He can't quite make out what is happening inside, so he pulls out his trusty spyglass in an effort to get a better look. He can see a large number of people inside. It's the majority of the townsfolk. He can see one or two gunmen standing guard inside. Doc smiles, thinking to himself, '*This is even better. We'll have less to worry about now. These folks will be safe and we won't have to worry about hurting innocent bystanders.'* He continues to look through his spyglass at the hills beyond the town. He can see Allen and the others on a far hill. He figures they are only twenty minutes or so from town.

Allen and the posse have just come over the hill, the last hill between them and town. Allen looks over at his remaining deputies. Okay guys, it's do or die time. He looks over at Steve. "You take two men and go to the gunsmith's building. I will take Billy and the boys to the jail." Then he looks at Wes, "You can accompany me and these boys to the jail." He stops his horse. "Okay boys, when we get up there to that cattle pen, we split up. Once we reach our spots, we will work our way through town from there."

Steve looks back at Allen. "I hope Doc, Levi, and the Braves took care of their part of the plan. "Cuz if they didn't, it's going to be a short and one sided assault."

"I didn't hear any shooting or explosions; I'd say they were successful," Allen is quick to point out.

Steve adjusts himself in his saddle, preparing for the next step of the plan and says to Allen, "For our sake, I hope so."

As the men get closer, they can hear and see that the town is full of activity. They reach the pen; they stop and look toward town. Even at that distance, they can see the rogues and scoundrels working feverishly to be the one to collect the bounties on Billy, Doc, and Allen. They see them taking cover behind wagons and tables which they have set up on the street and the boardwalk in front of the stores.

Allen looks at his men. He is worried about them. He knows they didn't sign on for the danger they are about to face. He adjusts himself in his saddle, sits up straight, looks toward his faithful deputies, and says, "Okay, it's time. Let's ride boys."

Doc watches as Steve and his group head to the gunsmith's shop. He watches for Allen to get the boys safely locked down. The deputy accompanying Allen peeks out the front entrance of the jail. Once he is sure it is safe to exit, he begins walking up the boardwalk with his back against the wall. That is the sign Doc needs to know; it's time to take out the unsuspecting men below.

Doc makes eye contact with Little Bear and Levi. He raises his hand and throws it forward. The invasion begins. Little Bear has his brave light the fuse on a dynamite loaded arrow. Little Bear pulls back on the bow and aims the arrow down at a table on the boardwalk where three men have taken cover. The fuse burns down and the dynamite explodes, sending parts flying. The fuse was short enough that the dynamite explodes almost instantly on impact. Glass flies from the windows of the storefront. Wood pieces from the porch and the table fly in every direction.

Men in the street and other areas take cover immediately and start firing at will. They keep firing, although none of them know where or what to shoot. A big and tall man in a large black hat steps out of the telegraph office. Doc recognizes him immediately.

The big man yells out, “Stop shooting! Wait until you have something to shoot at!” Just then, the brave lets another arrow fly and another explosion exterminates two more bounty hunters, causing more shooting and bullets to fly everywhere.

The man steps out again. “I told you idiots; stop firing until you have something to shoot at!” He steps out to the edge of the boardwalk and leans against the rail. He commands, “Okay, I want you cowards to step out to the center of the street and show yourselves!”

Doc stands up and leans over the edge of the roof. “That’s you, ain’t it, Walter?”

The big man hears where the voice is coming from and looks up to see a shadow looking down at him. “Yes. But who the hell are you?”

Doc stands straight up with his arms out stretched, exclaiming, “Your target!”

At the end of his statement comes a single rifle shot. Levi’s perfectly placed shot places a new hole in the man’s head. He drops into a crumpled heap in the street.

Gunfire resumes and Doc’s rooftop is peppered with fire coming from every man on the street. The braves shoot a few more exploding arrows into the street below. This technique keeps the gunmen running for cover. Their continual movement from place to place is making Doc and Levi’s efforts to drop them in their tracks much easier

Allen is standing in the passageway between the jail and the diner. He looks out across the street to see Steve already engaged in the battle. He joins Wes under the ledge where he has taken cover. They peer out and start to fire at the men on the boardwalk, taking out one at a time.

Steve is right in the thick of the firefight with both pistols blazing. He runs out of bullets so he ducks back inside the gunsmith's shop and grabs all of the ammo he can carry. He goes to the back of the shop, and with the other deputy, goes out the back door. The deputy gives Steve cover fire while he runs with the ammo to help Doc with his rooftop shooting. The deputy returns to the front of the store to continue the street level battle.

Steve pops his head over the roofline. He smiles as he announces, "Your back up has arrived." Doc doesn't answer; he only nods. Steve steps over and asks Doc, "What can I do to help? I mean, besides shoot?"

Doc is reloading and returning fire. "If you'd reload as I empty, that'd speed things up for us." Steve makes his way on his hands and knees over to Doc. He puts down the boxes of shells and starts reloading. Doc returns to the gun battle. As he reaches back for a fresh rifle he asks, "Steve, did you have any trouble getting into town?"

Shaking his head as he reloads the empty rifle, he answers, "No. With you guys doing all that exploding and shooting, they have no clue that we are here at all."

Taking a pause between shots Doc looks over at Steve and says, "Well, I think they know we're here now!" He winks at Steve and continues to return fire. Steve throws Doc a reloaded rifle and Doc tosses Steve the empty one. Doc looks over at the rooftop where Little Bear is still shooting arrows loaded with dynamite.

Little Bear sees two men shooting at him from a second story window of the boarding house. He draws back his bow, his brave lights the fuse and he lets the arrow fly. The fuse falls out in flight, the arrow sticks in the window frame just below the outlaw. The man looks down, laughs, and continues to shoot at Little Bear.

Doc sees the arrow still sticking in the sill with the dynamite attached. He takes aim at the dynamite and fires. The bullet is a direct hit, igniting the dynamite; and the top half of the building is gone.

Doc smiles as he looks at the spot where the outlaw used to be in the window and says aloud, "I bet you're not laughing now." Then He laughs.

Steve looks over at Doc and says, "Doc, man, you're a cold S.O.B."

"Thanks, I am glad you finally noticed," Doc replies. "Now if you don't mind, how about not talking; just keep reloading."

Little Bear stops flinging arrows long enough to exchange a glance with Doc. He gives Doc a big smile and a thumbs-up. Doc gestures the same in return.

Doc looks back over his shoulder at Steve. "Would you mind handing me a stick from over there?" Steve grabs a stick of dynamite and hands it to Doc. Doc lights it and tosses it into the wagon, set against a building across the street, where five men are hiding. It explodes, taking the wagon and the men with it. "I've had just about enough of you five. Hope you have a blast!" Doc comments.

Doc looks down to see Allen running from the passageway next to the jail and up the boardwalk to the telegraph office. Giving Allen cover fire as he moves to the door, Allen is able to jump through the telegraph door, pistols blazing. Once he is assured the room is clear, Allen turns around and reappears in the doorway, shooting at an outlaw hiding behind a barrel across the street. The man behind the barrel makes a run for it. Allen's bullet finds its mark and the man goes down face first on the boardwalk.

Levi looks over at Doc, holds a stick of dynamite above his head waving it, and points to a group of outlaws behind another wagon in the street. Doc smiles, and puts the rifle into shooting position and nods. Levi lets the dynamite fly. Just as it is right above the band of men, Doc shoots, exploding the dynamite and ridding the town of six more bad men.

Allen looks back up at Doc and motions with his pistol to the building next door. Doc throws two sticks of dynamite, one in the middle of the street and one in front of the building two doors down. Doc then motions with his rifle for Allen to go. He then shoots the stick in the middle of the street and when Allen starts to move, Doc then shoots the second stick. Allen dives in the door, and shots are fired. Allen once again safely reappears in the doorway, and fires across the street at another outlaw.

Just when it looks like they have control of the fight, twelve more outlaws can be seen riding in from the far end of town. The men are creating their own cover fire, as each of them fires a pistol from each hand, aiming and shooting at the rooftops. They get to the front of the saloon and dismount their horses in an effort to run inside. One of the braves across from the saloon fires an arrow into the boardwalk as five of the men are trying to head into the saloon. The men see the arrow too late. They go flying off the boardwalk as the dynamite explodes.

The shooting seems to slow, if only for a moment. Then a single shot can be heard. The target of the bullet is one of the braves on the roof with Little Bear. The impact of the shot causes the brave young Sioux warrior to fall from the roof to the dusty street below. Levi, Doc, and Little Bear stop shooting and look at their fallen ally. The moment is cut short by another flying bullet whizzing through the air.

Seeing the young brave fall causes something to overload in Doc's head. The man snaps; without any cover-fire Doc heads down into the street. He starts shooting at the villain, and then starts down the street gunning down outlaws as if they are bottles on the fence rail on his practice range back home. His shooting causes the outlaws to head for cover faster than his pistols can shoot. Doc runs out of ammo so he dives behind one of the wagons to reload. Levi and Steve continue to provide cover fire as Doc and Allen work on cleaning up the street.

Doc looks across the street at Allen and yells, "Okay, this is enough horsing around! I say let's clear this town of the scum that has taken it over!"

Allen leans his head out of the doorway he's ducked into. He looks at Doc to respond to the acclamation, but is stopped by the vision he sees. The expression upon Doc's face is startling to him. It is an expression more merciless than he has ever witnessed. The sheer blackness in the man's eyes is giving way to an utterly evil man within. Allen shutters at the sight. All the while he is thinking to himself, *'I never want to see that face again.'* Allen comes back to reality and shouts back to Doc, "I'm ready if you are."

With that response, Doc jumps up, steps out from behind the wagon, and starts picking off outlaws wherever they are hiding. Walking and shooting as he goes, Allen is firing as fast as he can, but Doc downs everyone he aims at before Allen can even pull his trigger. As Doc is working his way back to the other end of the walkway, he nears the general store. Allen signals him that there are three men inside. He nods back and indicates he is going in. He jumps through the general store's glass window, much to the surprise of the men inside. Doc lands on his feet. Within his reach is one man. He reaches for his knife and inserts it directly into the man's chest. Doc reloads his pistols, takes the dead outlaw's pistols, and sticks them in his belt behind his back.

Knowing there are two more men, he starts his silent search of the store. He hears a noise from the rear counter of the store. On his way to the noise, he finds two more pistols. He picks them up, looks to see they are loaded, sticks them in the front of his gun belt and continues toward the storeroom. The other two men have already snuck out the back door.

Allen has been watching the storefront for several minutes now. He has not heard a single gunshot; so he reloads, making sure he has all twelve rounds. Just as fast as his two legs can take him, he heads for the store to help, or even worse, save Doc. He jumps in through the already broken window. He announces his entrance as he lands on his feet, only because he didn't want to be on the receiving end of Doc's aim. "What's the plan, Doc?"

Doc steps out of the storeroom. He is rolling his pistol's cylinder to make sure it is fully loaded. Clicking the cylinder closed, he says, "I am going to walk through the front doors of that saloon and kill every no-good murderous SOB in there."

Allen steps in front of him. "Don't you think we ought to wait for Steve and Levi?"

Pushing Allen aside, Doc says, "I tell you what; you wait for them. I'll clear the way." Doc slowly walks out of the store to the saloon. He has his back against the wall as he slides slowly toward the doorway, going toward the corner window of the saloon. He peers in the window. A shot is fired at him, makeing him jump back. He looks up and over at Little Bear on the roof across the street. Little Bear has his bow pulled back and is looking at the corner of the saloon. He lets an arrow fly just as a man comes around the corner, stopping him in his tracks. Doc looks up and gives another nod, acknowledging a job well done. He tries to peek in again. He can see at least six men on the first floor, taking cover behind overturned tables, and another five on the upper balcony. He can see another one behind the bar. Doc looks back to Little Bear and makes a motion for Little Bear to shoot a stick over the saloon so that the explosive lands behind the building. Little Bear nods and grabs an arrow, lights the dynamite and fires over the saloon so that it lands in the alleyway.

The explosion is just the distraction Doc needs. He breaks through the front doors. Doc sees things like they are in slow motion. He is shooting both his pistols at the same time, working the room from outside in and bottom to top. Outlaws drop with every shot, before they can even get a shot off. After Doc runs out of rounds in his pistols, he lets them drop. He reaches into his belt for the pistols he found in the store. He starts taking quick aim at the men on the balcony and those coming out of the upstairs rooms overlooking the street. Shot by shot Doc continues with the town's cleansing. After all of the men are dead, Doc scans the room to see if any of them can still pose a problem. Two men come running in the back door, guns a'blazing, only to be blown back out by the fire from a shotgun Doc picked up from one of the dead men in the saloon.

Levi, Steve, and Allen come busting in the saloon together, shoulder to shoulder, guns drawn. There they stand, watching Doc behind the bar, pouring them a drink. He holds up his shot of whiskey and says, “Well, it’s about time you three showed up.” He drinks his shot, and then slams the empty glass on the bar. He looks at Levi and says, “I am truly sorry, Levi. I do believe it was quite rude of me not to leave you anyone to play ‘outlaw games’ with.”

The three holster their weapons and step up to the bar. Levi is laughing at Doc’s comment. “That’s all right, Doc. I do believe I had enough fun outside to last me.” Levi pauses, crosses his arms, and then raises a hand to rub his chin as he ponders the thought in his head. “Oh I’d say at the very least, I have had enough fun to last me twenty-four hours.”

The four of them start to laugh. Little Bear and his braves cut the moment of humor short as they come running through the doors. “I hope you’re having a fine time here but it is not over. You need to know there are ten men riding into town from the west. They are taking the exact same trail as Allen and the others did on their way here. I think they are tracking us.”

Allen slams down his shot glass, throws a hand into the air, looks at the ceiling, and says, “Will this never end?”

Levi pulls out his pistol and begins spinning it in his hand, like the trick shooters do in their routines. “I sure hope not. Whaddaya say, Doc? Let’s go out there and see if they have the stones to face us.”

Doc walks over to pick up the pistols he discarded in the saloon fight. After reloading his four guns, he places them back in his holster and belt. “Well Levi, what are we waiting for? Let’s go and deal with this in short order. Who knows, it could be fun.”

Allen is shaking his head and looking at the two men. “What you two call fun is what I call crazy. You actually want the conflict. If you two are set on getting these guys, at the least don’t go and get yourselves killed. Remember, you are still required to help me to escort our prisoner, Billy, back to Lincoln.”

Doc looks over at Levi, gives him a wink, and with a grin on his face says to Allen, “Well Allen, after all, they did track us all the way here; and I would hate to disappoint them. Let’s have another shot. Then we’ll see to this.” After Doc and Levi down their shots, Doc looks at Allen and says to him, “We’ll be right back.” He motions for Levi to come with him, and they head out the door.

Levi and Doc walk out of the saloon and into the street. They both stand ready as they watch the men ride up at the far end of Main Street. The men stop by the gunsmith’s shop. Each dismounts and makes the rest of the distance up the street on foot. There is not a single sound heard in the town. There are no voices whispering in the shadows. No one is shooting. The ten men walk up the street with their hands ready at their sides.

Doc and Levi stand waiting for the approach. Levi leans over toward Doc, making certain not to lose sight of the men. “I will take the five on the left and you take the five on the right.”

“Why don’t I take them all? And you just relax and have a seat?”

Levi shakes his head. “No, not hardly, my friend. You had all the fun by yourself in the saloon. I am not going to let you have all of the fun out here too.”

"Alright, I guess I can share some of the action."

The men stop about twenty feet from Doc and Levi. A couple of them push back their coats to reveal their guns. A tall man in the middle begins to speak, "I am Colonel Jefferson Pitts of the Pinkerton Agency. We are here to take Billy. Now move out of the way and we might let you live."

Levi looks at Doc, then looks at the Colonel and comes back with, "Well Colonel, that's mighty nice of you to give us this opportunity to hand over our prisoner. However, I believe that we will just keep our prisoner with us. It would alleviate you of any burdens or additional duties."

Pitts points a finger in the air as if he is pointing a finger into Levi's chest. "I don't know who you think you are, boy, but I'm telling you if you don't move and hand over the boy; I will personally end your pathetic life!"

Levi gives a deep evil glare to the Pinkerton. Glancing back and forth at the line of men, he introduces Doc and himself. "I think before this confrontation goes further you gentlemen deserve to know who it is you intend to send to hell." Levi reaches to his hat brim and takes hold of it, tipping it slightly. "How do you do, gentlemen? My name is Levi Calaway." Removing his hand from his brim, he motions toward Doc, "And this fine gentleman to my right is John, or as you would know him, Doc Gray."

The men begin to look uneasy, knowing the reputation of Doc and his friend Levi. Pitts is tapping the ivory handled pistols. "I really don't care who you are. I'm telling you both, you have one minute to make your decision."

Levi looks at Jefferson's hands as they tap the ivory handles of his pistols. Speaking softly he shares with Doc, "You know, Doc, those ivory handles would look quite nice on my pistols."

Doc mocks Levi. "I think that's just what you need to make your guns look a little more 'big city.' I think I remember hearing somewhere that those handles are what all the Marshals and Sheriffs back east have on their pistols."

Levi shoots a look at Doc. Doc just winks back. Levi looks back at the Pinkerton in charge. "Well Mr. Pitts, I don't think we'll be giving in. So why don't you men just ride out of town now? Oh, and you can just leave your pistols right there where you are standing, Colonel." All of the men tense up. Jefferson's tapping gets faster. "And if you don't want to cooperate peacefully, my friend and I can just gun you down right here."

Jefferson, not going to be intimidated by Levi, pushes up his hat brim just a bit. He takes in a deep breath and, letting it out, says, "I guess I will be the one to end the career of Doc Gray and his associate, Levi."

Doc sweeps his black duster back behind his holsters. "Jefferson, are you going to draw anytime soon or are you just going to keep flapping your gums and bore me to death?"

Jefferson waves a hand toward Doc. "In due time, my friend, in due time. Just wait a little bit and I will send you to join your wife and kids."

The feeling inside begins to rise to a boil within Doc. In less than a solitary breath, Doc draws his guns and starts firing. In a flurry of gunfire, the Pinkertons begin falling as fast as you can blink. Each one of the men creates a cloud of dust as he hits the street. After the ninth man falls, Levi is still trying to clear leather. That's when Doc takes aim at

Jefferson, shooting both pistols from his hands. Doc looks over at Levi grinning. "I left a little fun for you."

Levi, re-holstering his pistols, tells his partner, "Thanks Doc, really, thanks, but shooting an unarmed man is not exactly what I had in mind."

Having heard the commotion, Allen comes running out of the saloon and toward them, chambering a shell in his lever action as he approaches. Levi shouts, "Don't shoot him; he is not armed." He turns to face Allen. "You need to go back into the saloon and let the big boys handle the dirty work."

Allen stands almost toe to toe with Levi and exclaims, "I am trying to keep Billy alive! If this is going to go on like this, someone else needs to go down and help the deputy in the jail protect him, in case someone gets past you guys!"

"Well, go in and protect him then. Look Marshal, we don't know if there are any outlaws left in town. You need to send Little Bear up to the Livery to make sure there are no outlaws up there. Then, we need to think about the people in the church. We don't know if they are still being held hostage." Allen turns around and walks back to the saloon to direct the others to follow through.

Doc hasn't taken his eyes, or his guns for that matter, off Jefferson, through that whole exchange with the Marshal. Glancing Levi's way, he comments, "Don't you think you were a little hard on the Marshal?"

Levi takes a few steps toward Jefferson, shaking his head as he answers. "No, not hardly. We need to snap him out of the attitude he seems to have, and this may be the way to do it." He reaches for Jefferson's hands and ties them together.

Doc lowers only one gun, holstering it. "But by belittling him?"

Levi leads Jefferson over to a hitching post and ties his hands to it. "Frankly Doc, I don't know what else to do. His attitude has made him become more of a problem instead of a partner or an asset."

Doc steps over closer to Jefferson, still holding a gun on him. "I think he's a little afraid of dying on this job. It's a big one you know? And having or feeling a little fear is not always a bad thing."

Levi squats down over Jefferson's ivory gripped pistols. He picks them up, admiring them before putting them in his waistband. "That may be so Doc, but only as long as it doesn't affect your job or decision making."

Doc adjusts his hat while looking Levi squarely in the eye and says, "He will be fine. Levi, you just leave the Marshal to me." He redirects his attention back to Jefferson. "Now Jefferson, I have a job for you. I want you to ride to Avoca and give this message to Sutton. I want you to tell him: 'I'm coming and hell is coming with me.' Think you can handle that?"

Levi is shocked. He asks, "You are going to leave this piece of crap alive?"

Doc holsters his pistol and reaches for the ropes tying Jefferson to the rail. "Yeah, I need someone to deliver the message to Sutton, and who better than a conquered Pinkerton to tell him that all of his plans have failed?" They walk the Colonel back to his well-outfitted horse. Doc unties his hands and informs him, "We'll be keeping those pistols of yours. You just get on your horse and ride before I change my mind."

Jefferson mounts his chocolate steed. Sitting atop he looks down at the two lawmen and points at Doc. "This is not over, Gray. Trust me;

you'll get yours, and soon. You should have killed me when you had the chance because that was likely your last."

Doc just smiles at him. "If you are stupid enough to be in Avoca when I get there, I will grant you your wish." Jefferson slaps his horse with the reins and rides out of town.

Levi pulls out Jefferson's pistols and with a smile spins both pistols, playing trick-shooter again. With a big smile he looks at Doc and says, "Nice balance. I think I will keep these, after all. At first it was a joke, but they are remarkably nice."

"I see what you're thinking there, partner," Doc agrees. "I think I'll hang on to the ones I acquired in the saloon as well. You never know when an extra few pistols will come in handy."

"I think from now on I'll use these as my primary guns," Levi comments, still playing with the Colonel's pistols like a little kid with a new toy. "I'll save mine as my backups. Now let's go into the saloon and have Allen pour us a whisky or two."

Taking the lead to the saloon, Doc says, "Sounds good; all this shooting has given me a powerful thirst."

Levi and Doc walk back into the saloon and belly up to the bar. Levi looks at Allen behind the bar, "Hey barmaid, how about a shot and a beer for me and my men?"

Allen gives him an angry glance. "How about you get it yourself, funny-boy?"

Levi steps around the bar and grabs a bottle of whiskey and a glass. After pouring himself a shot, he holds it up toward Allen and replies, "Alright, I'll pour my own. But the next time gun play starts up, Doc and I will guard the prisoner and you can clear the way."

To Levi's surprise, Allen shoots back, "That sounds fine with me."

Levi grabs a bar cloth and starts mimicking a bartender by wiping a glass. He looks at Doc. "So what will it be, stranger?"

Doc grins and replies, "Just give me a beer, Levi."

Everyone sits around the saloon after dragging the bodies of the fallen outlaws to the undertaker's shop. They are enjoying the quiet and a drink. When the saloon doors fly open, they respond with lightening speed, drawing weapons and jumping to their feet. They replace their weapons almost as quickly when they realize it is the Mayor followed by many of the townspeople. They are all overjoyed at the peace now restored to their small town.

The Mayor walks up to the Marshal, extending his hand for a handshake. "I really don't know how to thank you, Marshal; we were afraid those men were going to kill us all."

Allen shakes his hand and says, "You should not have any more trouble from those men, and I think when we leave all of your problems will be behind you."

"I sure hope so," The Mayor replies." We are not used to this kind of violence, but I am a little worried about how we are going to rebuild our town."

Doc gives the man a slap on the back and says, "Don't worry about that; I am sure I know where you can get a loan to rebuild."

"Thanks Doc, but I am not sure we would have enough money to repay a loan."

"Did I say loan? What I meant to say was I will make sure you get the money to rebuild your town, Mayor."

"Well thank you Doc, but where are you going to get that kind of money?" The Mayor asks.

"Don't you worry about it, mayor; I know a man who is about to feel very generous," Doc replies.

Levi comes out from behind the bar, bringing out a deck of cards. He sits down at a table and starts shuffling. He indicates to the Marshal to sit with him, saying, "Well Allen, I think we should have clear sailing into Lincoln."

"I don't know about that, Levi," Allen says. "I think there will probably be another attempt or two. I think when we hit the hills between here and Lincoln with the tree and bush cover and the dugouts in the rocks, there are some good spots for an ambush. And that Pinkerton, Colonel Pitts; I don't think he's going to take this lying down."

Levi starts dealing out the first hand of cards to ease the tension saying, "Well, at least we can have a relaxing game of cards before we have to hit the sack."

The Mayor and the others bid good-bye and the posse all sit down for a quiet, friendly card game. Allen is looking over his hand, switching cards around in his hand. Without glancing up, he asks, "Doc, are you going to let someone win a few hands tonight? Or are you going to clean us all out?"

Doc shrugs, tosses a couple of coins into the center of the table and answers, "I haven't decided what kind of mood I'm in tonight; we'll just have to play and see."

Steve throws two cards into the center of the table and says, "I will take two." The men play for a few more hours until Steve pushes himself away from the table. "I can see I am out classed here and I am going to leave before I am completely broke." He turns toward the door, saying over his shoulder, "I'll see you boys in the morning."

When Steve leaves, Little Bear joins the game. After a few hands, he's feeling the pain of Doc's success at the table. He folds on a hand, saying to Doc, "Take it easy on me, Doc; I still need some traveling money."

Doc shakes his head and laughs a little. He looks at Little Bear and says, "I'll try and go easy on you. I already have most of Allen's and Levi's money."

The game goes on for a few more hours until Allen speaks up. "I don't want to break up the party but we do need to get an early start. Little Bear and I will take first watch. Doc, you and Levi will relieve us in about four hours; that will give us a few hours of sleep before sun up."

They all go over to the hotel; Allen and Little Bear keep watch in the lobby while Doc and Levi go upstairs to get some sleep. Allen keeps pacing back and forth, looking out a window overlooking Main Street every few minutes.

After about an hour Little Bear has enough of Allen's pacing. He stands up, puts a hand against Allen's chest, stopping him in his stride. He pats the man's shoulder saying, "Marshal, you need to relax and have a seat; we have this under control."

"I have a bad feeling about this," Allen says. "Things aren't over. I am sure we're not out of the woods yet."

The two of them sit for a while in silence. Then there is a noise from upstairs, followed by four shots. They hear Levi's voice ring out, "What? You thought you were going to catch me off guard? Fat chance."

Little Bear takes off running up the stairs and finds Levi standing there in his room, wearing only his long-handles and his gun belt. Little Bear almost laughs when he sees the view. He asks, "Do you always wear your gun to bed, Levi?"

Levi holds his pistol on the dead man caught halfway in the window. Without turning to Little Bear he replies, "It just seemed like the thing to do tonight and as it turns out it was a good idea."

Doc comes running out of his room, toting a peacemaker in each hand. He steps in the room, asking, "What the hell was that shooting all about?"

Levi puts his weapon back in his holster and replies, "It seems there were a few outlaws left over and they thought they were going to take me in my sleep; I guess I ruined their plans." He turns to Doc and comments, "Well Doc, whaddaya say? Since we're already up, we may as well take over so that Little Bear and Allen can get in some sleep." Doc nods and returns to his room, grabs his belongings, and gets dressed.

As Doc is leaving his room, he catches Levi as he starts to go down stairs. Doc smirks and clears his throat before saying, "Levi, you might want to put some clothes on before you go down for guard duty."

Levi looks down to see he is still in his underwear. "Oh yeah, I will join you in a few minutes. There's the matter of that dead guy in my room I need to take care of."

"You get dressed; the braves and I can clean up your room," Little Bear points out.

"Thanks, Little Bear. I really appreciate that." Levi turns and heads back into his room to get dressed.

A few minutes later Levi walks downstairs to the lobby dressed and ready. He joins Doc and Allen seated in the chairs by the front windows. The three men sit quietly sipping coffee. Levi uses the time to study them. The three of them have been friends for some time. To Levi, Doc always seems dark yet still in control; as for Allen, the energy emanating from the man isn't the same. He seems uncomfortable and tentative.

Doc tells the other two he is going to double check things outside while the two of them are able to keep an eye in the lobby. Allen and Levi remain quiet while waiting for Doc's return.

Levi breaks the silence, saying to Allen, "Relax, this will be over soon enough; we are almost to Lincoln, and then your part in this will be over. Then you can go back to easier work. Maybe spend a little more time ranching."

Allen shakes his head slowly, not moving his gaze from the windowpane, and says, "I don't get it. I just don't get it."

Levi leans against the banister, and then asks, "What is it, Allen, that you don't get?"

"You, I don't get you. You don't have any problem with all of this killing?"

Levi sips his coffee and then replies, "Well, I guess I always wanted to be a cowboy growing up and now I am getting the chance to live out a dream."

Allen stares down into his cup. "There is a big difference between being a cowboy and one of the territory's most notorious gunfighters."

Levi pats Allen on the shoulder. "Don't worry, Allen, I won't let anything happen to you. Just keep your head down and stay behind me; just relax, pardner, okay? Now go up and get some sleep."

Doc returns a few minutes later after he has checked around outside. Levi reaches for his empty cup, motioning it at Doc to ask if he wants one; he nods yes. Doc sits across from the Marshal, and then looks more closely at the expression on Allen's face. Allen looks nervous and anxious. "Hey Allen, what's going on, something wrong?"

Allen nervously grips the arm of his chair. He looks at Doc with an exhausted stare and says, "I just want this over. I don't know that I can take this anymore, John. I just need all this to be over and go home." Allen bows his head and puts it in his hands.

Levi is walking up the hallway and can hear them talking. "Am I interrupting something?"

Allen looks at him as if he has seen a ghost. "No. I guess I'm just tired and need a good night's rest."

"As I said before, Allen, take your tired bones upstairs and get some rest. Doc and I will take care of anyone else stupid enough to try and get in here."

Allen takes in a deep breath and exhales loudly. He puts his hands on the arms of the chair and rolls his grip on the arms for a moment. Then as he gets up, he says, "Alright, you're right, Levi; I just need sleep. Good night and try to stay safe."

"You just get some sleep and don't worry about us," Doc assures Allen. "We live for this kind of thing."

Without saying another word, Allen walks up the stairs and goes to his room to get some much-needed sleep.

Levi takes the seat across from Doc. "Is Allen going to be all right?"

"Yea, he is just tired, that's all," Doc replies. "He hasn't slept well since we started this job. I think there's more to this job than he was prepared for."

"We don't need to be worried about one of our own losing it when we get in the middle of a gunfight," Levi points out.

"The Marshal will be fine," Doc shoots back. "You just keep your mind on the job at hand."

Levi leans back and then forward, resting his elbows on the arms of the chair. "That's what I am concerned about. You know as well as I do that there will be more between here and Lincoln than we have already faced."

"Yes, I know," Doc agrees. "The area between here and Lincoln is Sutton's last chance to stop us. There are too many deputies in Lincoln to try anything once we get there. However, I have an idea. Let's say 'an ace up my sleeve' so don't worry."

Levi puts his elbows on his thighs and leans in to listen more closely to Doc. "Are you going to let me in on this?"

Doc quietly replies, "I have sent Fred and Bud on ahead to Lincoln for a little help."

"I was wondering where they went," Levi comments. "Truth be known, I figured the two young pups had enough of this and ran off."

Doc grins, and looks into the empty cup in his hands. "No, I thought we would need a little help getting into Lincoln so I sent them on ahead to enlist some others to assist in our cause." He winks at Levi, giving him a wry sideways grin.

Levi quietly slaps his knee before saying, "You never cease to amaze me, Doc."

They sit waiting and watching until time for the others to rise. The others start stirring just before sun up. They all mount up and head into the sunrise, heading to the fate awaiting them on this last leg of their journey.

18

The men ride side by side making a wide line riding into the sun. They are approaching an area that calls for scouting ahead. Levi, Doc, and Little Bear ride ahead, to scout for any trouble that might be waiting for them.

Levi looks toward Doc and asks, "Why is it we are always the ones up front in the middle of all the action when the others are always a safe distance behind? Don't get me wrong . . . . But seriously, why are some always responsible for this and others are left in the back?"

Doc looks at the man with a surprised expression on his face and replies, "Would you want it any other way?"

"I suppose you're right. You have a point there, Doc."

"We will take care of whatever comes our way, and do whatever needs to be done," Doc points out. "We will continue with our destiny, the way we always do."

"You mean shoot first and ask questions later?"

"Yep, that's seems to be working so far," Doc remarks.

Little Bear splits off from them and rides out. He comes riding back to Doc and Levi like his horse's tail is on fire. "Doc, they are right behind me. Sutton's henchmen are just over the hill. They shot at one of my men and they started after me."

Levi, with the usual grin he gets right before a fight, says, "Keep on riding back toward the rest of the posse. Tell the others of what is ahead. Doc and I will take care of this." Levi quickly scans the landscape, and then starts shouting directions. "Now Doc, get on top of that rock over there and I will go into those trees and we will surprise them."

Doc climbs to the top of a large rock while Levi crouches down in a grove of cedars. Doc spots five riders coming in fast. He holds up five fingers to Levi and points in the direction that they are coming from. Levi nods and takes aim in the direction Doc points. The men are shooting toward Little Bear when Doc opens up with his rifle. Levi takes aim at the first rider, watching him fly off the back of his horse. Levi aims at the second rider, but all he sees is a horse without a rider. He pulls his rifle down to look at the remaining three horses. They too are rider-less. He steps out of the trees and tosses his rifle down "Damn-it Doc! Why do I even need to carry a gun if you're not going to let me use it?"

Doc hollers down from the rocks, "Sorry, pardner. I didn't intend to take a shot away from you. I had a shot, and I took it."

A shot came from somewhere in the distance. A piece of the rock flew off six feet below where Doc was standing. He ducks back behind the rock. He peers out around the rock in the direction of the sound. He sees a muzzle flash followed by the sound of the shot and a ricochet off the rocks again. He looks down and yells at Levi, "Hey Levi, toss me my long rifle, will yah?"

Levi grabs Doc's long rifle off his horse and tosses it to him, saying, "Here you go," then ducks for cover himself.

As Doc catches his rifle, quickly he loads it and sets the sights. Taking aim, he pulls the hammer back and squeezes the trigger. Levi positions himself to be able to see the intended target. Looking through his spyglass, he says to Doc, "You nailed him. He dropped like a rock. He won't be giving us any trouble." Doc takes out his own spyglass and scans the landscape, to discover a hiding outlaw perched in a tree in the distance. Levi is still looking through his spyglass when he sees the next man to lose in a fight against them. He exclaims, "Doc, do you see what I do?"

Doc is adjusting his sights and says calmly, "Yep. I see him. I have him in my sights."

Levi keeps a watch on the man. "If you can take him in one shot, I'll buy you a new hat."

"You got it," Doc responds. "Levi. I take size seven and a quarter." Doc squeezes the trigger and the outlaw takes a quick trip to the ground.

Levi takes down his spyglass and rubs his eyes. He looks up at Doc and says, "Well I'll be. I have never seen anything like it."

Doc looks through his spyglass again, scouting for more henchmen. Without looking down at Levi, he asks, "What's that, Levi?"

Levi starts looking through his spyglass as well. “That shot… I have never seen anyone shoot that far. That shot must have been over a thousand yards.”

Doc laughs and comments, “When you are done being amazed, you want to catch my Sharp so I can get down?”

Levi steps out and stands below Doc, yelling up at him, “Oh yeah, toss her down.” Doc tosses his long rifle down to Levi and then climbs down to see Little Bear come riding back with the rest of the men.

Allen rides up to Doc and Levi and says, “I thought you had some trouble?”

Doc put his rifle away and replies, “No trouble at all. Just a few men who wanted a scalp to take back to their camp, and Levi and I didn’t think Little Bear was ready to give it up yet.”

“Very funny, who were they?” Steve asks

“Do you have any idea who they were?” Allen also asks.

“I don’t know, we couldn’t get a word out of them,” Levi replies as he picks up his rifle and puts it back in its sheath on his horse. “Well, I do think I heard one say ‘ouch’ when he fell off his horse; does that help Marshal?”

Allen shakes his head and replies, “Look, I am trying to find out who we are up against.”

“We? Don’t you mean who Doc and I are up against? Levi smarts off. “As I recall you were always about a mile or two behind the action.”

“Levi, Marshal, we have a job to finish,” Doc interrupts. “How about you leave the bickering for the women in the quilting and embroidery circles?”

“Alright Doc, what do you suppose we do?” Levi asks.

“Well Levi, the same thing we have been doing; protecting our prisoner, protecting each other, killing outlaws, and then collecting the bounty on the ones who have rewards,” Doc points out.

Well, now that you put it that way, what are we waiting for? Let’s get moving,” Levi says.”

Doc looks over at Allen as he mounts up, “Marshal, let Levi, Little Bear and I get out a ways and then follow. If you hear shooting, stay where it’s safe for the prisoner. We’ll have it covered.”

Little Bear rides up to Doc and says, “My braves and I will ride around to the right of the hill while you and Levi take the creek around to the left and we will meet on the other side.”

“That sounds like a plan to me; how about you Levi, anything to add?” Doc asks.

“No, but keep an eye on the trees and the hills. Doc and I were shot at from men on the high ground.” Levi points out.

“Okay Levi. We will keep our eyes open. See you on the other side,” Little Bear says.

They ride their separate ways. When Doc and Levi get into the middle of the creek, Levi spots a man up ahead behind a rock. “Doc, get down; there’s a man hiding behind a rock up there.

They both dismount. Doc grabs his long rifle and climbs a tree to get a better shot. As Doc is getting ready to pull the trigger, another man rides up and talks to the man behind the rock and both men ride away.

Doc climbs back down and says, “Levi, I am going to go right over the hill and provide cover for you and Little Bear.”

“You be careful up there; there’s no telling what may be waiting for us on the other side.” Levi warns Doc.

Doc rides about half way up the hill, dismounts, and ties his horse to a bush. Taking both rifles and the extra pair of pistols, he begins to crawl up the hill. He is almost to the top when he sees a large rock formation with a man sitting against it. The man is watching in the direction Little Bear has ridden. Doc slowly works his way to the rock. He crawls around from the man's blind side. When he has the man within his grasp, he reaches out swiftly and quietly puts the outlaw to sleep.

When Doc looks down at the prairie floor below him, he can see another group of outlaws in a camp just below them. He counts about twenty-six men milling about the small camp. In the middle of the camp, there is a tarp. He can see that there is something large under it. Doc instinctively reaches for his spyglass and focuses in on the tarp. He can now see the item hidden under the tarp; it looks like a cannon.

Just as he starts to process the situation, he sees movement on another hillside washout. Doc moves his spyglass to get a better look. He discovers a man with a badge, and the man is using a spyglass to look right at him. Doc removes his badge and holds it out for the lawman on the opposite hillside to see. The lawman waves his hat in acknowledgement. When Doc sees the man replace his hat, ten more lawmen step up to the edge of the hill.

Levi makes his way up the hill behind Doc to the large rock. Just behind him are Allen and the rest of the men making their way up for additional cover fire.

Doc looks at the others. In a regretful tone, he breaks the news. "The Marshals and other lawmen from Lincoln are across on the hill." Doc points in their direction. "However, things are a little different than we planned. There is a group of men who are camped out down on that floor. There are over twenty, and they have a cannon. They are definitely determined to stop us from reaching Lincoln."

Allen lowers his head and starts to feel anxious again. He asks Doc, "Great. What do you suggest we do now?"

"We use their weapon against them." Doc points out.

"And how do you suppose we do that?" Allen asks.

"Where there's a cannon, there's gunpowder. And where there is gunpowder; there is an explosive device," Doc answers as he turns toward the others. "Levi, do you think you can get a stick down there beside the powder keg?"

"You tell me when to send it and I will get it there," Levi answers.

At that moment, a ranger from the other group of lawmen takes charge and yells down to the men "You men in the camp. You are surrounded. Drop your guns and get your hands up."

No sooner, does he finish his demand on the villains then all hell breaks loose. The sparks from the guns light up the sky like fireworks on the Fourth of July.

Doc looks over at Levi. "Now would be as good a time as any to throw that dynamite." Levi throws the unlit stick and it flies ten feet over the keg. "It will only work if you get it close to the keg, Levi."

"I know, I know. I am doing the best that I can under the circumstances," Levi points out as he reaches for another stick.

"Well try again before they . . . ." Doc is cut off by the sound of cannon fire; he looks up to see the blast of a cannon ball hitting the side of the hill. "Now get this one close before they figure out how to aim accurately with that thing!"

Levi rears his arm back saying, "Alright, here we go"

The dynamite lands a foot away from the powder keg. Doc aims his lever action at it and squeezes the trigger, sending a bullet right into the stick. The stick goes off, taking out the keg, cannon, and the two men with the cannon as well.

Having made the odds even, Levi and Doc prepare to start picking men off one by one with their rifles.

While Levi is reloading his rifle, he comments, "At least these guys are smart enough to put some wagons down there for cover."

"Maybe they are getting a little better at this. But really, it doesn't matter," Doc says.

"How do you mean?" Levi replies.

"You still have dynamite, don't you?" Doc asks.

"Yeah," Levi answers.

"Well then, start throwing!" Doc commands

"Oh hell, yeah!" Levi exclaims.

Levi reaches in his saddlebag and starts to throw. When each stick hits the ground, Doc shoots it before it stops rolling. With each blast, outlaws go flying. After a few explosions, the men still left alive have their hands high in the air screaming, 'we give up.'

The Marshal, rangers, and deputies from the other hill, ride down into the valley, put the outlaws in chains and on the wagons from the camp and set out for the jail in Lincoln.

Allen climbs back on his horse, looks at Billy, and says, "I think this is finally over. You are going to be cleared of all wrong doing; you can go back to the farm and get back to your regular life."

With a feeling of relief, Billy says to the Marshal, "I'm really looking forward to plowing the field and not dodging bullets everyday."

Levi rides by Allen and Billy. "If you two ladies are done, can we get back on the trail? I am getting a powerful thirst."

Doc and his group of men ride down to join the marshals and rangers to escort their prisoners and Billy back to Lincoln.

The buildings of Lincoln are coming into view. The mood of Marshal Allen's men begins to improve. Then to their surprise and to the others, Doc is the first to say, "Damn, it is so good to be home again!"

Both posses stop at the Marshal's office. Everyone ties their horses up to the rail out front and takes their prisoners inside. Allen, Doc, and Levi pay special attention to protect Billy until they get inside. Steve, Wes, and the other deputies take the remaining five outlaws into a cell.

Allen steps over into the adjoining office to speak with the Circuit Judge, the Honorable Judge Matthew Nix. Seated across his desk is the Territorial Governor. Allen is surprised to see the Governor. "Good evening, Judge, Governor. I'm surprised to see you in Lincoln, Governor."

The governor looks up from the desk. "I got a wire you would be here soon; and after the kidnapping incident, there is no way I would miss this event!" The judge pushes a document across the desk to the governor. He reaches over, takes it, signs it, and hands it to Allen. "Marshal, this is a document for Billy. It's giving him a full pardon."

Doc reads it and smiles.

Allen reaches into his vest pocket, removes Billy's bill of sale, and gives it to Judge Nix. "Here you go, Your Honor. This should prove Billy bought those cattle legally and that he is totally above board with the whole thing."

The two men walk up to the Marshal's desk with Allen. The Governor starts explaining, "We have been talking to Billy's uncle, Horace. He had a very interesting story for us. He said that Mr. Sutton has been behind all of the trouble we have been dealing with around here, including the cattle rustling." He looks at Doc. "John, I'm sorry to hear that he was the spearhead behind the slaughter of your wife and sons."

The Judge hands Doc a warrant that reads: Wanted for Murder, Theft, and Conspiracy: Richard Sutton. The Governor grabs the warrant and the marshal's pen off the desk, writes something on the warrant, and hands it back to Doc. He leans over and whispers something in Doc's ear. Doc nods, reads it, smiles, and puts it in his vest pocket. He looks over at the others saying, "Levi, Little Bear, we need to get going. We have business that needs tending in Avoca."

Levi and Little Bear head out the door to get some fresh horses while Doc walks over to Allen, puts his arm around him, and walks him to the back of the office.

"Allen, I know you're tired of the fire-fights and basically don't care for the all out gun-play. So, why don't you stay here?" Doc suggests. "That way you can keep an eye on Billy until it's all over. Maybe even check in on Amy and Audra?"

They leave the Marshal's office and begin to walk down the boardwalk. Doc says to Allen, "Hey, while you're here, could you make sure everything is ready for the players when they come to town. They'll be here in three days."

Allen pats Doc's shoulder. "Good call, John. I'll see things around here are ship shape. You men watch yourselves going after Sutton. I'm sure he's ready and waiting for you."

"Pardner, let me tell ya' somethin'; what I am about to do to that man… You or anyone else has no reason to see," Doc says as he and Allen shake hands. "I'll be back in time for the show. You give my best to Audra and tell her I will see her just as soon as this is over."

Doc makes his way down the street to the livery. There he meets Levi, Little Bear and the braves. Levi is walking out front with two horses. "Here you go, Doc. I figured this big white stallion would fit this trip perfectly."

Doc laughs, and then says, "I see where you're going with this but I don't think Sutton is smart enough to figure it out."

"You and I know what it means and that's what counts."

The men climb on their horses and ride out of town, heading to Avoca and their 'unfinished business. Levi, riding beside Doc, says, "What's the hurry to get to Avoca?"

Without taking his eyes off the trail, Doc replies, "I figure if we get there a day early, Sutton will not be prepared for us. I hope we can get into Eagle under cover of night, get some rest and leave again as soon as it gets dark, no one will even know we were there."

"Someone will when we check into the hotel," Levi comments

"No, it will stay a secret," Doc points out. "Sherry and her father, Arlen, run the hotel and they are friends of Allen's. They can be trusted."

"If you say so," Levi remarks. "Well, we better get a move on if we are going to make Eagle in good time so we can catch a little shut-eye and be gone before daylight."

The men pick up the pace and continue to ride after sunset. Little Bear sends one of the braves ahead to assure their safety. A few minutes later, he rides back to the group and starts talking with Little Bear.

Little Bear rides back to Doc and says, "He says there are campfires up ahead with many men sitting around them. He has found a safe passage around them where we will not be seen."

Doc thinks about the situation and agrees with Little Bear's decision. "I think it's an excellent idea to skirt around them this time. If we do this, we won't be bringing attention to ourselves, thus letting Sutton know we are coming."

"I guess you're right Doc," Levi agrees. "But you know, we'll have to deal with him and them sooner or later."

"This time I would like to see it be later than sooner," Doc replies. "Like after we've dealt face to face with Sutton."

Levi nods in agreement and says, "Hey, by the way, share what the Governor said to you."

Doc reaches into his vest pocket and hands Levi the warrant. Levi opens it up and reads what the governor wrote, dead or alive.

Levi looks up from the warrant. "I guess I don't have to guess what you're going to choose."

Doc grins and says, "I am not going to kill him. My friend Little Bear is going to handle that job for us."

"Why are you going to let Little Bear kill him? After all Sutton ordered the killing of your family," Levi asks as he hands the warrant back to Doc.

"Even though the tribe is primarily a peaceful people, Little Bear knows ways of torture we have never even thought of," Doc explains.

"Oh. Well, in that case I can see your point," Levi agrees.

Doc spurs his horse and slaps it with the reins. "Now let's quit lolly-gagging and get to Eagle.

"There's a dried out creek bed surrounded by many trees that we can take around the men into the north side of Eagle," Little Bear points out to Doc and Levi.

The men take to the creek bed and ride around Eagle as quiet as a mouse. They are able to make their way to the back of the hotel undetected. Doc climbs down off his horse and makes his way in the back door of the hotel. He sneaks up the short hall and can see Sherry sitting at the desk. He whispers, "Psst, psst, Sherry; it's Doc I need to talk to you for a minute."

Sherry turns to face Doc, surprised to see him. She motions for him to get down under the desk. She looks down at the man crouching beneath her. "It's not safe for you in town. Sutton's men are all over looking for you. They know you made it to Lincoln. So they are prowling everywhere waiting to take you down."

"Are any of them staying here?" he asks.

"No, not after you cleaned out the hotel in Arrow Bluff," she replies.

"We need a couple rooms for the night and a place to keep the horses out of sight."

She takes him by the hand. "I will have my father cover the desk and I will take you to our house where you can hide your horses and spend the night. I will come and check on you around four in the morning."

Sherry goes to talk with her father while Doc goes out to fill the men in on the plan. After just a few minutes, Sherry comes out the door. Doc helps her on the back of his horse, and they ride out to the family's farm.

As they approach Sherry's farm, Little Bear takes the initiative, leans over, and says to Doc, "Let the braves and me ride ahead and see if the farm has any surprises in store for us."

"Good idea," Doc acknowledges. "We will hole up here in the apple orchard until you return; but remember, you have to take extra precaution not to alert anyone of our presence. If you do find anyone, let's try to take care of business as silently as possible, shall we?"

Little Bear smiles at Doc and says, "We shall. But then, don't we always?"

"You do have a valid point there," Doc points out "Be safe, my friend. We will be right here waiting."

Little Bear and his braves ride out into the dark with Sherry's directions to check out the farmstead. It is not long and Little Bear returns. "There were four men waiting for us. We were able to change the odds in our favor. Two of the braves are holding one of them prisoner. He is more than eager to talk. He's talking faster than a man should know how to."

The rest of them ride up to the homestead. Doc can see the lone outlaw hanging by his feet, begging for his life.

"I'll tell you everything I know; just don't kill me," he is saying.

Doc walks over to the man and asks, "Just what kind of information do you have that may be worth your life?"

"There are men all over Eagle waiting for you," he quickly says.

Doc cocks his pearl handle six-shooter and says, “We already know that; try again.”

“In Avoca there are many gunmen and Sutton has hired four professional gunfighters,” the man continues to say. “They are all over town waiting for you.”

“That is something new and quite useful,” says Doc, letting down the hammer slowly.

Doc and Levi are talking over the plan for the next leg to Avoca when they hear the outlaw say, “Is anybody going to cut me down? I told you all I know.”

“Cut him down, take him inside, tie him up, and gag him,” Doc says to Little Bear. “We can’t afford to have him escape and tell anyone we are here.”

Little Bear and a brave cut the man down and walk him inside the house. Doc and Levi follow them inside with Sherry right behind them. They tie him spread eagled on a bed and make sure he is gagged, and will not be moving soon.

“You men make yourselves at home,” Sherry says, “Mama is sleeping; but she will help you, so just wake her. I’d love to stay, but I think that will draw attention; so I think I need to get back to the hotel before someone misses me. I will take one of my horses so no one will suspect anything. I will ride out in the morning, around four, and make sure you are up.”

Doc hugs the sweet girl. “Thanks for everything, Sherry. You won’t need to come out. Little Bear will make sure we are up and ready to move out. Like I said, thanks for all that you have done for us. We’ll see you on the way back.”

"Okay I'll go on back," Sherry says. "It was nice to see you're still up to no good, Doc. Ya'all be careful now, okay?"

"Yes, we'll try our best not to get killed," Doc says as he walks her to the door.

She opens the door and looks back at Doc and says, "You be real careful. Mr. Sutton is not a nice man and he will be ready for you."

"I'm ready for him as well," Doc assures her. "After what he did to my family and other people, and the families he has destroyed, I am more than ready."

Levi smiles and looks over at Sherry as she stands in the doorway. "The only person that should be worrying is Sutton. I have known Doc for awhile now and I have never seen him this intent on getting a job done."

"Alright then, good luck and good night." Sherry walks out the door climbs on her horse and heads back to town.

Doc walks over to the outlaw and gives him a final warning. "If you are a good boy, you might just live to see the sunrise. If you cause us any trouble, my friend Little Bear over there will take offense and simply put an end to your miserable life. Do you understand?" The bound and gagged man nods. "Okay then. Little Bear, you take first watch; the rest of us will try to get some sleep."

"The braves and I will switch off taking watch," Little Bear replies. "You and Levi just sleep through the night. I will wake you when it is time to leave."

Levi and Doc go up the staircase to get some sleep before they head into Avoca during the wee morning hours.

19

The moon descends in the nighttime sky over the town of Eagle in the Nebraska Territory.

Little Bear goes up the stairs and knocks on Doc's door. He opens the door, announcing quietly, "Doc, it is time."

Doc looks up at Little Bear, smiles, and sits up. "Thank you. Is Levi up yet?"

"No, I thought I would let you do that," he answers. "Sherry showed up about an hour ago. She's cooking us breakfast."

Doc smiles, thinking about Sherry. She has always been a good and faithful friend. As he puts his boots on, he says, "I will go and get Levi up and we'll be down shortly."

Doc walks across the hall to wake Levi. Just as he is about to reach for the door and open it, Levi steps out into the hall, saying, "Mornin' Doc, are you ready to end this little saga of yours?"

"I tell ya buddy, I have never been more ready than I am right now."

"We'd better be getting' us something to eat first," Levi suggests. "When we're done eating we'll hit the bank and make a substantial withdrawal. I think the bank will have a banker available to oblige."

"Sounds good." Doc agrees. "Sounds like a good plan there. Count me in."

They walk downstairs and enter the dining room where Miss Sherry has the food already on the table. "Hurry up, fellas, before all this food gets cold."

Doc doesn't hesitate and plops right down. "I sure am ready for some of your good cooking." He looks over at Levi and smiles. "Levi, Miss Sherry is probably one of the best young ladies in the kitchen! I tell ya we hate to leave Eagle without having a plate of her eats. You're gonna love this!"

After finishing their meal, Doc and Levi push themselves back from the table. Levi is rubbing his belly. He looks at his hostess and says, "That sure was good, Sherry! Doc didn't lie about your cooking. I am almost sorry we have to leave. I could eat like this every meal. There is a job to finish. So maybe after our job is done, we'll have to visit for something from your kitchen." Levi stands up, puts his hat on, and then pinches the brim to tip it to the young woman. She smiles back. Levi turns and exits the door to the backyard.

Doc is already outside on his horse. "Little Bear, I need you and your braves to scout ahead. Levi and I will be a short distance behind."

Little Bear holds a hand up to say good-bye. “We will ride up ahead and make sure the path is clear.”

Doc looks at Levi and tells him, “Levi, grab our prisoner and make sure he’s bound and gagged; we don’t need him to alert anyone of our presence. We’ll keep him with us. That should insure that our arrival will be a surprise.”

The rest of them mount up and head for Avoca. Under a moonlit sky, they ride in absolute silence.

The sun is just starting to rise, lighting the dark night sky in the East. Little Bear rides back to Doc and Levi. He tells them, “I have seen the town from on top of the hill. The town is still asleep, but there are a few people moving about on the streets.”

Doc stops and looks around, noting landmarks. He starts pointing around, giving directions. “Little Bear, I think I will have you and a couple of braves go around and come in from the East. The third brave I want to stay with our prisoner. And Levi and I will approach from the west.”

“Sounds fine, Doctor John,” Little Bear acknowledges. “See you in town in a little while. Remember, there are men waiting just for your arrival, with their guns ready.”

It is still morning when Doc and Levi ride into the town of Avoca. The activity they see is very little compared to the normal activity in this town. Without a single incident, they ride to the livery. The blacksmith waves as Doc and Levi ride in. The two men put their horses in a stall and return to the doorway, to meet back up with the brave who is monitoring their prisoner.

When Doc steps out the door, he and Levi come face to face with five hired professional gunfighters, standing in the street waiting. The man standing in the middle looks right at Doc. He is a slight fellow. He has gray in his whiskers, and his skin shows years of saddle time in the sun.

He points at Doc. "Are you the man they call Doc Gray?"

Doc stops and prepares for a shootout. Doc gives the man a cold long stare before answering, "Yes, I am. Just who wants to know?"

The man reaches up to the brim of his bowler hat. His smooth black leather gloved hand tips his brim. After tipping his brim, his expensive glove returns to an 'at ready' spot by his waist. "My name is Slade. I have been hired to come here and put down a man with your name."

Levi is only a few steps behind Doc. When he walks out of the livery, he sees the odds and jokes with John. "Hey Doc, I thought they had four hired guns; looks like there are five. Hell, this may be a little more fun than I thought it would be. Things just may get exciting after all!"

Doc doesn't move his stare from Slade. "Seven, if you count the two men who are positioned on the hotel roof."

Levi snaps his head over to look at the roof. He doesn't see anyone. "Where? What do you mean? I didn't see or hear…where?" Levi asks with a little bit of confusion.

"These cowards put two shooters on the roof top of the hotel, Doc says. "Little Bear saw them heading up when he looked over the town from the hill, so his first move was to have a visit with them when he came into town. He took care of them. Trust me; they won't be a problem for us now." Doc points at the gunman. "Now Mr. Slade, what were you saying about killing me and Levi?"

Mr. Slade is looking around nervously, realizing he may not be at the advantage he thought. "I uh, I was saying we are here to . . . ."

Levi cut him off by stepping in front of Doc, "Did I hear you say you were here to kill Doc? Well, I have to say that as his friend I kind of take offense to that."

Doc pats Levi on the shoulder and has him step over and stand beside him instead of in front. He moves his riding coat back, exposing his pair of pearl handle guns. All of the gunmen jump and reach to pull out their own shooters. Slade motions for them to settle down. Doc looks down at the ground, at his feet, for a moment before proceeding. After a minute he says, "Well, Mr. Slade, I tell you what." Doc slowly and deliberately removes a pistol from his left holster. He opens the action and ejects all six shells onto the ground. He closes it. He spins it in place and then slowly bends down, placing the pistol on the ground without removing his eyes from the line of men across from him. After standing back up, he continues speaking, "I will make things more even. For this confrontation I will only use one gun." He nods to his partner. "Levi, you take the two on the right. I will disarm Mr. Slade and make the other two eligible to move into boot hill."

Levi rubs his hands together. "That sounds like a deal. But the one whose final man hits the ground last is buying the first round."

Doc nods. "You got a deal, Levi. Why don't you just go on up to the saloon and get the drinks ready?"

"Whoa, Doc! We haven't even started our little contest and you think you are going to win? Doc, I beg to differ."

"Well Levi, I am going to apologize to you." Doc still maintains his gaze with Slade.

Levi looks a little confused. "What do you have to apologize f. . . .?"

Before Levi gets his last word out, Doc pulls his remaining pistol and starts fanning the hammer; the two on the left fall, then the two on the right go down. Mr. Slade has yet to clear leather.

Before he pulls his guns Doc warns him, "If you want to live through this day, Mr. Slade, I suggest you get your hands off those pistols."

Mr. Slade pauses with his hands on the handles of his guns. He keeps his eyes locked on Doc Gray. He opts to put his hands in the air. Levi quickly steps over, puts the end of his gun barrel in the man's chest, and removes the pistols from his holsters, placing them in his waistband. Doc bends down, picks up his pistol from the ground, and puts it back in his holster.

Reaching into his pocket, Doc pulls out a silver dollar. He flips it up into the air to Levi. He tells Levi, "Take our new friend, Slade here, to the saloon and buy him a beer. The braves can go with you two. I'll meet you there shortly. Little Bear and I have to stop at the bank to make a withdrawal."

Levi is tying Slade's hands together; he pauses and looks over his shoulder back at Doc. "Are you sure you don't want me to go with you?"

Doc nods as he turns away. "Yes, I am sure. I need you and the braves to keep an eye on our prisoner and our horses, and keep Slade busy so I can deal with Sutton."

"Alright," Levi says. "We'll be at the saloon when you're done."

Doc and Little Bear make their way down the street to the bank. When they reach the front, Doc pauses before climbing the steps. He and Little Bear exchange looks, then in tandem they ascend. Doc grabs the doorknob and looks at Little Bear. "I need you to keep people out of my way and out of Sutton's back office. So when we get in, you empty out the room and I'm going all the way in, okay?"

"I will make sure no one gets hurt and that no one comes in to interfere," Little Bear informs Doc.

The two men enter the bank, to find four people in the bank conducting their morning banking. Doc walks up to a teller. "Is Mr. Sutton in today?"

The man behind the counter in the teller's cage smiles and says, "Good morning, sir. He is in today. However, he is not taking any appointments today."

"That's alright; he should be expecting me." Doc walks past the teller's cage and opens the door. He steps into the cage and up to Sutton's office door. He turns and looks back to see Little Bear empty the building. After watching everyone step outside, he turns back to Sutton's door, kicking in the door. Sutton is bent over, putting papers into a cabinet. The sound surprises him and he looks up to see Doc standing there.

Doc works hard at controlling his anger. Through clenched teeth, he says to Sutton, "Stand up, you no good Son of a bitch! You and I have some unfinished business to attend to."

Sutton stands up. He produces a pistol from the file drawer, pointing it right at Doc. "Hello John, it's been a long time. Yes, I believe we do have some unfinished business as you say. I know my unfinished business was not having you killed when I had those men kill your slut of a wife and those spoiled, good-for-nothing kids of yours!" Sutton steps out around his desk and stands in front of it, to stand face to face with John. "However, I am a little surprised to see you here. I say, you don't learn fast, do you? I thought you would be smarter than this. Hell, at least now I get the pleasure of killing you myself. That should make you happy too. You'll be reunited with your little family."

Doc smiles and chuckles; "You think you have the upper hand, do you?"

Sutton smugly replies, "After all, I am the one holding the gun."

Sutton never saw Doc's hand move. Doc draws his pistol, shoots the gun out of Sutton's hand, and puts the gun back into his holster. He smiles at Sutton's expression of surprise. He asks, "Who did you say was holding the gun?" Doc takes a couple of steps into the room. He keeps his hand on the handle of his gun. "You people make me sick. I mean sick! You think you are better than everyone else. You think you can take anything you want because somehow you think you are above the rules. Let me tell ya buddy, I am here to set you straight, right here and right now!"

"Well Doc, you know, without those guns you are just a little man, a little man whom I will be glad to teach a lesson."

Doc takes off his guns, looks over at Sutton, and tosses them out of his own reach. Doc holds his arms out even with his shoulders and says, "Guns are off now. What do you say there, Sutton? How about we just settle this man to man?"

Sutton charges at Doc. Doc dodges with moves like a matador. Sutton charges past Doc and flies headlong into the wall. Doc grabs him, and like a rag doll, tosses him onto his desk. Sutton slides off the desk. He attempts to stand, staggering to his feet. Just as he stands up, he is greeted with Doc's fist to his jaw, sending him back over the desk again and down onto the floor. Doc grabs him by his lapels, lifting him to his feet and begins beating him senseless.

Doc is having visions of the day that changed his entire world. With every swing, every blow he delivers, he sees his wife and boys hanging in the oak tree in front of his home. Every time he picks the man up to hit him, Doc can see the men who assaulted his beautiful wife. His anger increases each time he pulls back his fist, beating Sutton severely.

Just when he has beaten Sutton unconscious, he hears a voice. The voice tells him, 'he has had enough.' He stops in mid swing. He looks at the man. He releases Sutton, and Sutton drops like a bag of potatoes and lands on the floor out cold.

Doc walks over to the door and opens it, only to find Little Bear, with his back to it, and the town Sheriff yelling at him to open the door. Doc steps through the door, greeting the Sheriff. "Good morning, Sheriff; how are you today?"

The Sheriff tries getting closer to the door, but Little Bear is still holding him back. "It will be a lot better if you let me in there, Doc."

Doc takes out the warrant and hands it to the sheriff. "Here is the warrant for Sutton. Levi, Little Bear, and I are taking him back to Lincoln for trial."

The Sheriff grabs the warrant to read it. "Look Gray, I think I can handle the transport of Mr. Sutton to Lincoln. Why don't you just go on home and leave this matter to me?"

Doc grabs the warrant back and puts it back in his breast pocket. "I don't think so, Sheriff. I will be overseeing his transport if it's all the same to you. I think we are capable of handling this. Now, if you don't mind, we need to get Sutton down to the saloon."

Little Bear and Doc carry Sutton down to the saloon. When they enter they find Levi has tied Slade to a swivel chair and is spinning him around and around. He's questioning Slade. "Okay, dirt bag, are you going to tell me what I want to hear or are we going to do this all day?" He looks over at the doorway, seeing Doc and Little Bear holding the unconscious, lifeless body of Sutton; he smiles.

Doc and Little Bear toss Sutton onto the bar. Doc motions to the bartender and demands, "Give me a bottle of your cheapest whiskey." The man hands Doc a bottle of rotgut. Doc opens it and pours it on the bloody face of Sutton.

Sutton comes around, spitting up whiskey and screaming in pain. "You are going to pay for this, Gray." With a rap to the side of Sutton's head with the butt end of Doc's pistol, Sutton is silenced once again.

The Sheriff enters the saloon with five deputies, with their guns drawn. He bellows to the men in the saloon, "Hold it right there, Doc! Sutton is my prisoner and you will release him to our custody!"

Doc puts a hand on his pistol; again he repeats what he told the Sheriff when they were in the bank. "I already told you once, Sheriff. I don't think that is going to happen. I aim to see that Sutton gets to Lincoln in one piece and stands trial, a fair trial."

A young man standing with the sheriff laughs. "I know your reputation, Doc. I think it's all hogwash. Look around; it is five on two. And I know I for one ain't afraid of you."

"Are you afraid of Indians?" Doc asks.

The kid points at Little Bear and says, "Him? No, why do you ask?"

Doc thumbs at Little Bear and says, "No, not this guy." Pointing to the corner of the bar behind the lawmen, he gives them the instructions, "Turn around." The young deputy turns to find the rest of the braves standing there with their tomahawks in their hands. Doc finishes the conversation with, "It does change the odds a little, doesn't it? I suggest you, the others, and the Sheriff drop your gun belts; and I recommend doing it now."

The Sheriff and the other men drop their gun belts to the ground and put their hands in the air. Doc points to Little Bear and the braves and says, "Little Bear, take these men and our other prisoners down to the jail. After you lock them up, leave a brave posted as a guard, and for our friends Slade and Sutton here, I want an armed guard at their cells. We can't afford anyone getting to them, to shoot them or break them out." Little Bear and his braves escort the men down to the jail.

"Now what do you want to do?" Levi asks, "We have Sutton in custody."

Doc drinks a shot, places the glass on the bar, and starts for the door. "Levi, I have a little business I need to attend to. I will meet up with you a little later. It might be a good idea if you double check around town for any who aren't residents and see them to the jail, if possible."

"Sounds good," Levi acknowledges. "I'll meet you at the hotel restaurant in an hour?" Doc nods and steps out the door of the saloon and starts down the center of the street, walking without worry.

Doc reaches the telegraph office. When he enters, he finds a man behind the desk. The man smiles and stands to greet him, "Well hello there, Doc. I assume you were successful in getting the warrant served?"

"How did you know about that?" Doc asks.

The man leans on his elbows on the counter. He smiles and says, "I am the man in charge of the telegraph. I know all the in-coming and out-going news."

Doc lets out a half chuckle. "Good point. I guess you would know all the news." He takes a deep breath and exhales loudly. "Now, for the reason I stopped in. I need to send a message to Marshal Dan Allen in Lincoln."

The man nods, reaching for a pencil and a paper. "Alright Doc, what do you want me to send?"

Doc looks at the sheet to watch the man's dictation. "Marshal Dan Allen, U.S. Marshal's office, Lincoln; Dan, I need a posse of men. I need you to bring them to Eagle before seven tomorrow morning. Sign it John Gray."

The man reads over it and then says, "That it, Doc?"

Doc reads it over too; nodding with approval, he tells the man, "Yep, that'll do it. I will be at the Hotel restaurant eating lunch. When you get a reply, please let me know."

The man turns, sits down, and prepares to start tapping out the message. "Sure thing, Doc. As soon as the Marshal sends his reply, I will be right down with it."

Doc walks out of the telegraph office and sees Levi in a heated discussion with a man across the street. Doc makes a beeline over to see what all the commotion is about.

"Levi, what is the yelling all about?" Doc asks.

"This gentleman is wondering why we took the Sheriff and his deputies to jail. I told him the Sheriff is crooked and belongs in jail."

"Well sir, I don't think your Sheriff is necessarily a crook or bad man," Doc points out. "I say he is an average guy, who is a little misguided."

The man looks at Doc, interested in what he has to say. He asks in a level tone, "Well, you tell me exactly what he did to get himself thrown in jail."

Doc inhales loudly and exhales even louder. "Well, he didn't exactly 'do' anything. However, at this point in the situation, with men out to kill any lawmen who have been sent to take Sutton and anyone associated with him to jail, being in jail right now is more for his protection. You have to understand that there are some really bad men running around these here parts, and the jail is the safest place for 'good' guys too."

"Well, should I be concerned for my family with all these bad men about?" He asks.

"It's probably not a good idea to spend time out and about on the streets. You really should keep your wife and children inside, I say for at least the next couple of days. You can do something to help, actually. If you'd go up to the jail house after dinner tomorrow afternoon and release the Sheriff and the deputies, that would be great."

"I will do that for you, Deputy Marshal," the man agrees.

"Thanks," Doc comments. "Like I said, till then go home and keep your family out of harm's way."

The man turns around and hurries down the street and around the corner. Levi slaps Doc on the back. “You definitely have the gift to convince someone of something they will not ordinarily believe. You have a gift for gab.”

“Whatever do you mean, Levi?” Doc asks.

“I was about to pop him over the bean with the butt of my pistol and take him to jail when you showed up.”

“Sometimes it’s better to talk your way out of trouble,” Doc points out. “Now let’s go down and get something to eat.”

After the men finish dinner, they head down to the jail to talk to the Sheriff. They are about halfway to the jail, past the telegraph office, when the telegraph operator runs out and stops them. He hands a wire to Doc.

“Is it from Allen?” Levi asks. “What does it say, Doc?”

Doc smiles at the man; while taking the telegram from him, he unfolds it and reads it. “Yes, it’s from him. Dan says they will come into Eagle from the Southwest. They should hit Farley’s barn west of town at around seven o’clock tomorrow morning. They will spread out and cover the town to the East.’ That will pin down those guys we dodged on the way here. That should work perfectly, absolutely perfectly!” Doc let out a cackle sounding little laugh.

Levi rubs his hands together and gets a fake fiendish grin on his face, before commenting, “Sounds like things are looking up for us.”

They continue down the street and enter the jail to talk to the jailed Sheriff. Doc pulls up a chair and sits down outside the cell. He takes off his hat, holding it in his hands as he addresses the lawman. “Sheriff, I wanted to come down here and let you know why we had to jail ya’all and to tell you the importance of why we are the ones to see Sutton extradited to Lincoln to stand trial."

"This better be a good explanation, Doc," the Sheriff says, pointing a finger at Doc through the cell bars.

Doc nods, understanding the man's point. "Look, here's the deal, Sheriff. Sutton is responsible for a good many crimes, the largest of which is the massacre of my family. He is also responsible for foreclosing on land which is not in default; he keeps and adds these lands to his ranch to increase his number of acres. He is the mastermind behind some of the herds of cattle being rustled and behind some of the herds which have their brands altered or changed. He has methodically orchestrated each of these offenses."

The Sheriff looks at Doc in disbelief. He runs a hand through his hair. Then he makes the statement, "You better be a tellin' the truth. Are you really sure about this, Gray?"

Doc looks at the floor, nodding his head. He tells the rest of the story slowly. "Unfortunately, Sheriff, I am absolutely telling you the truth. I wish this was all a dream. Ya know? We could all wake up and I'd still be doctoring in Lincoln. Everyone would be going on with their lives and they would still have their pieces of ground for which they got their loans." Doc looks out the window, and stares out for a minute. "Sheriff, we have witnesses to some of the meetings between Sutton and his henchmen. We also have the documents Sutton kept of these meetings. We have the bill-of-sale that Billy received from the now dead cattleman from Kansas. The cattleman from whom he is accused of stealing is conveniently dead by a hired gunman, a gunman hired by

Sutton. He has been trying to kill Billy, Marshal Dan Allen and me since we left here with Billy over a week ago."

"I can't believe all of this," the sheriff shoots back. "This can't all be true. I had no idea these things were happening. The only story I received was from Sutton. I guess if he's really guilty, he wouldn't tell the truth to me now, would he?" The Sheriff glares across the jail at the cell on the other side of the room."

Knowing what is going through the Sheriff's head, Doc continues to hold his head down and not look the same direction the Sheriff is. He knows deep inside what is right; even if he'd rather just string up Sutton himself, dangling him over an open pit of flames, letting him burn alive, just a little at a time. The Sheriff throws down his hat, snapping Doc's thoughts back to reality. Doc clears his throat. "Yes, well it seems like anyone who tries to help us accomplish our task gets added to Sutton's list of intended targets. Here in jail is the safest place for you right now, while Sutton's men and hired guns are walking the streets."

The Sheriff nods and says, "You could be right about them still walking around; Sutton's reach is far. Just let us out when you leave town. But meanwhile, aren't we sitting targets here in jail too?"

"You're right; you could be too vulnerable here locked up and unarmed," Doc agrees. "I didn't think of that. We'll post a guard here through the day and into the afternoon tomorrow. We will also have someone release you and the boys when it's safe. But this will only happen as long as we have your word not to interfere."

"Doc, you have my word," the Sheriff agrees. "I wish you and your men the best of luck getting this piece of dung to Lincoln for trial."

Doc gets up and steps outside the jail. He pats Little Bear on the back. The two are just having a relaxed conversation when Levi interrupts/ “I am going over to the saloon for a bit before I retire for the day. I was thinking about a little whiskey and a card game or two. Anyone else up for it? Want to go up there and get into a card game?” Doc and Little Bear both shake their heads. “Alright then, I will see you boys in the morning.” Levi heads off for the saloon.

Doc gives Little Bear and the braves their instructions for the night’s watch, then jogs up the street to catch up with Levi. When he catches up with Levi, he slaps him on the shoulder and says, “I’ll walk up to the saloon, buddy. Even though I rarely pass on a good card game, I think I need to head over to the hotel and rest a spell.”

“Suit yourself, Doc. I am going to have a couple of drinks and play a few hands before I call it a day.”

“Good luck, Levi; I will see you in the early hours.”

20

In the early pre-dawn hours, the silence is overwhelming in Avoca. The peace is broken by the sound of spurs, Ping, ping, and cha-ching. Doc and his band of deputies are heading down to the jail to take Sutton to Lincoln to stand trial. Doc and Levi enter the jail to see Little Bear putting Mr. Sutton in irons for the trip.

"You are never going to take me alive all the way to Lincoln," Sutton says, staring straight at Doc.

"That's fine," Doc shoots back. "If you want, we can just shoot you here and deliver you dead; it really makes no never mind to me. How about you, Levi?"

Levi reaches for his 'new' ivory handled pistol. Pulling the pistol from its resting place, he opens the cylinder, spinning it an extra couple of times for effect. "I prefer the second option. I really don't care to listen to this wind bag all the way to Lincoln."

Doc walks across the room to the washstand, grabs a washcloth, and hands it to Little Bear. "Here, gag Sutton. I don't want him giving our position away."

Levi walks over to the Sheriff's cell, unlocks the door and allows the Sheriff and his men out. "Now Sheriff, we trust you not to interfere. However, if you or any of these men do, I will not have a problem stopping the interference. Am I clear?"

"I promise we'll stay out of your way," The Sheriff replies. "None of the boys or I will be leaving town anytime soon. You have my word."

Levi steps out of the way, allowing the men to reclaim their freedom. "I will hold you to that, Sheriff. Can you hold our prisoner until the judge gets here?" Levi is standing in the jail doorway, watching Doc.

"That will not be a problem, Levi," the Sheriff answers. Levi turns to face the Sheriff and purses his lips to give the impression of a smile. "Good luck getting back to Lincoln; I am sure Sutton still has a few tricks up his sleeve," the Sheriff points out.

Outside, Doc and Little Bear escort Sutton to a horse waiting outside the jail. They throw Sutton over the horse, forcing him to ride all the way to Lincoln draped over it on his belly. The man still tries to squabble about things with the gag in his mouth so Doc walks up to him and helps him to take a nap, using the butt of his pistol.

The men start to ride through town. Doc has been surprised at the resistance or lack thereof in Avoca. His only conclusion is that Sutton never expected them to reach him. He probably figured the others would have done them in, so they would never reach Avoca anyway. In a very short time, they reach the open land between Avoca and Eagle. Doc looks in Little Bear's direction and says, "Levi and I will go scout up ahead and you and the braves stay back with Sutton. If he gives you any trouble, thump his skull with the butt of your rifle." Doc pauses before saying, "Aw hell Little Bear, if he gives you trouble scalp him."

"Are you sure you want to scout, and not stay here with this pile of manure?" Little Bear asks.

"Yes, I think I want to scout," Doc answers. "Running Wolf and Running Water taught Allen and me well. I haven't been doing any scouting since we left Lincoln. I think now would be a good time." Doc turns around to look at Levi and says, "Levi, come with me. If we do run into trouble, four guns are better than two."

Doc and Levi ride ahead into the night. There is a full moon so the two scouts have to be a little more cautious so they are not seen. Levi decides to make the time pass by having a conversation. "So Doc, when did you have all this training in scouting?"

"You would not believe me if I told you," Doc replies.

"I don't know, Doc. I have heard about some strange things in the time I have spent on this earth. How hard would your story be?"

"Okay, here's the story. I lived with the Sioux Indians for a period. It was with Running Wolf and his people. Dan was with me. He also lived with them. During the time we lived as part of their tribe, they showed Dan and me some valuable things on how to survive in the wilderness."

"Well, that's not so hard to believe," Levi points out.

The story was interrupted by what the two men could see up ahead. "Levi, look up ahead. You see the lights of Eagle? Look around the perimeter at all those campfires. I think they figured out how we got by them the first time."

"Well, how are we supposed to get through this time?" Levi asks.

Doc stops his horse. Pulling a match from his pocket, he lights it to see the time on his pocket watch. Looking at his watch, he says to Levi, "Okay, we have about an hour before Dan and his posse hit Eagle from the West. Let's head back to Little Bear and put the rest of our plan together."

Levi turns his horse around and gives her a kick and says to Doc, "Well Doc, let's ride back to Little Bear and make good time of it. The more time we have the better."

Levi and Doc ride back to where Little Bear and his braves are, to let them know what they found.

Doc starts to express his plans. "Little Bear, there are many campfires around Eagle. They spread far to the North and South. We will not be able to go out around like we did with Sherry's help because we are meeting Marshal Allen. I think we will just go through town, right down the middle of Main Street."

Little Bear smiles about how Doc is trying to be so cautious. "It is not like we have not done that before," he points out.

"That's true," comments Doc. "However, Marshal Dan will be coming from the west any minute now. So we need to close in." At that moment Sutton gives a muffled laugh through the gag he has in his mouth. Doc rides over to him, whips out his pistol, and smacks him upside the head again, leaving him unconscious. Doc follows it up with, "Laugh at that!"

The men ride to the edge of Eagle where they run into gunfire. They dismount and take cover at the blacksmith's on the edge of town. Levi dives behind a pile of wood and yells out, "I think they were waiting for us, Doc."

"You think?" Doc snaps back.

"I can't get a clean shot at any one of them," Levi yells again. "How about you, Little Bear?"

"No. I can't either," he answers. "They are hiding very well. I saw the Marshal and his posse ride in. I think they are pinned down by the jail."

Doc does a quick log roll across the floor to Levi. And when he reaches him, Doc says, "I need your pistols."

"What kind of crazy plan are you contemplating?" Levi asks.

Doc gives him the cold calculated evil stare and says, "I'm going to ride through the middle of town and try to shoot as many as I can. When I do, they will likely jump cover to shoot at me. At that point you shall have a clear shot at them."

"If you do a stunt like that, you are going to be shot," Levi warns Doc as he hands over his extra pair of pistols.

Doc puts the pistols in his waistband and starts out for his horse. He looks over his shoulder at Levi and says, "Not if you shoot them first."

Doc jumps onto his horse, takes the reins in his teeth, and rides down main street pistols blazing. Outlaws jump out from cover to get a better shot at Doc. Dan, Levi, Little Bear and the rest of the posse are picking them off as fast as they stand up. Doc gets to the end of Main Street and rides into the livery to reload. As he enters the Sheriff's shed where they have their horses, he sees Allen shooting down the street. He says to Dan, “Marshal how’s your day going?” Doc dismounts and starts reloading all six pistols from his belt.

“That was the stupidest thing I have ever seen anyone do; what were you thinking?” Allen replies.

Doc finishes reloading, remounts his horse, and answers, “You thought that was stupid; watch this.”

Doc rides out of the shed, and once again, his pistols are firing as fast as he can. Outlaws are falling back as he rides by them. As Doc gets back to the blacksmith’s, there are only a few outlaws left in town to fire back.

Levi is astonished at what he has just witnessed and says, “Doc, that was the wildest thing I have ever seen. I can’t believe it worked.”

Doc reloads the pistols, hands Levi back the pistols he borrowed from him, and says, “You have to have a little faith. Levi.” He looks at Levi, Little Bear, and the braves, takes a deep breath and says, “Now, let’s clean out this town.”

They make their way through town, cleaning it of undesirables and meet Allen and his group in the middle of town. Doc looks back at Little Bear and says, “Why don’t you go back and get Sutton from where he’s chained. I want to buy him a drink.”

Levi laughs and says, “Good idea, Doc. I’ll buy him a round myself.”

Little Bear returns with the braves carrying Sutton. They drag him into the saloon and throw him into a chair. Levi grabs a beer off the bar asking, “Doc, may I buy him his first round?”

“Yes, be my guest,” Doc answers.

Levi takes Sutton's gag off. He holds the mug up to Sutton as if he is going to let him take a sip, only to lift the glass and send the amber liquid streaming down Sutton's face.

Sutton spits out beer and swears, "I am going to kill you all."

Doc walks over to the drenched man, showing him the butt end of a pistol and asks, "Do you want to take another nap?" Sutton shakes his head no. "Well then, keep your mouth shut."

The marshal steps up to the bar, making the announcement, "The first round is on me boys; belly up."

The drinks are flowing in celebration of a battle won. Doc walks over to the door and peers out toward the street.

Levi, close behind, asks, "Doc, what's the matter; you look like you just lost your best friend?"

"My friend, this part of the journey was too easy. It makes me wonder," Doc answers. "What's next?"

Levi sips his beer, pats Doc on the back, and replies, "I think the worst is behind us, my friend."

Still looking for undesirables on the street, Doc says, "I hope you are right; but just in case you are not, I think I will take Little Bear and go for a walk around town." Doc motions to Little Bear.

Little Bear walks over to the man. "What can I do for you, Doc?"

Doc points to the street, telling his friend, "Why don't you and I take a walk around town to make sure we didn't miss anyone?"

"Alright, I will be with you in a minute. I have to tell the braves what we are up to."

Doc and Little Bear walk out of the front doors and start down the street to make their rounds. He asks, “Little Bear, what are you going to do when this is all over?”

“I have some hunting to catch up on, and I have missed being with my people for all of the spring festivities,” Little Bear replies.

“I am sorry about that, but we could not have pulled this off without you,” Doc points out.

Doc and Little Bear walk through town. For the most part things are quiet. Little Bear catches movement out of the corner of his eye. He elbows Doc, pointing to an alley, and says, “There’s a man who just slipped into the alley up there.”

Doc nods in acknowledgement, then whispers, “I’ll go around back; wait for my signal and then go in carefully.”

Doc goes around back and whistles to signal Little Bear that he is in position. Little Bear enters the darkened alley and moves in between the crates and wagons parked there. Doc is coming in from the opposite direction when a man backs into him. Doc looks down at the man and asks, “Can I help you?”

The man turns to see Doc standing there. He turns pale. “Doc, I didn’t know it was you.” The man passes out right there in front of him.

Little Bear comes walking up to Doc and says, “I notice you have that effect on a lot of people.”

“Yeah, it seems that way, doesn’t it? Let’s take him to the Sheriff’s office and drop him off.”

When Doc and Little Bear open the Sheriff’s office, they see Marshal Allen there, putting Mr. Sutton in a cell. “I will put you in here until we are ready to leave. 'Cuz if you keep mouthing off, you'll be giving Doc just one more reason to kill you."

"Now Marshal, I would like to think I have a little more self-control than you are giving me credit for," Doc points out.

Surprised to hear Doc's voice, Allen jumps. He turns around and says, "Doc, what are you doing here?"

He shoves the semiconscious man into a cell, slamming it shut. "We are dropping off this here prisoner for the sheriff."

"Good, I've got a couple of guys to keep watch inside and out here. They will switch off sometime during the night. I was thinking of heading up to the hotel and getting a hot meal and a room; would you like me to get one for you too, Doc?"

Doc turns back toward the doorway and replies, "Yeah, that would be great, Dan. Little Bear and I are going to walk back to the saloon for a couple more drinks. Would you be so kind as to bring my key over?"

"You bet. I'll see you in a little while," Marshal Allen replies.

Little Bear and Doc enter the saloon to see Levi dancing on a table to a fiddle player playing, 'Old Susanna.' Doc shouts, "Levi, what the heck do you think you are doing?"

"Well Doc, if you can ride through the streets with everyone shooting at you, then I figure I can dance on a table or two."

Doc and Little Bear start to laugh at his out of time dance. Doc says, "I guess you have a point there, Levi. Have a good time but don't be getting carried away. You need to be sharp for our ride into Lincoln tomorrow. We may still have some surprises waiting on the trail."

Levi sips his beer and still keeps dancing, saying, "Doc, from what I saw today, we have nothing to worry about. Hell, I think you just might be immortal."

Doc holds a beer up to his lips and sips a bit, telling Levi,
"I think we have had a string of good luck, but that may change so be ready."

Levi holds his glass of beer up to toast Doc and says to his friend, "Doc, you worry too much; have a beer, and enjoy our victory."

Doc and Little Bear walk over to the bar and grab another beer. They are sitting down to watch the entertainment when Allen walks into the saloon. Looking up at Levi dancing on the tabletop, he smiles and shakes his head. He walks over to where Doc and Little Bear are sitting.

Handing Doc and Little Bear each a room key, he says, "Well Doc, I think our journey is almost over."

Doc sets his beer down, points a finger at Dan and says, "Don't get too complacent, Dan. We still have to get Sutton to Lincoln."

"On our way here we did not see any of Sutton's men."

"That does not mean there won't be any of them there tomorrow. After this drink I think I am going over to the hotel and get some rest; when do you want to head to Lincoln, Dan?"

"First thing tomorrow morning; you get some sleep, Doc. We can handle keeping Sutton out of trouble."

Doc stands up and walks to the door. He turns back, tips his hat, and says, "Alright, I will see you in the morning."

As Doc walks out, Levi climbs down off the table and takes Doc's spot. "So Dan, did you run into any trouble on your way here?"

"No, we did not see anyone."

"Well, maybe the worst is behind us," Levi comments.

"I sure hope so. I did not sign up for all of this," Allen points out.

"Is it getting to you a little, Dan?" Levi asks.

"Yes, I believe it is. I don't know how you and Doc can do this day in and day out."

"Well, I have been doing this all my life and I guess I have gotten used to it," Levi points out. "As for Doc, he has to do this to avenge his family."

"You're probably right," Allen agrees. "I hope after we bring Sutton to Lincoln, Doc will be able to get back to his old self. I don't know him anymore."

"Dan, Doc has been through a hell of a lot in this last year. Things of this magnitude are bound to change anyone."

"Yes, I suppose you are right. Well, what do you say we call it a night? It has been a long day and the morning is going to be here before we know it."

21

As the sun peeks over the horizon, the town of Eagle is bustling with activity. Even at such an early hour, people are up as if it's the middle of the afternoon. People are in town to get their weekly supplies and to see Sutton hauled off to Lincoln.

Doc and Little Bear are in the livery, saddling the horses. When they are finished Doc says to Little Bear, "Little Bear, why don't you go up to the hotel and get everyone up; I will go over and get Sutton up and ready for his trip to the Lincoln courtroom and the Lincoln gallows."

"Are you sure you don't want me to get Sutton and you go up and wake the men?"

Doc shakes his head no and says, "It'll be alright; I promise he will be alive when you get back."

Little Bear takes off up the street as Doc makes his way over to the jail. As Doc enters the jail, Sutton is still asleep in his cell, and the Sheriff is pouring himself a cup of coffee. "Morning Doc, would you like a cup?"

"No thanks, Sheriff. I need to get Sutton and get on the trail toward Lincoln; but thanks for offering, and thanks for keeping an eye on Sutton for me."

The Sheriff sips on the steamy liquid and says, "No problem at all, Doc. I pretty much napped in the back room there on that bed. To tell ya the truth your friends over here did most of the work."

Doc looks out at the street at the men. "Yeah, they are good help. If they would not have been with us, we would not have made it this far. Well, I need to get Sutton up and ready to travel."

"I will go and get him up and into irons for you, Doc."

The Sheriff walks over, unlocks the cell, and rousts Sutton "Mr. Sutton, it is time. Sutton rolls out of bed, scratching his eyes. "Where is my breakfast? I refuse to be treated like this."

Doc walks over to the cell and says to Sutton, "You'll get your breakfast when we get to Lincoln."

"I won't move a muscle until I get some breakfast."

Doc grabs for his pistol. Sutton puts his hands out in front of him so the sheriff can place the irons on him, spouting off, "Keep that mad man away from me, Sheriff."

"I see you and Sutton are getting along well, Doc," the Sheriff says, half laughing.

"We 'were' getting along right up to the point where he killed my family. I made a promise to Dan not to kill him; I can't break a promise, but this is one I wouldn't mind breaking. So I recommend, Sutton, that you get your ass going before I have to apologize to Dan for breaking my promise."

Doc walks out with Mr. Sutton in front of him and the braves following behind. The braves throw Sutton on a horse. His hands are hanging on one side, with his feet hanging down on the other. They ride over to the livery to meet up with Dan, Levi and the rest of the posse. Once everyone is ready, they mount up and hit the trail toward Lincoln.

Sutton has some time to think about how he can escape. When it appears that no one is paying attention to him, he tries sliding off his horse. He fails to take into account the shackles on his ankles. He hits the ground with a thud, and can't get up off the ground. The sound catches everyone by surprise. To no one's surprise Doc, Levi, Little Bear, Wes, Steve, and of course Allen all stop, spin around, and have two guns drawn and cocked faster than Sutton can take his next breath. Sutton just kneels there in the dirt.

Doc hops off his horse and grabs Sutton, bringing him to his feet. Doc grabs the horse Sutton was on. He calls over to Levi, "Hey Levi, would you give me a hand getting Sutton back on this horse so we can keep moving?"

"Sure thing Doc, more than happy to but I am a little surprised he is alert. I thought you might have given him another one of your magic sleeping treatments."

"He just about got one when we were leaving the jail but I decided to give him an option. He opted to behave. Now, I'm thinking he may not be worthy of another option."

They get Sutton up onto his horse. This time they tie his hands to his feet under the horse's belly and they continue on their journey to Lincoln.

Dan is leading the way when Levi rides up beside Doc and says to him, "There must not be any trouble ahead or we would be up front in the lead." Doc laughs and agrees with Levi.

It is a short ride into Lincoln compared to the past rides from town to town. They arrive in just a few hours.

As they ride down 'O' Street, Lincoln's main street, crowds have gathered to watch them come. Men with guns join their posse and are acting as escorts on all sides of their group. The first half dozen of them are waiting on the road outside town. Then a couple of men at a time wait to join, as they get closer to the Marshal's office and jail.

When they finally reach the square, people are standing along every inch of the block. They are applauding. They stop in front of the jail. Doc climbs off his horse and ties it to the post out front. He helps Dan get Sutton off his horse. The gathering of people are calling Sutton names and chanting to see Sutton hanged.

Dan steps onto the boardwalk and stands on the edge of the horse trough. "Now listen, everybody!" He whistles loud, gaining the attention of the angry mob. "We are going to put this man in jail and he will stand trial for what he has done. I want everyone to go home. We will take care of this matter."

A man in the crowd yells out, "Marshal, we want to see this man swing for what he has done, and I say we do it now! Hang him from the big oak at the West end of 'O' Street." The crowd yells and moves forward. Levi grabs Sutton and shoves him inside the jail. Doc steps in front of the trough, in front of Dan and yells, "Look people! Back off! No one wants to see Sutton swing more than I. Regardless of our personal feelings, he will stand trial. The trial will be immediate. I recommend you all go on about your business. There will be a formal announcement of the trial's outcome by the Mayor; until then all of you go home!"

The crowd begins to disperse with low rumblings as they leave. Dan shakes his head, looks at Doc and asks, "Why is it that everyone listens to you and ignores me?"

"I don't know," Doc replies. "Maybe it's my good looks." Doc puts his arm around Dan and continues, "Now, let's go inside and finish this job so we can finally relax."

The two men walk into the jail to find the Judge and the Territorial Governor standing there staring at Sutton. One of the Deputy Marshals is removing his hand irons and chaining Sutton's shackles to the cell doors.

The governor walks over to Sutton's cell and says to him, "For what you did to my daughter I ought to kill you right where you stand. I am going to enjoy watching you swing for your crimes." He starts to walk away but stops, turns around, and steps into the cell. He glares into Sutton's eyes, and then throws a right hook connecting with Sutton's jaw, knocking him into the Deputy. Sutton grabs the Deputy Marshal's pistol and swings it toward the Governor.

When the sound of the gun's hammer being pulled back is heard, Doc, Levi, and Dan, all draw their pistols and fire before Sutton can pull the trigger. The bullet from each of the men's pistols lands where it is aimed. A surprise to them was Little Bear. He, in that same split second, flips his tomahawk out, landing it the middle of Sutton's chest. For a split second, Sutton glances around at the men. He looks at Doc last. Doc locks glares with him.

The look on Sutton's face goes blank. Doc gets an eerie feeling. He sees a woman standing in the cell with Sutton. She is smiling and waving. It is Julie, his sweet dear Julie. She waves and blows him a kiss. He almost reaches for her, but she disappears just as quickly as she appeared.

Doc knows that she is at peace now. He feels the release of it all as he watches Sutton collapse onto the floor in a pool of his own deceitful blood.

The judge looks down at the dead man. "Well fellas, I guess my job here is done. As far as I see, justice has been served. Why don't you have one of your deputies drag Sutton to the undertaker? I'm taking these men down to the restaurant and buying them a hot meal and a whiskey."

As the men walk out of the Marshal's office to go over to the restaurant, there is a crowd of men waiting in the street, wanting to know what all of the commotion was. Voices of men are asking, "Doc, what happened in the marshal's office?" Another says, "Who got shot? Was it Sutton?" Someone else shouts, "I hope that Bastard's dead!"

Doc holds his hands up to quiet them. Clearing his throat, Doc tells everyone, "Well, it seems like Mr. Sutton was in a hurry to get his trial over. We granted his wish. He was found guilty of all charges filed against him." Doc no sooner made that statement than the jail door opens, and the deputies step out dragging the lifeless and bloody body of Richard Sutton. The crowd goes silent. They open a path for the men taking Sutton to the undertaker's. The crowd erupts; the air is filled with loud cheers.

One of the men pats Doc on the shoulder. "It serves him right, after all the pain he brought to this area. Maybe now you can put all of this behind you. After all, we still need a good doctor around here."

Doc smiles and says, "Maybe I'll have to open up the doors and dust off the instruments. We'll just have to wait and see what's in store for me next."

At the end of the street, right by the diner, a man dressed in black steps out. His hat is dipped low, concealing his face. The man says, "Hey Doc. Doc Gray. You should prepare to meet you maker. You killed my brother. I am here to set things straight."

Everyone quietly steps aside. Doc slowly slides his coat behind his pistols. He addresses the man. "Boy, you just better go on. Go on into the saloon, have a drink, and cool off. I am sorry if I killed your brother. But know this; I have not shot anyone who did not deserve it."

The man walks closer to Doc. "You better be prepared to defend yourself, or you will die where you stand."

Doc senses something familiar about the man's voice. He looks more closely and notices he is unarmed. He walks closer to the man in black and asks, "Will? Little Willie is that you?"

"Ah shucks, John. I can't fool you, can I?"

Doc exhales loudly and says, "That attitude you just gave me almost got you killed, boy. I suggest you don't ever do that again."

Pushing up his hat brim, he says, "Yes sir, Doc, sir"

Doc reaches over, grabs the kid, and gives him a hug. "Gentlemen, let me introduce you to a friend of mine from college. This is Will Boone. He is with the drama troop which performs the plays, with singing and dancing shows." Levi shakes the man's hand then pats him on the shoulder as they enter the diner, telling him "Boy, you don't know how close you came to ending up six feet under in boot hill."

Will smiles and shares the story. "We arrived last night. I wanted to be the one to tell John we had indeed arrived, so I came over to let Doc know we were in town and ready to perform. I thought it would be funny to do it that way; looking at it now, it's not such a bright idea."

Levi laughs and replies, "Yes, you certainly could have done it differently; never mind that, come with us. We are going to get a bite to eat; over dinner you and John can catch up.

After a good meal, Dan looks over at Doc and says, "What do you say we go over to the hotel? I know someone who has been waiting for your arrival. She said something about riding lessons."

Doc laughs and replies, "Yeah, I suppose I had better not keep her waiting any longer." Dan and Doc get up and head over to the hotel to see the proprietors of the hotel and talk a little business.

As they enter the hotel the girls are hanging drapes on one of the side windows. Doc looks over at Allen and elbows him. He kind of speaks loudly as he clears his throat, "Excuse me, ma'am. We were wondering if you might have a room for the night." The girls, busy with their decorating, don't turn to look.

Amy answers with her back still toward them, "I will be with you in just a minute; we have to finish this before the big celebration tonight."

Allen smiles and asks, "What celebration is that?" He is surprised she doesn't recognize his voice.

Still preoccupied, Amy says, "It's our grand opening and we have a traveling theatrical group performing special for the occasion."

Dan winks at Doc, throwing an elbow at him. Talking to Doc, he says loudly, "Well, that sounds like it will be a wild time in the old town tonight. I don't think that's for me. I am kind of tired. I really wouldn't mind a hot bath. What do ya say? Maybe we should just go out to the Triple-J Ranch? What do you think, Doc?"

Audra spins around on the chair she was using, to see Doc standing there. She leaps off the chair and into his arms. She plants a kiss on him. "I was so worried that I would never see you again. Then I heard one of the men say you went riding through Eagle with everyone shooting at you. What in the hell were you thinking?"

Doc holds her close and gives her a spin, swinging her around a couple of times. "I was thinking I had to get Dan back in one piece so your sister did not kill me when I came back." He kisses her again, squeezing tight. He puts her down and starts looking around the grand entry of the old hotel. He is impressed. "You two have been working very hard! This hotel looks great! I mean, just fabulous! It reminds me of the upscale ones back in Boston."

Audra smiles proudly. She hugs him again. "Thank you, John. But we have had a lot of help."

"Do you need any help with the last minute things?" Doc asks. "I'd be glad to help if there is anything you need."

She grabs him by the arm and leads him to the desk, handing him and Dan each a room key. "No. We really don't need any other help. It's almost done anyway. Now, you and Dan go get a room and a bath before the celebration gets under way."

Amy takes Dan by the hand and says, "Your rooms are on the second floor. The bathhouse is on the first floor, right by the kitchen. I will have one of the men get them ready with plenty of hot water right away."

Dan and John finish with their baths and head up to their rooms to get changed for the big grand opening celebration. As Doc and Allen emerge from their rooms, Doc looks over at Allen. "Wow, you clean up pretty good."

Dan looks John over, saying, "Well thanks, you don't look so bad yourself. Let's go down and celebrate the end of another job well done."

When they get downstairs John sees Audra and she looks like an angel from heaven. "Audra, you look beautiful tonight, like the sight of the first snow of winter, so clean and pure."

She feels a rush of excitement coursing through her. "Why Dr. John Gray, you are making me blush." She takes him by the arm and whispers in his ear, "Tonight you and I have much to celebrate. And we have a lot to talk about."

As if he has no idea of what she means, he replies, "Really? Should I be worried?"

She caresses his coat lapel, bats her eyes at him, and answers, "No, no need to worry, my love. You deserve everything you are going to get tonight for a job well done."

Dan and Amy are right behind Audra and Doc entering the dinner theater, with all of the guests already seated and enjoying a fine meal. Doc and Allen pull out the chairs for their dates and seat them at the table, then take seats themselves. The night is filled with music, dancing, and short skits; and as he promised Bonny, Doc is right up there with them. Surprising Audra and Amy with another facet to this man named John Gray.

Allen is laughing, knowing his friend Doug in most ways has returned from within this man Gray. After the celebration finally wound down, and all of the guests have retired or left, the foursome climb the stairs, making their way to the second floor.

John opens the door to their room, allowing Audra to enter. She removes her hat, placing it on the table. Pulling the pins from her hair, she releases her mounds of auburn hair. She shakes her head, then looks at John and says, "I am so proud of you for bringing that man to justice and making sure everyone gets their deeds back and their loans straightened out."

Doc removes his hat and gun belt, hanging them from the bedpost. "I thought it was only fair to make sure all of the wrongs and injustices Sutton inflicted on these people be set right." John reaches for the girl standing before him. Bringing her close to him, he says, "Now come here; we have a little catching up to do."

As the sun peeks through the window and glistens off Audra's auburn hair, Doug thinks to himself that this is the right thing to do. It is what is needed for Doc to help him get over the tragic loss of his family and to start anew with this wonderful young lady, Audra Lee Randolph.

He is admiring her in her natural beauty, when the door to his room flies open. He sees Levi standing there.

"Doc!" Levi shouts. "Hurry up and get dressed we have to go right now!

For years, the legend of Box Butte Canyon had been told about a Native American Tribe unable to get to their Spirit world.

It was said that the beating of drums could be heard in the distance, with visions of braves appearing on painted ponies of gold.

This epic tale of adventure starts with Doug and Allen on a fishing trip with their friend Steve. Without warning, Doug and Allen find themselves thrust back into the yester years of the 1800's.

Unsure why they were there, the Legend unfolds and leads them on a mystic journey of helping to right a wrong, in doing so they learn the ancient lost art of humanity, and discover that things are not always as they seem.

Available now from Four Star Publishing

www.bookstore.fourstarpublishing.com

Coming Soon

"Doc get up! Come on we got to go!"

With that single sentence, a new story starts for our men:
U.S. Marshall Dan Allen, Deputy John "Doc" Gray, and
U.S. Marshall Levi Calaway.

This new story of adventure will take you east through Missouri, Iowa, and to Chicago. You will venture through the picturesque Black Hill of South Dakota.

The trio with help of their band of men set out on yet another adventure to set right things that are wrong.

They are in pursuit of a man who has stolen a very important document. This document is a treaty between the Sioux Tribes and the U.S. Government. But before the Sioux Chief or the President can sign it, it is stolen.

In this story you will meet all of the people who are part of the extended "family" Marshall Allen and Doc have all across the countryside. Wonderful, helpful people wanting justice for the men responsible of the crimes that are happening around them.

Peace can come to us all if we can ***Save A Nation!***

Made in the USA